S0-BIY-569

Spine damage 3/11

DATE	ISSUED TO
AF Hei	$ 26.95
APR 1 7 2008	
JUN 1 9 2008	
JUL 0 3 2008	
JUL 2 8 2008	
FEB 2 0 2009	
SEP 1 5 2009	
NOV 1 7 2009	
MAR 0 3 2011	

© DEMCO 32-2125

The Rose Legacy

*Also by Kristen Heitzmann
in Large Print:*

Halos
Twilight

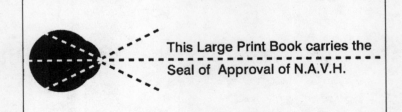

The Rose Legacy

Kristen Heitzmann

Thorndike Press • Waterville, Maine

Published in 2005 by arrangement with Bethany House Publishers.

Thorndike Press® Large Print Christian Historical Fiction.

The tree indicium is a trademark of Thorndike Press.

The text of this Large Print edition is unabridged.
Other aspects of the book may vary from the original edition.

Set in 16 pt. Plantin by Christina S. Huff.

Printed in the United States on permanent paper.

Library of Congress Cataloging-in-Publication Data

Heitzmann, Kristen.
    The rose legacy / by Kristen Heitzmann.
      p. cm.
    ISBN 0-7862-7857-9 (lg. print : hc : alk. paper)
    1. Italian Americans — Fiction. 2. Women pioneers —
Fiction. 3. Colorado — Fiction. 4. Large type books.
5. Christian fiction. I. Title.
PS3558.E468R67 2005
813'.54—dc22   2005012477

To Trevor
for your laughter, your zeal,
and your exuberance.

Thus will I bless you while I live;
lifting up my hands,
I will call upon your name.
As with the riches of a banquet
shall my soul be satisfied,
and with exultant lips
my mouth shall praise you.

Psalm 63:4-5, New Am.

As the Founder/CEO of NAVH, the only national health agency solely devoted to those who, although not totally blind, have an eye disease which could lead to serious visual impairment, I am pleased to recognize Thorndike Press* as one of the leading publishers in the large print field.

Founded in 1954 in San Francisco to prepare large print textbooks for partially seeing children, NAVH became the pioneer and standard setting agency in the preparation of large type.

Today, those publishers who meet our standards carry the prestigious "Seal of Approval" indicating high quality large print. We are delighted that Thorndike Press is one of the publishers whose titles meet these standards. We are also pleased to recognize the significant contribution Thorndike Press is making in this important and growing field.

Lorraine H. Marchi, L.H.D.
Founder/CEO
NAVH

* Thorndike Press encompasses the following imprints: Thorndike, Wheeler, Walker and Large Print Press.

One

It is a fact that the human heart differs from all other species. While its function to the body is that same of all animals, its participation with the human soul is both rhapsodic and fatal.

Rose

June 7, 1880

With a hollow crack the wagon lurched to the side and lolloped like a large lamed animal. Yanking on the reins, Carina DiGratia set the brake with one deft foot and brought it to a grinding halt. She pressed a hand to her chest while her heart pounded in her throat. A quick glance to the left made her head swim.

It was not that the grade of the road was so steep, but rather that it wound upward until it brought her to a dizzying height that overlooked the chasm below — a chasm filled with teeth ready to chew and swallow her. She closed her eyes and resisted the swelling fear. Nothing in the traveler's guide she had read mentioned a road more fit for mountain sheep than human travel.

Praying the brake would hold, Carina jumped down and snatched up a rock the size of a Bantam hen. This she shoved behind the wagon's outside back wheel, then she hurried to the other side. There, between the wagon and the rock wall of the canyon, she crouched to survey the damage. Loose rungs and a cracked felly that rendered the wheel worthless. This after everything else! *Perchè?* Why?

She stood up and kicked the wheel's rim. The shock of the blow jarred her shin up to the knee and she gasped in pain, gripping her leg and hopping backward. Then she balled her fists and stood still, feet planted, and scowled at the wheel as though that could make it right.

Carina should have known that the old wagonwright was cheating her, the way he wouldn't look her in the eye. She had sensed it but ignored her feelings because she trusted. Always she trusted! The old man had thought her a fool, and she had proved him right. She pressed the heel of her hand to her forehead and paced behind the wagon, halting well short of the edge.

Turning, Carina shaded her eyes with her hand and surveyed the trail that snaked up the canyon wall. She should be grateful; a broken outside wheel might have tipped her over the brink. Her stomach lurched at the thought, and she stumbled, gripping the wagon bed.

She edged around the side of the wagon to the large umber mule harnessed there and ran her hand along the enormous dusty back, then tangled her fingers in his wiry mane, taking comfort in his company.

"Bene!" And in English, "Well! What now, Dom?"

He snuffled her hand, the stiff whiskers of his velvety muzzle tickling her palm. His deep brown eyes looked wise and sympathetic, but he had no answers . . . in English or Italian. He was only a mule. Carina felt very alone.

She unhitched the harness and led him over to the pink granite wall of the canyon where the thin shade would succor him for the moment. Half a mile down and half a mile up, the trail widened, but here, perched on the side of the mountain, it was scarcely the width of the wagon. Naturally the wheel broke at this precarious location. Carina raised an open hand to heaven. *"Grazie, Signore."*

A thin, sparkling stream seeped from the rock wall and ran across the road. Flecks of black and white stood out from the darkened pink granite, catching the sun like facets of gems. She glared at the rut that had jolted the wheel. It wasn't much of a rut, but large enough to find the flaw in her wheel and expose it, causing the awful hollow pop, the sudden dip and lurch that had sent her heart to her throat.

Carina glanced down over the edge to the

blue and white water rushing far below, the pointed spires of pines along its banks, the long stony slope, clifflike in pitch. She had avoided the sight these last miles as the road dug its way more steeply and sharply up the side, climbing away from the creek's edge, toward the blue expanse of sky.

What was she doing? She signed herself with the cross, then sank to the ground where trail met wall. Above her, a single stunted pine sprang from a crack in the rock amid a shock of dry buff-colored grass. Its stringy roots dangled at her back, a lacy veil where the earth had fallen away from the stone. A precarious perch, yet it clung there and grew.

That tenacity, that spirit. Did she not possess the same? Had not Papa said so from the time she was small, calling her *tigre*, his little tiger cub? She didn't feel like a tiger now, so far from home and family. But she must. She must make the fight rise up inside. So the wheel was broken, the road narrow, the canyon steep . . . Would she be defeated by so little after coming so far?

She need only wait. This was the road to Crystal, Colorado, the diamond of the Rockies. A magic city where dreams came true. She felt her chest swell with hope and determination. From the branches above, a crow cackled. She didn't care. Let the foolish bird laugh. She would show it what Carina DiGratia was made of.

The shade was no more than a foot's width under the noonday sun, but it cooled her. For the last several hours, the sun had burned from a sky the azure blue of *Tía* Marta's bread bowl. The travel journals were right to declare the air thin at this elevation. She must be higher than ten thousand feet now that she was near the summit of the pass. Dom's heaving breaths and her own were witness enough.

She dropped her head back against the mountainside and untied the wide-brimmed hat that Mamma had sent. She wanted to see clearly, without the brim blocking her view, no matter how frightful the prospect. Again thoughts of the steep drop invaded her mind.

So she was not good with heights. She had known that already, ever since Divina lured her onto the roof when she was only four. Carina closed her eyes and heard her sister's voice. *"Do not lean so, Carina. Carina, don't . . ."*

Opening her eyes, Carina rubbed her forearm. The break had healed well, the youthful bone knitting easily. But the fear had stayed, though she tried again and again to conquer it. And she had never forgiven Divina that. She sent her gaze across the valley to the opposite slope. So why was she

11

now on this mountaintop? Why did she tempt God?

Unbidden, another memory came, sharp and clear as though etched onto the plate of her mind. Voices, low and soft, through the barn wall where Carina pressed close to listen, a dim shadow in the moonlight. Murmurs and quiet laughter, a whisper and an answer, deeper and far more dear, sending shards of broken dreams, jagged and piercing, to Carina's heart.

How she had screamed, cursing them as they scrambled apart in the hay. The names she had called, thrusting her thumb into Flavio's chest when he tried to excuse the inexcusable. And Divina, Divina laughing behind her hand. That, too, she would not forgive.

Even now, the humiliation, the hurt was as fresh as that night three weeks ago. She had prayed, *What do I do? How do I endure this?* She had begged God for an answer, and there, the very next morning, had been the advertisement: a home and opportunities. Grazie, *Dio,* it was her answer. So here she was, climbing the mountain into the sky, half a continent from Sonoma, California. If Flavio wanted her, let him come and prove it.

She raised her knees and dropped her elbows into the skirt draped between them. There she rested her chin, eyeing the beige linen hem. Bent that way, the bones of her corset pinched her lower ribs beneath her white cambric blouse. She couldn't sit long. Smacking her palms on her thighs, she stood up and tossed the hat into the wagon bed, then paced, considering her dilemma.

She could unload the wagon and have Dom drag her things one at a time up the slope, except maybe the rocker, the bedding, and the dishes. . . . But then what would she do with the wagon? Not even the sturdy mule could pull a three-wheeled wagon. Yet she couldn't leave it there in the middle of the road. Though it was small, at this narrow point only two men abreast could pass it on one side.

And tipped as it was into the wall of the canyon, she wasn't certain the damaged wheel could be removed and replaced. Could the wagon be disassembled and hauled down? She jerked her head at a sound and peered down the trail. A large wagon was climbing, pulled by a team of four powerful horses — the front two a pair of sprightly matched blacks, the next two even larger, caramel brown with white markings. Clydesdales, surely.

A single driver urged them along, sitting high in front of the load of cargo meticulously covered and tied behind him. She did not think he had seen her as he maneuvered the horses onto the narrowing incline and started up the cut. No matter. He would reach her soon enough with such fine strong horses.

Surely this wagon was sent by God. She recognized the gift. "Grazie, Signore," she breathed with no sarcasm, no scolding this time. She brushed the dust from her skirt and waited, the breeze catching her hair and tossing it. Carelessly, she caught the rippling strands with a hand and held them back from her face. Dom raised his head and brayed as the stranger drew in rein behind her wagon, encircling them in dust like fog off the sea.

"Whoa." Sitting high above her on the wooden box, the man touched the broad brim of his hat but didn't remove it. The high noon shadow hid all but the jut of his chin and the mane of light brown hair that hung impudently to his shoulders.

Shielding her eyes, Carina squinted up. "Good afternoon." She made her voice strong. If it came to dickering, she would not be cheated again.

"Wagon trouble?" His had a strength of its own.

"A broken wheel."

The man gave only a cursory look to the damaged wheel, then eyed the trail above and the drop-off to their left. "Bad place."

Carina nodded toward the load behind him. "You have a spare?"

"Not that size."

She noted the difference between his immense wheels and her own with a sinking heart. But maybe there was something else to be done, some repair possible, some . . .

He leaped down from the box and strode over to inspect the damage more closely. His hand found the discoloration on the felly where it had cracked. "Wheel was flawed."

"The man who sold it was *disonesto*. A crook."

The stranger stood up, and Carina got a brief look at his face, rough shaven with a full mustache curving to his jawline. When he tipped his hat back and wiped his forehead with his sleeve, she glimpsed gray eyes before he turned away.

He walked to the front of the wagon and looked up the trail, then patted Dom and stroked his muzzle with a soft hand. He eyed the splay in the legs and heaving sides. "Your mule couldn't have pulled much longer anyway. Not at the summit."

"He's very strong."

He didn't argue, just looked up the trail again. "Your husband shouldn't leave you alone out here, even to go for help. This isn't exactly civil country."

Carina drew herself up. "I am traveling alone." That would give her credence and establish her equal footing. She wouldn't

15

tell him that her own papa had seen her to San Francisco and put her into the care of Guido and Antonnia Mollica, related by marriage to the Ghirardellis themselves. Together they'd taken the long and tedious Southern Pacific Railroad to Salt Lake City, where she'd been handed over to Anna and Francesca Bordolino, maiden aunts on Mamma's side. They rode the Union Pacific to Cheyenne and the Kansas Pacific into Denver. Only then was she deserted to find a means of travel up this godforsaken road. None of which this man needed to know.

Carina held out her hand. "Miss Carina Maria DiGratia."

He made no move to take it, just eyed her blankly and, she thought, a little darkly.

Feeling foolish, she withdrew her hand and waved at her cargo. "How much to haul this?"

He rubbed his chin with the back of his hand, then passed by her to the wagon bed. "As you can see, ma'am . . . Miss DiGratia, I've a full load of freight, all that my team can manage."

So he meant to dicker after all. Bene, she would dicker. Carina walked to the pair of blacks. Their necks steamed with sweat, but their ears were high and no white showed around the dark eyes. They were work horses, but fine nonetheless. "They seem strong and healthy enough."

16

"They are. And I mean to keep them that way. What do you need more than anything else?"

Carina turned to her own wagon. She eyed the trunk, the rocker, the rolls of bedding and feather mattress tied up with string, the dainty iron bed frame, the crates of books, dishes, and pans, jarred tomatoes and wheels of cheese, her *nonna's* silver, the leather satchel. She reached for the last item automatically, then grabbed the rose-patterned carpetbag.

He had indicated one thing, but she cleverly took two. He made no argument, and that heartened her. She might have the better of this after all. He took the satchel and swung it up, then wedged it behind the box. "Be careful . . ."

If he heard, he paid no mind. He tossed the carpetbag onto the box and hoisted her up with the same care. From her high seat, Carina watched him take Dom by the reins, ease him along the edge, and tie him to the back of the freight wagon. That was the limit of this man's charity, she supposed. Now he would bargain for the rest.

She would let him speak first; otherwise she would sound too eager. But he said nothing, merely walked around to the front of her wagon and worked the wheels to the left, then came around the back. His silent purpose unsettled her.

17

As much as she hated to start the dealings, he left her no choice. "Now we'll discuss the cost to haul the other things?"

"Nope." He put his shoulder to the back end of the wagon, lifted and pushed, straining hard for a moment, then easing as it started to move.

She suddenly realized what he was doing. "No! Stop!"

Carina leaped down from the seat, landing on her knees in the dust, then rushed to the edge of the trail as her wagon plummeted down the slope. It struck the ridge and shattered into pieces, her belongings smashing and tumbling to the creek below. Through the air, the straw hat sailed, ecru ribbons fluttering. Her head swam even as the anguish clutched her heart, leaving her breathless and stunned.

"Whoa." The perpetrator of destruction caught her arm and tugged her backward as the loose gravel slid away beneath her feet.

Incensed, she wrenched free, anger suddenly eclipsing the hurt. "*Sciocca!* Fool! You have lost me everything I own!" Stiff splayed fingers accented her point. "I don't have even a change of clothes."

"Then you should have chosen your trunk." He turned for his wagon.

And now she *was* a tiger. She snatched up her skirt and followed him, waving a hand in his face. "How could I know you meant

18

to send my things over the side?" She couldn't bear to think of them there, smashed and scattered. She could only think of lashing this . . . *briccone,* this knave, with her tongue.

He spared her scarcely a glance. "You had the trail blocked. I have freight to deliver."

How dare he? Mamma's rocker, the books, everything that had meant enough to bring all the way from Sonoma, California, to Crystal to build her dream. . . . Pain left her with no answer, save a sob that collected in her throat.

He moved to lift her again to the box of his wagon, but she thrust his hand away.

Undaunted, he motioned to the seat. "You'd better ride along."

"No, grazie." She forced the words through clenched teeth.

He looked down the road behind his wagon, then shrugged. "Suit yourself." He walked around to the back and untied Dom, whose saddle was gone with the wagon, of course. The mule wore only the harness bridle and looked at her mournfully as though that were his fault. The freighter held out the rein. "Stage'll be along shortly. I suggest you don't wait."

Bene! Now he was giving advice? Again the anger threatened to bring tears. She took the reins and eyed with dismay the

19

height of Dom's back. In her skirt, without a stirrup . . . The man stooped and made a step with his hands. With pleasure, she stepped on him, wishing to kick as well.

Astride, Carina held the reins and waited while the freighter mounted the box of his wagon and whistled to his team. Too late, she realized her mistake as dust rose and took hold of her. Choking and fanning her face, she remembered her bags tucked carelessly behind his seat. "Wait! Stop!"

The creak of wheels, the rattle of harness, and the clomp of hooves kept him from hearing. Or perhaps he chose not to. She turned back and saw the stagecoach below just starting the narrow climb. The roof was covered with passengers, all men, and she could only suppose the seats inside were filled as well. As it neared, she saw more clearly what manner of men sat atop: rough, desperate-looking men. She now guessed what the freighter had meant.

With no choice but to follow in his dust, she kicked her heels and Dom plodded up the winding road. Patient, steadfast, and long-suffering, Dom had come with her all the way from Sonoma, first by train from the wine country to Denver, then pulling the small purchased wagon into the mountains without complaint, though it was more than one beast should bear. She clung to him now with her heels as tight as her nerves.

Around a bend and down the slope a short way, she saw the remains of a horse, its ribs bare to the sun, old flesh clinging like tattered rags. She shuddered and looked away, thankful Dom's strength had never failed her. He plodded on, though it seemed each hoof was weighted down and each breath a struggle.

She urged Dom forward. The road dipped down briefly and grew rough with craggy pink boulders bubbling up from the white dirt. Just ahead, the horses drawing the freight wagon strained, and their driver urged them in low tones but did not apply the rein or whip. Here was her chance, and Carina took it, drawing up alongside.

"Stop. Hold there. You have my bags." She motioned to the seat beside him.

He looked over his shoulder as though the bags had climbed there themselves, then reined in his team. With a swift motion, he heaved the carpetbag free and tossed it down to her. She caught it with a solid thud to her chest, then looked up as he readied to fling the next.

"*Don't* throw it." Just like Mamma, she put generations of Italian matriarchs into that command, and it rang with Mediterranean fervor no man could ignore.

He stopped, and leaned down with the bag, and she snagged it from his grasp. "Thank you."

"Sure you don't want a ride?"

She ached already from riding bareback on Dom's bony spine. But she shook her head and stuffed the bags before her on the mule's withers. *Don't show the hurt, nor even the anger. Show him nothing. And don't cry.* She put up her chin. "No, I don't want a ride. But I will go before you now, as I make less dust."

He sat back, his head half-cocked, and allowed her to pass. Now she need only follow the road. She may have lost her belongings, but not her purpose. Had she not a deed in her bag and a future ripe with possibilities? With a nudge of her heels, she urged Dom on, upward again, closer and closer to the sky, then at last around the bend that crested the pass.

Carina caught her breath at the majestic grandeur before her. The valley opened up, encircled by mountains. One snow-streaked peak was reflected in the glassy blue lake beneath it, the line of contour repeated in exact detail. Bright, frothy green climbed the feet of the range, blending into the darkened crevices thick with pine. It was virgin beauty so fresh it suspended the motion of her chest and sliced through her rancor to the soft part of her spirit.

Dom dropped his head to graze on the grass beside the road, but Carina could not pull her eyes from the vision. This place, like none she had seen before, would be hers. This beauty, reward enough for what she had lost. Surely, surely this was the place of dreams after all.

She pulled on the reins and set Dom a steady pace. That must be Mount Pointe, and according to the traveler's guidebook, Crystal was not far past the lake. Her spirits rose at the thought of reaching her destination. Perhaps there was even some recourse she could take for the loss of her property. Perhaps the freighter could be made to pay damages. The thought sharpened the pain of knowing she had lost more than things. She had lost the remembrances of her memories.

Yet not everything was gone. She clutched the leather satchel closer to her chest. She had almost left it, should have left it, but could not. It was foolish, like holding a burning coal. But she held it, letting it burn.

For two hours she rode downward into the valley, eagerly looking about in spite of her discomfort. She drank in the scenery like an elixir, a tonic for her loss and fury. Even Dom seemed to sense it and bobbed his head as he walked. The air, breathable now, was shockingly clear and invigorating, acting on her mind and lungs in a healthful way. Oh, she had made the right choice. No matter the hardships.

As she left the lake behind and climbed again into a cleft valley, she slowed the mule in dismay. The denuded slopes ahead looked obscene, the trees hacked down and dragged away to the sprawling clutter of clapboard, canvas, and dust that could only be Crystal, Colorado. It was worse, far worse than Fairplay, where she'd spent the night before, thinking it was a poor relation to the city that would greet her this day.

Carina stared, unbelieving. Unlike the illustrations in the travel guide, Crystal was a stubbled wound in the ripped and quarried mountainside. A scar, a disfigurement. She felt the injury as to herself. How could this be the place of her dreams? The diamond — it was flawed, crushed, fouled. She felt the greed ooze from the shafts and diggings, the infection that had taken hold and was boring into the mountain's heart.

She felt stripped, like the very slopes. This . . . ugliness . . . was not what had brought her a thousand miles from Sonoma, California. *What was I thinking?* This was not a place of dreams. It was a nightmare. And for the first time, she questioned her good sense.

Two

Is there any pain an enemy can inflict that compares to that done by a friend?

Rose

The freighter had caught up to her as Carina lingered, stunned. He went by without a word, passing between the first shacks and tents along the rushing stream. She tasted his dust again as he maneuvered around the stumps in the road. They were everywhere, the remainders of trees used to build the shaft houses and mining works on the hill-sides, the log cabins and businesses, and the tall fronts of the stores along the main street.

Dully, Carina followed as best she could, the entire way clogged with mules, wagons, and teams. The noise was unbelievable after the mountain silence. She choked on the dust, though it was the least of the smells that assaulted her. With a sudden yank, she reined in as the freighter before her lurched to a stop behind a braying mass of mules, smaller than Dom and mean-tempered.

"Get on, now!" He swung his hat at the beasts and they shied away enough for him to pass.

Realizing he was her best hope, Carina

stayed close behind. As they pushed through, the mule skinner turned a gap-toothed grin her way and spat. She turned away and scanned the buildings on the near side. Two were of brick — the Crystal Hotel and the Miner's Exchange Bank. A few were stone, the rest pine logs and clapboard.

She had time to study them in detail as the traffic on the street reached an impasse. She would do better on foot. Scanning the signs within sight, she found the livery stable across the way. She turned Dom and urged him through the crowd to the far side of the street and back half a block.

A tallow-haired boy waiting in the door-way took Dom and her payment inside. She would not leave him long, only until she had found her house and seen whether it had a shelter for the mule. Standing be-tween her bags on the street, she held her ears against the din, then realized there was no help for it.

She dropped her hands and considered the situation. It was on the opposite side of the street that the most important buildings stood, and behind them the more perma-nent dwellings. That was where she would find her house, not among the shacks and tents sprawled on either side of the swiftly rushing creek.

Carina grasped her bags and plunged into the masses filling the street, hearing spatters of German, Spanish, and Italian — though less familiar Southern dialects of *abruzzesi, ciociari,* and *Sicilian* — among the English. But she didn't stop to look even when she reached the far boardwalk. Thank God she'd had the presence of mind to grab her carpetbag, or the deed, the key, and her bank notes would be at the bottom of the canyon with everything else.

Briccone! She spared a dark thought for the freighter, then pressed between the unwashed bodies milling in and out of the doorways of saloons. She had counted three in a row: the Boise Billiard Hall, the Gilded Slipper, and another called Emporium that smelled foul. There were others beyond those, gaming halls as well. Her teeth suddenly clamped together from the jolt of a man who nearly knocked the breath from her in passing.

"Pardon me, ma'am." He was gone as the last word left his mouth, melting into the crowd of matching coats, felt hats, and canvas pants.

She refastened her grips on the carpetbag and satchel and continued. Coming to the corner, she searched for a street marking and found none.

"Step right over this way, little lady. I see you are a woman who cherishes her complexion." The speaker wore a ruffled white shirt and suspenders, reminiscent of the

27

hawkers at the fairs back home. His head bore only a trace of hair in brown strings across the shiny crown. "Such flawless skin deserves only the finest handmade soap you will ever have the pleasure of using." He held out a bar, motioning her to come close.

As she took a step over, he held it to her nose. "Have you ever smelled anything so heavenly?" Its scent was lost in the cooking odor of the stall beside him, where the man stirring the pot looked to have foregone soap for years.

"Just fifteen cents for a bar of this heavenly blend. . . ."

Carina set down her cases, reached into her pocket for her coin purse, and felt only the empty pocket lining. She felt again, then checked the other pocket. "I've lost my . . ." Her mouth fell slack. "That man . . . that man who hit me. He took my purse!"

"Ah." The hawker shook his head. "Not a grand welcome to the Crystal City, my dear. Here. Take the soap. A small measure of my sympathy."

Carina's palm felt numb as he placed the bar upon it. A bar of soap to ease the injustice? Would it wash away the foul deed? But that was unfair. It was not this man's doing. "I must report it."

"Can you give a description?"

"He was perhaps a head taller than you, rough shaven and . . ." She couldn't remember any more. He had passed quickly and, in truth, looked no different than all the others.

The hawker laughed. "Could be any man in town, beggin' your pardon."

It was not a laughing matter. Twice now she had been robbed. First the freighter, now a common pickpocket. She would report them both. But for now, she was thankful her currency was in the carpetbag. "Could you tell me what street this is?"

"Some call it Walker, most call it Central, ma'am, though you won't find a sign either way. There's not a street marker in town, but I can direct you anywhere you need to go."

"I have a house on Drake." She reached into the carpetbag for the deed. "There's no number, but I have an illustration." She held it up and he studied it, then gave a low chuckle that disconcerted her more than anything else.

"Drake's the next block down. Turn right to find this place and good luck to you."

Luck. *Mine had better change soon.* "Thank you." Carina tucked the deed and illustration back into the bag and lifted her luggage. She pushed her way across the side street and started along the next block.

Suddenly the boardwalk dropped out from under her, and she stepped down hard to the section of walk a good foot lower than the last, at least for the length of the meat market. Then it jumped up again for the span of the drugstore. Each business seemed to build its own walkway in whatever manner it deemed best. But for the congestion, it would be easier to walk on the street, dust and all.

Her ankle sent a twinge of pain when she stepped again, but she ignored it. A feeling of unease grew within her, and she wanted to get to the house. She wasn't fool enough to expect it would look as good as the picture, not anymore, but the soap hawker's chuckle had been unsettling.

She rounded the next corner and quickly sidestepped the dentist who unfolded a chair and stood a sign against it. *Extractions, caps, and other.* Carina shuddered. She had a healthy fear of losing her teeth, and the thought of losing them there on the street corner with God knew what to deaden it and passersby gawking and gaping . . .

Carina bumped into a woman — no, a girl — but her eyes, and such meager clothing . . . The girl shoved by, but as she passed, a man in stained overalls grabbed and kissed her. The girl slapped him smartly across the face, and Carina wanted to cheer. Even if she was poor he had no right.

But then the girl leered. "You'll pay for the next one." She licked her lips and passed on.

Carina was shocked. She'd heard of such women, of course, but had never laid eyes on one. And so young!

"Hall Street hussy." The man rubbed his cheek and spat.

Carina looked away. Her head ached. The air suddenly seemed too thin, and whatever bracing effects she had imagined were gone with the dust, the noise, the smell, and the degradation around her. Where was the magic touted in the advertisement?

She scanned the dirt street ahead. At least it had less traffic than the main thoroughfare. Her eyes lighted on the house, her house. It had to be the one, tucked between Mae's Boardinghouse and Fletcher's Stationery.

It bore a vague resemblance to the illustration she carried in her pocket: single story, clapboard, a front window. The chimney had been an embellishment by the artist, as had the shrubs, shutters, and scrollwork trim. Even the paint had been false.

It was, as promised, centrally located near the happenings in town. Had she known the happenings would be so loud and vulgar, she would have thought twice. But now she wanted nothing more than to go inside and close the door behind her. Her heart cried out for sanctuary and peace.

Carina made for the house, smaller than

the picture had made it seem. Still, the front room would do for a table and bed — had she a table and bed any longer — and there was a cookstove. She could see its pipe extending from the roof as she gamely climbed the two front steps. She set down her load and found the key in her carpetbag.

She inserted the key, but the door wasn't locked. Puzzled, she pushed it open and looked in. The pinewood floor was cluttered with blankets and smelled of rank tobacco, the brown splatters on the walls verifying the source. She frowned. Could it be the wrong house?

She checked the advertisement. No. Her house was located between Mae's and Fletcher's businesses. This was the only house pressed between the two large buildings. She looked about again, disgusted by the filth. What were squatters doing in her house? Footsteps on the stairs behind her caught her attention, and she froze.

"What do you want, lady?"

Fear, like a slow spider, climbed up her spine as she faced the spiteful glare of the burly man before her. One side of his lip was drawn up like a cur by the scar that ran to his cheekbone. Beside him stood two others dressed in canvas pants and flannel shirts. Their hands were black with grime, and the same covered their clothes and boots.

With an effort, Carina kept the fear from her voice and drew herself up. "This is my house. I have the deed. . . ."

"No, it ain't." The first man spat, hawking brown spittle to the floor at her feet.

Animale! Though disgusted, she refused to step back. "And I have the key." She thrust it out on her palm.

With a swift motion he snatched it, leaving a black smear in its place. "No, you don't. Now get out." He shoved past her with an elbow. The other two followed.

When the door closed with her outside, she stood there on the step, her heart thumping in her chest, her hands clenched at her sides. It was not to heaven she'd come, but hell. Her head ached and tears blurred her vision. Well, she would see about this! The house might not be much, but it was hers. She had lost her luggage, her furniture, her coin purse, and now her temper. She would *not* lose her house.

Grasping her cases again, Carina made her way back to Central Street. She passed the Crystal Hotel and Fisher's General Mercantile, then the Miner's Exchange and Rudy Mitchell Clothier. Two doors down, she found the sign she needed. *Berkley Beck, Attorney at Law, Land Agent.*

Carina pushed open the door and strode through the empty room to the desk in the center, then she dropped her bags and hit the bell on the desk. There was a thump from under the desk, and a male voice swore.

Carina bent and looked underneath as the man in a gray linen suit sat back on his heels and held his head. His clean-shaven face screwed up in pain, then smoothed immediately as he looked up at her with wide blue eyes and smiled. "Pardon me. You gave me a start."

"And a knot by the sound of it."

He climbed out from under the desk and stood. "I lost the nib to my pen. It went down the crack there, and I was trying to retrieve it."

"I'm sorry."

"Please . . ." He indicated the chair before the desk.

Arranging the case and carpetbag on either side of her, Carina sat.

The man straightened his coat and hooked a thumb in the pocket of his vest, as though posed for a portrait artist's camera. "I'm Berkley Beck. How may I be of service?"

Carina pulled out the deed and handed it to him with the illustration and advertisement. "This is my house. Six weeks ago I bought it, and now three foul-smelling men have taken it over."

Berkley Beck almost smiled, then conformed his features and reached for the deed. "I see. Well, you do have a bit of a predicament." He scrutinized the paper closely. "Whereas the deed seems legal . . ."

"Seems?"

"Well, at first glance . . ."

"Is it not the legal deed to the property I purchased in full?" It had required the extent of her personal funds to make the purchase. Once Papa had seen her resolve, he had provided for the trip, but little more. The rest had been up to her.

Mr. Beck set the deed on top of the other papers covering the desk and took the chair behind it. "There are certain technicalities here, Mrs. . . ."

"DiGratia. Miss Carina DiGratia."

He reassessed her momentarily. "You see, this particular property . . ." He returned his attention to the illustration. ". . . must have been vacant for a time."

"It should have been vacant. I've only just arrived."

"Yes, but you see, if a property is vacant —"

"The property is not vacant. It is unlawfully inhabited."

He flicked the edge of the paper. "Yes, I see your point, Miss DiGratia, but . . ."

Carina stiffened. "Are you saying you can't help me?"

"No, no. I'm not saying that at all." He

patted his hand over the blond hair parted in the middle and slicked back from his face. "What I'm saying is, your claim has been jumped."

Carina waited. What on earth did that mean? She was angry, disillusioned, and uncommonly tired. All she wanted was a place to get clean and lie down. "I'm willing to pay for your services," she stated, though she had no idea what those services might cost. To her knowledge, no one in her family had been involved in litigation. They did business with their own and handled differences with loud voices but no courts.

"Miss DiGratia." His eyes went over her, liking what he saw, she knew by his expression. He stood and walked around the desk with a bit of swagger. "You are in the finest legal hands in town." He reached for her own hand and brushed it with his lips. "I assure you if anyone can assist you, it is I."

Carina withdrew her hand. "Then you will get my house back?"

"I'll do my utmost. But you look completely exhausted. Would you care to continue the discussion over supper? No charge, of course." He flashed a set of unusually broad and straight teeth.

Carina fought the unexpected tears. She was weary, had no place to stay, and dared not refuse his offer. She needed him. Besides, she was hungry. She dropped her gaze to her hands. "Is there someplace to lodge until they are out of my home?"

"I will personally vouch for you. The trouble, of course, will be vacancy." He assisted her to her feet. "But we'll see what we can find." He tucked her hand into his arm. "Your bags will be safe here in the office. No need to carry them along." He led her out, then turned the key in the door.

"Thank you, Mr. Beck." She returned a faint smile.

"Things will work out. You'll see."

Carina followed him into the lobby of the Crystal Hotel. The lobby was not large, but well enough appointed with gold-flocked, white silk wallpaper and brass lamps. She looked up the stairs that led to the rooms as Berkley Beck rang the bell.

"Yes, Mr. Beck?" The clerk shoved his spectacles up his nose with one finger and eyed them through the small oval lenses.

"Any vacancies, George?"

"You got to be kidding. On Friday night?" His glance at Carina brought the fire to her cheeks, then he turned back to Mr. Beck. "You needing a . . . room?"

"Miss DiGratia has need of a room."

George eyed her again, his eyes through the spectacles like the enlarged gape of a fish. His mouth, too, opened and shut like a carp tasting a pond's surface. Then he turned back to Mr. Beck. "I'm full up. But

Swisher moved out of Mae's 'bout an hour ago. Went to stay on the Mary Jean since he struck ore. Try over there."

"Very good. Keep us a table for supper, will you?" Berkley Beck took Carina's elbow and rushed her out. "Let's just hope we're in time."

In time? And the room had only vacated the hour before? Carina didn't ask. She only wanted to wash the dust from her face and teeth and lie down someplace quiet. Her stomach growled, as she had not eaten since early that morning, and she was light-headed and dizzy. Supper was necessary.

When Mr. Beck turned onto Drake, she refused to look at the house next to Mae's that should have been hers by now. She shivered. The evening air had chilled with the setting of the sun, chilled more swiftly than she would have expected. She was glad for the warmth of the front hall they entered. Its smooth pine walls had a golden hue that caught and held the lantern light like amber.

Carina's eyes landed on the innkeeper. Mae Dixon was perhaps the largest woman Carina had ever seen. The dimples on her cheeks would have swallowed half of Carina's pinky finger, and no less than three rolls connected her chin to her chest. A grizzle of mostly gray hair was knotted behind her head, and her earlobes were thick and curled under where they met her skin. But most impressive were the eyes, thick-lashed and nearly violet.

"Well, Berkley Beck, what have we here?" Mae's throaty voice was thick as butter.

"Mae, Miss DiGratia needs a room. Legal matters keep her from claiming her rightful property next door."

She raised thin eyebrows. "The Shipley place? Whew. Even you'll have a time ousting the Carruthers."

"Nevertheless, oust them, I will. In the meantime . . ."

Mae shook her head and the neck skin swung. "Swisher moved out not an hour ago. But I have a man holding the room on a ten dollar deposit."

Berkley Beck reached into his vest and took out twenty dollars. "Miss DiGratia's first week and a little something on top."

Mae Dixon pressed her hands to her ample hips. "Are you bribing me?"

"One hand washes the other."

"When I need washin', I use the pump."

Mr. Beck flashed his teeth, conceding the point. "For Miss DiGratia's sake, then."

Mae fixed her strange purple eyes on Carina, shrugged, then turned to the wooden boxes on the wall behind her. She slid the key from one and handed it over. "Number eight."

Carina silenced any protest. She was in

39

no position to be sanctimonious. The man who had put down the deposit would fare better finding another place than she could.

Pocketing the key, Mr. Beck turned to her. "We'll collect your bags after supper. Would you like to have a look at the room first?" He led her away from the counter. "I daresay you'd better keep it, even if it's not to your liking. It was a terrific stroke of luck to find one open."

"It wasn't open."

"It wasn't occupied . . . yet. Possession is nine-tenths of the law."

The room felt overly warm. "So now I've done what the Carruthers did to me — jumped that man's claim?"

"Miss DiGratia —"

"Please." Carina raised her hand. "Don't explain. I only know that I . . ." Her head suddenly swimming, she swayed against him. She closed her eyes, only vaguely aware of Berkley Beck supporting her back outside.

He was speaking, but his words sounded faint and meaningless. ". . . the elevation. Your blood will thicken after a time . . . so thoughtless of me."

The cold air cleared her head, and she looked up with an exhaled breath. "I'm better now, thank you." She released his arm.

"In a few days you'll adjust. Can you

make it back to the hotel for supper? I could borrow Mae's hack, but it's more trouble than it's worth trying to get through now that the sun's down."

"What do you mean?"

"The miners, of course." He directed her attention to the swarming street. "Three thousand men at last count, or very nearly."

Where had they all come from like ants from the ground? The sight was over-whelming. Carina shook her head. "I can walk."

The din that had been considerable during the day was now far worse, increased by the raucous noise that passed for music blaring from the saloon doorways they passed. Gambling parlors and every other commerce dependent on the miners had stepped up their efforts to lure the men in.

Carina was thankful for Mr. Beck's sturdy arm as he shouldered them through the crowd. The dining room at the Crystal Hotel was packed, all but the table held for them. As Berkley Beck seated her, she wondered why someone had not stolen their table as he had done the room at Mae's. Maybe with Berkley Beck it only worked one way, and for that she should be grateful.

She took the menu handed her by the red-haired woman whose lips pressed in a hard, tight line. The skin at either side of her mouth was creased and craggy like quarried granite.

"Thank you, Mrs. Barton." Mr. Beck took his bill of fare with a smile.

The woman did not return the smile nor speak but merely walked away. Carina sighed. The menu swam before her eyes, and she pressed them shut. She could well believe Berkley Beck's speech about thin blood. The walk over had left her winded, and her heart was still pounding.

"The ham steak with redeye gravy is exceptional."

Carina closed the menu. "Thank you."

The ham steak *was* exceptional. It was the first good thing she had experienced. That, and Mr. Beck's kindness. Wiping her mouth, she looked up at him. When he smiled, his face seemed thinner, scarcely framing his broad mouth, but he was handsome in his own way.

His dark eyebrows contrasted with his blond hair, and she wondered if his beard would come in dark as well, though he bore no shadow by which to tell. Unwillingly she thought of another whose blue black shadow would be well under way by this time of night, whose dark melting eyes matched his swarthy complexion. She pushed away the thought.

"Feeling better?" Mr. Beck's blue eyes were amused.

Carina realized she hadn't spoken since the meal was served. She laughed. "I've been discourteous."

"Nonsense. You needed to eat. I'm only glad it met with your approval."

With the food warming her stomach, Carina felt almost punchy. "You've been so kind."

"My pleasure, I assure you. And now I'll see you back to your room. You have need of a good night's sleep." He stood and pulled out her chair.

"Have they brought the check?"

"They'll charge it to my account."

So he was a man of standing. Good. She had done well to find him. Carina waited outside while he ducked into his office for her bags.

He came back out in a moment. "Have you a trunk somewhere?"

Somewhere *inverità*. "That is another matter I must discuss with you. On the road up, my wagon broke a wheel. A freighter sent it over the side with all my belongings."

"Deplorable bad luck."

Carina ducked under a low-hanging sign where the boardwalk dipped to a lower level. "But what can be done? Must he pay damages or . . . or . . ."

"Unfortunately, it does state in the miners' bylaws that the wagon road must remain open. Any blockage is forfeit. Heinous

43

as it may seem, the freighter was within his rights."

Carina frowned. "Why should he be allowed to deprive me of my goods to pass by with his?"

Mr. Beck stopped at the base of Mae's steps. "He shouldn't. But he is. The road is critical, and yours is not the first wagon to meet that fate. I'm terribly sorry."

Carina saw his sincerity, but it changed nothing. She turned as a man stormed out Mae's door, his flaccid cheeks red, fists clenched at his sides. He blew past them with neither a glance nor word, but Carina was certain it was the man whose room she had usurped.

She felt a twinge of remorse, then realized she had only acted as did everyone else in this place. She would have to stop regretting such actions if she were to survive in Crystal City.

"Never mind," Berkley Beck murmured. "He'll find someplace else."

She smiled, more grateful than she could say to have found Mr. Beck. Though he had wrongfully usurped the room, it was more than anyone else had done for her. Bene. She would take it. Mr. Beck had won it for her. And one thing she knew. Berkley Beck would never have cast her belongings down the mountain, whatever the bylaws said.

He took the staircase ahead of her,

stopped outside number eight, and fished the key from his pocket. Then he opened the door to reveal a space the size of a horse stall, stuffed with a cot, washstand, and coat hook. The side walls were stretched canvas, stained and mottled. Carina took it in with one glance, and her expression must have said more than words.

Berkley Beck set the carpetbag and satchel inside the door and stepped back out. His voice was gentle. "In the morning we'll see what we can do about things."

She nodded and watched him down the stairs. Then she went into the room and lifted the carpetbag to the cot. Thankfully it contained a nightgown and change of undergarments, her pig bristle toothbrush and tooth powder, and a hairbrush. Only those things she'd needed readily at hand.

The black leather satchel she placed under the cot. She would not think about that now. She looked around the room again, slowly circling it with her eyes, very close to tears. The morning seemed a long way off.

Three

What joy in the sunshine. What glory fills a bird's throat that infects the air with song. I am awakened to the wonder, and I will open my ears and close my eyes, the better to listen and feel the sun's glow.

Rose

Carina woke with a crick in her neck. The room was cold, and the blanket smelled of whiskey and something worse. She shoved it away from her face, disgusted, then rubbed a hand over her eyes and sat up. The sun's rosy glow filled the tiny window like the rose-painted panes in the cathedral at Turin, where she had visited once with her papa when she was very small.

Carina felt a pang for the old country, something she seldom felt, as she'd been so young when they left. It was the newness, the unfamiliar room, the shock of all that had gone wrong. She had wakened earlier than she might normally after taking most of the night to fall asleep, yet not early enough by the sounds of commotion beneath the floor.

She would have snuggled back in and forgotten it all but for the smell of the blanket and the lumps in the ticking. She tried to remember if she had ever slept on straw before. Played in it, yes — sliding and tossing it until she was prickly with hay dust. But slept on it? Maybe on the ship. Certainly not since.

Frowning, she reached back to rub the stiffness from her neck, still surprised she had slept at all through the continuous din of the night. The lace edge of her cotton batiste gown brushed her cheek, and she closed her eyes, thinking of all the things she had lost on the mountainside. Her anger brought her fully awake.

She sat up and swung her legs out, then wrenched them back immediately as a mouse skittered across the floor. Once her heart stopped pounding, she watched the creature. Unlike the rodents she had seen before, this one had pale toffee-colored fur with fat white cheeks and large black eyes. Its ears were pink shells. When it stopped at the corner and raised up to sniff the air, she could see its whiskers trembling in the morning light, fragile as spider threads.

Sliding her legs out once again, she leaned closer to the mouse. "Good morning, little *topo*." It tipped its head, took one good look, and ran. Carina dropped to her knees beside the cot, closed her eyes, and murmured, "Grazie, Dio, for this day. Keep me from the Evil One and all his ways. And if you don't mind . . . give me my house today."

She crossed herself, touching her forehead, her chest and each shoulder, secure that nothing evil could pass that shield — or at least after yesterday, hoping so. Then she stood and ran her fingers through the tangles of her hair. She took off her gown and carefully folded it back into the carpetbag, then tied on her corset and slipped the skirt and blouse on from the day before. Taking the pitcher from the stand, she went out of the room.

Downstairs she found Mae setting out plates of hot cakes as fast as she could on the long wood-plank tables lined with men. Carina touched her arm as she hustled by on her way back to the kitchen. "Excuse me. Where do I get water?"

"The pump's out back." Mae swung around. "But wait a moment."

Carina watched her cross the room, fascinated by her graceful rolling gait.

"Take this with you." Mae pulled a pistol from beneath the desk. "Those Carruthers are bad eggs."

Carina looked at the pistol in Mae's soft palm. She must arm herself to gather water to wash? What had she gotten into? She clasped the cold metal of the gun.

"There's enough men in town totin' hardware that a girl with looks like yours better watch her step. What are you anyway, a Spaniard?"

Carina frowned. It was true the combination of Papa's northern coloring and Mamma's darker features was unusual. But a Spaniard? "I am from Italy, though now I am American . . . like you."

"Well, you're just exotic enough to attract more attention than you want."

Carina slid the gun barrel into the waist of her skirt. She had never before handled a weapon, but she was glad for it now. "Thank you."

The air was frigid as she stepped outside and looked cautiously about. She saw no sign of the Carruthers while she filled the pitcher at the pump, but the skin on her neck crawled, thinking they could be watching from the house, her house.

Exotic? There were Italians in Crystal. She had seen them, heard them on the street as she passed through the day before. But they were *contadini*, southern peasants, not northern Italians from the Kingdom of Sardinia like her papa. They came to America with nothing, came to escape hardship, but they were ill-equipped to rise to higher status. Could they be, as Papa said, so entrenched in hardship they clung to it?

She had not known such hardship, and she crossed herself in gratitude, then reached for the pump handle. She had not even known hunger, thanks to God and her papa. Angelo Pasquale DiGratia was an educated man and a gifted physician. He had been famous in Salerno, a friend of Count Camillo Benso di Cavour, prime minister to Victor Emmanuel II, king of Sardinia-Piedmont.

And he was well respected in Sonoma. With his classic patrician features, blond hair, and blue eyes, his knowledge of seven languages, four of which he could read as well, and, most of all, his ability to heal . . . ah, Angelo Pasquale DiGratia was a great man. She felt a homesick pang. Oh, Papa.

With the full pitcher, she made her way back to the boardinghouse. Inside her room, Carina scrubbed with the vendor's soap, then brushed her hair into a dark, rippled veil down her back. Closing her eyes, she tossed it softly back, feeling the length of it brush the top of her thighs. Loose like this, it was her finest feature, or so Flav—

She jerked her head upright. She would not think of that. Her hair dried while she brushed the dust from her blouse and skirt and donned them again. Once she was dressed, she twisted and clipped her hair at the nape with the horn barrette her mother had given her.

First she would check on Dom. She would have to leave him at the livery until

Mr. Beck got her house back. But she would see Mr. Beck directly. After that, she would attend to the task that burned most fiercely.

Carina pulled the door closed behind her. From the tumult downstairs she guessed Mae was still serving food, and when she reached the stairs, she saw it was so. The benches, made of a single log hewn lengthwise and supported by thinner crossed logs, overflowed with more men than Mae housed.

Every table was filled, and as fast as Mae shoved platters of meat and hot cakes down, they were devoured. Like slopped hogs, the men ate, then took up their hats and walked out. There was no refinement, no leisurely enjoyment. She pictured her own papa at the breakfast table, his shirt white in the gentle sunlight, his motions elegant, relaxed, his smile quick as his laughter. Even her brothers with their pranking did not match this . . . coarseness.

Watching the miners, her hunger left her. Though the smell of fried bacon and woodsmoke teased her nose, Carina shook her head. Even were there room for her, she would not join them. She slipped out unnoticed.

The morning air had a bite, though the June sun climbed up the clear sky. It seemed to have no power yet to warm the day. As she turned onto Central Street, she passed three boys scrabbling in the sawdust swept out from the floor of the Boise Billiard Hall. Carina wrinkled her nose at the smell of whiskey, vomit, and tobacco spittle in the sawdust, but the boys seemed oblivious. One jumped up and hallooed, gripping a coin above his head. The other two dug their fingers in with renewed fervor. She looked away.

Empty ore wagons, hauled by mules or horse teams, made their way out to the mines. She turned toward the stable. *Tavish Livery and Feed*. A sign to the right of the door read:

City transfer & hack line
Expressing and hauling

And on the left:

Boarding horses a specialty
Horses let by the day, week, or month
Carriages to Wasson Lake
and all points of interest
Fine saddle horses.

Inside, she strained in the dim light. Dom was there, and beyond him, she saw the freighter's blacks. So he was in town somewhere, no doubt delivering his precious cargo. He who made free with her own precious things. Dom whickered as she reached for his muzzle.

"Help you, lass?"

She turned to the wizened ostler, so bent his head was no higher than hers. His knuckles, like crab apples, gripped the harness he held. A pang for Ti'Giusseppe seized her, and she swallowed the lump of longing in her throat. "This is my mule."

"Ah, the one with a will of 'is own, now."

"He was trouble?"

"Not an animal alive gives Alan Tavish trouble, lassie. I have the way with them, ye see."

She smiled, sensing the same affectionate passion for creatures her Ti'Giusseppe possessed. That, at least, she could be glad of. Dom was in a good place.

"Are you needin' 'im hitched up, then?"

Hitch him to what, rubble on the mountainside? She frowned to think of her belongings crashed to pieces and felt the hurt and anger still inside. *Oofa!* Enough. What was done was done. "Thank you, no. But I will need him saddled . . . if you have a saddle?"

"I do, but not a lady's."

"I can ride astride." As she had with Flavio too many times.

"Then I'll get 'im ready for ye."

"Thank you. I'll come back." Carina

blinked as she stepped back outside into the brightness and headed across the street.

"Watch it!"

She jumped back from the irate driver and his string of shaggy mules straining with a load of ore.

"Lose yer purty head if you don't watch out!" He spat a brown string.

Carina raised a bent arm topped with her fist. "Animale!" Twice now she had been spat at by tobacco-chewing brutes. Animals! Not even Ti'Lorenzo, who always held a plug in his cheek, American-style, had ever spat in her direction.

Gathering her skirt, she crossed through the traffic and started down the uneven boardwalk to Berkley Beck's office. When he didn't answer her rap on the door, she tried the knob. It held fast. Surveying the street, she saw no sign of him among the growing crowd, so she made her way to the Crystal Hotel.

Unlike the night before, the dining room was empty, though by its condition, it had been well used earlier. The miners must rise with the sun, or more likely from the noise last night, they simply stumbled from the gaming halls back to their diggings in the mountainside.

Only Berkley Beck lingered at the corner table, engrossed in a newspaper. The coffee steam from his cup drew her irresistibly.

At her approach, he jumped up. "Miss DiGratia."

"Good morning, Mr. Beck."

"Please." He held the chair for her.

Carina sat.

"May I order you breakfast?"

Her appetite had not returned. "Only coffee."

"That I have already." He turned over a white china cup and poured from the pot beside his plate.

Carina sipped slowly, breathing the aroma. A pang of longing seized her for Mamma's coffee and cake. She could almost breathe its fragrance, and her mouth watered at the thought. No one matched Mamma's *tarelle*. She sighed.

"I trust you spent a restful night?" Mr. Beck's voice was sincere.

She raised her eyebrows. "A loud night, but I did make a friend."

"A friend?"

"Yes. A fat-cheeked fellow."

He raised an eyebrow. "Did this fellow have a name?"

"Topo, I guess. He skittered under the floor board before I could make his proper acquaintance."

"Aha." Berkley Beck laughed. "You'll find the rodent population thriving. There's not a cat in town. Are you sure you won't eat?"

Carina shook her head. "Thank you, no. I came to find you. I went first to your office."

"I'm afraid I do dawdle over breakfast. A terrible habit, but one I cultivate nonetheless. I apologize."

"There's no need."

"Now that you've found me, I can only hope it wasn't all business." Again his broad teeth flashed.

She returned his smile. "I'm anxious to have my situation resolved. I had expected to be settled in already, and today I meant to find employment."

"Employment, Miss DiGratia?"

She took out the advertisement that had appeared in the same paper as the one for her house and held it out to Mr. Beck. "You see here? Professional opportunities for women. Contact Madame LeGuerre."

Mr. Beck's eyes went abruptly from the advertisement to her. "Unless I have misread you, Miss DiGratia, these are not the professional opportunities you seek."

"What do you mean? It says training provided."

Mr. Beck folded the advertisement and covered it with his hand on the table. "I would encourage you not to pursue this avenue further."

"Why not?"

"Madame LeGuerre is a . . . well, a madam."

Carina looked at him blankly.

"A woman of the night."

Her eyes widened involuntarily. "You mean this is . . . but . . ." Carina spread her hands. Was it possible? Yet another error? "I didn't know. I purchased a house. I intended to learn a profession — not that profession. I . . ." She sagged in her chair. "I don't know what to do."

He would tell her to go home, that Crystal was no place for her. And he would be right. Oh the shame, to go home to Flavio's taunting. . . . Hadn't he said as much, calling her a foolish girl? He'd been angry, irate that she was leaving. But he was right. What would she do now?

Mr. Beck laid a comforting hand over hers. "Miss DiGratia, I would be happy to engage you as an assistant."

She started. "An assistant?"

"You no doubt noticed the deplorable condition of my office."

Now that he mentioned it, she did recall the cluttered desk and the stacks of books and papers along the wall. She had been too stunned by her situation to consider it before, but now . . . What were her choices?

She looked into the earnest face before her. "Are you doing this out of kindness, Mr. Beck?"

"Yours would be the kindness, Miss DiGratia. I'm a desperate slob."

57

That would not be so different from Mr. Garibaldi, whose books she'd kept. "Have you enough business to afford —"

"Heavens, yes! I'm over my head with claim disputes, property settlements . . ."

"Such as mine?" Carina raised the challenge pointedly. She couldn't let him forget.

"Well, yes, as a matter of fact." He smoothed back his hair.

"Then it will be some time before you settle it?"

Beck sipped his coffee, dabbed his lips with the napkin, then folded and laid it over his plate. "Miss DiGratia, you have my word. I'll move with all due haste. But . . ." He straightened. "I won't mislead you. It will be involved."

Carina's heart sank. "Involved means time."

He nodded regretfully. "My concern is that the transaction you made on the house may be as misleading as this one." He patted the folded newsprint beneath his palm.

Her anger flared. How had she been so duped? Was she a dunce, an imbecile? *Innocente!* Again she had trusted!

Glancing up, she saw the freighter who had destroyed her wagon. It had to be the same, his brown hair hanging to his shoulders, the mustache jaunty and full. He stood in the doorway looking like a Corsican pi-

58

rate, even without a gold ring in his ear and a sash at his waist. He'd acted one, too. It was piracy he'd practiced on her, no matter his reasons. Her blood burned at the very sight of him.

He turned when the red-haired woman Mr. Beck had addressed as Mrs. Barton hastened to his side. She looked like a different woman, all sweetness and joy, the craggy sides of her mouth folded back around her smile, revealing long ferretlike teeth. "Quillan Shepard, bless you. You've brought my order?"

Quillan Shepard. A rogue embodied, and this woman transformed from a silent malcontent to a doting aunt. Carina couldn't help but stare. Bless him? How could anyone bless such a man?

Mrs. Barton took the box from him, no sign of her tight-lipped grimace now. "Have a seat, and I'll fix you something hot before you take off again."

He shook his head. "No thanks. No time for it."

Of course not, Carina thought. He's much too busy to perform normal human functions. Sustenance and kindness must not interfere with commerce for such a one.

"Well, you can't take that pass on an empty stomach. If you won't spare the time, I'll pack something up."

"It's not necessary."

She laid a hand on his arm. "I insist."

Quillan Shepard's sudden smile transformed him, though it was brief and a little indulgent. Carina fumed. She would not be taken in. A mouse who considers the smile of the snake is soon made dinner. She had been naive yesterday, but she was no longer. She turned away and caught Mr. Beck's gaze. Had she betrayed her contempt?

Carina drained her cup, and Mr. Beck offered her more. She shook her head. "No, thank you."

He replaced the pot and threaded his fingers together. "Now then, if you accept my offer . . ."

"I accept."

His face brightened, the brows pulling up abruptly like a marionette's, the eyes wide and satisfied. "Good. Very good. As for compensation, the best I can do is pay your room and board and perhaps a dollar a week beyond."

"Mr. Beck, you're too kind." Relief washed over her. It wasn't much, but it was a start.

He raised her hand and kissed it. "I'm very sorry for your misfortune, Miss DiGratia. Whatever I can do to ease your situation . . . it's my pleasure, I assure you."

Carina felt the warmth of his lips on her fingers. "Thank you." From the corner of her eye she saw Mrs. Barton tuck a wrapped parcel into Quillan Shepard's hands.

"Will you come to the office now?" Mr. Beck's breath lingered on her fingers.

Carina pulled her gaze from the now empty doorway. "I have an errand today."

"Then have dinner with me."

She laughed. "Mr. Beck, you are shameless."

"Guilty where you are concerned, Miss DiGratia." He stood and pulled out her chair.

Carina preceded him outside. The day had warmed, she saw, as she stepped into the sunlight. It would likely get as hot as yesterday, the heat with the strange sharpness she had not felt before. As Icarus flying too close to the sun, had she, too, melted her wings and was even now falling to earth?

Four

To rise to higher joy is to risk a deeper
sorrow. Do I dare reach for the sun?

Rose

Carina went back to her room and stripped
the sheet from her bed. One look at the stains
on the mattress made her wish she hadn't.
How Mamma would have scrubbed the
ticking to keep it fresh. She balled the sheet
under her arm and went downstairs.

"Where you heading with that bed sheet?"
Mae called from behind the desk.

"I have some things to collect, but I won't
harm it." Carina edged toward the door,
wondering how it could matter.

"See that you don't. Things come dear up
here."

If they were dear, why did Mae take such
poor care of them? But it wasn't for her to
judge. She would be careful with the sheet,
but she could think of no other way to take
care of her business. Carina found Dom
ready for her as Alan Tavish had promised.
"I've no place to keep him at present. Will
you board him for me?"

"Sure and don't worry. He makes a fine
companion in the wee hours."

Did the rheumatism keep the old ostler awake? Carina took her eyes from the crab-apple knuckles. "I'll likely have him all day. Is there a feed bag?"

Tavish shuffled to the wall and unhooked a bag, then filled it with oats. He then filled a water pouch and tucked them in one saddlebag while she shoved the sheet into the other. "There now. That'll keep 'im."

"Thank you." Leading Dom outside, she nearly collided with Quillan Shepard, coming for his horses, no doubt.

He stepped aside, and, with a snort, she tugged Dom's rein and passed. Holding the mule steady, she mounted. The sooner she was gone the less likely her tongue —

"Miss DiGratia."

She reined in and turned back to him. The fact that he remembered her name was more annoying than gratifying.

"If you need things replaced, I'll pick them up for you." His hair blew across his shoulders in the breeze.

"I will find whatever I need in the stores, thank you."

"Not at my price."

"Oh, I see. You mean to profit from throwing my things over."

"If you buy directly from the wagon, I'll charge you my cost only. If you go inside any store here, you'll pay six times the rate."

"Do you so gouge the shop owners that they must raise the prices so high?"

"Most of the cost of business up here is what it takes to get the goods from the train to the town. I think you have sense enough to see that."

"Sense enough?"

"Well, anyone who takes up with Berkley Beck can't have too much sense. Good day, Miss DiGratia." He tipped his hat and went into the stable.

Carina kicked Dom harder than she intended, and he leaped forward. He kept the pace only a short while though, then slowed to his usual plod. The noon sun was peaking overhead when Carina approached the steep, narrow strip of trail that had cost her so much. The pitch of the rocky slope dropping away from the trail made her head swim before she even neared the edge.

Keeping her focus on the dusty trail, she made her way to the spot where the wagon had gone over. She dismounted, closed her eyes and gathered her nerve, then looked down the plummeting slope to the destruction below. Fragments of wood and fabric cluttered the rocks and sparse trees.

She was *pazza* to think of going down there. What if she fainted or blacked out? What if her vision blurred and her head spun? What if she, like her wagon, plunged . . . Carina pressed her hands to her face, then with renewed resolution squinted through her fingers.

Was that . . . it was! A crate wedged between a spindly tree and the boulder it sprang from. Could it be her books? It looked intact, and that excitement bolstered her. She pulled the sheet from Dom's saddlebag and braved the edge. If she looked just where her feet were and no farther . . .

The first step was the worst. It was the only one she had to think about. After that she moved without thinking, sliding, catching herself, and sliding again. She scraped her palm and banged her elbow before grabbing hold of a handful of scrub and stopping her fall. She was only halfway to the ridge, but already she found the remains of the rocker.

It must have flown off before the wagon broke up. She lifted one rung and smoothed the dust off with her fingers. The ache started in her chest. They were only things. She had known when she started out she might lose them one way or another. It was just that she had come so close. And the rocker held such memories of Mamma rocking and crooning in its embrace.

Tears welled up in her eyes, and she blinked them away. Quillan Shepard. Could he not have added her things to his load? She had brought so little. Did Mr. Quillan

Shepard think there was no room for even her meager lot? Would she have added so much to his horses' toil?

Carina ran her hands down her blouse and skirt. Small boned. *Delicata*. Even though her angles had filled in as her mother promised they would, she lacked her sister's soft plumpness. She stood only five foot four inches — hardly substantial. And her trunk, her crates, her few pieces of furniture . . . could it have been so much?

She sighed. She was tired and hot, bruised and scraped, and not in her right mind. But she was not going to be beaten. She would salvage whatever she could, and what was lost was lost.

Standing, she slid away from the scrub and landed on her backside. She should stay that way, but she couldn't risk the only skirt she had left. With her hands spread to the sides for balance, she regained her feet and scrabbled down the slope to the ridge where the wagon had struck and gone to pieces.

Beyond that ridge the mountain dropped sheer to the creek bed below. The scene wavered. She felt herself falling and looked quickly away. It was only a trick of her mind. She must not let it confuse her, or she would indeed fall.

A short distance to her left, the lidless trunk lay on its side with a few items of clothing. One was the blue denim skirt she

66

had sewn for the trip. It appeared sound, and she dropped it into the sheet with a camisole and blouse. The lace on the silk blouse was badly torn but maybe not past repair.

She made her way along the precarious ridge to the tree growing from the split boulder. There was indeed a crate of books wedged there, and while the crate was broken open, it hadn't spilled its contents. Like a greedy child with a candy jar, she dug out every book and piled them into the sheet, then hung it on her shoulder and tugged.

At the weight of it, she nearly lost her footing. Carina dropped the bundle and groaned. She would never make it up the slope with it. That meant more than one trip up and down, again facing the chasm below. But would she rather lose her books? She peered up the steep expanse of rock, scattered pines, and pale golden grasses.

Her chest lurched. A figure appeared at the crest, his long shadow spreading down the slope like molasses. She closed her eyes. What a sight she must present to Mr. Quillan Shepard.

She settled in against the tree as he started down, not sliding in a straight line as she had, but cutting back and forth as he descended, keeping his footing and dislodging as little of the slope as possible. He could not have missed the fresh gash of rockslide and dirt she had left in her wake.

He came to a stop beside her and tipped the broad brim of his hat. "Miss DiGratia."

"I don't require your assistance."

"It's my pleasure, I assure you." One corner of his mouth twitched. Was he mocking her with Mr. Beck's words? What sort of man was he to gloat over her misfortune?

He looked back and forth along the ridge. "You're scavenging your belongings?"

Narrowing her eyes, Carina raised her chin. "I do not scavenge."

Frowning, he eyed the sheet tied up around what she had already found. "You can't mean to haul that entire crate of books."

"I do."

He smiled crookedly — not at all the smile he'd given Mrs. Barton. "May I?" He reached for the sheet and, to her dismay, untied the top and reached in.

"If you drop so much as one book over, I'll . . ."

"What?" He raised an eyebrow at her.

Carina imagined herself shoving him hard, over the edge and down. She saw the rush of air catch his hat, his hair flying up, and his arms wheeling as he plunged downward . . . The thought brought on a feeling of vertigo, and she turned away.

He pulled out a leather-bound copy of Dickens and flipped it open. " 'It was the best of times; it was the worst of times.' "

Carina brushed the loose strand of hair from her face. "That was my papa's."

He didn't comment, only slipped the pack from his back, undid the leather clasp, and pulled it open. Then he moved the books from her sheet into the pack until it was full. Only four remained.

What was he doing? What was this gesture? A guilty conscience? He certainly had cause for one. "How did you know I was here?"

"Saw your mule." He reached into the branches of the pine and retrieved a petticoat with eyelet trim.

Carina snatched it from him.

He shouldered the pack. "See what else you can get into that sheet. Don't try to go up without me. From the looks of your trail down, you're lucky your neck's not broken already." He started up, traversing the slope as he had before, as surefooted as a goat.

Leaving the sheet spread open on the ridge, Carina crept back along its edge to a clump of bushes. The small, fuzzy, gray-green leaves on the branches were thick with feathers where her mattress had met its end. The rest of the bedding must have gone over the edge, maybe even been carried away by the creek below. Hooking her arm around a spindly pine trunk beside the bush, she chanced a look down. There at the water's edge was her iron headboard.

She swayed and regained her balance, then scooped up a shawl and camisole without even checking their condition. Farther along the edge, she found the shattered remains of two lamps, utterly useless, and a battered kettle, salvageable. One iron pot and its lid were caught in a bush, and she dug into the branches to retrieve her hand mirror.

It had been a gift from Papa for her sixteenth birthday. Cradling the smooth, curved frame in her palm, she caught her reflection, repeated in angular fragments by the slivers. The sun, glancing off the shards, pained her eyes, and she set the mirror on the shawl. It was useless, but she wouldn't leave it there like so much rubbish.

Seeing nothing more, she carried her finds back to the sheet. There she laid the pot and kettle and mirror among the remaining books as Mr. Shepard returned. The camisole and petticoat she tucked under the skirt, blouse, and shawl, unwilling to give him a second glimpse of her lacy whites.

He eyed the large iron pot, then bent and worked it into his pack along with the lid. "There's a ladle behind you, and I'd wager that box holds silver."

Carina spun, crouched down beside the bush he indicated, and clapped her hands together, forgetting everything in her excitement. "It is! It's Nonna's silver, and . . ." As she reached, the ladle slid off the edge and sailed down . . . down . . .

Her head spun, and she felt the box slipping from her fingers. Something gripped her arms, then her waist.

"Whoa, lady, don't faint here."

Coming to her senses, she shook off Quillan Shepard's arms. "I do not faint. It's . . . high places."

He looked over the edge, and she felt her insides jelly.

"Please." She pressed a hand to her forehead. "Don't lean."

Again he crooked an eyebrow. "You're serious, aren't you?"

Carina turned away. How Flavio had taunted . . . until he saw it truly hurt her. She dropped her chin. What should it matter? She could live with it. What business was it of anyone else's?

Mr. Shepard eyed the slope up. "You must have wanted your things awfully bad."

She didn't answer, knowing tears would choke her voice. She stooped down and fingered a broken shard of china. Her blue willow plate. He heaved the pack to his back and climbed again without further comment.

Buono. She wouldn't look a gift horse in the mouth by refusing his help, but she wanted none of his sympathy, if he was even capable of that. She searched the ground on either side, but there was nothing else. Carefully she laid her nonna's box of silver forks, knives, and spoons on the sheet, then tied it tightly. She hauled it to her shoulder and looked up. With a deep breath, she started to climb.

It was not as easy as Quillan Shepard made it look, but she followed his example, going at an angle and keeping her feet sideways to the slope. At least she did not have to see the drop below. The worst part was turning to cut back the opposite way. Each time, she lost ground and sent the dirt cascading down. Once she caught herself with an outstretched hand to keep from going with it.

"Hold up." Quillan Shepard left no room for argument.

She stopped climbing and waited for him to meet her. When he reached for the filled sheet, she handed it over but couldn't resist saying, "I'm not helpless."

He shouldered the sheet. "Now keep upslope from me, and I'll break your fall if you come loose."

Near the top there was no choice but to scrabble with hands and feet. Carina reached up. Suddenly Quillan Shepard thrust her aside with the back of his arm, caught her on his knee, and fired the gun that flashed from his holster.

Carina cried out with the gun's report, clamping her hands to her ears, which left her hanging from his knee. He swung his arm under her ribs and pressed against the slope, digging his boot into the ground to stop their slide. She shrieked and struggled when the spasming snake body flipped over the edge and dangled from a rock at her cheekbone.

"Stop!" He flung the snake aside with the barrel of the gun and tightened his grip on her ribs.

Carina's heart pounded against his forearm as she sucked in ragged breaths and stopped fighting. Her ears rang, and her stomach turned at the bloody ooze left on the stones. She was thankful now for the hollow in her belly. Breakfast might not have remained inside.

"All right, use my knee for a step." His voice was strained but firm.

Carina obeyed, though she would not reach blindly for the edge again. She climbed onto his thigh just above the knee and pushed herself up to find herself eye-level with the gaping, fanged mouth of the snake. She lurched back instinctively, but Quillan Shepard's hand was firm on her spine, allowing no retreat.

His gunshot had severed the snake's head, and it lay there as though unaware the rest was gone. Cringing, she pulled herself up, then twisted around and sat, ignoring as best she could the tan-and-gray plaited snake head lying in the dirt. Her breath came in long, shaking lungfuls.

Quillan Shepard climbed down to where the sheet bundle had fallen, then made his way back up. When he reached the road, he nudged the snake head with his boot toe. "Don't touch it yet. Poison's still good."

Carina flashed him a glance. Touch it? She scrambled to her feet. "Is it a rattle-snake?"

"It is. You seem to have a way of attracting snakes, Miss DiGratia."

So he was back to taunting. She would not ponder what he meant. The gun was holstered on his hip. She had not noticed before that he was one of those who carried a gun, but she was deeply thankful now. "You saved my life."

"One bite doesn't usually kill, but you're in a whole lot of hurt. 'Course, if he'd gotten a neck hold . . ." He dumped the sheet on the trail.

Carina shuddered, glancing once again at the jaws of the snake spread so wide they almost doubled back. The fangs stood out like needles.

"Keep it if you want. It's powerful medicine to some." At her incredulous look, he shrugged, then kicked the head over the side, where it tumbled to meet its body.

"How did you know it was there?"

"The rattle. Didn't you hear it?"

In her scramble she had heard nothing. But why elaborate?

He yanked open the sheet and emptied its contents beside those he had already taken from his pack. He looked over the assortment, though, to his credit, lingered less over her underthings than the pot and kettle and books. "How're you getting all this back to town?"

She motioned to Dom, expecting his criticism, but it didn't come.

He studied the pile, then began arranging the items in the sheet. "You'll want it balanced so the mule doesn't strain something."

Noting his kindness toward the animal, she softened in spite of herself.

When he had the load divided, he tied up the ends and fixed the makeshift pack over Dom's back. He checked its fit, then came back around. "Can't hurry him with iron pots and Dickens banging his flanks. It's hard enough to expect him to cross the summit two days running."

Carina's back rose again. "I won't."

"Well, then, I guess you're set." He gave her a hand to mount and checked the fit of the pack again. "At his pace . . . a couple, three hours to town. Should have plenty of daylight."

She nodded, taking up the reins, and looked about for his transportation. He pointed down the road. At the first spot wide enough for two conveyances, his team and wagon waited, the load once again carefully tied under a tarp. He must have passed Dom, then left his wagon and walked back up.

"Couldn't block the road."

His gray eyes pierced, and she heard the unspoken defense of his previous action. Without another word, he started down.

"Wait!" Carina called.

He half turned.

"There is something you can get me."

He waited.

"A gun." The thought had sprung to her mind and now surprised them both. Let him think her pazza. She would not be caught again without protection.

He cocked his head. "Any kind in particular?"

What could she say? She knew nothing of guns but thought of how Mae's had fit into her palm. "Something small to carry with me, as I've already been robbed, cheated, and nearly snake-bitten."

He turned slowly on his boot heel, then walked away. Carina tugged Dom's head

76

from the dry patch of grass he was working on and started up the trail. She glanced down once from the top, but Quillan Shepard had reached his wagon and did not look back.

Quillan released the break and took up the reins. When he'd seen Miss DiGratia's mule at the edge of the road and the slide she had taken down, he half expected to find her battered body at the bottom of the canyon. The sight of her clinging to the tree, scrabbling for her belongings, was one that wouldn't leave him soon.

It occurred to him now that the things he'd discarded had meant something to her. Meant a lot, maybe. The thought didn't sit well. Maybe she wasn't what he'd taken her for, but how was he to know she didn't trade on her looks, which were considerable. A woman alone, young and lovely. Only one thing drew them to a place like Crystal.

Apparently not Miss DiGratia, however. Even so, on the worst stretch of road, his horses pressed to their limit and his load calculated to the final pound of machinery for the Silver Belle shaft works — and add to that the stage riding his dust and its clientele whom he'd watered with in Fairplay . . . No, there hadn't been a choice. His conscience stung only a moment. There hadn't been a choice.

He nickered to the horses, and they started off. Too bad she had fallen in with Beck. But she'd catch on soon enough, though Beck was putting on a good show, the hand-kissing especially. Quillan snorted. He edged the horses to the left for the turn, then settled in for a long ride.

Time alone on the road, alone with his thoughts. He felt a vague annoyance that they clung to a black-haired waif with coffee-colored eyes, large and defined and beautifully shaped in her likewise well-formed face.

He rubbed his jaw with his palm and pulled his thoughts toward something else, something to recite maybe. Looking around him, he settled his mind on William Blake. *To see a world in a grain of sand* . . . He bent his memory to the task, mastering his thoughts, forcing them down an avenue of his choice. That was better, and definitely smarter.

Five

What I know is little to what I hope to know. What I feel is already too much.

Rose

Carina slowed as she reached the bottom of the dip. Dom exhaled through his nostrils and choked. She dismounted and checked the balance of the load across his flanks. Quillan Shepard had divided it well, but in the sheet it was still an ungainly and uncomfortable load. Dom turned his large mournful eyes on her, and she stroked the side of his neck.

Blowing a strand of hair from her eyes, Carina scanned the distance, trying not to think of Quillan Shepard's remark. Was it too much for the mule to cross the summit again today? She could just make out the bare slopes that held Crystal City. Behind it, the sun was setting in brilliant streaks of orange, casting the mountains in shadow.

She turned back to the mule, jacked up her skirts, and remounted. Dom started forward, wheezing. What was wrong with him? He had worked hard before, was no stranger to it. This could not be more toil than pulling the wagon mile after mile. Still, she dismounted and walked around to his head.

Foam circled his mouth at the bit and his head hung heavy. "What is it, old man? Why can't you walk? Am I too much for you to carry, too?" She stroked his soft muzzle. "Very well. I'll walk, and you will carry my books. It's not so far, now. Come." She pulled gently, and he followed, head low and coughing until again he resisted the rein.

"Come. We cannot stop here. Slowly, *sì,* but come." She tugged. As the sun nestled behind Mount Pointe, the evening chill penetrated her blouse, and when Dom balked again, she released him.

"All right. We'll rest." She walked around to the sheet and rummaged for the shawl she had scooped up with the other clothes. It was snagged with branches and grass, but she picked them off and wrapped it over her shoulders.

The hollow in her stomach grew more insistent as she crossed her arms against her chest and watched the sky fade from gold to gray. She would have eaten by now if Dom were more cooperative. She eyed him sullenly where he stood, not even grazing, just heaving softly and hanging his big head. "*Disgrazia,* you should be ashamed." There was still plenty of light to see by, but without the sun's rays, the air grew cold. They had to go on.

She walked over and felt his neck again. It was damp with sweat, and he shivered. Was he ill? Somewhere in the trees behind her, an owl gave a throaty cry. She was not afraid, but the wild loneliness of its call sent a shiver up her back.

Setting her chin, she took Dom's bridle. "Gidd-up."

He followed two paces, then stopped. Pressing her head to his neck, she whispered, "Please, Dom. *Per piacere*."

He stepped forward, one pace, another.

"That's right." She held his head between her hands. He followed slowly. At this rate, they would not reach Crystal before dark, but they were moving. Then Dom stumbled and balked, yanking her arm.

Carina bit her lip in frustration. Why was everything going wrong? Just when she thought the worst had passed, it was something new. She looked into the darkening sky. "Why, Signore? Do you have to strike my mule? It is not enough that I lose my things, my house?" And so much more that she wouldn't put into words.

She dropped to the side of the road, folded her arms around her knees, and laid her forehead down. Thoughts crowded in, thoughts she had fought for weeks. Thoughts of Flavio, his smile, his eyes like dark velvet, the sound of his voice when he said her name.

The sound of his voice saying Divina's name! Carina clamped her ears with her hands and fought the tears. She would not cry. She was too angry to cry. But the tears lodged in a hard knot in her chest. Was it pride to resist them? To hope, however vainly, that things might come right, could come right if only . . . ?

Would he come? Was she worth a thousand miles to him? She slapped her knees with her palms. What if he did? Would she accept him now, knowing what she only suspected before? Why did her heart linger so? Should it not repulse her for what he was?

Carina stood and slid the loaded sheet from Dom's back. Keeping it balanced as Quillan Shepard had tied it, she hung it across the back of her own neck. The weight pulled her head forward, and try as she might, she couldn't tolerate it. Slipping the load over her head, she dropped it to the ground, yanked the knots open, and spread the sheet.

The pot could go, and the kettle. Until she had a kitchen she would not need them. She carried them beneath the trees and tucked them into the undergrowth, then went back to the road. The silver she would not part with, nor the books, where the weather would spoil them. She laid them in two stacks and padded them with the clothing, then tied up the middle as it had been and tried again.

Please, Signore. A small favor. It was

heavy, painfully so, but she would do it. She straightened herself under the weight of her load, took Dom's bridle, and walked. He followed without protest now that she carried his load. Maybe he had rested enough. Maybe he sensed she had no patience left. Maybe . . . God had listened.

By the time she reached the first outbuildings, her neck was a burning probe down to her lowest back, and her legs could barely keep from buckling. Instead of going down the main street like a gypsy peddler, she cut off toward Mae's, every stumble on the rough ground a torment.

She reached the boardinghouse steps but could not climb them. A single lamp shone from inside, and Carina focused on that as she bent and slid the load off her shoulders. The pain of bending was so extreme, she almost cried out. Pulling herself up by the railing, she made it to the door. With the side of her fist, she banged and waited. It wasn't long, but it felt like forever.

"Door's open. I always keep it open." Mae pulled it wide, and the light sprang from the hall, silhouetting her enormous shape. "What in the name of thunder's happened to you?"

Carina swung a weary arm toward the sheet, then felt her knees buckle as they had threatened to all day. This time the chasm was only as deep as the floor.

Carina blinked against the light. A man's face swam into view, and Mae's, like a round moon, behind him.

"Here she comes, now." He smiled, removed the spectacles from his nose, and slid them into his vest pocket. "Well, young lady. It appears you overtaxed yourself."

Carina glanced around the room, papered in soft cream and beige. There was a photograph of a blockish man on the wall before her, and wilting flowers adorned a painted vase on the table.

"Is she all right?" Mae's tone was surprisingly warm.

"I think so. Pushed herself too hard, especially being new to the elevation."

Carina stared at him, trying to piece together where she was and why. "Where's Dom?" Her voice sounded as thin as whey.

"Dom?" Mae cocked her head.

"My mule."

"Tied up out back."

Carina closed her eyes. Had she ever been so tired? She forced the lids to rise again. "Alan Tavish . . . he'll know what to do for him. . . ."

The doctor stood. "I'll see him to the livery on my way."

Carina's eyes closed of themselves, and she gave in to the warmth and the darkness.

Like a great mother hen, Mae swooped upon Carina the next morning. "You'll not budge from that couch until I say so." She swung a tray with broth and brown bread spread with apple butter onto Carina's lap. "You're gaunt as a ghost. When's the last time you ate?"

Carina thought about it. "The night I came in. I should have been back for supper with Mr. Beck, but Dom . . ."

"I thought as much. Don't you know board comes with the room?"

Carina nodded, feeling foolish now for not eating with the men. The motion sent a fresh wave of dizziness. "My head . . ."

"Ten thousand feet, child. Ten thousand feet above the sea. Think about that."

Carina did think. Could that have affected Dom as well? She suddenly pushed herself up. "I must see to my mule."

"Doc took him to the livery. Old Tavish'll see to him."

Carina believed that, but there was more she must do. "Mr. Beck is expecting me."

Mae shoved her gently into the cushions, then settled into the horsehair wing chair across from her. "As you've mentioned him, I'll tell you. He was here twice last evening asking for you."

"I was supposed to meet him for supper."

"Well, he'll get by that." Mae winked,

and the folds of skin scrunched up around her violet eyes.

The innuendo was clear and annoying. Did Mae think she had come all this way to find a husband? And that she would jump at the first man who offered a hand in her plight? Carina sipped broth from the bowl. The bread she couldn't stomach yet. "I'm to be his assistant."

"Oh? Well, he'll hardly expect you, being that it's Sunday, and I have specific orders not to let you out of the house today. Dr. Felden's orders."

Carina sighed. The relief she felt shamed her. This weakness of body was foreign and frightening. Crystal was not a place to be weak. She'd seen that much already.

"If you'd rather, I can help you up to your room. But you're welcome to stay here."

Something in the way Mae said it tugged Carina's heart. Was the woman lonely? She thought of the evenings on the porch with Mamma, Tía Marta, Lucia Fiorina, and old Tía Gelsomina, who was not a true aunt but Divina's godmother. And Divina, of course, unless she had better things to do, like sneaking away with other women's sweethearts.

Mae heaved herself up. "I have a few chores, but I'll be in calling range. In a while we'll chat, but for now you rest."

"Mae . . ." Carina sank back into the pillows. "My books . . ."

"And your silver. There by the couch." She pointed. "I figured they were important if you nearly killed yourself hauling them in."

"Thank you. I hope the bed sheet . . ."

Mae waved her hand. "None the worse for the wear." She headed out of the room.

Carina bent and ran a hand over the clothbound copy of *Don Quixote*. Lifting it to her chest, she closed her eyes, too tired to read but not releasing it. Her mind floated to a sun-kissed land with sloping vineyards ripening beneath benevolent rains. And a dreamer knight, neither old nor confused, but her own darkly handsome Flavio sang her name . . . *Dulcinea*. And she rose up on the song, became the song, and for a time . . . forgot.

Carina woke when Mae slid the book from her chest. The lamps were lit, and the window was dark. She sat up. "Have I slept the whole day?"

Mae chuckled. "You have. And I've brought food. Nothing fancy yet, just good solid bread and broth."

"You're too kind."

Mae handed her the bowl. "Kindness has a way of coming around again."

Carina sipped the broth. "It's good. I'm hungry."

87

"And you have color in your cheeks. To-morrow you'll feel like your old self again. Just takes a while to build up the blood. After that the climate's right healthful. At least that's what they tell the tuberculars." Mae reached for the chair to settle in but stopped at the knock on the door. She heaved a sigh and went out.

Carina heard her outside the door. "No, Berkley Beck, you can't see her."

"Now, Mae . . ."

Carina could just picture his expansive teeth and "butter won't melt" expression. He wouldn't get past Mae, though. Carina would bet on it.

"You can see her tomorrow."

"I only have a small thing or two to say —"

"Save your small things for the mornin'."

"You're cruel, Mae Dixon. Can't you see I'm sick with worry?"

"Worry? Hah. It's lovesick you are, and that'll keep. Good night, Berkley Beck."

Carina cringed. She must put an end to that talk immediately. The door opened, and Carina caught just a glimpse of Mr. Beck's face before Mae closed the door behind her.

"There now. If absence makes the heart grow fonder, he'll be right fond in the mornin'."

"It's not fondness between us. It's business. Maybe legal business. Maybe my house next door —"

Mae waved her hand. "Honey, you aren't gettin' that house back. You may as well put it out of your mind."

Carina sat up. "It belongs to me. I paid for it. I have the deed."

"You have *a* deed."

"What do you mean?"

Mae laughed. "Half the deeds in town are forgeries. Claim jumping is a sport up here. The only way to have your property is to keep possession. And that ain't easy."

"You have yours."

"I'm a landmark. Anyone comes in here raisin' Cain, I pull the pistol. Besides, the men won't give me trouble. They like too well the way I run things, leavin' the door open all night and fillin' their bellies at my table."

Mae cracked the knuckles of both hands, tapered hands that seemed too small for her. "Still, if I don't stay on my toes . . . Why, there have been people who built all day, went to sleep, and woke to find their work pulled down and someone else's building in its place."

"But how can they —"

"Because they do."

Carina sank back into the cushions. "Mr. Beck would have told me."

Mae raised her eyebrows and shrugged.

"Well, maybe. He's given you a job, you say?"

"Yes."

"That's what brought you here?"

No. But what would Mae think of her true reasons?

Mae shook her head. "I guess you know what you're doing, but Crystal's not exactly abounding with opportunities for women. Though that's not to say that those of us with a mind to it can't make it happen."

"I intend to." Crystal may be far from what she expected — worse than she could have dreamed — but she was here now, and she would make the best of it.

Mae nodded. "Well, put on the feed, then, so you won't be passing out on the porch."

Carina bit into the bread, coarse and brown and heavy. Not at all the crusty white loaves the size of her thigh that Mamma had sliced and drizzled with thick green olive oil, vinegar, and salt. Carina sighed. If the Carruthers had not taken her house, she might even now be baking a loaf . . . but the olive oil and vinegar were gone with the tomatoes and wheels of crumbly black-rind cheese.

She had lost all of the things she would have used to make a home. How would she replace them? Work. By earning enough to buy again what she needed. "I hope Mr. Beck won't change his mind."

"I'm sure he won't. He had a daisy in his lapel."

Carina frowned, but Mae laughed, a thick mezzo laugh that shook the rolls at her neck and squeezed the pouches almost shut around her eyes. It was a contagious laugh like Mamma's, a laugh that wrapped around and squeezed you. In that moment, Carina wanted to hug her, to grab Mae's arms and dance, throw back her head and laugh as she had with Mamma when she was very small. But that was the Italian, not American, way.

"I remember when Herb Dixon came courtin' the first time. He was so nervous I thought he'd faint same as you did right out on my floor." Mae laughed again.

Carina turned to the picture on the wall, a small, square, unremarkable man with thinning hair and round, guileless eyes. "Is that Mr. Dixon?"

"We were married only a year. He took a fever and died on me." Mae wiped her eye. "Twenty-nine years, and I still miss him. He hardly ever spoke, but he listened. A warmer-hearted man I never knew."

Carina quaked suddenly. Twenty-nine years! Eight more than her full age. Could the hurt last so long? "He brought you up here?"

"My nephew did. Mr. Dixon left me with a handsome sum, and my sister's son had a use for it. So we moved up to Placerville and staked a claim."

"Placerville?"

"The remains west of town are Lower Placer. We lived in Upper Placer, farther up the gulch. It was hardly more than a gulch camp at its best, forty-niners who staked out here instead of haulin' all the way to California, fifty-oners who'd failed in the sunny gold fields of their dreams, slogging homeward and snagging on the Rockies with enough dream left to dig in once again. Then others trailing in for one reason or another."

"Did you find gold?"

"Sure. Dug the riverbed all day long, sluicing gravel for a handful of dust. Then Matthew had enough of it and went his way, but I had the mountain in my blood. A new rush of folks were startin' to work other gulches. Let's see, that would've been '59. They weren't just lookin' for gold in the creeks. They were surveying other metals and coming in with machinery and real know-how. I had a head for business. Where there were men, there'd be a need for a roof and food for their bellies."

She chuckled. "I was never in much romantic demand, not after Mr. Dixon. And not a one ever suggested such. They knew better."

Mae patted her belly. "But I kept a good

house for them that wanted such. The first was a tent in which twelve men slept in six cots taking shifts. They had regular meals same as I give them now, though the accommodations have improved."

Not tremendously, Carina thought. She handed Mae the finished dish tray. "Will you stay here always?"

Mae shrugged. "I have nowhere else to go. And I've come to know it here. Leastwise, it knows me."

It was good to be known, respected, Carina thought. Mae had dug into the mountain and found her place. It was possible. But was it what she intended for herself?

Six

How can one change a moment passed? Even a moment that should never have come.

Rose

The next morning Carina felt stronger than she had in days, having slept through the din without waking. Maybe she had grown used to it. Maybe Mae's care had fortified her. She rose from the couch, washed, and dressed, then with a deep breath left the haven of Mae's rooms.

Mae was serving breakfast on the long tables in the dining room, hot cakes and pork sliced thick and fried. Sweat beaded Mae's forehead, and her cheeks were flushed and red. There was a greasy sheen to her hands as she plopped a plate down where Carina sat awkwardly between two men who had made room for her.

Carina eyed the crisp, blackened bacon and spongy hot cakes with thoughts of Mamma's sausage and peppers, fresh bread and milk. She picked up a charred stick of bacon. With a sigh, she said a silent blessing, then, like the men around her, she devoured it.

After eating, she took the box of silver and made her way down Drake to Central Street. As she reached Berkley Beck's office, the door opened and a gruff, sour-faced man pushed out. He neither looked nor spoke to her but grumbled under his breath. At least he didn't spit. She went inside.

Berkley Beck stood immediately. "Miss DiGratia. I'm overcome at seeing you so hale. I was terribly concerned." His hair was smoothed back and parted, his suit uncreased, but he wore no daisy in his lapel.

She breathed her relief. "Thank you, I'm quite recovered and ready to work. But could you recommend a safe storage for this?" She held up Nonna's silver. "My walls are canvas."

He eyed the box. "Certainly. I have a small safe; though if you don't mind, I'll keep its location to myself."

She handed him the wooden box. Whatever place he had would be more secure than a room with a door that locked but walls that could be cut with a knife. She hadn't risked the steep slope only to have some ruffian steal the silver from under her bed.

He set the box on the desk. "As you see, I'm prepared for you." He motioned to the crude desk he had placed opposite his own. "It's not pretty, but it'll have to do, I'm afraid. I regret we haven't more room. Un-

95

fortunately, my living quarters take up the balance of the space behind the office. At some point I hope to move, but until then . . ." He spread his hands.

"This is fine, Mr. Beck. Only show me what you need me to do."

"Yes, of course. Well, for a start I thought maybe you could bring some order to these papers." He looked sheepishly over the piles.

Carina eyed the mountainous range of stacks along the wall. Mr. Beck's office was not as meticulous as his dress and demeanor. He obviously paid better heed to his person than his work. She thought of Papa's clinic, spotless and orderly, everything in its place — though sometimes Papa's thick, shiny hair stood in graying blond spikes and his collar protruded at odd angles. Still, Mr. Beck seemed earnest enough.

She returned her gaze to him. "Will you excuse me?"

"I beg your pardon?" He rested his hand on his vest.

"I have a thought for filing your papers, but I need to get something."

"Oh. Yes, of course. Come and go as you please. You'll find I'm frequently out myself, so here is a key to the front door." He held it out.

Carina's eyes widened involuntarily. Mr.

Garibaldi had watched her like a hawk. Never would he have trusted her with a key. Yet Mr. Beck handed her his now, and they had only met two days before. She tucked it safely into her pocket.

As she went outside again, Carina half smiled to think how Mr. Garibaldi had hollered when Papa told him she was leaving. He was Papa's cousin, and she had done his books as a favor to Papa, since the cousin's eyes were so crossed he saw double. All she had heard from him were complaints until she was leaving, and suddenly she was invaluable! Irreplaceable! How could Papa think of letting her go? What sort of father was he to send a daughter so far?

But Papa did not holler back. He was a man of mild temper, above displaying emotions even when his parental judgment was questioned. His voice stayed low, his countenance unruffled. *"My daughter is twenty-one years old. She may choose her path."* And that, even though it made his heart ache to be losing her. Mr. Garibaldi blustered and swore. Papa never did either.

Only Mamma hollered and slapped. She had married above her class because of her beauty. Now Carina did smile, recalling the story told again and again as the women sat together, baskets of mending beside them. How Papa had come to treat Nonna's illness, laid eyes on Mamma, and fallen in love.

He could have married higher, but the little dark-eyed beauty was all he could think of. Nonna's own reputation had soared with the catch made by her daughter. The other widows came to her for advice. How can we marry our daughters well?

"She is too lazy," Nonna would say, or "her mind wanders," or "she eats too much *dolci*." So they would think it was her training that had made the match for Mamma. But Nonna knew it was Mamma's lovely face, her smile, her laugh that brought her good fortune.

Carina frowned. That was not always the case. Of the two DiGratia daughters, she most resembled Mamma in all those things, but it was Divina whose fortune had been won. Not won! Stolen. Divina had stolen her good fortune.

She kicked a stone and traipsed back to Mae's kitchen. There, she gathered the empty crates outside her door. They smelled a little of salt pork, but the waxed paper linings had kept them free of grease. With the linings gone, they would do nicely for the job.

She returned to the office and set about organizing the papers into the crates. She tried filing them by type of complaint, then found that almost all dealt with claim disputes and filed them by date instead. Her own claim she found no trace of, but she had only sorted through a small portion by the time her stomach wanted food. Had the elevation turned her into a voracious wolf?

Mr. Beck had been out most of the morning, but he returned now, slightly breathless but with a jaunty step. "May I buy you lunch?"

Recalling Mae's assumptions, Carina filed the paper in her hand, then met his hopeful countenance. "I think it best if we keep to business, Mr. Beck."

He raised his brows, surprised. "I see."

His expression remained pleasant, and she hoped he did see. She had left everyone she cared about — left them with one thought, one hope in her mind. And no one, not Berkley Beck or anyone else, could replace them. She dropped her chin. "Thank you for understanding, Mr. Beck."

The color rose slightly in his cheeks, but he smiled, though without showing his teeth this time. "Of course, Miss DiGratia." He turned on his heel and left.

Propped up by his crutch on the street corner, Cain Bradley shook his head. The look on Berkley Beck's face could sour milk, no two ways about it. He felt a cackle seize his throat and indulged himself. Oh, how the mighty have fallen. . . . Perhaps it weren't right to delight in another's misfortune, but something had stuck in Beck's craw, and Cain hoped it choked him.

Cain glanced heavenward. *No offense, Lord, but even you had your moments with the scribes and Pharisees, callin' them whited sepulchers, all clean and tidy on the outside but inside full of dead men's bones and all corruption. Well, I'm a-lookin' at corruption right here and now.*

He leaned forward on his leg stump, encased in the leather cup above the wooden peg, and watched Berkley Beck advance. Beck ignored his presence. As he passed, Cain raised his crutch in mock salute and mumbled, "Whited sepulcher."

Carina went back to Mae's for lunch. The fare was stewed beef and potatoes, bread with no butter, and strong coffee to wash it down. Only a handful of men came in for it, and after they were served, Carina joined Mae at the kitchen table to eat.

Mae dunked a chunk of bread in her gravy. "So how was it working for Mr. Beck?"

Carina toyed with the stewed beef, tough and flavorless, though it had cooked long enough to cure leather. "He's kind, but not very tidy."

Mae smiled. "He needs a woman for that."

Carina ignored her obvious intent. "A

man who takes pride in his work is capable of his own orderliness."

Mae snorted. "Show me that man, and I'll show you a fool. Why, Mr. Dixon couldn't wipe his own shoes. But that made me more valuable, you see. I liked doing for him."

"So now you do for other men?"

Mae shrugged. "A body needs a purpose." She stood and took the plates from the table. Carina followed her outside the back door. Mae slid the dishes into the massive wooden washtub, then plunged her arms in to the elbow. The water was slimy with grease and soap, one hardly better than the other, and Mae didn't seem overly concerned with the task.

She swiped a plate with a nubby cloth. "There are plenty here who need doing for. It's a regular city to be sure, bursting its seams with dreamers, though the amenities are a little slow in coming."

A little slow? It was the most backward place Carina had been.

Mae sloshed the plate into the rinse tub. "Where other cities have gas lights and all such folderol, Crystal residents are hauling water and burning coal oil, kerosene, and candles. My stove burns wood and most of the food, too, as the regulator door's unpredictable. But it could be worse. The tent dwellers cook on open fire pits."

"Why don't they build? Bring in gas and water lines?"

"It'll happen. Just now the miners are trying to prove Crystal's here to stay. Though folks have been scratching around here nearly a decade, it's only been this last two years they've had real success. The water runs too close beneath the surface, and until they brought in the new hydraulic equipment, the mines flooded and made the deeper ores unreachable."

Mae pulled the plate from the scalding water and laid it on the board to dry. "Now it looks like they'll make a city of it yet. It's rough, but it has the makings of something more. You've seen the crowds, and it's not just miners. Folks are bringing culture. The Selman Theatre has acting troupes and opera stars, though the best show last year was when Fred Little strung a rope from the weather vane on the Crystal Hotel to the ridgepole of the livery, then walked it. Dead sober." She laughed.

Carina tried to imagine it and failed, her head spinning with the thought. What sort of fool would tempt fate so when it was bad enough having to face normal heights?

Mae rocked back on her heels. "Maybe it's my lack of sophistication that keeps me in a place like Crystal. But frankly, the world's changing too fast. I like it simple. Fry and serve the hot cakes, scrub the

102

dishes. Wash the linen off the bed of the man who gives it up; spread it for the next one."

Carina frowned. It sounded dreary to her. "You don't get tired of it?"

"Not really. There's always new faces. New stories. I learn the men's names because I have a head for it. I hear their stories. Some I believe because I've been there myself. Some, I know, are no truer than their dreams. Though one man in fifty does make his dream happen."

"One in fifty?" Carina's heart sank. One in fifty was not good odds for her own dream.

"That might be generous. See, it takes more than luck. It takes know-how and perseverance. The ones who come thinking there's gold lying on the ground just waiting to be picked up — well, they scratch around a little, then give up."

She had a neat row of dishes drying now, catching the sun and breeze. "But the ones who find good ore and either sell out or have the wherewithal to make the mine pay, they're the lucky ones." She pointed a finger. "Still, they rub shoulders with the down-and-out and remember where they came from. It's the wives they bring up who are less inclined to recall."

Mae rocked back on her heels. "I have no time for them — would-be society gals with ridgepole noses. They think their husbands' sudden wealth makes them somehow different from the rest of us."

Carina thought of her own family, generations of titled wealth. Papa's own fame and his daring move to the Americas. Did Mae consider hers a ridgepole nose?

"Give me good honest work, bellies to feed, and dishes to wash. I want no part of their causes and complaints."

"Don't you get lonely?"

Mae eyed her slowly, the sun catching in her gray-streaked hair pulled into a knot behind her head and lightening the violet of her eyes to a pale amethyst. Carina thought for a moment she had offended her with the question. But then Mae sighed.

"Well, sometimes I long for a listening ear and someone to laugh with. But I learned long ago not to trust in human companionship. People die. Plain and simple."

Pressed tighter than a can of smoked oysters that afternoon in the crowd at Fisher's General Merchandise, Carina vowed to avoid Monday mailings. Due to the arrival of the weekly post delivery, she had waited more than an hour already. And why? She did not expect a letter yet; she only had one to send. Its message was simple and optimistic, penned on paper purchased at an extravagant price from Fletcher's Stationery.

Dear Papa,

I promised I would write when I was settled. It is very beautiful here in Crystal. The mountains are majestic. I am assistant to an Attorney at Law. There is a misunderstanding regarding my house, but he will soon have it taken care of. I board with a woman named Mae. Everything is fine, so tell Mamma not to worry. My love and prayers to both of you.

Your devoted,
Carina

"Five dollars to anyone in the front who'll swap places." The man waved a paper bill over his head.

"Make it twenty," another yelled back.

Carina smiled, understanding their sentiment. The man in front of her returned her grin. He was missing a front tooth, and she wondered if the dentist on the street had extracted it.

He pulled the slouch hat from his head. "I'd offer you my spot, but it's only one closer."

The man in front of him half turned. "She can have mine. That's two better."

Carina shook her head, but a third man called, "I'll swap you, ma'am." He was halfway to the window, and the temptation was too great. Carina left her place and pressed forward, her letter home clutched to her breast.

"Thank you." She took his place in line, and he received the rib nudges of the men all the way back to hers. There were decent men in Crystal, hardworking and mindful of their manners. None of these men carried guns. They wore patched and faded shirts and trousers. The grime of real work lined their fingernails.

Their faces were homely, their hair ill-kempt. Some wore the look of greed, others desperation, and some a forlorn helplessness. Were they hoping for letters from home? Did they have wives and children? Would they sit in their tents or their rooms tonight and pore over each word their loved ones left behind?

Carina reached the front. Seventy-five cents for her letter to be carried. Shaking her head, Carina paid it and hustled away from the post office. When she reached the downstairs rooms at the boardinghouse they were deserted, but she found Mae upstairs changing the linen in one of the canvas-walled guest rooms. From its condition, the boarder had little care for clean linens.

Black grime caked the floor from the door to the foot of the bed, as though the man had dragged through the opening each night and flopped to the bed without ever turning to the side to dress or undress or wash. In fact, the washbasin stood dry and unsullied.

Mae tossed her a skimpy pillow while she stripped the bed. "Through for the day?"

"Mr. Beck had meetings to conduct in the office. Has this man moved out?"

"You might say. Fell down a shaft and broke his neck. That's why I take rent in advance."

Carina's mouth parted in surprise. It seemed unlike Mae to be so callous when she had shown such kindness to her. "Has someone taken the room?"

Mae wrenched the mattress up and shook it once, then let it fall. "Why? You lookin' to move?" She spoke in short-breathed sentences.

"No." Carina shook her head. "I just expected the room would be taken quickly."

"It is taken. By the man who had a deposit on yours." At Carina's flush, Mae gave her chesty laugh. "Don't you think I gave in to Berkley Beck's swindling. It was for your sake I let that room go. I told Mr. Turner he'd have the next vacancy." Mae huffed as she scooped up the linens from the floor. The blood just under her florid skin rushed to her cheeks like a flood.

"Let me take those for you," Carina said automatically. Mae's forehead was dappled with drops of sweat, and her chest rose and fell with the exertion of changing only one bed. She was an older woman and not well. It was natural to help her. When Mae dumped the load of soiled linens and foul smelling blankets into her arms, Carina gathered it staunchly against her. "Where do you want them?"

"Out back to scrub." Mae pressed a hand to her lower back.

Carina caught a look, almost puzzled, in Mae's features. Had it been so long since anyone had lifted a hand for Mae? A pang of fear seized her. Could she, too, spend her life alone, forging her place on the mountain without family or friends?

The thought was too foreign to consider. There had always been an overflow of close relations, distant relations, friends of relations. Always people to scold and instruct her, to berate and encourage, to argue and to rush to her defense. Here on the mountains she had none of them, no one.

"Have you grown roots on the floor there?"

The smell of sweat and rotten wool stung her nose as Carina hauled the bedding down the stairs and out the back door. Seeing the washtub, she dropped the linens in a heap beside it. Not for anything could she offer to scrub them. She looked down the street to the corner where a crowd was gathering.

"What is that, Mae?"

"Someone stumpin' for something." Mae poured a steaming kettle of water into the tub. "Go on before your curiosity burns a hole in you."

Carina sent a smile back over her shoulder, then headed for the street. Was it only three days since she first fought her way through the crowds and the din and the smell of Crystal's streets? Now she knew to carry no more than a few coins at a time and to shove back if she was shoved.

She was small enough to insinuate herself through the burly, lanky, and broad-backed men on the street. A scattering of color revealed a painted woman here and there, along with a few serious-faced wives. When she pushed her way to the front, she saw a man literally standing on a stump in the street, the tallest and stoutest of those he had to choose from.

One hand waved as he spoke, the other hung by a thumb in his silk vest. "I tell you the boom is on, and Leadville's the place. Silver by the barrel in the magic city, just waitin' to be dug."

Carina glanced at the old peg-legged man beside her. "Who is that?"

"Horace Tabor along from Leadville. The city in the clouds, he says. He's stealin' our thunder, don't ya know."

"What does that mean?"

"Grubstakin' miners to hop with him over to Leadville."

She didn't understand a word, but Carina looked at the sharply dressed man on the stump, his charismatic presence drawing the circle of men in like the throat of a whirlpool. His largely protruding mustache danced up and down on his lip as he spun the pied piper's tune with words.

"The railroad's comin' through. General Palmer's narrow gauge. It's the real thing, boys. Leadville's got it all."

Carina looked around her at the men's faces, some skeptical, some aglow. Would they go? Would these men leave their diggings here in Crystal and rush for the silver this Horace Tabor claimed was lying there in Leadville for the taking?

"Gentlemen!"

Carina turned as Berkley Beck's voice rose over the din. He had taken a stump beside Tabor that, with his own height, raised him a head taller. "Leadville is a veritable metropolis. What's there has been taken. Why, by last count there were ten thousand men. Would you work for someone else like common laborers?"

He swung his arm to include all the landscape. "Here in Crystal you can be your own man. Stake your own claim. This is your future."

"Sure," the old man at Carina's side muttered with a wry twist of his mouth. "Crystal's the promised land, don't ya know." He cackled softly.

Carina noted a hint of derision as he eyed Mr. Beck with pale robin-egg eyes.

"There's plenty of future in Leadville." Tabor boomed his voice over Beck's. "The richest square mile in the Rockies. Fortunes to be made, riches you'll never find here. I know, boys. I've walked these hills since '60. This gulch'll go the way of Placerville, a little surface metal, then nothing. But Leadville . . ."

"Crystal is not Placerville." Berkley Beck smiled as though reproving a child. "Why, assays are coming in every day with high content silver and gold both. We're only scraping the surface, and the deeper we go, the better it gets. Gentlemen, your place is here — Crystal, Colorado." Berkley Beck stepped down from the stump as though that was the final word and nothing more needed saying.

Horace Tabor shrugged. "You men know the odds. Why not grab for a sure thing?" He, too, stepped down and was pressed into the crowd and hauled to the saloon. Clearly some of the men liked what they heard from him better than Mr. Beck's promises.

Carina searched the street for Berkley Beck, but he must have returned to his office. It was nothing to her if the miners went

111

to Leadville. Let them clear out and make the streets passable. Ten thousand men in Leadville? It was bad enough with three thousand in Crystal, though how they had managed to count with all the coming and going, she had no idea. For all she knew, it might be no more than Mr. Beck's best guess.

Seven

Of all life's betrayers, the heart is the worst. It flutters with joyful anticipation, leading down paths better untrod. Now that I know my heart, I must never follow it again.

Rose

Quillan Shepard balanced the single-shot derringer in his palm. It was small and light. It would fit Carina DiGratia's hand, but she would have to be close enough to smell a man's breath to make her only shot do any damage. With the roughs getting bolder and the constabulary turning a blind eye . . .

He handed the gun back. "Not likely she'll hit much with only one shot."

"There is the Remington over-under derringer, double shot . . ."

"What do you have that'll pack a punch without taking her arm off?"

The man replaced the derringer and held out a Sharps 4-Barrel Pepperbox. "Thirty-two caliber rimfire. Brass frame case, steel barrel with gutta-percha grips. It's used, but fine condition." He fingered the hard rubber grips molded into leaves and vines and curlicues.

Now that was more like it. Quillan took hold of the pistol. Not a revolver, but a sturdy weapon with four shots instead of one or two. Thirty-two caliber rimfire cartridges would rarely prove fatal, but one ought to stop a man in his tracks, especially with four shots.

Quillan examined it for defect, felt the balance in his hand, and looked down the sight on the barrel. "How much do you want?" He haggled on the price and made the deal, then went back out to the wagon, loaded and ready for the trip up the pass. He pulled himself onto the box, clicked his tongue to the horses, and slapped the reins on the backs of his first relay of horses.

It was all so natural to him, he went through the motions now without a thought. He had a good head for this work and the constitution as well — not so tall he had to hunch, but straight and muscular and sound. The sky was clear, the day warm, but not too warm thanks to the breeze off the mountains. He settled in and made the drive from Denver to Morrison without a hitch.

There he loaded on cargo from the railhead and started on. He'd change horses twice and spend the first night in the open; the second in Fairplay. There he'd pick up his leaders, Jack and Jock, and the wheelers, Peter and Ginger, all four of which he owned outright. He saved them for Mosquito Pass, as it was nearly winter conditions up there, and they were the most reliable. Also, he liked having the blacks in Crystal for his use in town.

As he drove, he recited William Blake's *The Marriage of Heaven and Hell*, which he'd read the night before, exhausting the collection of Blake's works he'd purchased in Denver. It bothered him he couldn't get one of the lines right, and he felt impatient with himself. The drive seemed longer than it had for some while. Normally he liked the stretch of time alone with his thoughts, liked the spread of blue sky, the craggy heights, the call of a hawk overhead.

But he was antsy today. He'd been five days out of town, three driving and one making purchases, then delayed another in Denver waiting for the box of vaccine to arrive. Now every new delay worked on him like sandpaper. He turned his mind to the cargo he hauled, none of it pre-orders except for what he'd taken from the train.

He'd chosen everything else, things rare to the folks of Crystal, things that would be appreciated and sell well. Except the gun for Miss DiGratia. Guns were common enough in the mining town that was outgrowing its decency. Though most of the miners still went about unarmed, the rough element and the guards hired to keep them off private claims were heeled well enough. Not that guns were the first mode the roughs chose. They were still thugs, preferring their fists and clubs.

Quillan's own revolver was a necessity, as was the rifle he kept under the seat. Riding the route alone for days at a time left him open to robbery and other such interference. Not to mention beasts of nature such as the rattler he'd beheaded with a single bullet. A .45 at close range was deadly.

He considered the piece of hardware he'd purchased for Miss DiGratia. The same gun in town would run her five times as high. He ought to charge a commission, as he wasn't exactly replacing something she had lost. He'd wager he hadn't sent a gun down the mountain with her things.

He took only a short stop to eat his dinner and switch the horses, then started off again. He'd drive until nightfall, then sleep under the wagon, so tired he'd hardly feel the ground. Hard work didn't bother him. He'd rather be working from the onset of day to the sinking of the sun than sitting idle. *"Idleness is the devil's tool,"* he thought wryly, picturing the pinched face of the woman who'd drilled that lesson in. That and plenty of others.

But he'd taken it to heart, working sometimes just to spite her. Most of the time, though, he worked because it suited him.

Diligence was a virtue he came to naturally, and one that had brought him this far. He didn't expect to drive a freight wagon his whole life, but for now it was a lucrative opportunity.

Quillan smacked the reins. He was making good time, but he was still eager to reach his destination. That was not a good sign. If he started chafing the distance, he wouldn't last long as a freighter. And as he had purchased his own rig and outfit, he intended to last. Still, he pressed on farther than his usual night camp, then stopped, cared for the horses, and unrolled his bedding.

Sliding under the wagon, he expected to drop right off into the honest sleep of hard labor. Instead, he lay wondering how much extra the horses could have managed if he'd added Miss DiGratia's load to his own. It was sheer foolishness, but somehow the question kept insinuating itself into his mind. It made sleep less than enjoyable.

Rising before the sun, Quillan started on again and made Fairplay by evening. He spent the night in the Fairplay House as he did most every trip by arrangement. In the morning he hitched up his own team and began the home stretch. Though June had been dryer than usual, there were still drifts of snow along the pass. But the road was

117

passable, and aside from putting on a heavier coat, Quillan kept on as he'd been.

It bothered him that his impatience hadn't passed, though he'd slept better than the previous night. Taking a winding section of the road, he edged the horses closer to the canyon wall, away from the edge. The weight of his load stayed firm, with no shifting as he made the next turn. He prided himself on that. A freighter's first loyalty was to his load.

He heard horses coming up behind and turned. Stevens and McLaughlin's stage. The four-horse team pulled the Concord coach briskly until it was right on his backside. Quillan maintained his pace. He had the right of way. If he lost his load over the side, it was his responsibility to get it back up. If the stage lost its load, as the saying went, the driver only had to bury it.

The road widened past the turn, and Fogerty, the stage driver, hollered, "Comin' around." Quillan pulled in as close to the side as he could manage, reined in, and waited while the twelve passengers disembarked. They held the ropes tied to the roof and walked alongside to counterbalance it along the edge while Fogerty angled the stage around the wagon.

Sometimes Quillan thought the rope business was more to impress the passengers than for any actual need, though it was true the stage was more easily maneuvered empty. The passengers waved as they passed him on foot, then reboarded the stage. They were a motley assortment as usual, mostly rough men coming to stake a claim, one woman who looked sour as bad milk, and a swell or two.

The last would be cut down to size before long, for Crystal City was no respecter of pomposity. A man could have money or not, good luck or bad. But if he came into town with a high opinion of himself, he didn't keep it for long. There were too many newly rich and too many changing fortunes each day.

When he made it into Crystal late that afternoon, the buzz of the town was well under way, it being Friday. Quillan had hoped to beat the weekend madness, but the extra day in Denver had cost him. Now it would take much longer to make the deliveries. Fighting his way through the crowds, he stopped first at Ormsby's Drugstore with the extracts and tinctures. He made a handsome profit on that load, having finagled items hard to come by at the best of times. But Ormsby could afford it. Doc Felden would get the one precious box of smallpox vaccine, no extra charge.

He headed next for MacDonald's Sampling Works. He had a scale for them, as theirs had not been weighing accurately. He knew Gavin MacDonald was too Scotch to order a new scale, but Quillan would make the man believe it a bargain and see it put to use before someone got shot. A bad scale was unforgivable in these parts.

In just over two hours he had all but the last of his deliveries made and the money collected. The last was Miss DiGratia's. The gunsmith had thrown in a leather shoulder holster, though Quillan doubted Miss DiGratia would wear it. Nevertheless, it was wrapped in the package with the gun, and he took it from beneath the box. He made his way on foot through the incoming miners to Drake Road.

Mae Dixon watched him from the porch like a well-fed cat. "Well, well. Quillan."

"Hello, Mae. I have a delivery for Miss DiGratia."

Her violet eyes took on a decidedly feline glee. "You can leave it at the desk."

Quillan cocked his head. "How would I get payment?"

"She can leave it at the desk."

He took the steps up. The cool evening air ruffled the hair on his neck. "All right."

"Then again . . ." Mae nodded to the street. "You could hold still a moment."

Quillan turned as Carina DiGratia lifted her skirt and stepped off the end of the boardwalk. He saw only a flash of booted ankle, enough to confirm that her leg bones were as delicate as the rest of her. He noted the blue denim skirt they'd rescued from the mountain and a fresh white blouse with a lacy ruffle like moth's wings down the front. Was it the torn and ragged blouse she'd scavenged? If so, she'd done admirably by it.

She carried herself sprightly enough, unaware of an audience. He'd wager she had money, or at least she'd come from it. She didn't look the hard-luck kind, come to find riches in the Rockies. Especially not by the means most women found it.

He was surprised now that he could have thought so. There was an air of quality he'd missed on the road, a certain strength of spirit and breeding. She was like the dainty, dark Morgan horse he'd seen in Golden, small-boned and light-footed. If he pressed his imagination, he'd see her prance and bob her head as that filly had.

But now she looked up and saw him, dark eyes suddenly large. He wished she wouldn't startle so every time they met. It made him feel less than respectable. He tipped his hat. "Miss DiGratia."

Mae heaved herself up. "I'll leave you two to settle business." She went inside and closed the door that had stood open to catch the cross breeze.

As Miss DiGratia climbed the steps, Quillan held out the package. "Your order." She took it without comment and pulled open the paper. The gun was holstered, and she slid it out and tried the feel of it.

He could see it was a good fit, but even a small gun had weight. Her wrist didn't want to support it until she firmed the muscles and stiffened her arm. "You know how to use it?" he asked.

"I understand the mechanism. I don't need the holster. . . ."

"It's no charge. Came with the gun." He handed her the box of rimfire cartridges that hadn't come free. "If you haven't used a pistol . . ."

"I'm certain I can learn. What do I owe you?"

Why did he feel like a robber when he named his price? He'd hardly put anything on top for his trouble. It was recalling her on that slope, picking up the flotsam from her wagon . . .

She held out the holster. "Take off a dollar and you can resell this."

She was bartering? He tucked his tongue between his side teeth and eyed her, her head tipped up to meet his gaze squarely, shoulders back. What good was it to sell a holster without a gun to fill it?

"It's a deal." His voice was a stranger.

She nodded her satisfaction and turned for the door. "The money's inside."

Quillan leaned on the porch post. "I'll wait here." Raising his hat, he shook back his hair. A cricket sang from under the porch, and he could smell Mae's cooking. Maybe he'd eat here tonight. Though Mae seated more than she roomed, he was early enough to get a place.

And if he could get past Miss DiGratia's defensiveness, he might even teach her to shoot. She "understood the mechanism." He laughed softly. Point and shoot. That's what she needed to know.

Upstairs, Carina pulled the bills from the carpetbag. There were few enough left, things coming, as Mae said, dear up here. She smiled at how she had improved Mr. Shepard's price for the gun. His face showed he'd not expected it, but it was only one small part of all he owed her.

Taking the money, she went down. Mae was nowhere to be seen, but the aroma of dinner filled the lower rooms. Stewed beef and potatoes. Always stewed beef and potatoes, though twice a week onions and carrots would be added, and once a week it was bear meat in the pot. Carina tried not to think about it.

How she longed for the rich smells of sausage and spicy tomato sauce thick with basil and garlic and oregano. But no one else seemed to care. As soon as the sun dipped below the peaks, the men would come to eat. Like locusts.

She stepped back out to the porch. "There you are, Mr. Shepard." She handed him the money.

"I prefer Quillan." He took the bills and tucked them into his shirt pocket without counting. "Shepard's only loaned to me."

Loaned? How could a name be loaned? Was it not passed down with pride, father to son, regardless of station? "Loaned, Mr. Shepard?"

"In a manner of speaking."

"What were you called before it was loaned?"

"Quillan."

Carina studied him, looking, as Papa would have said, under the skin. For a moment, she glimpsed something, but it was gone too soon. She felt as though she had intruded, and he'd put her out like a stray dog nosing where it didn't belong.

"Have you plans for supper?" A smile quirked his mouth. "Mr. Beck, perhaps?"

Mocking again. Bene. "Mr. Beck is my employer."

He raised his eyebrows to that. But before he could respond, a crowd of miners drawn by the scent of food rounded the corner of the porch. They climbed the two low stairs and swarmed between them to the door. She recognized three of her fellow boarders, Elliot, Frank, and Joe Turner, whose room she had taken, but who now

124

slept in the dead man's bed. Each tipped his hat in turn.

Four others she knew but couldn't remember their names. The rest were strangers. When they had passed, she found Quillan Shepard gone. Looking down the street, she saw him striding away, no doubt thinking already of the next business he would transact.

Later that night Carina joined Mae at the sink. She rinsed and dried the dishes that Mae swabbed in the water, thick and cloudy with soap and the remains of the stew. How many plates had been filled and emptied? As there was no time to wash dishes during the meal, when the plates ran out, those waiting were served on the dishes already used. Carina would never eat unless she was in the first seating.

Carina felt the grit beneath her boots. How long since the floor had been scrubbed? Why would Mae allow such filth in her own kitchen? Carina knew the mice came out at night and ate the scraps that fell. Their traces lined the floorboards. Did Mae not notice or care?

Carina pulled a plate from the steaming rinse tub and wiped it. "I won't need to use your pistol again. I bought a gun of my own."

"That's what Quillan brought you?"

Just Quillan. "Yes." She stacked the plate and took up the next, the tips of her fingers smarting in the scalding water. "Why does he not have a second name?"

"He has one. Just prefers not to use it."

"Why?"

Mae shrugged, then hauled a stack of plates to the shelves and slid them into place. She clicked her tongue, shaking her head. "Don't know how he does it. Those long days on the wagon with no one but himself for company."

Long days alone. She pictured him walking away from the crowd. She pictured his smug smile. She didn't want to picture him. She had wanted Mae to talk, to fill the silence. But Quillan Shepard would not have been her choice of topic. Carina turned the plate and dried the back side. "Why doesn't he take a partner?"

"Can't say, really." Mae slid the next plate into the rinse basin. "It's not that he isn't liked."

"Perhaps he doesn't like in return."

"Oh, I don't know that I'd say that."

Carina started a new plate stack. "He doesn't like Mr. Beck."

Mae laughed. "Honey, most of Crystal doesn't like Mr. Beck."

"That's not true. He is always treated with respect. People come to him for help." She pictured the magnanimous smile, the crates and crates of legal cases he had handled, cases she had only just succeeded in bringing to order. "His table is always held at the hotel, no matter how many others are waiting."

Mae laughed, deep and heavy.

"He is kind. And *he* did not push my wagon over the cliff."

Mae's eyes widened, but her chest still rumbled. "Is that what happened? Quillan sent your wagon over?"

"Mr. Beck says he had the right, but I say, *beh!*" Carina curled her fingertips to her lips with the word, then flung open her palm.

Mae stilled the chuckle. "Well, Quillan's a strange one. Comes and goes like the devil's on his heels."

"Maybe he is." Carina crossed herself.

Mae laughed right out again. "You're a strange one, Carina DiGratia." She seemed to settle inward. "But I'm glad you've come."

Carina sensed the warmth in the words within her own breast. Her throat filled with tears, and at that moment she could have cried out her homesickness and the hurt that had sent her on this crazy flight to Crystal, Colorado. But Mae hung the washrag and left the kitchen. Carina guessed it was closer than Mae had come in a long time to speaking her heart. Why it should be to her, she couldn't say.

127

Carina boiled water and scrubbed the floor with green lye soap. On her knees, she remembered each member of her family and blessed them one by one: uncles, aunts, godparents, grandparents living and deceased, and her brothers, Angelo, Joseph, Vittorio, Lorenzo, and Tony. She blessed Mamma and Papa. But she did not bless Divina, nor did she allow a thought for Flavio.

Quillan set the half-eaten plate of beans on the ground before the brown-and-white mottled dog. Resting his forearms on his knees, he sat back against the crate inside the tent wall. "Thanks for dinner, Cain."

"Nice of you to stop in." Cain Bradley raised the left stump of leg that ended at the knee and adjusted the flannel pant leg, tied in a knot at its base. "Don't get around too easy now."

Quillan nodded, absently stroking the dog's ear like a swatch of velvet between his fingers and thumb. The animal had lapped the beans in three quick strokes of his long pink tongue, then collapsed at his side in bliss.

"You got to get you a dawg."

Quillan half smiled.

Cain waved a finger. "I mean it, now. Man needs a dawg near as much as vittles."

"Don't have time for a dog." He stroked the underside of the animal's jaw until it rolled over and suggested its belly. Quillan rubbed the matted fur along the ribs and soft tissue between.

"Now that's just the thing. A dawg makes you slow down, take time for livin'."

"I'm livin', Cain."

"Yeah, yeah. You and that half 'count son o' mine." Cain scratched his own side clear up to his armpit.

"He's bringing in the ore." Quillan patted the dog's belly.

"And spendin' twice what he takes out in the saloons and bawdies."

Quillan shrugged. "You only live once."

"I don't see you throwin' yer gold down the gully."

"Don't have time."

"Son, when yer sixty-eight, you can talk to me about time." The old man slapped his hand on the crate at his side. "What are ya? Twenty-three, twenty-four?"

"Twenty-eight."

"Hah. You got more years left than a porcupine's got needles. You ever been skewered by a porcupine?"

Quillan grinned. "No, can't say I have."

"Man alive, it hurts worse'n almost anything 'cept losin' a leg." Cain rubbed the stump.

"I'll remember that." Quillan curled his hand around the dog's forepaw. "You got everything you need, Cain?"

"What man alive can say yessir to that? I make do on what the good Lord allows me."

And the Lord allows you precious little, Cain. Quillan glanced about them. "Well, then is there something I can pick up for you?"

"Tobaccy. Bull Durham, for smokin', don't ya know. It's a vice, but the Lord Jesus ain't perfected me yet."

Quillan patted the dog's neck, then pushed himself up.

Cain's eyes followed him. "You're off again, then?"

"Bright and early."

Cain shook his head. "There's such a thing as too much comin' and goin'. Ain't natural."

Quillan shrugged. "It's my job." He shook back his hair and put on his hat. "I'll be back with that tobacco." He stooped to exit the tent.

"Thanks for stoppin' by," Cain hollered after him.

Quillan waved, then started for his own tent. The wagon stood behind it, already loaded with ore to leave at the smelter on his way out. The horses were in the livery, fed and rested, and he pulled open the canvas door flap and went inside his tent. It was only slightly larger than Cain's, but sewn and treated by a man named Levi so that it repelled the rain like duck's feathers.

And unlike Cain, he lived in it by choice, not necessity.

He pulled the cash from his vest pocket and knelt beside the bedding neatly tucked around the straw mattress on the canvas floor. Pulling aside a flap of canvas, he touched dirt, then found the edge of the box with his fingertips. He lifted it, dropped the money inside with the rest, and laid the lid in place.

Smoothing the canvas, he sat back on his haunches, considering the disguise that hid his stash. He didn't know how much was in there, made a point not to count it, a small defiance of his dependence on it. Not dependence literally. Once the money was in the hole, he never took it out. He used what he needed for food and essentials before he put the remainder under his floor.

But it had a hold on him nonetheless. It was his means to personhood, his proof of worth, his guarantee he would never again be indebted to anyone. He smiled grimly at his weakness. No, he did not throw his gold down the gully as Cain said. He buried it under his floor for a tomorrow that might never come.

But then again, it might. Quillan rubbed a hand over his eyes, stretched, then settled into his bedding. He rolled to his side and tucked an arm under his head. Morning would come soon enough.

⋆ ⋆ ⋆

Staring at the tent flap after Quillan left, Cain felt a familiar pang. What was it about the young man that stirred him so? Though he knew the parts of Quillan's past that they'd talked of directly — and some few that Quillan might not even know — it wasn't that. It was in the fabric of the man himself.

Everyone had flaws, and Cain was sure Quillan was no different. But there was in him a basic goodness, try as he might to hide it in nonchalance and sometimes downright surliness. Quillan had a good heart, though maybe he showed it more often to an old cripple and his wayward son than most others. Still, there was a shell around that goodness like a limestone geode holding the crystals inside where none could see.

Why? And why did he resist the Lord's call? Cain knew it was so. Soon as the name of Jesus came up, Quillan got all quiet and closed up, then skedaddled. It was sure enough the quickest way to show Quillan Shepard the door.

Cain reached down and grabbed his soft, worn leather Bible. He held it in one palm and caressed it with the other as a man might the warm cheek of his first love. Quillan was like the rich young man who came to Jesus asking, "What must I do to be

132

saved?" The man walked away sad because he couldn't do the one thing the Lord required . . . give over himself.

Had nothing to do with riches, really. That was just where that story-man's heart lay. Quillan wasn't wrapped up in worldly goods, but his worth was bound up somewhere and locked away where the good Lord couldn't get at it. Cain shook his head. "I cain't figure it, Lord."

Quillan followed the rules. He treated men decently. Fact was, he had an overworked sense of justice. Quillan said it hadn't used to be that way. As a youngster he'd broken every rule there was to break — a regular hellion, taking pleasure in the scowls the congregation gave the "preacher's son." Cain could hardly picture it.

But Quillan had a brush with the law that turned him quicker than a hornet shies a horse. What was it he'd said? The thought of doing time, of being locked into one place unable to get out, was enough to put him on the straight and narrow for good. Cain shook his head. It must be part and parcel with being such a fiddle-footed man, never staying put long enough to cool his heels.

But Cain suspected a deep tenderness in Quillan. He had seen it more than once. Quillan had a gentle hand for the dog, a keen wit with D.C., and most of all, the heart to reach out to an old man fool enough to get his leg blown off. Not to mention the way he always dug in for the underdog and those suffering some injustice. That's what had gotten him crosswise with Berkley Beck to start with. And now he was as committed to upholding the good as he'd been to thwarting it in his youth.

He did good, and he cared. But Quillan did it all without grace. Cain opened the Bible and pictured Quillan in its pages. Some of these words had to be the key that would open his heart and let out some of the pain. Cain knew where it came from, some of it, anyhow. No one with a start like Quillan's could be free of hardship, not in this life. Cain just wished he could help. He thought if only . . . But then, he hadn't succeeded so well with his own boy either.

He swallowed that bitter truth with a familiar sadness. The Lord knew his own son, D.C., had been hearing of God's glory all his life by Cain's own mouth, and where was the boy now? Cain didn't want to picture what den of sin the boy wallowed in presently. Sometimes it was just too hard.

He lay down wearily on the cot. What with the worry and the jumping ghost pains in his leg, sleep was elusive. That came with age, he'd been told. Didn't seem to make much sense, though, when he spent so much of each day tuckered out. Unlike

D.C., who didn't seem to need sleep, not if the hours he kept were any indication.

In the first dim light of dawn, Cain strapped on his wooden leg and took up his crutch. He pulled himself up by one pole to balance on another. The sorry thing was, the wooden peg would outlast the joint in his good leg.

He limped out of the tent, ducking under the flap, and headed for Central. He'd look there before searching Hall Street. It was more likely gambling than women that kept the boy out all night. The women of Hall Street didn't linger.

He teetered along on the crutch up the slope from the creek, past the livery, and onto the boardwalk of Central Street. It didn't take his old eyes long to realize the dusty heap in the road was his boy. Nineteen years old and hardly the smarts of a coon. Robbed, no doubt. Beaten maybe. Chastened? Not hardly. Cain shook his head. He'd give him what-for just as soon as he cleared him from the wagon road.

Eight

Time is an undying enemy. No matter how much you put behind you, there is always more. I think eternity the cruelest joke of all.

Rose

From her window, Carina watched the old man shake the lump in the street. With his crutch he struck him once on the backside, and the younger man scrambled to his knees. There must be strength still in the old one's limbs, for he heaved his companion onto the boardwalk, and she lost sight of them behind the corner of Fisher's Mercantile.

What was she doing watching some old man pull someone from the gutter? One week in this place and she ached for home. Why was she here? If she asked him, Papa would send her money to go home. She could ride down with a freighter. . . . No, not that, but somehow. Dom would carry her. Anything to go home, away from this place, these strangers. To see her own people, hear their Italian voices raised in laughter and song, the warmth of their hands, their hugs.

She pressed her forehead to the grimy

glass and imagined how Mamma would welcome her, tears shining in brown eyes wreathed with creases, arms strong and thick. She had dreamed all night of the ones she'd blessed and wakened with an aching longing. How they would pet her and soothe her, scold her for leaving, then crush her with hugs and kisses and cry on her neck!

Carina wanted to cry herself. But if she once gave in to the ache, she would undo all her plans and run home. Yet how could she? She held a hand to her throat where the aching lodged. If she went home now, it would spoil everything.

The old man resurfaced, pushing the other ahead of him. He, too, reminded her of Ti'Giusseppe, her great-uncle on Papa's side. Indomitable, fearless, yet gentle as a dove. The young man wedged his head between his palms. From her vantage he looked weak, tottering, forgettable. But then it was the old man who stumbled, and the young who reached out his arm.

Coiled together like that they passed from her sight. Carina sighed, feeling alone and foreign in a way she never had before. All that she knew — the lilt in speech patterns, an expression in the eyes, shared memories and expectations, simple generations of being — all had been left behind, a thousand miles away.

She felt thrown into a stew, and she

137

couldn't find another of her kind anywhere in the broth. She had gone into exile — self-imposed, though not chosen. What had seemed to her bruised heart a dramatic, even romantic severing, was now only dull reality. Who was there to see her brave defiance? She had thought to make a home in Crystal. To show Flavio, to show them all, to show the world. How could she know, pampered daughter of Angelo DiGratia, that the world didn't care?

She dropped to her knees beside the cot, folded her hands, and rested her forehead on her peaked fingers. *"Il Padre Eterno . . ."* Shaking her head, she closed her eyes. "Please bless Mamma and Papa and Great-Uncle Giusseppe. . . ." Her voice broke before she could name the others. "Keep me from the Evil One." The words were empty. As empty as her hope. "And give me back my house today." It had become a litany.

Pulling on her boots, Carina frowned. She should buy a pair of slippers for walking in town, but she had been shocked by the prices in the stores. The choices for women were few and so high priced she had refused to spend her dwindling cash on shoes when she already had one pair of boots. But they were hot and heavy travel boots, not walking shoes. All her slippers had gone over the side with her wagon, thanks to Quillan Shepard.

Somehow the loneliness and displacement she felt this morning seemed centered on his single rash act. If not for him, she would have the things with which to make a home. She would not be living in a stall with canvas walls and changing in the dark so that her form would not show through to her neighbors. She would have her clothes and her furniture.

But not my house. The thought crept in unbidden. Losing the house was not his doing. But it seemed possible that it was, as though he'd started the misfortune and it grew from there. If he had not destroyed her wagon, her entrance to Crystal would have been as she expected. She would not have been robbed, and maybe, *possibilmente,* the Carruthers would not have run her off.

That was the way of things. Good brought good, but evil did likewise. Once misfortune began, it stayed like an unwanted guest. *Inverità,* her misfortune had begun before she lost her wagon. But she would have stopped it, had stopped it. If not for Quillan Shepard, things would have happened as she planned.

She went down the stairs and found Mae kneeling in the flower bed along the porch, grunting with each thrust of the handspade into the hard earth. The clumps of bachelor's buttons and daisies looked pale and tired, leggy in their search for air and water.

"If it don't rain soon," Mae spoke without looking, "this ground will be hard as mortar. Hand me that pail, will you?"

Carina lifted the pail, careful not to slosh the water on her skirt. Mae took it and poured it around the flowers. The cuts she had made with the spade sucked the water in, and Mae nodded. "That's better." She smeared mud across her forehead with the back of her hand. "Month of May was a running muck, but this is the driest June I can remember."

A freight wagon rumbled by, raising a cloud of dust, and Carina recognized the long brown hair beneath the hat. Mr. Quillan Shepard, off early and about his business as usual. Frowning, she turned away.

Mae rocked back on her heels. "You know, in these parts folks need a thick skin. You can't let one offense eat you up."

No? Carina pinched off a broken daisy and raised it to her nose. Was it not human to harbor a hurt, to nurse a wound? She should take injury and not remember? Not return it in kind? "Quillan Shepard. You know him well?"

Mae pushed herself up, breathing hard. "Don't know that anyone can say that, though some try, some who wouldn't know

140

the truth if it hit them in the face. But then, tales here grow as tall as Mount Pointe."

"What tales?"

"Rumors, is all. Nasty rumors."

Carina quirked an eyebrow. "Rumors start from truth."

"Or spite."

"Spite? Toward such a compassionate man, so charitable?" She waved a mocking hand as she spoke.

Mae rested her hands on her hips. "You have a sharp tongue."

Carina turned away. She felt sharp this morning, lonely and cross. If people talked about Quillan Shepard, it was his own fault. "I am not deceived."

"Then you're a first." Mae pinched a dried straw-colored bachelor's button from the stem and tossed it.

"Has he been here long?"

Mae leaned on the porch railing. "He's been freighting to Crystal for a year or so."

"And before?"

"Don't know much besides that he was born in Placer."

"In Placer? Where you mined gold?" Carina turned back, curious.

"Oh, I see that look." Mae tucked a gray, kinky strand of hair into the loose bun at her neck. "Listen, I'm not a tale spinner, especially that tale."

Especially that tale? Now Carina was more

141

than curious. What was Quillan's story? And more, how could it benefit her to know? Carina dipped her head obediently as she would to Mamma's scolding, a look of compliance, surrender even, but inside . . . She turned toward the street.

"Where are you off to?"

"Mr. Beck is expecting me." It was true. Though it was Saturday, he worked a six-day week and expected her to also. She shrugged. It would change soon. When the time was right, when things came right, she would need him no longer. Soon . . .

Berkley Beck rose from his desk as she entered. Carina approached with the easy confidence she had developed since Mr. Beck no longer courted her affections. It was business between them, and she knew how to conduct business.

His expression was purposely indifferent as he pulled a heavy black ledger to the center of his desk. "I'm going to be out most of the day, Miss DiGratia. This stack needs to be entered into the ledger." He rested his hand on the papers beside the book. "You're welcome to work here at my desk."

She nodded, then with sudden boldness asked, "Mr. Beck, where are the city records kept?"

He tipped his head. "What sort of records?"

142

"Births and deaths. Claims . . ." She spread her hands innocently.

He shrugged. "The courthouse keeps that sort of thing. It's public domain. If you're concerned about your house, I can assure you —"

She raised her hand. "I know you will handle that for me, Mr. Beck. I'm simply curious. Would . . . the records from Placerville be there as well?"

"Placerville? Miss DiGratia, you intrigue me. What possible interest could you have in old Placerville?"

She dropped her gaze to the wood of his desk. "If someone were born in Placerville, would those records be . . ."

"As far as I know, the records are intact. Everything was moved here when Placer closed down." Berkley Beck walked around the desk and leaned on it sideways. He studied her a moment, his blue eyes cool. "Two heads are better than one, as they say. Perhaps I can help."

"Quillan Shepard." Carina bit the words.

The blue eyes turned glacial. So the bad feelings went both ways. Mr. Beck ran a slow finger over his chin. "What's your interest in him?"

"He relieved me of my belongings on the road." It sounded petulant even to her.

As he nodded cognition, did she imagine also satisfaction?

"What are you looking for exactly?"

"I don't know." And she didn't. As Mae said, she should leave it alone. But would she?

He spread his hands regretfully. "Had I known it was Quillan Shepard who robbed you of your belongings, I might have handled things differently from the start."

"How differently?"

"I'm afraid it doesn't matter now. Too much water under the bridge, as they say. Still, it never hurts to be armed. Find out what you can and we'll see what we can do about it."

Carina nodded. Was it not exactly what she'd thought herself? Even hoped?

"In fact, the ledger can wait."

Though his smile was unchanged, his eyes took on a feral gleam that caught her short. But then the look was gone. She had imagined it, and his smile was as guileless as before.

"I insist. You've worked miracles in here." He gave his arm a grandiose swing, then caught her hand and brought it to his lips, warm and soft, a gallant gesture. "You must know how grateful I am."

He was close enough for her to smell his hair pomade, feel his breath on her fingers. It was beyond the boundary she had set, but Carina did not rebuke him. Mr. Beck could no more stop his courtesy than Mr. Shepard his lack thereof. Perhaps they could help each other after all.

Thinking about it as she walked to the courthouse, she became more convinced than ever. Mr. Beck had standing. He could prove a powerful ally in a place like Crystal. If she found anything worthwhile, she would tell him.

When Carina arrived at the two-story frame courthouse, the caretaker unlocked the door. The two judges and the others in the building didn't work Saturdays as did Mr. Beck. And that was just as well. It pricked her conscience to pry. But she meant only to learn what others knew. It was public domain, Mr. Beck said, free for the knowing.

She was shown into the room off the courtroom, then the caretaker left her alone. She looked up the records for Placerville that had indeed been moved when the old camp died. The official records started in 1851, but there were no listed births. As Mae had said, Placerville had been little more than a gulch camp with a handful of men, discouraged forty-niners, and those who had never made it as far as California.

She turned the page and ran her finger down the columns, skimming to the *S*'s. No Shepards listed under births. She checked again, then went on to the next year and the next. After the sixth year, she leaned back, her brow furrowed. Perhaps Mae was wrong.

She flipped back to 1852 and went through the births from the beginning, when a name jumped out at her. Quillan. No surname attached. It was as he'd said. *Com'é strano.* How strange. His parents were listed as Wolf and Rose, again with no family names. What did it mean?

Carina turned to the section for deaths. Running her finger over the page, she found Shepards. Four of them, all children. There must have been an epidemic, for the number of deaths rose dramatically, all within a two-month period. She puzzled that only a moment, then closed the book and replaced it.

Next, she took out the directory of land claims. This was a tedious search, as they were organized by filing date, not name. But in the summer of 1851, there was a claim filed in Wolf's name and called the Rose Legacy. Carina studied the land claim map, took out a handkerchief, and scribbled the rough location.

It was in Upper Placer, farther up the gulch than Lower Placerville and farther still from Crystal City. She tucked the handkerchief into her pocket and replaced the book. How many times had she been told to mind her own business? What good would it do to see where Quillan Shepard was born? What concern was it of hers?

She recalled the fervor in Mr. Beck's eyes. Was there something to know that might help them both? Knowledge was power. She had lost too much by not knowing, not wanting to know. *Innocente.* She would not make that mistake again.

From the courthouse, Carina made her way down the impossibly crowded street to the livery, hoping by now Dom was healed and acclimated. And indeed, he greeted her with bright eyes and an eager snuffle. She pressed her hands to the sides of his bony head and stroked his ears.

"Are ye takin' me companion, then?" Alan Tavish stepped out from behind the carriage he was polishing.

Carina smelled the linseed oil on his hands. "Is he well?"

"Well as ever. He only needed rest."

"Then we're going sightseeing." Carina spoke to the mule's muzzle. It wasn't truly a lie. She hadn't been out of Crystal once since she'd come, except to retrieve her belongings, and that could hardly be considered a pleasure ride.

"A bonny day for it. Not a cloud."

Carina thought of Mae's wish for rain as Alan Tavish slid the bridle between Dom's teeth. He had given her loan of both it and the saddle for a flat rate thrown in with the mule's keep.

"Where did ye plan to ride?"

She could say she had no plan, really, but that would be blatantly false. She knew exactly where she meant to go. "I thought I'd see old Placerville."

"Nothing but ghost houses and abandoned mines there, lassie."

And one mine in particular. She was tempted to ask him what he knew of the Rose Legacy but didn't. He was too gentle a soul and would likely scold the same as Mae. Besides, she was losing her resolve, and one more person telling her to mind her own business might be enough. She shrugged. "It might be interesting."

"See ye don't fall down a shaft." He waved a gnarled finger. "There's ghosts enough without adding yerself to their number."

"I don't plan to go into the workings." That much she promised herself.

"Aye. But the whole ground up there's been gophered, except maybe the center of town."

Carina stroked Dom's muzzle. "I'll be careful." And she would. She had no intention of doing anything foolish or dangerous. It was curiosity that sent her up, but curiosity did not always kill the cat, or there would be no cats left in the world. She didn't remind herself that there wasn't a single one in Crystal.

She led the mule out into the bright June sunshine. The mountain freshness enlivened both her and Dom, and she felt again the healthful energy in the air. Mr. Beck had not suggested she take her search this far, but she guessed he would not object. What was between Mr. Beck and Quillan Shepard was not her affair, but as he said, two brains were better than one.

With the location of Wolf's Rose Legacy mine in her pocket, Carina started up the gulch. Once outside Crystal's scar, the beauty enfolded her. The light had the illusion of motion — never stagnant, but alive with possibility. The breeze tickled the aspens and the chartreuse leaves trembled and danced so that the grove seemed insubstantial, like a mirage that might vanish when she approached.

Carina almost imagined she was riding simply to enjoy the view. But in just short of an hour, she came among the abandoned buildings of Lower Placer. The empty windows stared at her, vacant reminders of lamp glow that had burned a welcome in years back. Strings of fabric reached out in the breeze, beckoning her gaze. What wife had hung those curtains to make the rough cabin a home for her man?

The old hotel was two stories, with brick

chimneys and a balcony across the front, not unlike Mae's, though larger. The upstairs door still held twin arched windows, amazingly unbroken, though the wood around them was cracked and splintering. How quickly the mountain was reclaiming the town.

A quarter century ago it was built, fifteen and it was burgeoning, ten and that life had dwindled. Now it was gone, though the memories clung to the graying remains. Had one of these houses been Mae's? Why hadn't she asked?

Dom's hoof crushed a fragment of a teacup in the road. Someone had drunk from that china. Someone's lips had touched its rim. Where was that person now? She had an overwhelming sense of time as she gazed at the ancient stones of the mountain that had seen the different peoples come and pass away. The mountain would outlast them all.

A small gray rabbit darted under the sagging porch of a building from which a sign swung on one hinge, creaking. *Mater's Saloon and Entertainment.* Wasn't there a Mater's Saloon in Crystal? Some things didn't change. They just moved down the mountain.

She came to the first crossroads and stopped, then pulled the handkerchief from her pocket and shook it out. She studied the layout she had scribbled from the map, then gazed around her. This had to be the turn. She pulled Dom's head around and urged him up and away from the cracked and sagging buildings. She crossed the creek where it was wide and shallow.

On the other side, the trees thickened as she went, some obviously original growth, unmolested by the miners. Probably they were too small at the time to be of use, but now they had grown into tall thin giants. She found the lichened boulder that marked the edge of the Gold Creek Mine and the spring behind it pouring from the mountainside to join Cooper's Creek, which ran down the gulch alongside Crystal City. How far did it flow, growing bigger and stronger, joining and parting with other waters? Yet here was its start, or at least a portion of it, straight from the mountain, gushing out with amazing force.

She looked past it to the broken and rusted workings of the mine that burrowed into the mountain. According to the records, the ore from this hole had been exceptionally rich, grossing $250,000 its first year. The mine had changed hands three times but was one of the first to play out, bankrupting the last owners.

Carina turned south and cut up the new gulch at a rough diagonal until the ground leveled out before jutting up a sharp rocky face. Turning in the saddle, she eyed the town below. She could see the single inter-section like a cross in the center, down and to her right, but the slope was gradual enough at this point not to dizzy her head.

That couldn't be said for the next climb. Maybe she'd gone far enough. Why should she ride all the way to the top? Hadn't Mamma warned her time and again that cu-riosity led to trouble?

What good would it do to pry into the past of this Quillan Shepard? And what could she possibly learn from an old mine that might have been his papa's? It would be no different from what she saw here, no more revealing than all the gray skeletal buildings she'd passed already.

She looked up and sighed, then thought of Mamma's rocker splintering on the slope, heard the bare explanation with no apology or remorse. Her jaw tightened. She would know what manner of man did such a thing without regret. Had he spawned from the same greed with which his father robbed the mountain? Wolf. He was a predator, and he'd sired a predator son. She started to climb.

So he helped retrieve her books. An op-portunity to gloat. So he shot the snake. It was his own neck at risk as well. He did bring her the gun . . . for profit. She must learn to see behind the obvious. How foolish she had been. Innocente. But you did not put your fingers to the stove twice. Flavio had taught her that. This time, she would be prepared.

Carina skirted the stony face around the turn and along the shallow shelf until she saw the hole in the mountainside just to the left of the rock wall. Unlike many of the shafts drilled downward by hand or animal-driven whims used also to draw out the soft ore, this one appeared to have been picked by hand into the mountainside. Raw strength and stubbornness had opened this mine.

It must have held surface ore for someone to quarry it so. She couldn't tell how far the tunnel penetrated. A small circle of ground was cleared around the opening with a rough path leading away. The Rose Legacy. No sign to that effect, but it must be. The timbers that shored the tunnel appeared sound, and she approached the hole. Stopping at the outer framework, she stared a long while.

It was dark and cool and dry inside. Animal droppings showed occasional use, but there was no evidence of regular occupancy. It was silent and deserted. What had she thought to see? What could a hole in the mountain tell her? Nothing.

She had seen no records of ore from the Rose Legacy. That meant nothing of itself.

The smaller producers were not necessarily kept track of, and she had hardly read all the accounts. Had this hole yielded gold, brought fortune to Wolf and Rose? Had it been guarded or squandered? Who were they, and why did they not use their names?

She turned. A short distance away, among the trees, a stone foundation rose like teeth from the ground. Carina dismounted and led Dom over. The stones were roughly laid, stacked with no mortar. She dropped Dom's reins and paced it off. Eight feet by eight. She bent closer, noticing the inside of the foundation was blackened. Fire?

Had the cabin burned? Had fire swept the mountain? There was no sign of fire in the landscape she had passed. None in the town, nor the Gold Creek Mine below, nor even the timbers in the Rose Legacy. This fire must have been only here. Carina sat on the foundation wall and stared straight ahead. Then with a deep breath, she looked down.

Her stomach coiled and her head swayed. She was leaning, falling . . . No! She gripped the rocks on either side. It was Divina's doing, this plaguing fear of heights. Divina then, Divina now. Oh! Was there no end to her malice? Carina clamped her hands over her ears, hearing again her sister's laughter at being caught with Flavio, Carina's Flavio, as everyone had known since they were children. She balled her hands and thumped them on her knees.

No more. She would not wallow in self-pity. She forced her gaze down again, made her mind face what was there. The buildings below looked like a toy town she had once seen at a traveling fair. One slip and she would tumble down, shrinking as she went until she joined the ghosts that stared from the dots of windows. The vertigo was too much, yet if she could conquer it, would she not show Divina? Show her what? Divina was a thousand miles away, in Sonoma . . . with Flavio.

Carina pressed her palm on the rough stone edge. The pain kept her conscious as she looked away and down. Had not another woman looked down from here day after day? Had she not borne a son inside these walls? Maybe held him in her arms and looked out from the door? Maybe seen the town lying out below her and not been afraid?

Who was she, the woman who had lived in this high place of stones laid in a square to mark her presence. And where was she now? Carina looked around her. What was left to show that a woman had lived, loved, and birthed her son in this place? Rose. Rose who? Why were there no surnames? Rose and Wolf. Had they died here?

Carina crossed herself suddenly and

stood. She had been wrong to come. Whatever secrets this burned-out square held, the mountain would keep as its own. Gathering Dom's reins, she swung herself to his back. She kept her eyes on his neck and mane as he stepped gingerly down the rough path. He was surefooted, but the way was steep.

Carina moved her body to his stride. He had been hers since her fourteenth birthday, a young mule then, strong and sure. A gift from Ti'Giusseppe. And she loved him more because of that. She glanced down the slope, then quickly closed her eyes and let Dom carry her. Another day she would face the fear. Another day she would beat it.

For now she had only to get away, to leave her speculation and leave this high place. She was not meant to soar, but to keep her feet on the low places, planted on the level ground. Bene. She knew now from what humble beginnings Quillan Shepard came.

So he acted the big man. She knew better. Secrets of birth were seldom redeeming. His must be shameful indeed to have so much mystery. She raised her chin, feeling smugly satisfied, then paused. She sounded like Divina, always disparaging, looking for the bad, the weakness in someone. Where was her *indole mite*, the sweet temper Papa had praised, calling her *dolce angelo*, his sweet angel?

She frowned. Sweet angels were betrayed.

Sweet angels were laughed at. *Oofa!* She must open her eyes, see people as they are. She must not trust what they seemed to be, what they wanted her to see. She had trusted before, trusted those closest to her, and now? Look at her now.

Feeling the grade change, Carina opened her eyes. After the pristine wildness of the Rose Legacy, Placerville seemed squalid in its decay. Too bad the fire had not consumed it as well. She imagined the catcalls from the saloons, the tobacco spit and animal leavings in the street, the grubby children . . . was Quillan one of them? Again the curiosity stirred. What did she care?

Carina kicked Dom's sides, and he headed down the road toward Crystal, lengthening his stride until her hair flew out behind her and the rush of air stole her breath. Dom's chest was sweating and heaving when she reined in at the livery. Leaving the mule for Mr. Tavish's boy to rub down, she hurried off to balance Mr. Beck's ledger.

As she entered the numbers into neat rows beneath Mr. Beck's figures, Carina noted his exact script. Unlike his office, Mr. Beck's ledger had order — meticulous figures beside neat descriptions of services rendered. Catching her lower lip between her teeth, she flipped back the pages to the date of her arrival. Had he entered her case?

Once again she was trespassing on information, but she had started the day prying, so she may as well continue. She searched the page of entries for June seventh. There was no sign of her charge against the Carruthers, no listing of her claim dispute. But then, he had charged her nothing so far. No money taken, none recorded. But why had he not yet required payment from her? Would he collect upon completion?

She looked around the room. Where could her own deed and paper work be? She had filed the backlog, those cases successfully and less successfully completed. She had filed the ongoing disputes and even some he was not sure he would represent. But she had not found hers. Surely she would have seen and noted her own name beneath the date and type of claim.

Maybe in sensitivity he had filed it himself. It was possible. She sighed, looking up from the desk when the door opened. She had expected Mr. Beck, but the man was clearly not he. Standing even shorter than she, with a curvature of the spine and small rawboned face with protruding teeth, he looked like a ferret with dark, darting eyes.

"May I help you?"

"I'm looking for the lawyer." He waved toward the sign outside the door. "Berkley Beck?"

"I'm sorry, he's not in."

"Does he handle property disputes?"

Carina had to smile as she waved to the crates along the wall. "He does."

"Well, I have a house . . ." He stomped forward and shoved a paper at her.

Carina's jaw fell open as she stared at the very same property advertisement she had carried with her to Crystal City. Her heart sank when a deed swooped into place beside the illustration, replica to the one she had turned over to Mr. Beck herself.

She looked up at the little man and read in his eyes the anger she had felt in his place. If this man had a deed to her house, how many others did as well? And suddenly she was not sorry for him. He was a threat, an enemy. "Mr. Beck cannot take your case."

"What do you mean? Why not?"

"There are other lawyers in town. See one of them." She shoved the papers back toward the awful little man and thought for a moment he might explode with the blood rising to his face like a flood.

He snatched up the papers. "Well, I will then." With sharp, quick steps he went out.

Carina sagged in her chair. Mr. Beck might not approve of her sending business away, but how could he represent both of them? It was hers first, forgery or no. She had paid her money and would not be cheated. And the moment Mr. Beck returned, she would let him know that.

Nine

If the eye is the window to the soul, and from the abundance of the heart the mouth speaks, why can't we all be blind and dumb?

Rose

Carina walked home without having seen Mr. Beck. Her head ached and the anger she had controlled for days was burning inside. How many times could the same house be sold? How many deeds were out there for her property? Her ride up the mountain was all but forgotten in her renewed frustration. What did she care for a burned-out cabin on a forsaken mine? It was real walls she wanted, a floor and ceiling of her own.

"Hard day with Mr. Beck?" Mae came around the corner, her arms full of wood for the stove.

Carina remembered Mae's earlier words. *"Half the deeds in town are forgeries."* Well, Mae was right. Carina had been cheated. How many more people would take advantage of her?

She didn't answer Mae's query and didn't offer to help. As she passed the kitchen door, the smell of stewed bear and potatoes turned her stomach. She pushed out the back door and headed for the pump, then, furious as it gushed out icy cold, she slammed the handle down and stalked toward town.

Across Central and through the tents and shacks, she came to a low stone building at the side of the creek. She pressed the hair back from her face and went inside. The steamy, slightly sulfur aroma teased her nostrils. The air was damp and moisture beaded the walls.

A tall woman appeared and stretched out her palm. Carina laid a coin there, and without speaking the woman took a thick, rough towel from a stack and motioned her to follow. Carina did. Having learned of the hot spring's existence, she would splurge, never mind the cost.

The woman turned the corner like a sleepwalker, her face long and square as her shoulders and hips. As she walked, the brown braid barely stirred between her shoulders, and Carina was intrigued. How did she hold herself so straight? Carina tried to mimic her, then stopped when the woman glanced back.

"Watch your step."

She speaks, Carina thought as she started down the uneven steps into the dark stone cave. Inside the first alcove was a small circular stone basin, and steam rose in wisps from the water. There were four such caves, Mae had said, each bubbling up independent of the others, yet so close together the one entrance served them all.

The woman set the towel down on the ledge, tugged a curtain across the opening, and left her. Alone in the dim lantern light, Carina stripped off her dusty outer clothing. She touched the water with her toes, then jerked the foot back. Gingerly, she stepped again into the steaming water, then lowered herself slowly and sighed. How long had it been since she'd indulged in hot soaking water?

She cupped a handful and let it stream through her fingers, imagining Divina across from her with a palm full of suds. They had covered each other in suds, then splashed them off with such noise and giggling that Mamma would run in scolding and end up laughing, nearly as wet as they. Carina was surprised at the happy memory of Divina. They were few enough.

She sank down into the pool until the water cradled her chin and crept up the back of her head. Closing her eyes and pinching her nose shut, she ducked under. She could feel her hair swirling on the surface and shook her head side to side, then came up.

"Hot?" The woman had returned with a bar of soap that smelled of clove.

Carina nodded. "How does the water come out hot right next to the icy creek?"

"It comes from a crack in the earth's crust. The creek is runoff from the snows higher up."

"The creek also comes from a crack in the rock. I saw where it started. Only it's cold."

The woman shrugged. "I guess some comes out hot, some comes out cold. There's places in the creek where it runs both hot and cold."

"Really?" Carina glanced up to verify the truth in the woman's eyes. That intrigued her to think the water had a life of its own, playing some game of nature they could enjoy, if not anticipate. She pointed at the soap. "Is that for me?"

"If you want to use it." The woman held it out. Her pale hazel eyes were almost ex- pressionless, as though spending her days in these caves dulled her, sapped from her some energy vital to life.

Carina reached for the soap. "Is it extra?"

"Twenty-five cents."

"Extortionary. But why not. In my skirt there." Carina watched her dig into the skirt pocket for the change, then turn, straight- ening like a sapling after a breeze.

"You're new."

The words were soft, tentative, and Ca- rina guessed more personal than the woman

163

was used to. She knew what was meant but considered it figuratively, feeling as though she had just been hatched or birthed into a new and unrecognizable world. She thought how naive she had been eight short days ago, driving her wagon toward a dream. Within hours she had been stripped of all but her determination. Now she was learning, learning to fight, to win.

"Yes."

The woman nodded, and a small spark of life touched her eyes. "My name's Èmie."

Carina realized she was younger than she'd first thought, nearer her own age than not. Perhaps outside the caves she was not so blank, so stiff and pale. "I'm Carina DiGratia."

"You have lovely hair, Carina DiGratia, the way it ripples like that."

An ache started as Carina recalled Flavio coming upon her once in the swimming cove. He had stood on the side and stared at the rippling veil laid out across the water's surface as she floated on her back. *"One day I will marry you, Carina Maria,"* he had called from beneath the over-hanging palms. And she had dived under and swum through the salty waves with strong strokes, laughing inside because she knew it was true.

She swallowed the pain. "Thank you."

Èmie eyed the hollow at the base of Carina's neck. "Father Charboneau will say Mass tomorrow."

Carina touched the silver crucifix that hung there, hot against her skin. Why did she suddenly feel uncomfortable? "A priest? In Crystal?"

"He's many things. Priest, prospector, even a boxer at the fairs. He goes between the mining camps and cities. He's been serving these mountains since Placerville."

Carina shivered in spite of the steaming water. A priest from Placerville. But for one street corner shouter, she had heard no mention of God except in blasphemy in this godless city. Of course, she had spent the last Lord's Day in bed. She couldn't know what kind of observances had occurred while she slept.

The melting soap felt silky in her palm as Carina pressed it to her neck. "But I've seen no church." She thought of the Spanish mission church in Sonoma with the white stucco towers and the arch that held the massive bell, where the black-scarved women had streamed each morning, she and Mamma and Nonna and all her tias and some men among them. Not a man would miss Sunday Mass, but only a handful went daily. Carina had gone to please Mamma, yet she wondered some-times why Mamma went.

Èmie started for the cave's opening.

165

"There isn't one. Father Charboneau has a small cabin west of Spruce and Central. We meet there."

Carina's heart sank with the news. "Which one is Spruce?"

"Just past Drake."

Closing her eyes, Carina rubbed her face with soap. The melancholy that had settled on her in the ruins of Placerville returned. Her soul required she attend, but her heart quaked at the thought.

Sunday. Quillan lay back on the mattress, arms folded behind his head. A day of rest. Even he had to take it sometimes. His body needed it. Too many long days in the wagon were enough to warrant a break, and tomorrow he'd be better for it.

Not that he could lie there completely idle. He reached for a book he'd purchased on his last trip up. *Tales From the Brothers Grimm*. A collection he hadn't read as of yet, being something that would not have been approved in his youth. The Book of Job, the Psalms and Proverbs, Deuteronomy, Leviticus, and the Gospels had made up most of his expected reading.

The dime novels and works of Hawthorne, Cooper, and Edgar Allan Poe were confiscated when found, though he had become adept at hiding them. He thought of the precursor to the hole under his present

166

canvas floor. He had loosened the floor-board under his bedstead and replaced it so carefully that his book cache had remained hidden until he left home at thirteen.

Quillan rolled to his side and flipped open the cover of the book. It was sheer pleasure to lose himself in tales of inconsequence, even absurdity. Unbidden, he thought of Miss DiGratia and her sheetful of books. Had she lost others from the wagon for which she risked the mountain? He frowned.

She should have claimed them, then. He would have carried whatever she named most dear. What did she have in the black leather satchel that meant more than the wealth of books she went down the mountain for? He'd like to know what caused her queer expression when he made to throw the satchel down to her.

Maybe it was fragile, but he hadn't heard any clinking inside, nor felt anything but soft padding between the leather sides. He hitched his shoulder to capture the down pillow into the crook of his neck. Whatever it was, she had demanded it be handed to her in that smoky voice of hers with a tone that left no argument.

It was something she valued, no two ways about it. So he had saved it for her. He should credit himself for that. The rest was forfeit, not through malice, as she seemed to think, but necessity. The wagon road had to stay open. Too many depended on it for their livelihood. He turned the empty leaves to the first page of the initial story, *Make Me Shudder*. That should prove entertaining enough, he thought with a wry smile.

Somewhere a bell rang, the sort that was fixed to a base and struck with a hammer. Though it wasn't the deep heavy throat of a tower bell, it sent a cold spear down his back nonetheless. Somewhere, folks were gathering to pay homage to an invisible being who meted out justice and punishment with the heavy hand he had known all too well in the flesh.

Though no church building had yet been raised in Crystal, the faithful gathered where they could. There were the Methodists and the Baptists down by the creek, the Catholics over on Spruce, Anglicans in a small house west of town, a handful of Saints sent up from Salt Lake to enrich the coffers of their believers, and of course the Jews, though they met quietly Saturday nights without bells and incense. Fools every one.

Quillan rolled to his back and rested the book on his chest. Unbidden, the words came to his mind. *Blessed is the man that heareth me, watching daily at my gates, waiting at the posts of my doors. For whoso findeth me findeth life, and shall obtain favour of the Lord. But he that sinneth against me wrongeth his own soul: all they that hate me love death.*

He heard his small voice reciting it in the darkness of wooden walls closing in around him, not seeing from where the blow would come. The smack of wood on flesh. *"Again. Repeat it."* With his groin liquid and his knees locked, the words coming from his lips again, and the blow sending hot fire to his flesh. *"Again . . ."*

Quillan closed his eyes and shut out the sound of the bell. The stories would not be enough. He needed to *do* something. He rolled restlessly to his feet and stood.

The worst part of having only half a leg was not being able to kneel. Cain slumped on the bunk and rubbed the stub. *I suppose you understand, Lord, seeing as you saw fit to remove it.* He bowed his head and folded his hands. He'd join with other believers later into the morning, but just now he had the Lord to himself, and that's the way he liked it best.

In a pitiful voice that couldn't hold a tune, he sang a hymn from his childhood and felt his spirit rise. How close the Lord was every time he thought to look. How near and how faithful. No shadow of death, no veil of tears could keep him from God's love. Cain knew it as surely as the sun would shine, and it pained and confused him that others found it so hard to believe.

Cain could hardly think of a time he hadn't known the comfort of God's presence. There'd been times of loss, hard times, sad times. But those times had brought him close to the Lord and swelled his faith, not weakened it. It just didn't make sense any other way. Who could ever face life alone? Cain wasn't strong enough for that.

That's all I ask, Lord. That whatever comes my way, you don't leave me alone to tackle it, don't ya know. He opened the black leather Bible and slid the ribbon to the center of the spine, then ran his finger to the section of the page that held the Twenty-third Psalm.

The words were imprinted on his mind as indelibly as on the page, but he liked seeing them when he read, knowing that some inspired saint, some lover of the Lord, and maybe David himself had written those words in a moment of ecstasy, knowing God's intimate love. Cain's cup overflowed.

The priest didn't show his age. If it was true he'd been ministering to the mountain towns since the days of Placerville, he had to be nearing fifty. But he was a robust, dark-haired man with little thickening in his trunk and strong, muscular arms, a boxer's arms roped with muscle.

Carina saw them holding the chalice high,

the wide sleeves of his vestments slipping back as he intoned the Rite of the Eucharist. She closed her eyes. Did she dare take part in the sacrament? It had been so long, but until she would forgive . . . She felt the anger coil around her heart, serpentine in strength. Though it hurt, something inside welcomed it, embracing her wound and nurturing it. She would rather hurt than forgive when Divina had laughed.

Èmie stood beside her, rapt and angelic, hardly recognizable as the same woman from the caves. Her skin was pale, her hair lifeless, her face plain and narrow, yet there was a peace about her, a simple joy. Carina swallowed the ache. Where had her own joy gone?

She glanced about. They were pressed close in the crowd of mostly Irish and Italian men, along with a handful of wives. She could see the women's resentment in their eyes when the men pressed forward, introducing themselves to a fellow country-woman, "I am Umberto Mancini, Lorenzo Belli, Mario Lasala . . ." She knew what the wives thought of a young woman here alone, a lure for their husbands and sons.

I don't want them. You can have them. They are contadini, *peasants.* Where did these thoughts come from? Had she not followed Papa's example of good deeds to the poor, felt compassion for those less endowed by

171

the Creator and downtrodden by life? Had she not done small works of kindness from her earliest days for just such as these? Why now did she disdain them so?

Èmie went forward to kneel before the priest, who seemed to grow in size and stature, holding out the Eucharist to Èmie's tongue. Carina's heart pounded in her chest. Her own tongue could not receive the Christ. Her soul wrenched inside her at the thought, but she was not worthy.

It surprised her how it hurt, though it was her own doing. No. It was Divina's sin! Her chest constricted. She glanced up furtively as others filed forward, then pressed her eyes shut again and stood still on the pressed dirt floor of the cabin. She knew what was required.

She drew a long, slow breath. She could not forgive. Even if the pain lasted for years, she would not forgive Divina. She kept her head bowed as the priest spoke the benediction, then signed herself with the cross. She would slip away quietly. She had done her duty.

Èmie caught her arm as they filed outside. "Come and meet our priest."

Carina's throat cleaved. She did not want to meet him. He would know, would see the unforgiveness in her.

"Father Charboneau, may I present Carina DiGratia."

"Welcome, Carina DiGratia."

His handgrip was as powerful as she expected. His eyelids crinkled with the smile into pointed arches over blue gems, glittering warmth and genuine pleasure. In the sunlight she noted flecks of silver in the dark waves of his hair. "Thank you."

He expanded his chest with a deep breath. "It's a glorious day, isn't it? Like all the days in heaven. One golden moment after another."

Carina nodded dumbly.

Èmie seemed to have come to life, an awkward butterfly tasting the sun after too long in the cocoon. "Won't you join us for breakfast, Father?" She spoke to the priest but tightened her hold on Carina's arm, leaving no doubt as to her own invitation.

"I will. And have a word with your uncle Henri."

Carina tried to escape Èmie's hold, but it was firm. What choice had she but to surrender?

"Have you been here long, Miss DiGratia?" Father Charboneau strolled beside her.

So it began. He would question and probe, creeping closer and closer to the truth until he surprised it from her. *I hate my sister, Father. I wished for her to die.* "Only a week."

"Then I doubt you've seen much by way

of the sights." He tucked his hands into the pockets of his trousers and proceeded at an easy amble, so relaxed.

"The sights?"

"Wasson Lake, Beaufort Falls . . ." He spread his hands. "You are touring?"

What could she say? This was no pleasure excursion. What was it? A misguided, ill-fated flight from humiliation to . . . to what? Better he believe her here to enjoy the sights. "I did tour Placerville."

"Ah. Old Placer."

Now she would turn it on him, draw him out, away from her business. She stepped over a rut. "Èmie said you were there? Did you have a church?"

"No. I said Mass in Mater's Saloon."

"And you prospected for gold?"

He smiled with a quick glance to Èmie. "I did some prospecting, but the best gold I found was in the people. Amazing the nuggets lying beneath the silt of life's burdens."

She thought of her findings from yesterday. "Did you know a man named Wolf?"

It was faint, but she caught the unease behind his look of surprise. "I did."

"And Rose?"

His face softened, the flesh growing slack, brows leaning together, suddenly tired. "I buried them together."

So Quillan had been orphaned. Did that explain his borrowed name?

Èmie tugged her arm. "Carina, what are you talking about?"

Father Charboneau patted Èmie's shoulder. "A sad story, not unlike many others, though perhaps more vicious than some. A tale, however, that time has put behind those who carried on."

His meaning was clear, and his blue eyes pierced. He did not want her to ask more. Sensing that, Carina took it to heart. But she had accomplished her purpose. He wouldn't pry if she did not.

He started on with a vigorous stride. "I feel that frying pan calling me, Èmie. What I wouldn't give for a half-dozen eggs and the butter to fry them in."

"The best I can do is flapjacks." But she beamed as though even that was an honor to provide the priest.

Carina struggled to keep up. She was no competition for Èmie's long legs and Father Charboneau's powerful steps. By the time they climbed up to Èmie's cabin, she was hot and winded. She worked the pump, splashed the icy water over her face, then smoothed back her hair.

She considered slipping away, but that would be cowardly and a poor trick to play on a woman who had seemingly befriended her. In a place like Crystal, she needed all the friends she could find. Still, it was with some reluctance she went into the small two-room cabin behind the others.

The back door was open to the mountain, and Father Charboneau shot a look at Èmie. "It appears your uncle got wind of our coming."

"The smell of breakfast will bring him back."

"But not with his tail between his legs."

Èmie shook her head and turned to Carina. "Uncle Henri and Father Antoine have a long-standing dispute."

"Feud. Tempest. War." Father Charboneau rubbed his hands together in anticipation.

Carina noted the familiar name Èmie gave the priest. They must be long-standing friends. Bacon sizzled in the iron skillet as Èmie skewered the thick, ruffled slices and flipped them over. With that aroma filling the room and the coffee steaming on the stove, it was no surprise when a large, dour man appeared at the back door.

He growled when he entered and took his seat at the table. Even with his French saturnine scowl, Carina recognized a resemblance between him and the priest. Both broad shouldered, a little barrel-chested, blue eyed, and sharp featured. She glanced at Èmie, who nodded slightly.

"You look old, Henri." Father Charboneau pulled a stool to the table and hurdled it to land squarely atop.

"I work for a living."

"Ah. But I work for the dying, and that, without exception, is all of us."

"Save your preaching for fools like Èmie. Food, girl."

Èmie laid his plate before him and another for Father Charboneau. She motioned for Carina to follow her outside with theirs.

As Èmie sat down on the stoop, Carina dropped beside her and balanced the plate on her knees. "They're brothers? The priest is your uncle?"

Èmie nodded. "Father Antoine is Uncle Henri's youngest brother."

"Why do they fight?"

"Uncle Henri can't forgive Antoine's taking the cloth."

Not forgive a man for choosing the church? Was it not an honor any family craved, to have a son become a priest? "Why not?"

Èmie leaned close. "Because before he did, they were outlaws."

"What do you mean, outlaws?"

"Horse thieves."

Carina stared.

"It was before I was born. But as long as I can remember, I've heard Father Antoine going after Uncle Henri to repent and make restitution."

Carina shook her head. Horse thief turned priest. His own story was as black as anything she or Quillan Shepard had to hide. But she was hardly surprised. What else in a place like Crystal? "Why did the priest stop thieving?"

"They got caught. The ranchers strung them up from the only tree for miles around."

Carina stopped her bite of flapjack half-way to her mouth. "To lynch them?"

Émie nodded.

"What happened?"

"Father Antoine says God. A storm came with lightning and thunder. The ranchers thought that would spook the horses as well as a bullet, and their hands would be clean of it, so they left them there on horseback, hands tied and nooses on their throats." Émie circled her neck with her long, solid hands. "Can you imagine sitting there waiting for the horse to spook and . . ." She tightened her hands and sucked in her breath.

Caught up in the tale Carina pictured the scene. "They didn't spook?"

"They spooked. The lightning hit the very tree my uncles were hanging from."

"Then how —"

"It sheared the branch clean from the trunk. Father Antoine said it was a sign from God. Uncle Henri called it good luck.

But Antoine wouldn't steal with him again. He knew he was called, just like St. Paul being struck off his horse."

"So he became a priest."

Èmie nodded. "He went to France to study with the Jesuits. They made him a missionary and sent him back to America. Now he travels, looking for the worst, down-trodden, hopeless souls he can find. But he can't sway Uncle Henri."

Carina chewed the bacon slowly. So there was more to Father Charboneau than one might think. Horse thief, prospector, priest. What next?

After cleaning up with Èmie, Carina took her leave. She wanted nothing more than a lazy day with her head in a book. She had finished Cervantes for the third time. She pondered her choices as she wandered slowly down the hill to Mae's and found her out back in dishwater up to her elbows. The giant wooden tubs she used outside to wash and rinse the dishes in the daylight were almost as large as the pool in which Carina had soaked.

"Went to Mass, did you?" Mae sloshed a plate from the washtub to the rinse water.

"Yes."

Mae's hands were raw, but she didn't seem to notice as she scrubbed away. "I'm not denying Father Charboneau says a right nice funeral, but if it's preaching you want, bring yourself to Preacher Paine's tent revival."

Carina took up a towel and braved the scalding water for a plate to wipe. "Preacher Pain? And people come?"

"That's Paine with an *E*. And yes they come, and come back. He puts the fire in the brimstone, if you know what I mean."

Carina didn't. Neither did she care. She had done her duty, no more.

"Preacher Paine comes up every summer. There's a picnic first to sort of fatten the calf, then the tent meeting come evening. Most folks can't sleep after, unless they went forward and unburdened themselves."

Carina tried to imagine it. "Does everyone go?"

"Most everyone."

"Henri Charboneau?"

Mae snorted. "Not that one. Some go just for the show, but Reverend Paine hooks 'em." Mae dug a thumb into the flesh beneath her jaw like a fish yanked by a gill.

Carina was fascinated by the display. "How does he hook them?"

Mae laughed low. "You come see for yourself."

No grazie. Was it not enough to face the priest? A sudden thought struck her. "Do you know Father Charboneau?"

Mae heaved an iron skillet the size of a

wheel into the tub. "I don't suppose there's anyone here I don't know."

"Then you know he was a —"

Mae sank the skillet in the tub, put her dripping hands to her hips, and faced Carina. "We need to get something straight, right off. I don't gossip, especially about folks I might depend on for my life."

Carina flushed. Wasn't gossip part of life? Didn't the stories grow and grow better with each telling? Didn't it lend stature and long-suffering to the tellers and even the tell-abouts? Was it not a sharing of hearts and souls? Even Scripture said what was whispered in darkness would be shouted in the light.

"I don't hold with hanging people's lives out like laundry."

Carina frowned. Did dark deeds not deserve hanging out, and brave deeds not shine brighter? "Why is it wrong to tell our stories?"

Mae pushed herself back from the tub. "Nothing wrong in telling your own. Just not someone else's."

Carina considered that. How she had cringed when Divina told and retold of her falling from the roof, squirmed at the telling of her kicking Tony because she could not win the foot race. How they had laughed and called her Giusseppe's mule. Many times she had wished to shush Divina.

Could Mae be right? Could the very fabric of her life, of her person, of the people she knew and held most dear, prove faulty?

Before she could answer, Carina was cloaked with shadow — Quillan Shepard's shadow.

Ten

Is it possible to live someone else's life?
If so, I have left mine and entered the
mind and body of a stranger . . . whom I
don't much like, and trust not at all.

Rose

Carina jolted like a rabbit in the carrot patch,
certain he could see her guilt. She had pried
into Quillan Shepard's life. Like Eve after the
fruit, did she look different for the knowledge? Anger vied with shame. Had she
learned so much? No, but she had intended
to, and the guilty feeling wouldn't pass.
Mae's reprimand was a barbed hook, holding
fast against any excuse she might make, and
she pictured herself as Mae had been just
moments ago with a thumb hooked into her
jaw.

If Quillan noticed her discomfort, he
made no sign. He was clean and groomed,
his hair tied back and mustache trimmed
so its line ended just below his mouth and
no longer reached his freshly shaved jaw.
The sleeves of his cotton shirt were rolled
to the elbow, the collar open two button-
holes.

He tipped his hat. "Mae. Miss DiGratia."

Mae hunkered back. "Well, Quillan. What brings you around this time?"

"Unfinished business with Miss DiGratia."

Carina startled. What unfinished business?

"Mind if I steal her?"

"Steal away." Mae waved a sudsy hand.

Carina bristled. What was she — a horse, that they made her plans without her? "What business have you with me, Mr. Shepard?"

For an answer, he motioned to the pair of blacks, saddled and waiting by the wall of Mae's house.

Vanitoso. How confident he was that she would accept his inelegant invitation. But then, she could be grateful he wasn't a hand-kisser like Berkley Beck. Such behavior from Quillan Shepard . . . She cringed inside.

Bene. Let him tell her his business. Whatever his offer, she would refuse — and enjoy the refusing. He put a hand to her elbow as she slipped her foot into the stirrup and swung up. The black she mounted was strong with heavy hooves. A man's horse. A work horse. She could feel its strength in bone and muscle.

Quillan swung onto the horse beside her. "Ready?"

She felt a quiver of excitement astride the powerful horse. It had been long since she'd ridden a fine-blooded steed with a man beside her. Not since . . . She shook away the thought.

She would not consider it now in the presence of Quillan Shepard, whose gray eyes seemed to look into her soul, though he rode like stone beside her, offering no explanation, no congenial conversation. Whatever his plans, he kept them to himself.

She wouldn't ask, would not let him know she wondered. What unfinished business could he mean? There was no need to ride if he meant to haggle further over the gun. Besides, a deal was a deal. He would know that. What then?

There was nothing more on the mountain where her things had spilled. If he meant to sell her something, he would have brought the wagon, or at least presented it there at Mae's. Why the ride? The secrecy? Did he know she had looked up his records?

No, that was her own conscience accusing her. No one knew except Berkley Beck. Surely he would not have told Quillan Shepard. So she had gone to the mine — many others rode that way. She had found a trail and followed it. That was all.

Yet . . . Father Charboneau's expression played in her mind. If there was something, something to hide, and Quillan suspected she had pried . . . Oh, why was he there? Why would he not explain himself?

As they passed the last of the dwellings that fringed Crystal City, she could take it no longer. "Where are we going?"

"A record."

She glanced sidelong.

"I'd wager that's the longest you've gone without sating your curiosity."

She started to retort, but he interrupted with, "Wasson Lake."

"Wasson Lake? Why?"

"It's far enough away you won't be heard."

She tried to rein in, but her black kept prancing with his, neck to neck, defying her. Somehow Quillan Shepard controlled even the horse he didn't ride. Fear sprang up inside.

"I'm teaching you to shoot, Miss DiGratia." He gave her a crooked smile. "I don't deliver useless goods."

Her hands relaxed on the reins. He had done that purposely, used innuendo to frighten her. He was teaching her to shoot? Then he didn't know. Besides, what had she learned? That his parents had died. It was nothing to hide. But why had they borne no surnames?

"You have the gun with you?" He might have asked that before they came so far.

She brought up her chin. "I told you I would carry it. What use is it in a box somewhere?"

"What use is it if you can't shoot?"

She gave no answer.

"Can you ride?"

"Of course."

"Really ride?"

Was he challenging her? She felt the power in the horse beneath her, saw the ripple of muscle and sinew. This horse was not her slow plodding Dom, but that didn't mean she knew nothing of riding. "What's his name?"

Quillan quirked an eyebrow.

"This horse. What do you call him?"

"Jack."

"And yours?"

"Jock."

With a sudden motion, she leaned over the horse's neck and dug in her heels. "Fly, Jack!"

This time the horse sprang forward, and Jock quickly followed, the excitement of the race upon them. She felt Jock vying for control, but Jack had a nose lead on him, probably the difference between her weight and Quillan Shepard's. They pounded across the stony ground onto softer growth as the valley widened and leveled. The horses ran neck and neck, so closely matched in stride as to be one.

She tried to make Jack pull ahead, shrinking herself down and applying the rein. But he was either at his full speed or held back by something else; he resisted her prodding. Ahead, a low fringe of willow and swamp grass marked the line of a stream. She saw a narrow gap in the growth and headed for it. That was her chance. If she could edge him out . . .

Pressing herself lower to the neck, she caught hold of the saddle horn. The willows drew close. With only seconds to make her move, she bore down for the thrust, then raised up from the saddle. With a wrench, she was in the air, flying over Jack's neck and landing seat first in the tall, wet grasses. The narrow stream lapped her skirts.

Quillan swung his leg, leaped off his mount, and crouched beside her. "You all right?"

Frowning, Carina pulled herself up by Jack's rein. "What sort of horse can't jump a stream?"

"He can jump it. Just not without Jock. He thought they were pulling together."

Pulling together? And then she pictured them hitched to the wagon. Were they so trained they responded to him as one horse? What kind of power did Quillan Shepard wield over his animals?

"They're twin foals, you see. They almost think as one."

She ran a hand down the wet side of her skirt, feeling the damp all the way to her skin. "And you knew that would happen?"

"I suspected."

Bene. "But you said nothing."

"You might have reined in at the stream and called it a draw." He stuck his tongue in his cheek to keep from laughing.

She was not amused as she pulled wide her soaked, soiled skirt, the beige linen she had worn into Crystal. "You have a habit of spoiling my things."

He sobered only slightly. "The choice was yours."

Her anger flared. "As it was the first time?"

He met her eyes without flinching. "The first time there was no choice." He looked off to his right, toward the lake just visible beneath the peak. "This way." He started to walk, tugging both Jock and Jack's reins. She stood a moment, stubborn, then released a sharp breath and followed.

They walked along the stream, which was tucked so deeply into the overhanging grasses that only an occasional sparkle marked the water's path. She watched a bumblebee the size of a pecan hum over a globe of clover, then make its weaving way to the next. She would not be the one to speak this time.

"Ever pet one?"

She looked up, confused, and he pointed at the bee. He was teasing, of course. "Like touching the rattler's head?"

189

His mouth quirked. "It's safe. Especially if you find one dozing, late afternoon, evening." He straddled the stream and held out his hand. After a moment's pause, she took it, and he lifted her over the marshy ground.

His grip was firm and strong, but his voice low and silky. "You reach out nice and slow and stroke it right down the fuzzy back. You can almost hear it purr." There was playfulness in his eyes, something she wouldn't have credited him.

"I don't believe you, Mr. Shepard."

"Quillan." He gave her time to step away, then urged the horses across. They looked eager to join him again, as though his bidding was their delight. He started walking. "You think I'm lying?"

"I think you stretch the truth."

He shrugged. "Try it and see for yourself."

"And have a sting for my trouble."

He studied her a moment. "Only if you telegraph fear, Miss DiGratia."

She frowned. "I'm not afraid of bees. I just don't ask for trouble."

"No?" He sauntered past her a step and turned. "What sort of work do you do for Berkley Beck?"

His change of subject surprised and bothered her. What business was it of his? But then, what business were his birth and the death of his parents to her? Conscience demanded she answer. "I keep his records."

Quillan raised his brows. "His books?"

She shrugged. "I file his cases and keep his ledger if he gets behind."

He narrowed his eyes. "Where'd you get legal training?"

She scoffed. "What training is there to putting dates in order?"

"You only look at the dates?"

She wiped the dampness from her skirt. "They are all the same. Land disputes, claim disputes. Too many." She waved her hand. "I will not get my house back."

"Your house?"

She had forgotten he didn't know. Why should she tell him and reveal the depth of her ignorance, of her plight? She sighed. "After you destroyed my wagon, three men took my house."

Quillan stopped walking. "What three men?"

She made a scornful sound. "Carruthers."

"On what grounds?" There was something in his expression, some knowing, some . . . but then it was gone.

"I don't know." She waved her arm in frustration. "Mr. Beck thinks a fraud; Mae says forgery. It must be a forgery because another man —" She bit off her words.

"Another man what?"

She blew out her breath in exasperation.

191

"Another man had the same advertisement and deed. He came to Mr. Beck for help, but I sent him away. How can Mr. Beck get the house for us both?" Her voice rose to a petulant pitch in spite of her efforts.

Quillan stood slack-hipped. If he cared at all for her hardship, it scarcely showed. "Why did he go to Mr. Beck?"

"I suppose he saw the sign, same as I. Berkley Beck, Attorney at Law. Where else do you turn when you're wronged?"

Quillan looked as though he had an answer to that but kept it to himself. "Where's your deed now?"

"I gave it to Mr. Beck. He's handling it." Quillan snorted.

"I know what you think of him. But —"

He raised an arm and pointed. "That spot should do all right."

Carina followed his arm. Away from the stream, the ground had firmed into clumps of fine gold and pale green grass. Masses of kinnikinnick and red-berried bushes grew beneath the white-barked aspens amid thorny rock roses with pale pink blooms. The leaves of the aspens trembled in the breeze, twisting on their stems so that the sunlight glinted off them like paper-thin stained glass.

Quillan stopped walking when he reached the place he'd chosen. "Hand me your gun."

She pulled the gun from a deep pocket in her skirt and gasped when he wrenched it from her with such force it burned her hand. She jumped back, her eyes wide, her breath catching in her throat, his speed and power and brutality of motion overwhelming her.

He scowled. "Never point unless you mean it. You hand over your gun grip first."

She met his scowl with her own. "My finger was not on the trigger."

"You think anyone will wait to find out?"

She opened her mouth, then accepted the reproof in silence. With her gun in hand, he walked the horses to an aspen that stood to the side of the clearing and loosely wrapped the reins, then returned to her side. He slid the barrel forward and dumped the rimfires into his hand.

"Didn't I load it right?"

"You did." He slid them back in. "Now the firing pin rests on these so you can't bang it around. If I'd known you had it in a pocket . . ."

"You would not have thrown me from your horse?"

"I didn't . . ." He paused, rested the gun in his palm, and examined it. "No, I wouldn't have. My Colt revolver would have blown through your limb. This Sharps . . ." He handed it to her. "Don't take that chance again."

As though she had planned to fall from the horse. He was the one who knew, who watched to see it happen. No warning, no explanation.

He adjusted the weapon in her grip. His palm was callused, yet smooth from the rubbing of leather reins. "All right, pull back the hammer."

She did.

"Now, when you pull the trigger, the firing pin strikes the charge around the rim of the factory load. The fulminate of mercury ignites and sends a spark to the powder inside the shell. But then, you already understand the mechanism, don't you." Again his mouth pulled into a sardonic smile.

She didn't actually know all he had just told her, but she nodded anyway.

"Then shoot that aspen with the scar." He pointed.

She squeezed the trigger. The shot splintered the bark of an aspen some twenty feet off. Not the one she had aimed for.

"You closed the wrong eye. If you're shooting with your right hand, close your left eye. That gives you a straight line down your arm."

She raised both arms, centering the gun between them. This time the bullet grazed the side of the tree she meant to hit. He raised his eyebrows as her third shot took a chunk from its other side. The last one nicked a branch. She turned to face him.

He took the gun, extracted the shells, and reloaded. "Try again."

"Why are you doing this?"

"I told you. I don't deliver worthless goods." Quillan handed it back. "Try it from your pocket."

"Aren't you afraid I'll shoot my limb?"

"Don't hold the trigger when you pull it out."

She sank the gun into her pocket, then tugged it free and fired. She couldn't tell where the bullet hit, though she heard the faint click of it somewhere.

"Don't take the time to close your eye. Just pull it and shoot as though you're pointing your finger."

She put the gun into her skirt again, pulled it out and shot. It caught a branch of the aspen.

"Again."

She shot and missed. And missed again. He reloaded and she fired until they'd run through a box of rimfires.

"One more."

Her arms ached as she raised the gun for one last shot. She nicked the side of the trunk. Sighing, she extracted the shells as she'd seen him do. He dropped the last four cartridges into her palm. Still silent, she slid them into place, closed the barrel, and dropped the gun into her pocket. She rubbed her arm below the shoulder, knowing she had shown little aptitude for the weapon. Reluctantly she looked at Quillan Shepard.

"The trees better watch out." He smiled, his well-formed features and bent brows over dark-rimmed gray eyes looking more rakish than ever. A pirate's grin. A rogue's grin. Then it faded. "What you won't know until it comes to it is if you can point at a man and pull that trigger." His scrutiny delved deep, searching her, seeking her mettle.

She imagined herself putting a bullet into living flesh, recalled the time Papa had dug a lead ball from a man's side. He'd held it up between his pincers and said, *"Behold man's cruelty."* In spite of her papa's efforts, the man had died, poisoned inside by the wound. He'd come too late.

Looking now at Quillan Shepard, her voice shrank. "I hope it never comes to that."

His answer came, low and caustic. "Hope is for fools. Are you a fool, Miss DiGratia?"

She bit him back. "I am no fool. I am the daughter of Angelo Pasquale DiGratia, physician and advisor to Count Camillo Benso di Cavour."

Quillan Shepard eyed her darkly. "Do you think a lofty birth makes you anything more than you are?"

Her breath released in a haughty rush. "It makes me everything I am. If I were born a contadini, a peasant like . . ."

"Like what?"

"Like you."

"What makes you think I'm a peasant, Miss DiGratia?"

"Are you not?" She trembled with the accusation. She hadn't meant to go so far, but her anger dulled her instinct.

He started for the horses.

"What else could you be, born in a hole on the mountain, the son of Wolf?" She could think of no worse insult than a nameless parentage.

He turned, his face defined in chiaroscuro, light and darkness, like a portrait by the masters. A renaissance face: handsome on the outside, deadly within. "What do you know about Wolf?"

And now she trembled in earnest. She had gone too far, betrayed herself.

His jaw twitched. Above it, his eyes stormed, a fierce, deadly force showing itself in their depths. His voice grated. "My father was a savage, my mother a harlot. Is there anything else you want to know, Miss DiGratia?"

Quaking inside, she refrained from crossing herself. She could scarcely listen to such words, never consider applying them to her own mamma and papa. Yet he said it with such defiance, such loathing. Her voice wouldn't come, so she shook her head quickly, ineffectively, then watched his back as he untied the horses for their escape. He was, no doubt, as eager as she.

Quillan let the silence lie between them. What did Carina DiGratia know of the hole in the mountain — the Rose Legacy? Where had she learned his father's name? And why? There were some who knew, some right there in Crystal, but why would Miss DiGratia know? Had she asked? Again, why?

Quillan controlled his breath, forcing it to come in short, even spurts. He wished he could be rid of her, this woman who mouthed the name of Wolf, who shot it at him like a weapon. How could she know the very mention conjured thoughts and emotions too deep to contain?

They were too far from town. Why had he brought her so far? Some lingering guilt or misguided desire for gentle companionship? To keep their gun practice quiet, as he'd said? Or to make certain Berkley Beck caught no wind of his courting her?

Courting? Hardly that. Rather winning her trust to make use of her familiarity with Beck's business.

He refused to glance her way, that beautiful Italian princess who thought she could throw his past at him. How could she know? Mae? No. Mae kept secrets close to the vest. She had never betrayed him before. Beck? It was possible. She had Berkley Beck panting at her skirts like the miserable dog he was. But did he know? What use could that blackguard make of it? Plenty.

Quillan dismounted before Mae's porch. Miss DiGratia waited, no doubt her breeding requiring his assistance. He lifted her down from the horse, the feel of her narrow waist nothing more to him than any other piece of baggage he might haul. Her feet were on the ground, and he was free. He caught up the reins and pulled the twin geldings behind him. He should at least take his leave. Common courtesy demanded it.

But he kept walking. He never turned until he reached the livery and took the horses inside. Then he released the breath that had stagnated in his lungs.

"I dinna think a bonny day with a lass could bring such a face." Alan Tavish reached for the reins.

Quillan's scowl deepened. "What makes you think I was with a lass?"

Alan tapped the side of his head. "I keep me wits about me and me eyes open."

"Well, don't carry on like an old maid. It was business."

"Aye, I can see that by yer sour look."

Quillan dropped his chin. "Just reminded me why I prefer the company of men."

"She's a fetching lass, Quillan."

"She's a fury." Quillan patted Jock's wither and left Alan to the task.

Carina stood where he had placed her, firmly, silently. Not one word had he given her to ease the tension. And the look on his face — stark, embittered fury . . . She brought her hand up to finger the crucifix on her neck. *Madonna mia,* the man was *pazzo.*

Eleven

To think is pain; to remember, torment; but to consider the future — more than I can bear.

Rose

"You look as though you've seen a ghost."

Carina jumped when Mae spoke from the chair in the shaded corner of the porch, but she took the two steps up and joined her. Not a ghost. He was far too real for that. "I should know better than to trust Quillan Shepard to be civil."

Mae's laugh was little more than a mezzo rumble in her chest. "You don't look much the worse for wear. What did he want with you?"

"To teach me to shoot. He said he doesn't deliver useless goods."

"And that's a fact." Mae brushed an iridescent fly from her arm. "Takes pride in his goods. That's why folks pay his price with no thought even to bargain him down."

No? Had she not done just that with the gun? Her chest swelled at the thought. Only a fool wouldn't quibble. And he had accepted without countering, then presented himself as instructor. He was not the idol Mae thought him, only a man with a bad temper.

Carina leaned on the rail. A strain of birdsong sounded from the corner of the roof, and she watched the sparrow flit to the side rail. Mae held out a lump of fat from the bowl beside her chair, and the bird hopped closer.

"Come on, you little beggar. Come on over."

The bird's feet made tiny clicks on the wood as he advanced, cocking his head to one side, then the other. His eyes were shiny beads of onyx, his beak a delicate ivory point. Would he go all the way to Mae? Would he take the food from her hand? He puzzled it, hopped, puzzled it some more. Slowly Mae reached to the side and set the fat on the rail.

Carina held her breath. The sparrow hopped, bobbed his head, hopped again, then took sudden flight as a man rushed around the corner, knees and elbows akimbo.

"Mae! Mae, I can pay my bill." It was Joe Turner, who slept in a dead man's bed. "The Ulysses S. Grant hit ore." He swiped the hat from his head and crushed it to his chest. "Miss DiGratia, will you marry me?"

Carina startled. "Marry you?"

"It's all on account of you!"

She looked bewildered.

"You see, the night you took my room I was so angry I stomped off in the dark and started to dig. I didn't even look where. The next morning I figured I may as well keep digging there as elsewhere and, well . . ." He pulled a black chunk of rock from his pocket. "Here she is. Silver- and lead-bearing ore."

Carina smiled to think her wrongdoing had played a part in his good fortune. "I'm happy for you, Joe Turner, but you'd do better to ask Mae."

"Well, I would if she'd have me. But I know better than to expect it."

Mae laughed. "And right you are. My marrying days are done."

And I am already spoken for, Carina thought, then chided herself. *No longer, Carina. Don't be a fool.*

"Well, I'm off to have it assayed." He kissed the rock. "Wish me luck!" He plopped the hat back on his stringy brown hair and darted off.

Carina watched him run down Drake to Central, knees to the side like a gray cricket, then turned back to Mae. "I'm absolved."

Mae's belly rolled with the laugh. "And more. His blood's so thick with prospector's fever, nothing'll thin it save embalming fluid."

"I hope his strike is rich."

"You'll become a legend if it is. He'll

likely tell that tale all over town. You'll have folks asking you to put them out so they can find a hole just like Joe Turner."

Carina put a hand to her chest and strutted. "And why not? Haven't I the DiGratia good fortune?" She cocked her chin and tossed back her hair. "Perhaps I should dig a hole myself, as I, too, was put out of my house."

"Perhaps you should. But then you'd have to hire men to work it and grubstake them to boot."

Carina waved a hand through the air. "With my luck, they'll grubstake me."

"Grubstake? You're not thinking of deserting me?"

Carina spun at Berkley Beck's words, at once subduing her manner as he climbed the steps. It was one thing to prance before Mae, another altogether for Mr. Beck. "I was making a jest, Mr. Beck."

"I'm pleased to hear it." He smiled. "I came to say I'll be out of town several days, and I was hoping to leave the shop in your hands, so to speak."

"Of course. But what can I do without you there?"

"Just keep track of anything that comes in, and keep me alive to any new possibilities. I'll surely be back by Wednesday." He smoothed a hand over his hair. "I'll leave some small tasks for you at my desk."

Carina nodded as he left, but her mind was not on his small tasks. An uneasy feeling started inside. She should not have told him about searching Quillan's records. If Quillan Shepard knew she had involved Berkley Beck, he might prove more frightening yet. The look in his eyes . . .

"You swallowed the goat?" Mae leaned forward in her chair, causing a creaky complaint from the old rope seat.

The tone of his voice and the underlying power, the menace of his silence . . . "He frightens me."

"Berkley Beck? He's harmless."

Carina jolted. She had spoken without thinking, and it had not been to Mr. Beck she referred.

Mae continued, oblivious. "He thinks a lot of himself. Still, he'll likely do all right. Wouldn't be a bad match."

Carina frowned. "I'm not looking for a match, good or bad."

"Well, you sure couldn't tell it by Berkley Beck. He's an eye for you and no mistake."

Carina drew herself up straight. "Our relationship is business."

Mae rocked back and folded her arms across her bosom. "Hmm."

Quillan sat, unmoving, behind Cain Bradley as the old man jammed his crutch into the ground like a bishop's crook and drew his bushy brows together into a hedge. "What do you mean, it's gone?" Cain moved his pale eyes from one face to another.

D.C. met the gaze, then glanced off. "Just that, Daddy. It wasn't a vein or even a pocket, just a thin shelf and it's all used up."

So much for hope. Quillan had heard the same too many times to recall. Either a hole never reached ore, or it played out too soon. Crystal had too few rich strikes to hold on for long. Men were jumping to Leadville like fleas from one dog to the next.

"You're tellin' me there's no more ore in the Boundless Mine? No more a'tall?"

The boy shook his head, glum as a soaked marmot, and the two men behind him confirmed it with their own gloomy faces. Quillan hurt for his friend. This was not the sort of news a man took easily.

Cain leaned on the crutch, suddenly older than he'd been. "Well, maybe you just dug through the first part. What it wants is to go deeper, don't ya know."

The thin man behind D.C. raised splayed fingers. "We dug sixty feet to find the first ore, and it wasn't good grade anyhow. It's not worth searchin' deeper."

"Not worth —" Cain shook his head. "All that work, and me losin' my leg. And it's not worth searchin' deeper?"

"I'm sorry, Cain. You can keep diggin' if

you want to. The mine's two-fourths yours and the boy's. But I want out. I'll sell you my share, or I'll sell it in town."

"Sell it! You said it was worthless!"

Slow Jim shrugged. "It may and it may not be. I'm just tired of digging that hole. I've lost my faith in it, and when a man's lost his faith, the tunnel's too long and dark to make sense of it."

"So you're quittin'."

"No." Slow Jim stuffed his pockets with his hands. "I'm sellin' my share and goin' to work for Joe Turner. He's hit it rich. Some of the richest ore yet." He gave a crooked grin. "The DiGratia woman found it for him by putting him out of his room."

Quillan stirred. What was this? More meddling by that woman.

Cain sagged. "Well, what is it you want for your share, worthless as it is?"

"Eight hundred dollars, gold dust."

"Eight hundred!" The blood vessels stood out in Cain's forehead.

Slow Jim reddened. "That's what it'll cost me to jump in with Joe."

"Well, I hope you break your neck jumpin'. I don't have eight hundred dollars gold dust or horse manure. And you know it!"

Slow Jim looked uncomfortably at his companion. "Morty, here, wants the same. He's comin' with me."

Cain's throat worked up and down, but no sound came out. His face went gray, almost matching the pale blue eyes. "That right, Mort? You, too? After all we been through?"

"It don't make sense to stay, Cain. The hole's no good."

"You're askin' eight hundred, too?"

"Andrews got forty thousand for his. It's just down the way."

"His is producing." Quillan's voice was low and flat. "And that price was for the whole works, the buildings and machinery and proven assays."

The two men looked past Cain to meet Quillan's gaze. "There's greenhorns who'll buy our shares, none the wiser."

"And leave Cain to explain?"

Slow Jim colored again. Mortimer Smith shrugged one shoulder in eloquent embarrassment. They knew what it would do to Cain to be saddled with newcomers in a mine with no ore. Mortimer reached a supplicating hand. "You can sell out, too, Cain."

"And go where?" Cain wheezed the words, too used up to care.

Quillan stood up from the crate. "I'll give you eight hundred for both shares together, cash or gold dust. You can go in halves on a share of Turner's hole."

Cain's mouth gaped.

"But you're not a miner," D.C. started to argue.

Quillan ignored them both. "It's the best offer you'll get — honestly, anyway. Mort? Slow Jim?"

The two men conferred with their eyes, then sighed. "Eight hundred for both. We'll likely have enough for a second share before the month's out."

"If you'll wait here, I'll fetch you the money."

"Dust if you got it. Joe's wantin' dust."

Quillan pressed the hat to his head and went out. He hadn't intended to go by Cain's tonight. He'd been angry enough after leaving Miss DiGratia to kick his horse and spit. He'd done neither, but now he was almost as angry at himself. Eight hundred dollars for a worthless hole, and he'd sworn he'd never mine, never succumb to the lure of the ore.

He ducked inside his tent and stood a long moment staring at the canvas floor. It wasn't the lure of ore that made him do it. It was pity . . . and friendship. He dropped to his knees, his arms stiff and reluctant as he tugged the canvas free and felt the board beneath.

He wasn't reluctant lifting the board to drop his savings in, but it felt like lead to reach in and take some out. He could go back and tell them no deal. Cain would understand. Cain knew how he felt about mining. His own face had shown it. D.C. had blurted it.

He touched the pouches of gold dust stacked to one side, the bills on the other. His bank. His future. His worth. His fingers closed around two pouches, and he balanced their weight in his palm. About right. Maybe some from a third.

His hand rebelled, but he made it reach in for one more. Some of that one would go back. They'd weigh it, make the deal, and he'd return the rest to the hole. He again heard Cain's wheezing voice. *"And go where?"*

Quillan knew well enough what it was to be uprooted, to leave what you know for what you neither knew nor wanted. Hadn't he been dragged from place to place on the excuse of saving souls when all he wanted was a home and folks to love him? Eight hundred dollars was nothing to what some holes were going for. But then, this one was worthless.

He'd have to make them believe he doubted that, keep D.C. digging, maybe take on a man or two to help. Otherwise Cain would know he'd done it out of pity, and that would shame the old man. He'd cut out his own tongue before he shamed Cain.

It would cost plenty to keep the mine working, and D.C. couldn't do it alone.

Cain could hardly wield a pick with half his leg gone, blown off by a charge with a defective fuse. Quillan refused to consider the job himself. He would not under any circumstances scratch the ground for a living, nor willingly work a mine tunnel, especially one likely played out. The thought alone left a bad taste in his mouth. Well, he'd better get back and make the deal before either he or they changed their minds.

D.C. looked like he'd swallowed feathers, so badly did he want to question Quillan's decision. Quillan gave him no opening until the deal was concluded and the money exchanged.

Slow Jim and Morty took their leave, and Quillan stood with a forced grin and held out his hand to Cain. "Well, partner?"

Cain gripped it weakly. "You ain't got time for a dawg, but you got time for a mine?"

"I can't work it, Cain. You'll have to hire on someone to help D.C. My share's an investment."

"What if there's no ore like they said?"

"There is no ore." D.C. wiped his face and threw down the towel. "I tried to tell you, Daddy."

"But there might be. Deeper in."

D.C. shook his head. "That's what they all say. All the fools who don't know when to stop."

"And plenty of fools stopped too soon when the real pay dirt was only a few feet away." A vein stood out in Cain's temple.

"Easy for you to say. You don't have to tunnel it all day in the dark with nothing but a candle on your hat and another on the wall, and dank air in your lungs, your hands worked to the bone."

Cain scowled. "What would you rather do?"

"Anything!" D.C. threw up his hands. "I'd rather drag a plow behind a mule than dig in a hole like a varmint. I want out, too, Daddy. I want out so bad I could spit."

Quillan laid a hand to his shoulder, gripping perhaps harder than he needed to. "Consider carefully what you're saying, Daniel Cain. You're turning your back on something your father's put a lot of his life into."

"Then let him dig the hole! Let him blow his other leg off looking for ore that ain't there!"

Quillan's fingers dug harder. D.C. didn't know how good he had it with a father like Cain who cared for him. He saw the tightening of Cain's lips, the grim look of the eyes, almost opaque, a mask to cover the pain.

"You want to walk away, boy? Go ahead." Cain's voice was stronger than

212

Quillan expected. "Go ahead and push a plow, or get drunk and gamble your life away."

"Need money for that." D.C.'s chin was dropped so low to his chest he growled it.

"In the box. You can take all I got. I only wanted it for you anyhow."

Quillan stiffened as D.C. pulled away and grabbed the money box from the crate. He took out a thin stack of bills and ruffled them. With a frown, he put several back inside but kept the majority. Then he looked up at his father. "I just can't do it anymore."

Cain nodded. "Then don't."

As D.C. pushed past him and left the tent, Quillan felt defeated. Why had he spoken up? Cain would have been better off with new partners or leaving town with D.C. Why had he jumped in and given D.C. an excuse? Now what? They would have to hire men to work the mine, and Cain would need to oversee it himself.

"Are you up to this, Cain?"

Cain shrugged, letting himself down on the cot. "I'm gettin' too old to wonder what I'm up to, don't ya know."

Quillan sat down on an upturned crate, elbows to knees. "Maybe he'll come to his senses."

Cain shook his head. "Not sure he has any to come to."

Carina shrank back from the window, sickened by the violence she'd just witnessed. The brutality. And just under her window, so she could hear the thudding fists against the young man's flesh, the grunt of his breath, and his cries. Snatching her shawl, she ran down the stairs.

"Hey there! Where are you going?" Mae blocked her path.

"A man's been hurt."

"It's not your affair."

Carina tied the shawl on her shoulders. "He's just outside. You must have heard it, too."

"Doesn't matter what I hear or don't hear. I mind my own business."

Carina stared. Mind her business? She could ignore such a thing? "He's hurt. Badly."

"What's that to you?"

Carina drew herself up. "My papa is a physician. I know a little medicine. I cannot leave him there bleeding in the street."

"Well, you'd better leave him."

"As you left me when I fell senseless on your porch?"

Mae pressed her hands to her hips. "That was different."

"How different? He's been beaten and robbed."

"That's right. It's the roughs. And if you run out there, you'll be next."

Carina stared at the back door. Just beyond it a man lay, gagging on his own blood. She hardened her jaw. She would not leave him lying there. She had seen the men run off — brutes, big and ungainly. Carruthers? The thought jellied her spine. But she walked to the door, turned the knob, and pulled it open.

In the darkness she could hear him crying. Her heart twisted. Did a man cry? Even a boy so grown as he? She almost turned back inside, then remembered her bold words to Mae. She had to see it through now. She had no choice.

"Here. Don't cry." She hurried to his side. "Are you maimed? Is something broken?"

He groaned. "Leave me alone." He spoke through a thick and fouled nose. Broken surely. "I wish they'd finished it."

"Well, they didn't. But they might if you stay here crying."

He yanked his arm away. "Leave me alone." Then his eyes found her in the dark, and he wretched. "It was my daddy's money. Almost everything he had, and him all crippled up on one leg."

Carina felt her jaw drop. The same boy. The same one she'd seen only days ago with the old man on the crutch. The pair who had left her feeling so alone. She grabbed him by the shoulder. "Get up now. You need tending."

"I don't deserve it."

"Maybe not. But you need it." She tugged ruthlessly, and he struggled to his feet, wincing. She half dragged him inside, then kicked the door shut behind her.

Mae had a sheet spread on one of the long tables. "Set him there. How bad is he?"

"I won't know until we clean the blood off. I think his nose is broken."

Mae snorted. "So is most of the camp's." She strode away and returned a minute later with a basin of warm water and a towel.

Carina washed his face, wincing when fresh blood flowed from the nose unchecked. Though he screamed, she reformed the nose between her hands. She tore two small pieces of muslin from a roll Mae held, rolled them tight like cigarettes, and pushed them into the nostrils in spite of his hollering. They would hold the cartilage in place and keep the passages open while stanching the blood. He would have to breathe through his mouth.

She mopped the remainder of his facial cuts clean. None were severe enough to need sewing. "Help me with his shirt." Her fingers worked the buttons loose.

Mae frowned, but the man sat still and stopped complaining, likely dazed.

"I must see if there is bleeding inside." Carina pulled open the shirt. "Bring the lamp closer." She pressed his stomach with her palm and examined the ribs, then walked around to his back, again pressing with her palm and watching the flesh. "I don't think your organs are damaged."

"How would you know? Are you a doctor?" He spoke thickly through his blocked nose.

"Are you in need of one? Or simply of someone with better sense?"

He scowled. "I don't have to take this."

"Didn't you learn the last time not to walk alone at night?"

His head came up abruptly. "The last time?"

"The last time you lay in the street and your papa came for you."

He jerked around to face her. "What are you, a spy?"

"Not a doctor, nor a spy. It takes neither to recognize a fool."

He pushed her away and stood, his legs shaky, but his expression firm in spite of the cloth protruding from his nose. "I told you to leave me alone."

"You would prefer to lie down again in the street?"

"By Jove, I would!"

"Then by all means . . . ." She waved her arm. "Your bed is made. Go sleep in it."

He staggered toward the front door, gripped the knob, and nearly fell out when it opened. Without a backward look, he went out and slammed the door.

Carina raised her chin. *"Buona notte."*

Mae's laugh was so deep and full it choked her. "Land sakes, Carina. He'd rather face the roughs than your tending."

"So let him." She looked down at her blood-soaked blouse, all the thanks she'd get for her trouble.

"Is your father really a doc?"

"Yes."

"Not a poor man's doctor, I'd wager."

Carina raised her chin, reminded of Quillan's remarks. "He has served a king."

Mae let out a low whistle. "Well, well."

Carina softened. "He has also tended any who came to his door and many who couldn't come. And sat by the deathbeds of some too desperate to own a decent bed to die in." She met Mae's violet eyes, daring her to scoff, to ridicule her pride in her papa, her heritage.

Mae smiled. "Let's have a cup of tea. A toast to your victim."

"*I* did not break his nose."

"No, but you certainly put it out of joint." Mae caught Carina's arm through hers and laughed.

"It was his own stubbornness."

"And you'd know nothing about that."

Carina opened her mouth, but Mae had caught her squarely. Had not stubbornness and injured pride brought her to Crystal? No. It was heartbreak and . . . hope? Was hope, as Quillan said, only for fools?

Quillan reached for the gun holstered by his bed. "Who is it?"

The voice was unrecognizably thick and muffled.

"Who?"

"D.C."

Quillan swung his legs over and strode to the opening of his tent, gun in hand. He pushed the flap open. "D.C.! What have you done?"

"Nothing. Can I come in?"

"What's that in your nose?"

D.C. pawed the swollen flesh. "Cloth. Some woman shoved it there."

"Woman?"

D.C. scowled. "At Mae's. Some woman at Mae's."

Carina DiGratia. "She did this to you? Broke your nose?" Quillan wouldn't put it past her, though why D.C.'s and not his own he couldn't say.

D.C. shook his head and sank into the caned chair. "It wasn't her." He dropped his face into his hands and sobbed. "They took the money. They took Daddy's money.

I didn't even spend one cent of it. They took it all."

Quillan went cold inside. Part of him wanted to punch D.C. himself, part of him seethed at the roughs who preyed on the men of Crystal. Even those like D.C. who almost deserved it. It had to stop. "How much was it?"

"I don't know. I never counted it. I never touched it, not since I put it in my pocket." He groaned. "I can't go back."

"No, I wouldn't think so. Cain would add broken ribs to your broken nose."

D.C. hung his head. "I wish he would."

"Wouldn't get the money back. Only one way to do that."

"How?" D.C. looked up at him exactly as Cain's mottled dog did.

"Work. You work for it."

"But how?" D.C. spread his hands. "If I go back to the mine . . ."

"No. You've taken your stand. Now keep to it. You can work for me." Quillan tossed a rolled blanket to the floor of the tent. "Get some sleep. In the morning you learn the freighting business."

Twelve

A single moment of joy can slake the throat of a dying spirit. An act of kindness, no matter how small, becomes a mercy drop from heaven.

Rose

As she walked to Mr. Beck's office the next morning, Carina was surprised to see the boy she had tended seated high on Quillan Shepard's wagon. She stopped on the walk and stared. The daylight was less kind to the young man than the lamp had been. His nose was enormous, his eyes masked with blue swellings. He sat slouched and sullen, but whole.

He did not look up from the reins to see her, but Quillan Shepard did. His face was set, offering her nothing, not even his anger. But she knew it was there. Beneath his mask of indifference was the bitter fury that had frightened her so. She turned into the office, suddenly eager to see what work Mr. Beck had left her.

Closing the door brought instant relief. Mr. Beck's desk was cluttered as though he had tossed the papers there, then shuffled them about with his hands. Maybe he'd searched for something before leaving and had no time to put them in order. But then, maybe he had considered it her job to bring order. She sighed and took her seat.

Thankfully, she had the next few days to herself. What was it Quillan had said? *"You read only the dates?"* Perhaps it was time she learned better what it was Berkley Beck did. She took up the first page and started to read. It was tedious language at best, and after four or five pages, she lost interest. Better to file them and be done.

After the first several miles, D.C. was squirming on the box. Quillan wasn't surprised. A youth like that would chafe every mile of solitude. But it might give him the chance to think. Quillan could hardly blame him not wanting to be shut away from the sun day in and day out.

No wonder he was pallid and whining. Who could want to spend his life in a hole? Still, there were lessons for D.C. to learn, like appreciating what Cain had tried to do for him. It wasn't easy raising the boy alone, him coming so late in their lives that the mother had died in the birthing. What man could be father and mother both?

Quillan saw D.C. wince at the bump of the wagon but said nothing. It was for the kid to mention if he needed to. It was time he learned to be a man. Quillan hadn't planned to be the one to teach him, but it seemed to have fallen out that way. He supposed it was good D.C. had come to his tent last night. It would have broken Cain's heart to see him.

Quillan frowned. Somehow, some way, the lawlessness had to be stopped. But how? Marshal O'Neal had resigned the position. His constables ran the other way when it came to trouble with the roughs, and none of the miners seemed willing to stick their necks out and make themselves a target. If no one stepped up, there would be no opposition to the roughs at all.

But Miss DiGratia had stepped up. She had gone out into the dark and fetched D.C. inside for doctoring. He'd gotten the whole story last night from D.C.'s point of view, which probably wasn't far from the truth, especially her sharp tongue. They ought to elect her marshal and let her scold the roughs out of town.

He chuckled to himself, and D.C. looked over with a questioning brow raised.

"Just drive, D.C. Just drive."

Carina blew the straggling hair off her forehead and laid down the last paper in a neat stack. After lunch she would file them, now that they were sorted and the corresponding leaves put together. She pushed back the chair and stood, but her skirt snagged on the floor and pulled her back down.

She bent beneath the desk and freed it from the loose board that slapped back into place. No wonder Mr. Beck lost his pen nibs in the crack. The board had lost its nail. She held her skirt free and stood.

Her stomach was hungry enough for even Mae's fare. And they had begun a habit of lunching together, as few of the men came in for the noon meal. Most took the remains of their breakfast in packs to hold them until dinner. That left Mae and Carina to share a quiet, leisurely meal, her favorite of the day.

She met Èmie on the corner of Drake and Central. Though she had no intention of immersing herself in Crystal's social life, she had developed a fondness for Èmie Charboneau. She couldn't help pitying her, living with the dour, cross uncle and working in the hot springs. "Have you left your cave?"

Èmie nodded. "I snuck away. If Uncle Henri knew, he'd send me back directly. But I can't spend every minute in there. Some days I think I might as well be a miner."

Carina pictured the dark bath caves, the narrow tunnel between. She almost smelled the sulfur steam and heard the trickling on the walls. "At least your tunnel is clean."

"True. But it's dark and dank. I wish the springs opened to the air."

Carina caught her arm. "Come with me for lunch with Mae."

"I don't have money for it."

"You'll be my guest."

Èmie shrugged. "The worst she can do is throw me out."

"She won't. She likes too well to have the dishes washed for her while she dozes in the sun."

Èmie held out ragged hands. "I know well enough how to wash dishes."

"Then come along. Your sink awaits." The day that had started ruefully with the sight of Quillan Shepard and the damaged boy had suddenly grown bright. Carina looked upward. How had she taken for granted the brilliant blue of the sky, the warmth of the sun? She thought of Èmie sneaking away just to breathe the air outside, worrying her uncle might find out. Her heart moved for her friend. Yes, her friend.

"I think we should picnic," Carina stated. Èmie needed the sunshine, the brisk mountain air. When they reached the kitchen door, Carina pulled it open. "Mae, we have a sun swept canopy we can't waste. We must eat outside today."

Mae looked askance, then shrugged. "It's no skin off my nose. Eat wherever you like."

But Carina caught her arm. "You must join us. Just listen to the birdsong."

"That's a crow's caw."

But Carina tugged, and Mae carried their plates outside. Sitting together with Mae and Èmie on the back stoop after eating, Carina talked, pouring out her family history, her memories. She told tales of her brothers' escapades with skilled artistry, making them larger than life until Èmie's eyes shone. She spoke of Papa's work, his rise in Italy, his move to Argentina and on up to California, his importance in the community, yet his generosity and compassion.

"Not only does he doctor the people who can pay generously, but also those who bring only a loaf of bread or nothing at all. He takes his oath to heart and refuses care to no one. He is a great man."

She spoke of Mamma's beauty. "Even after seven children she is shapely, and that's no easy thing with such brutes of brothers as mine. Tony was the size of a young ox at birth. Mama called me a runt, coming after that. But either way, she was back in her skirts in weeks. She is the envy of all the aunts, as beautiful now as she was when Papa chose her." That wasn't strictly true, but very nearly.

"That's where you get it, then." Èmie smiled shyly. "My own mother was plain like me, but gentle and warm. I always remember how warm . . ." Her eyes brightened suddenly with tears.

Surprised, Carina wrapped an arm about

226

Èmie's waist, and they rested their heads together. Mae wore a distant look, thinking perhaps of family, perhaps of Mr. Dixon. "Family's important. Sometimes I wish I'd had one."

Èmie sniffed. "Sometimes I wonder if I ever will."

Carina suddenly ached so strongly for her loved ones she squeezed Èmie. "We must be family to each other." Fervent tears stung her eyes. She needed it so much.

Mae laughed. "Will you look at us? And in plain sight of God and all the world."

But Èmie and Carina held each other tightly. Carina raised her face to the sky. "Let them see. We are women. We are not meant to be alone."

That evening, Carina took some of Mae's load as her own. After keeping Mr. Beck's business through the day, she ate with the men, then scrubbed the tables and benches and swept the floors. The next morning before she went to Mr. Beck's office, she rubbed down the woodwork, chasing the never ending dust. Mae told her neither yea nor nay but accepted the help with silent gratitude.

And as they lunched in Mae's parlor, Carina was rewarded by Mae's own tales. How different they were, her stories of life in the camps and gullies she'd prospected. "Then there was the time winter surprised us in June. We were at the front of our provisions, so there wasn't much chance of starving. But mine was the only cabin, as I was the only woman. It took about two hours of blizzard before the men abandoned their chivalry and packed in with me. Didn't even need a fire, there was so much body heat inside my walls." Mae's buttery voice warmed at the telling.

"Each one had a pretty apology for barging in, but not a one offered to leave, even when night fell. That was in a time when getting caught with a fellow after dark meant disgrace or matrimony." She glanced at Mr. Dixon's picture on the wall. "I told them they'd have to ante up to see which one would get me, but they just guffawed and said, 'Heck, ma'am, we'll all marry you.' "

Carina's eyes widened.

"That made forty husbands, and what would the Mormons think of that? 'Course, not a one of them meant it, and I knew it and they knew it, and we all had a good laugh and spent the night warm and chaste. No, there was only one man for me, and him not much in some eyes. But that's how it is. The heart sees what the eyes miss." Her voice caressed the portrait of her plain husband.

"But listen to me going on." Mae pushed

her plate aside. "If I didn't know better, I'd swear you've bewitched me."

Carina spread her hands. "There's no magic here."

"Maybe not. But that's the most I've carried on in years."

Carina smiled. "Carry on, Mae. It's good for the soul."

When Mae laughed deep in her chest, Carina laughed, too. She felt a lightness inside that she hadn't known since arriving. And the lines on Mae's face seemed to smooth and lessen. Her labored breath came easier, and Carina wondered if she truly had worked some magic on the woman.

Only that night, when she trimmed the lamp and lay down in the darkness, did the aching loss return. *Oh, Flavio.* And when she slept, she dreamed her heart was an eye watching Flavio caress Divina's face and bury his fingers in her hair.

Wednesday morning, as Carina worked at the small desk across from Berkley Beck, she noticed his glances. He had watched her all morning since his return last night — not blatantly, but not furtively, either. It made her realize how much she'd enjoyed the days without him. Why? Was he not the first in Crystal to help her, to show her kindness?

She glanced up and her eyes met Mr. Beck's. He made no move to look away. Instead, leaning back in his chair, he tapped his lips with his pen. "Forgive me, Miss DiGratia. Nowhere in my absence did I find anything so pleasant to gaze upon."

"Mr. Beck, you turn a shameless compliment."

He smiled. "If only it furthered my suit."

She returned his smile but gave her attention to her work.

His chair creaked as he leaned forward. "By the way, did you find what you were looking for?"

She raised her brows in query.

"The Placerville records."

"Oh." She had tried not to think of that, still quaking when she recalled Quillan's anger. She gave a small shrug. "Nothing important."

"What if I were to tell you Quillan Shepard has things to hide?"

Did he think her blind as well as foolish? But her curiosity quickened, anyway. "Why would you do that, Mr. Beck?"

His smile was genuine this time, amused. "Why indeed, Miss DiGratia. Suffice it to say, there are things Quillan Shepard and I don't see eye to eye on."

That was hardly surprising. Quillan Shepard had said the same, though less politely. But she was intrigued in spite of herself, and it must have shown because Mr. Beck continued.

"What if I told you he was wanted for robbery?"

Her mouth dropped slack. Robbery? She pictured the flash of Quillan's gun severing the snake's head, heard the single report that did the job without error. So he *was* a pirate, an outlaw. She had not expected that, not with Mae singing his praises and a priest guarding his story, and he, Quillan Shepard, conducting himself like the king of Sardinia.

"You see, I did a little checking on my own the days I was gone."

"That was your business?"

"No." Mr. Beck laughed lightly. "I merely took the opportunity while I was about my business to aid you in yours."

"How can he come and go if he's a wanted man? Why doesn't someone stop him, arrest him?"

Mr. Beck stood and walked around his desk. "The warrant is old. And it's issued in the Wyoming Territory. Besides, more than a handful of the men in Crystal could boast likewise. Places like this draw the unlawful."

Carina's breath seeped out from slightly parted lips. And she had been alone with him. What might he have done when she angered him so? Her heart hammered her chest at the thought. "But if you know . . ."

Mr. Beck leaned forward, pressing his palms to her desk in a familiar manner, as though they were old friends, family. "I just think it might prove mutually beneficial for us to . . . share information."

The thought frightened her, especially recalling Quillan's anger at her prying. "I only learned that he was born in Placerville to Wolf and Rose, and that —"

"What!"

Carina had been about to say that he was orphaned, but Mr. Beck's whole demeanor had changed, sharpened.

"Did you say Wolf?" The black pupils inside his blue eyes seemed to widen.

Carina nodded, certain now there was some dark secret in Quillan's past.

Berkley Beck pushed off her desk and straightened. "So." He tapped his chin with the side of his index finger. "So." He was no longer speaking to her. "This is better than I hoped."

"What is? What does it mean?"

"More than you guess, Miss DiGratia."

"But —"

"We'll leave it for now."

Carina spread her hands. "I don't understand."

"No. But you don't need to. Not yet."

What was he saying? Why the secrets? Did he think to protect her? Had she learned more than she knew? Told more than she should? Why did she feel so uncomfortable?

"Miss DiGratia, do you have plans for to-night?"

His change of subject surprised and annoyed her. "No, Mr. Beck." Innate in that "no" was her refusal of what would come next. She was not here to be courted.

He cocked his chin and eyed her over his shoulder. "Then I'd advise you to stay inside. As you may have heard, Crystal has a new city marshal, Donald McCollough."

Again she was confused. She had heard the former head of the police had resigned, but what did the election of a new marshal mean to her?

"Trust me, my dear, and don't go out to-night. I assure you it's best."

He knew things he wasn't telling. But from the look on his face, she wasn't sure she wanted to know. She turned back to the papers on her desk.

He lingered a moment. "If you should learn something more about Quillan Shepard, it would be safer to bring it to me than elsewhere."

"Shouldn't the new marshal know he's wanted for robbery?"

"My dear Miss DiGratia. Two weeks is scarcely long enough for you to understand the workings of a city like Crystal. But for your benefit and your safety, I'd recommend you not rely too heavily upon the marshal, whoever holds the office."

His voice was gentle, reassuring. *Trust me, Carina DiGratia. Trust me.* She almost heard his unspoken thoughts. She didn't understand, but what choice did she have? Mr. Beck was in a position to get her what she wanted, to restore her property and provide the means for her to support herself. If it came to choosing sides, she would take the man who fought for her rights over the one who discarded them like her wagon over the side of the mountain.

Thirteen

Of all my sins, one stands out above the others. That I ever took my first breath.

Rose

Was she crazy? With scarcely three hours before sundown, even after Mr. Beck's cloaked warning, Carina rode again up the winding path to the Rose Legacy mine. What insidious speculation had Mr. Beck planted in her mind? Carina shook her head at her own foolishness. With what she had learned of Quillan's past and seen of his temper, she was pazza to go back.

What if he found her there? What if he, too, visited the sight of . . . of what? His parents' death? Was he an outlaw? A rogue certainly and secretive, showing nothing of himself, yet . . . She saw again the deadly rage. *"My father was a savage, my mother a harlot."*

She shuddered. He would not go to the mine, not honor their memory. A cold hollow pit formed inside her. Had anyone mourned them? Father Charboneau? Had his face not been merciful when he spoke of them buried together? Was the man of God more merciful than their own son, Rose's

235

child, borne from her womb and suckled at her breast?

Robbery. Could it be possible? Would Mr. Beck mislead her? What reason could he have? She left the gray buildings of Placerville behind and climbed. Ahead, she saw the small circular clearing, the gaping hole of the mine, the stone-toothed foundation. The Rose Legacy. What *legacy?* What was left of Rose's memory? To be called a harlot by her son? Such hatred, such malice. Could a person deserve it?

Yes. The venom coursed through her veins. Did Divina not earn such malice from her? And Flavio . . . Her stomach clenched. She didn't want to hate him. She'd loved him too long. But had she not cursed them both, shouting furious words of destruction on both their heads? And Divina laughing.

With a sigh, Carina slipped from the mule and rested her forehead against his neck, then left the mule and sat on the piled stone foundation. Long rays of sunlight shot through the trees, gracing the ground below with a final benediction. Carina looked down. She felt the spinning begin. She would fall to her death. . . .

She shuddered. No. It wasn't real. It . . .

"Are you all right, Carina?"

"Papa?" She turned, startled.

Father Charboneau wore a look of true concern. "Are you ill?"

She shook her head. What was he doing there? When he had used her name, it sounded so like Papa. . . .

"May I?" He pointed at the stones beside her.

"Yes. Of course." She pulled her skirts aside. Her head was clearing as she kept her gaze close, on the ground, on the wall, briefly on the priest. His expression was still concerned. She owed some explanation. "I have trouble with heights."

"Ah." He took his place beside her. "Yet you've climbed high."

She frowned. "Must I succumb to the weakness?"

"Certainly not."

"And you? Why are you up here?"

"I wander these hills. I've spent so many years walking from camp to camp, my legs don't know how to stay put."

Carina looked around, imagining him visiting Wolf and Rose in their tiny cabin. Had they received him? Of course they must have, he spoke of them so gently.

"This is the farthest mine up." He eyed her quizzically.

"Yes."

"The Rose Legacy." His look grew pointed. "May I ask why the interest in Wolf and Rose?"

What would she say? She could tell him anything. How would he know? But to lie to a priest? "I thought to avenge myself."

His brows came up, and the smile broke from his lips. His teeth were yellowed but strong. It wasn't a smile of disbelief, but surprise at her candor. "For what wrong?"

"Quillan Shepard sent my wagon down the mountain. I lost everything but what I could scavenge later. I thought to learn something to use against him."

"And are you given to revenge, Carina?"

No. Yes. Was she? Had she come to Crystal for revenge? To strike back, to hurt Flavio? She recalled his face, stunned and amazed that she would go so far, that she would leave him over such a small transgression. It was not small to her, and yes, yes she wanted revenge. On Flavio, on Divina, on Quillan Shepard. "Aren't we all?"

He tipped his head. "Perhaps. In our basest nature." He flicked the edge of an algae plate from the rock's surface beside him. "And have you found it, your revenge?"

"No." She had found only questions and an odd, brooding sadness. Thoughts of a son who could be an outlaw, the son of a wolf. And thoughts of a woman, Rose, that would not leave her in peace.

"Justice is more noble than vengeance. And far above both is mercy."

Mercy? What mercy was she shown? She

should be merciful to a man who destroyed her belongings? To another who destroyed her heart?

"Look there." Father Charboneau pointed.

Carina followed his arm to the sky, stretching an indigo silk blanket above them. In it soared an eagle, the slanting sun igniting the white plumage of its head. Its wings spread like fingers outstretched in blessing, peace and joy to all below.

"There is God."

Carina returned her startled gaze to the priest.

"And there." He pointed to the spruce, so old and thick with foliage its branches swooped down, then up again in graceful arcs, pale blue bristles capping their ends. "And even here." He put his hand to his chest. "Feel it."

Carina pressed a palm to her own heartbeat.

His voice was low, barely more than a whisper. "*Thump-thump, thump-thump.* Do you feel it?"

She nodded. "Are you a pantheist, Father?"

He laughed. "No. A realist. Nothing exists that God did not bring into being. Nothing happens that He doesn't allow. Not one breath, not one beat of your heart, not one flap of the eagle's wings."

"But the eagle isn't God."

"In true essence, no. But it is His signature. We can't see God, but we can know Him in His creation, in His people. God is all, in all."

Not all. She frowned. God could not be in Divina. Such cruelty, such shamelessness, such a mockery she made of Him, veiled and pious, the dutiful daughter, yet in the quiet of the night . . .

"You don't believe me."

"How can God be in someone wicked?"

"Wickedness is an action of the human will. God is wholly independent of it. He loves regardless, and because of that love, many come to goodness."

"But you can be separated . . ."

" 'For I am persuaded, that neither death, nor life, nor angels, nor principalities, nor powers, nor things present, nor things to come, nor height, nor depth, nor any other creature, shall be able to separate us from the love of God, which is in Christ Jesus our Lord.' "

She looked down at the town below. Though it twisted her stomach to look, the shades were silent. "But you can refuse God's love and deny it to another."

"Refuse, yes. And deny it, possibly. But God is relentless in His pursuit."

"As a wolf to a lamb?" She imagined God's teeth on Divina's throat.

"As a mother wolf to her lost pup." The

softness of his voice wrapped and permeated her anger, turning it back, dissolving it. This was not the place to harbor it, nor the time.

Carina met his eyes. "How did they die?"

He didn't ask who. "They burned."

She felt the blackened stones beneath her. "Could they not get out?"

"Their bodies were recovered clasped together on the bed they shared."

"They never woke?"

Father Charboneau looked out across the gulch, his eyes the same indigo of the sky. His shoulders rose and fell almost imperceptibly with the breaths he took. His hands rested in his lap, one curled into the other. The slanting sunbeams faded, the indigo deepening to violet. A star shone out a single light.

Slowly he turned. "Unless you care to sleep here tonight, you'd better start down."

Carina shuddered and crossed herself. "No, Father. I don't intend to sleep here." And she had stayed far too long. It would be dark soon.

He smiled, but the smile was dim, as though small joy could be wrung from him. She mounted Dom and started for the path, then looked back over her shoulder. "Where are they buried?"

"Up the mountain."

Higher still. And not in consecrated ground. "Good night, Father."

241

"God bless you, Carina."

Carina clutched the reins in her right hand, a handful of mane in her left. With her knees held to Dom's sides, she started down. The path cut sharply to the right, then meandered steeply down, and Dom grunted as he placed his hooves. Her head spun.

Down was always worse than up. Down afforded a view of what lay below. Each small glance made her stomach jump, sending quivers down her legs. She pressed her eyes shut, kept them tight. She made her body slack, letting Dom carry her down, trusting the old mule more than her own senses.

She would fall if she looked, die on the mountain. A shudder ran up her spine, bursting at the base of her skull. Eyes closed, she saw in her mind the burned-out foundation, pictured it with flaming walls, while inside Wolf and Rose lay clasped together. Why had they not run?

Where was the grave? Where did they lie? Up the mountain, away from Placerville. Why? *My father was a savage, my mother a harlot.* Were they outcasts? Shunned? Even with her eyes closed, Carina sensed the expanse of mountains about her, the immensity of star-speckled sky above, the camp below, tiny and unreal.

Had they gone down there to shop for

supplies, to visit, to lose themselves in the ragged humanity robbing the mountain? Or had they stayed to themselves, alone in that high place. . . . No, not alone. They had each other.

She blinked, catching a brief sight of tree-tops below and trunks around her. Something jarred her mind, and she opened her eyes. The trees were thicker than they ought to be, old growth undisturbed. Dom had wandered in his search of an easier way, but he followed no track she could see.

Carina hazarded a glance down the slope. Perhaps she should turn Dom, but which way? With her eyes closed she had lost her sense of direction. Better to let the mule carry her down, then follow the creek.

She didn't close her eyes again, instead keeping them fixed on Dom's mane and the ground immediately beneath them. Then the sound reached her ears. Running water . . . no, rushing, falling water. She came out of the trees and caught her breath. In the last of the light she saw the creek, white foam rushing from the narrow rocky crags, plummeting down with a roar to the rocks below.

It must be the falls Father Charboneau had mentioned. She stared only a moment, then took stock of her location. She was farther up the gulch than she'd ever been, but she could just make out the edge of

Placerville nestled below. She had lost time, but not herself. *Grazie, Signore.*

From a high peak somewhere something howled. A wolf? Shuddering, she crossed herself and turned Dom's head. *Wolf.* Did he haunt the mountain, unable to rest in unconsecrated ground? Did he howl his protest to the darkness? Her heart thumped inside her, hard enough to feel without a hand pressed there. She kicked Dom's sides furiously. Could he no more than plod?

There were only stars to guide her through Placer, past the spectral buildings full of eyes and whispers. A chill gripped her neck, running icy fingers down her spine. Something ran to her right, and her heart filled her throat. They were watching. The shades were watching. She felt eyes all around. And they knew her.

Her fingers fluttered up to her forehead. *In nomine Patris* . . . to her heart . . . *et Fili* . . . her left shoulder . . . *et Spiritu Sancti.* She touched her right shoulder, then gripped the reins and kicked Dom's sides.

Perhaps he sensed her fear. For once he galloped as she desired. Leaving the ruined camp behind, she drew deep, full breaths. Who was she to be afraid of empty buildings, shells of houses filled with mice? Afraid? *Beh.* Yet her heart still pumped and her ears were tuned to the darkness around her.

The running of the creek was a low comfort carrying her along. *I will not lose you. Only follow, follow, follow . . .* God is all and in all. If the eagle was God's signature, was the creek His voice? Carina shook her head. God was far above, somewhere beyond sight, waiting to judge her. The thought was less comforting than Father Charboneau's view.

Carina clenched her jaw. She would get a hearing at least. *You cursed your sister.* Yes. *You denied her my love.* She stole the love that belonged to me. *You cursed your love.* I didn't mean it. *You damned him to hell.* No. I only meant . . . oh, Flavio.

Carina dropped her face to her palm, and Dom slowed to a walk. The night deepened with every plod of a hoof. The darkness was complete. Only the stars glittered on the creek, Cooper Creek. Who in the world was Cooper? *One of the forgotten dead.*

Quillan waited, his breath no more than the air around him, his body still as darkness, unstirred by so much as a twitch. They passed within four feet, but he was nothing but shadow, the night, though starred, boasting no moon. He smelled the feral sweat of the predator upon them as they passed, also stealthy, but on the move.

As they crouched against the corner of the saddlery, he slipped to the side of the Boise

245

Billiard Hall. In darkness he waited for them to move. Four men burst through the swinging doors of the Emporium, arms locked, singing. Quillan knew they would not move yet. They weren't all ready.

Through the din, a sound met his ears. Hooves. Unusual this night. One of them? He turned and saw the mule approaching the livery from the gulch side. Even with no moon, he knew her form. What was Carina DiGratia doing out past dark — and alone? An errand for Mr. Beck?

His flesh twitched beneath his left eye. He waited while she entered the livery and came out again on foot. She should cut through the field and make directly for Mae's. But she didn't. She started down Central toward Drake. Didn't she notice the empty street? He felt his shoulders tense. Had she no better sense — but then, she didn't know the roughs were out to make their presence known.

Or did she? With a new city marshal "elected" that morning, there would be havoc tonight. They had scared off O'Neal and would show this one just how impotent the position was. Quillan frowned. And there was Miss DiGratia walking into the center of it.

Midstride, she changed direction and crossed the street, coming toward him. He pressed into the wall, not intending to be seen. He wanted faces and names, one in particular, and to get that he had to stay hidden. But she advanced, stepping quickly and lightly to the sidewalk, oblivious to her danger.

Doors swung and light spilled into the street carrying with it a man, in his cups, but thick-set and steady. He neither sang nor swayed but pressed his derby to his head and stepped off the walk heading toward the tents. A newcomer then, as Quillan didn't recognize him as a neighbor. His neighbors wouldn't be fool enough to walk out alone tonight.

Miss DiGratia's head came up, and she spied the man. She paused only a moment, but it was all Quillan needed. He sprang from the shadow, cupped her mouth with one hand, and pulled her tightly against him to the wall, whispering hoarsely, "You don't want to go on just now."

As she struggled, the men left their haunt and circled the derby in the street. The front man, a large, burly mass in canvas pants and sack-shaped coat, spread his legs and extended his palm. "Hand it over, Mick."

"And would ye like to ever git out of me way, befir I bloody yer nose."

Carina DiGratia thrashed, and Quillan realized he had blocked the breath from her nostrils. He adjusted his grip, but she fought him still. He tightened the arm across her ribs. Couldn't she see what was happening? "Keep still," he rasped.

The Irishman reached for his gun, but the second man clamped his wrist and wrenched it from him. The third leveled a kick to the Irishman's ribs. "The money, Mick."

Miss DiGratia shook her head side to side. Quillan felt her teeth on the pulp of his finger and yanked it free just before they drew blood. He spun and pressed her to the wall, trapping her with his body, one hand gripping her throat to cut off a cry.

She was small and ineffective in her struggle. Her face, turned sideways, was pressed out of shape, lips and cheek pushed askew against the wall. Her hand slipped down to her skirt, and, guessing her intent, he gripped the wrist without mercy. She must not reach the gun. He cursed himself for providing it. If she shot even once it would draw the roughs' gunfire.

Whoomp. A blow to the Irishman's belly and another to the jaw. Arms thrashing, the man resisted. But he was one to three. He was kicked to the street and two of his assailants sprawled on top, ripping the coat from his arms and digging fingers into any pocket they could find.

Quillan's struggle was not finished. Miss DiGratia tugged against his hold, gasping for breath through his fingers on her throat. "Don't move," he hissed in her ear. "Do you want them to hear you?"

She whimpered, and he loosened the clamp on her wrist. Two more men came from the shadows, watched for a moment the commotion in the street, then went inside the Gilded Slipper. A moment later they came out, dragging a man between them.

Staring over his shoulder, Quillan tried to make out the faces. He was too far, having lost the chance to draw nearer with Miss DiGratia's untimely appearance. Now she fought him like a wild thing, landing a backward kick to his shin. He grit his teeth at the pain.

From the far side of Madison Avenue a cluster of men joined the pair holding the dragged man to the street. One of these stood forward and, with a foot, raised the man's chin from the dirt. Quillan could not hear what was said.

Carina DiGratia bit his forearm, and he wrenched it back. She spun and clawed him with both hands while he scrabbled to keep his hold. Fury gave him strength, and he swung her to his shoulder and loped around the corner even as her invectives turned the heads of the men in the street.

They would come now, he knew. They risked too much not to. All of Crystal had known what this night would bring. Only those who defied the rough element were about, and they would be taught their mistake. With her fists banging his back, her legs kicking air, he ran. Ducking into the shed behind Fisher's General Mercantile, Quillan dropped her to the ground and held her there.

"You're either crazy or stupid." He spoke through clenched teeth, so angry he shook her. "You might have killed us both."

Her face was stark in the darkness, the whites of her eyes full rims around the darks. He felt her trembling. She was terrified. Of him. He jammed splayed fingers into his hair, loose now from the leather string he had tied it with.

Steps outside the door. He clutched her to his chest, resting a finger to her lips. "Not a sound." Her heart pulsed in her throat, but she made no noise louder than her rasping breath, which caught short when the door opened and a man peered in.

The darkness and clutter were all their defense. But they were enough. He closed the door and passed on. Quillan felt her go slack in his arms, and a flickering tenderness stirred inside. She had no reason to trust him, and he'd been brutal in his need to subdue her.

He let go his hold, and she sprang away, freezing when yet another hand found the door. It swung open and she gasped. Quillan tensed to spring.

"Carina?"

She jumped to her feet. "Mr. Beck." Her voice was thin with fear.

He stepped forward and gripped her hands. "My dear . . ." He sent a hasty look over the shed.

Though the starlight from the open door hardly lightened the shadows, Quillan closed his eyes to slits lest they catch the light and betray him. Not that it mattered. In a moment Miss DiGratia would do so anyway.

"What are you doing out?"

"I lost my way on the mountain."

"I told you to beware."

"I only meant to take a short ride."

"My dear, you're trembling." He cupped her elbow with his hand. "You must be terrified. There are bad things happening on the street. Bad men, as I warned you."

She nodded.

"You were right to run."

Quillan tensed. It would come now, her indignant retort that she had been grabbed and carried like so much grain. But it didn't. Instead her voice was small. "Who are they? What are they doing?"

Beck shook his head. "It's a travesty. The lawless terrifying the people. They're telling the new marshal he's as powerless to stop

251

them as the last man." He raised her chin with a finger. "Are you all right?"

"Yes."

"I'll see you home at once." He kept hold of her elbow with one hand and guided the small of her back with the other.

She stopped at the door. "Aren't you afraid to go out?"

"More angry than afraid. It's an outrage." A slick answer.

Quillan released the tension from his muscles. Beck was a better actor than he'd thought. He would indeed see her safe. Doubtless she trusted him to do so, though she had never asked what he was doing out there himself.

Fourteen

Is a violent deed more heinous than a violent thought? The thought and deed spring from the same spirit.

Rose

Carina's knees shook as she climbed the stairs to her cell of a room and shut the door behind her. She leaned back against it and closed her eyes, the jelly in her knees spreading upward to her chest and shoulders until her teeth rattled.

Opening her eyes, she raised a hand and stared at the bruising on her wrist, touched her throat, felt again the fingers there, muting her cry with a stranglehold. Not strangled, no, he had allowed the air to pass. Though he might not have. She had been powerless against him.

The pirate. The outlaw. What terror he struck in her, jumping out from the darkness like a demon spawned. She could believe him an outlaw. His arms were steel entrapping her, his hard weight crushing her to the wall. Her body had fought of its own accord, desperate to break contact with a madman. But was he?

Did he not keep her from walking blindly

into the thick of it? Mr. Beck had warned her to stay inside that night. Why had she ignored him? Going to the mine had so preoccupied her thoughts. She expelled her breath. She had not meant to be out past dark. Father Charboneau had sent her off in time. If Dom had not lost his way . . .

She brushed fingers over the damaged wrist. Quillan had protected her. The streets were bad enough any night. But this . . . to teach the new marshal he had no power? She passed a hand over her eyes, pressed the eyelids with her fingertips, then pinched the bridge of her nose. What man was pazzo enough to take the job?

An Irishman. Donald McCollough, Mr. Beck had named him. No doubt he was simply a man down on his luck enough to accept the impossible task. Had she not seen the brutality, cleaned the blood from one fool caught by the roughs? More mornings than not there was at least one body battered unconscious and stripped of gold. And others who had been less reluctant, therefore robbed but not beaten.

But nothing like tonight. Not in the open, dragging men into the street. Was there no safety? Quillan Shepard had kept her safe. A tremor shook her. How her heart had jumped! Could he not have spoken first? But that would have given him away. And would she have listened? Would she not more likely have run? What was he doing there in the shadows?

Her chest went cold. Robbery. Was he one of them?

Creeping along the wall, Quillan made his way from the shed back to the street. Three men lay there; one he knew would be the marshal. There were sounds of fighting in the alley behind the bank, shouts and fists, boots on ribs. He scanned Central. They would go on all night, but he'd missed what he needed to see.

Who had made the threat to the marshal? Who had warned him to turn a blind eye, then had him beaten senseless? He could only suspect, for Miss DiGratia had prevented his knowing. He frowned, still feeling the throb of teeth marks on his arm.

Quillan should have let her go, let her walk into it, should have let her see for herself what her foolishness wrought. He left the wall and ran across the street. He had lost his chance. Now the best he could do was make it to his tent without incident.

At least he hadn't been seen. He considered Miss DiGratia's silence. She hadn't given him away. Maybe she had finally realized he was helping her. Or maybe the sight of Berkley Beck brought such pleasure and relief she forgot him altogether. He snorted. Most likely the latter.

He traversed the darkened tent camp, most of the occupants wisely inside their canvas walls, not willing to make themselves a target for this night's activities. Stopping outside Cain's tent, he hesitated, then knocked on the wooden doorpost.

"Who is it?" The voice was D.C.'s.

Quillan was relieved to hear him there. He'd instructed him to stay with Cain tonight, but he wasn't sure the boy would follow that advice. "It's Quillan."

"Well, let him in, boy." Cain's voice, insistent and annoyed.

The flap opened, and Quillan stooped to enter.

Cain waved him in with a cup of coffee. "What in tarnation are you doin' out tonight?"

"Trying to get a look."

"You're crazier than a coon in a tail trap."

Not if he could have gotten a clear look as he'd planned. Quillan sat down cross-legged, and the mottled mutt sidled in next to him. "Something has to be done, and it won't come from our constabulary."

"Bunch of cowards." D.C. scowled, tossing a stale crust he dug out of his bedroll to the dog.

Cain turned to his son. "Can you hardly blame 'em? McCollough's likely had his head busted in, and the others are next if they so much as show their faces. If they know what's good for 'em, they're headin' for the hills right now, don't ya know."

Quillan clenched his fist. "That's why it has to come from us."

"You mean vigilante action?"

Quillan traced his fingers down the dog's neck where the crust had disappeared in one gulp. "It's been done before." He'd seen it. He knew how situations like this could escalate. He'd watched it in Laramie when his foster father worked the people into righteous anger against the sinful elements. Reverend Shepard had been crushed and confused when his words were made the excuse for violent repercussions that left three people dead.

Quillan shook his head. "But I'm not suggesting that. I hope it doesn't come to it."

"What, then?" Cain shifted his stump of leg on the cot and rubbed the thigh.

"If we can find who's behind it, name the perpetrators and bring them to justice, we can have an end to it."

"How do you intend to do that?"

Quillan raised an eyebrow. "I have a plan."

Cain's larynx jumped up and down his throat beneath the thin, slack skin. "You've got a plan."

"I'm not sure yet about all the pieces. But I'm working on it."

"What piece ain't you sure of?"

Quillan tipped his head down, unwilling to be misconstrued in this next part. "Carina DiGratia." He flicked his eyes up to see Cain's reaction.

Cain ran his tongue along the inside of his lower lip and said nothing, but D.C. flushed red and looked about to splutter something, only anything he said would leave him with egg on his face. Cain didn't know Miss DiGratia had doctored his son following one of his more shameful moments.

Quillan leaned forward. "You know whom I suspect."

"And you know I agree with you." Cain raised a knobby finger.

"If we can get someone inside, someone close to Beck, someone he trusts . . ."

"Carina DiGratia." Cain's nasal drawl made the foreign name sound almost comical.

"Think about it, Cain. She has access to his files, his ledger even. If we can learn whatever there is . . ." Quillan swung his arm.

"What happened to you?" D.C. pointed.

Quillan looked down to the spot D.C. indicated. Just below the roll of his sleeve, two semicircles of red gashes showed the work of Carina DiGratia's teeth on his forearm. He stared a moment stupidly, as though he didn't know perfectly well how they'd gotten there.

D.C. hunkered close. "Looks like some-one bit you."

Quillan looked from D.C. to Cain. "Someone did."

Cain's face suddenly sported red spheres on each cheekbone and on the bulb end of his nose. He drew his knee up to his chest and cackled. "Carina DiGratia."

Quillan hung his head. "I hate it when you do that, Cain."

Carina woke to a throbbing ache in her right wrist. She opened her eyes and exam-ined the bruise. "How . . . ?" Then it wasn't a dream. Her mind had conjured strange images again and again through the night: Quillan howling from the crest of the moun-tain, then seizing her out of the darkness, his hands like steel claws, his head that of a wolf, but the eyes . . . the eyes were Quillan's gray, fierce and searching as the talons seized her and they soared up higher and higher over the mountain that held his parents' graves.

Absently she felt her throat. It hadn't fared as poorly as her wrist. But she was thankful Mr. Beck had come when he did. She flushed at the memory of Quillan's hold, the iron forearm across her ribs.

She had felt it before when he shot the snake and held her dangling. He seemed to enjoy trapping her between himself and some obstruction. Well, she had given as good as she got. Sitting up, she brushed her fingers through her hair and recalled the feel of her teeth in that same iron arm. It was flesh after all.

She climbed out of the cot, and her heel bumped the leather satchel underneath. She dropped to her knees and looked but didn't open it. She knew the contents well enough. What had made her bring it? Some crazy hope that Flavio would regret his actions and come for her?

Sighing, she folded her hands. "Grazie, Dio, for this day and for protecting me last night." She paused. "Thank you for . . . for Quillan and Mr. Beck. And per piacere give me my house today."

She dressed and washed, then, taking up the letter she'd penned the day before, she went downstairs to the smell of pork and flapjacks.

Cain pushed open the swinging door with the head of his crutch. A complete abstainer, he nonetheless went inside the Emporium and made his way to the polished bar at the back. The place stank, but he'd smelled worse.

William Evans set up a cup and filled it with coffee, then gave him a haggard grin. "Mornin', Cain."

They had too many years of gold fields to

let their differences on drink come between them. William Evans was a good man, even if he peddled the devil's water now instead of scratching dirt. Cain looked around the room, most all the chairs in place, the sawdust undisturbed. "Seems you had a slow night."

Evans puffed his cheeks and blew the air out. "I expected it. The poor fools who didn't found themselves facedown in the street."

"And the new marshal?"

Evans shook his head, then scowled. "No better than the last. They'll have him right where they want him."

Cain sighed and sipped his coffee. "Poor fella. Keep electing honest men, and the roughs'll have their way every time. Need a regular thug to do the job."

"Anyone in mind?"

"I was sorta thinkin' you, Will." Cain raised his cup in toast.

Evans laughed. "I'd like to have a piece of them. But I got a family to think of now. It's not just me anymore."

Cain nodded, feeling gloomier than ever. "That's why you settled for business over pleasure."

"I'd hardly call crushing stone and shoveling dirt pleasure, though I admit it had its excitement when I was younger. No, Cain, I'd be no better than McCollough. Once a man has something to fear for — or rather someone — he's helpless."

Shouldn't be that way, Lord. Lettin' fear keep a man from doin' what's right. But who was he to judge? "You seen my boy lately?"

"Now, Cain. I can't play nursemaid to every runt that comes in here lookin' for fun." Evans leaned hammy elbows on the counter.

"I just thought you might'a noticed he's freightin' with Quillan these days."

"That so? What about the Boundless?"

"Morty and Slow Jim run out on her. Claim she's dry. Cain't hardly expect better from Daniel Cain. Quillan's my full partner now." Cain slurped the coffee.

"Quillan?"

Cain rubbed his mouth with the back of his hand. "For all it's worth. He won't touch a pick, don't ya know."

"Well, he can't hardly work a mine without folks connecting him to his pa, now, can he?"

Cain shrugged. "Don't rightly know why not. None of that affair was ever proved to any degree. And anyhow, the sins of the father cain't rightly pass on to the son when the son never knew the father."

Evans shook his head. "I don't know, Cain. That was a bad business, and memories are long up here."

"Not so long as cain't be set right."

Evans leaned close. "I heard it, Cain. You heard it yourself. It wasn't human."

Cain opened his mouth to reply, but Evans looked up as someone swung in through the doors. By William's scowl it wasn't someone he cottoned to, but Cain didn't turn. He'd learned to melt into the scene by not drawing attention to himself. Came in handy more times than not.

William Evans wiped down the bar to Cain's left and set up a glass. "What'll it be?"

"I haven't come to imbibe."

The voice was Berkley Beck's, and Cain wasn't surprised by William's poor welcome. Will's opinion of Berkley Beck wasn't high, and he had a quick-trigger temper. With William Evans as marshal, Berkley Beck would watch his p's and q's, even if he was in cahoots with the roughs.

Beck didn't take the stool but leaned an elbow to the bar and scanned the room. "I have business to discuss, though I notice yours is rather off."

Evans scowled deeper as he poured a cup and set it out. "Someone ought to take a shotgun and clean out the whole mess of them."

"I presume you mean the roughs."

"I mean everyone deservin'."

"Well, we have our marshal, though I haven't seen him this morning."

By the look on Evans' face, he was too

close to speaking his mind. But he only said, "You won't," then waved a chunky finger in Beck's face. "Doc put thirty stitches in his head last night."

"Thirty?"

"More or less. And that's not to mention a broken arm and all the other cuts and bashes. He'll be as worthless as the last."

Beck rubbed his chin thoughtfully. "Well, that does bring me to the business I mentioned. But . . ."

Through the corner of his eye, Cain saw Beck's gaze fall on him.

Evans crooked his arm and rested his chin on his palm. "Don't worry about him. That old coot's deafer than a post. Let's hear your business."

Beck hesitated, but Cain stared into his cup, then took a leisurely mouthful, swished it through his teeth, and swallowed. Turning, Beck gave him his back and leaned a little toward Evans on the counter. "What if I could assure that you and your customers would go unharrassed after this?"

Evans' dark woolly brows drew down until they joined. "And how could you do that?"

Beck's voice was smooth, reasonable. "I don't know that I can. But what if? Would it be worth something to you?"

"That's a big fat if." Evans looked skeptical and more than a little perturbed.

Beck rested his palm on the smooth polished surface of the bar and glanced briefly at Cain. "Let's say I can. And let's say it would cost you a hundred dollars a week."

"Bah!" Evans pushed off from the bar.

"What would you lose in revenues if every night became like last night? All the miners hiding in their tents, holed up in their rooms, afraid to go out . . ."

"They'll come back. Last night was on account of the marshal."

Beck smirked. "And of course he'll be ready for action tonight."

Evans' shoulders hunched. "Even if he's not, the men won't stay holed up long. They'll just watch their backs and each other's."

Cain almost grinned. William was goading the man, but it was a dangerous thing to do.

Beck's eyes narrowed. "Things will get worse before they get better."

"Is that a threat?"

"Of course not." Beck straightened. He pushed back from the bar. "But you'll change your mind."

"You're bloody crazy to think I will."

The flush crawled up Beck's neck. He looked once more in Cain's direction, and this time Cain turned a little, drained his cup, and watched Beck walk out with a stiff step.

"So that's his game," Evans growled. "I say who needs proof? You tell Quillan I got all the proof I need."

Cain grabbed his crutch and pulled himself up on his peg. " 'Therefore the ungodly shall not stand in the judgment, nor sinners in the congregation of the righteous.' "

"That's all well and good." Evans rubbed his chin. "But they sure seem to prosper in Crystal."

Quillan splashed the cold biting water over his arms and chest, rinsing away the soapy lather. He felt the stubble on his chin but decided against a shave. Reaching for the towel, he caught sight of a figure and turned to watch Cain make his slow, ungainly way to the creek side. "Mornin', Cain."

"Howdy, Quillan. You sleep last night?"

"Not much. You?"

"Not hardly a wink. Prayin', don't ya know."

Quillan didn't answer. If Cain wanted to believe God cared, let him. "D.C. up and ready?"

"Up maybe, but ready's another trick altogether."

Quillan splashed a last double handful over his face. "I want to make an early start."

"I spoke with Will this mornin'."

Quillan swabbed his face. "And?"

"Seems Berkley Beck's offerin' protection to them as can pay."

"Protection? From the roughs?"

"That's how I heard it. Will says to let you know he don't need more proof than that."

Quillan slung the towel over his shoulder and stood. "Maybe not where Beck's concerned, but there are others in high places. I want the whole nest clean. Leave one or two rats, and before you know it there's another infestation."

Cain leaned on his crutch and studied him.

"What?" Quillan asked, feeling uneasy under the scrutiny.

Cain crooked an eyebrow. "Just curious why it's so important to you."

"Shouldn't it be? Don't you want Crystal free of violence?"

"Oh yessiree. But it's not eatin' me up from the inside, neither."

Quillan jerked an arm into the sleeve of his shirt. "What makes you think it's eating me?"

Cain didn't answer.

"I just want to make Crystal a safe place for folks. The same as you do, Cain," Quillan said, pulling the shirt across his back and sliding the other arm in.

Cain nodded, but Quillan knew his thoughts. "There's no more to it than that."

"Okay."

"Send D.C. over."

"Will do."

When D.C. arrived a short while after, Quillan could see already the boy's ill humor. D.C. was silent, stewing no doubt about his fate as a freighter, which he seemed to like little better than mining. But there was money to earn. Even if D.C. didn't regret the debt himself, Quillan wouldn't let him forget it. Not when Cain had scratched and sacrificed so long for every cent of the money lost.

Leaving D.C. with the wagon, Quillan strode away from the tents. He walked along the ruts toward the street, quiet now and clear of bodies. He pictured the scene last night, and his jaw tightened. If he had just gotten closer . . . But then he couldn't have grabbed Miss DiGratia. He shook his head and turned toward the livery.

It wasn't the last chance he'd have to catch a look at the roughs. Unfortunately, it was the best chance he'd have, short of getting himself robbed. Even then he'd only see the plug-uglies and not the face of the one who had threatened the marshal. That would have been done personally, flagrantly.

Someone was spearheading the violence, though maybe not all of it. Maybe some of the pickpockets and thieves worked on their own. But last night was orchestrated, he was sure. And if he only had proof — he looked up and saw Berkley Beck heading for his office — he'd guess he knew the name to put to it. But it was still only a guess, thanks to Carina DiGratia.

He passed Beck without word or acknowledgment. Beck gave him the same. Theirs was a shaky truce. Quillan had been vocal when suspicions were raised against the man a year ago, suspicions that Beck was working a land claim scam, with the poor and unsuspecting getting the worst of it.

Cain had lost his first claim at Beck's hand and settled for the lesser sight of his Boundless Mine. Cain and the others had no mind or means to counter Beck's mumbo jumbo, and the snake had wriggled out of the accusations. Since then he'd been more circumspect, though hardly more honest. And Quillan guessed he'd learned who his enemies were, with Quillan Shepard heading the list.

Why hadn't Miss DiGratia told Beck he was there, hiding in the shadows? She could have, and it would have meant blows. Beck was hardly a physical match himself, but if he had others at hand — and Quillan didn't doubt that he did — it could have been ugly. Beck would have jumped at the chance to silence him, maybe for good.

Quillan crossed the alley and stepped back up onto the walk. Directly before him, Miss DiGratia rounded the corner, caught her breath sharply, and brought the letter she held to her breast. Just above the cuff of her sleeve, ugly blue marks glared in the morning light, and he recalled his hand gripping her wrist. Had he done the damage?

Her eyes were cautious, her lips unsmiling, yet not frowning either — simply a natural curve and delicate line. With her hair loose down her back, catching the morning sunrays in its black ripples, she was lovely, stunning . . . the marring bruise more accusing than ever. His throat felt like dust.

With one hand he took the hat from his head, allowing her a courtesy he gave very few. "Miss DiGratia . . ." His eyes found the bruise. "I apologize for my rough treatment last night." He didn't mention that his own arm still throbbed where she'd bitten.

Her lips parted, then came together again. She shrugged, bringing the hand down from her blouse and covering the wrist with the fingers of her other hand. "I shouldn't have fought you."

"You didn't know."

She tipped her head, and the hair swished back. It was incredible, really. He wanted to thread it with his fingers, just to feel its softness. He recalled the feel of her in his arms. That was something that shouldn't have

270

happened. He'd had no intention of holding her, but now he had, twice, though in duress both times.

He drew a long breath and replaced his hat. "Good day, Miss DiGratia." He breathed her fragrance as he passed. The livery was ten paces away. He could make it without turning. He was acting like a fool over a woman he had no interest in pursuing.

Why not? She was beautiful, if a little bony and long in the nose, intelligent, though not always sensible, and by all appearances principled, her choice of employers notwithstanding. But he was not looking for encumbrances. What in the world would he do with her? Aside from the obvious.

Carina released her breath. It seemed her ribs automatically froze in Quillan Shepard's presence. First her wagon, then the snake, then his terrible words. And last night's demonstration of his virile strength, the worst of all. She felt the tremor down her spine. Bene. In considering an outlaw, how was a woman to feel?

True, there was no *prova,* no proof. Nothing but Mr. Beck's words. Had he shown her a warrant? A poster? Anything? No. There was nothing. As she crossed over to Fisher's to mail the letter, her fingers trembled on the thin stationery. The words within filled her mind.

Dear Mamma, how I miss you. I am lonely for all of you. And Flavio most of all, though she didn't write that. *I am settling in now, learning so much. Crystal is* — how had she put it? — *so different.* Dangerous. Deadly. *I think of you always, especially when I'm hungry. There is no food here to compare with yours. But mostly I miss working beside you and the talking, talking, talking. I have made two friends, Èmie and Mae, and of course Mr. Beck, for whom I work. He is very gracious. There is a miner who thinks I made his fortune. Mae says I will be a legend.*

She had signed it with all her love and imagined Mamma crushing it to her breast with tears in her eyes. Mamma, who knew what Flavio had been to her, who only guessed what had come between them. *"Why, Carina? Why so far?"* Because I must. *"But what of Flavio . . . of your future?"*

And she had stood silent, knowing Mamma would defend Divina, would tell her to forgive Flavio. It was a man's way, eh? But it wasn't Papa's way. Mamma had never been betrayed, and Carina would not accept an unfaithful man. So why did she watch every day for his coming?

As always, Mr. Beck rose when she entered. "Miss DiGratia . . . Carina." His smile spread around his teeth and narrowed his face. "I may call you Carina?" He raised one dark brow.

Not him, too. Wasn't it enough to face Quillan this morning without Mr. Beck carrying on as well? "I think it's best —"

"After all, it's a small thing to ask. 'Miss DiGratia' keeps us at such a distance." He waved his hand between them. "You may call me Berkley."

Berkley. He was extending such an honor? By his expression, he thought so. She thought of Quillan's similar insistence. Somehow his wanting her to use his given name was different from Mr. Beck's. But what argument could she make? Mr. Beck had seen her safely home after Quillan's less than gentle treatment.

"Very well."

Mr. Beck came around the desk. "Carina, I'm devastated you witnessed that nasty business last night."

"Had I not been out, I would hardly have slept through it."

He shook his head. "I only hope it hasn't dimmed Crystal for you. I assure you I mean to do all in my power to make this city safe and prosperous."

He needed his street stump. It made him more impressive — and believable.

He hooked a thumb into his vest pocket. "In fact, I've been out this morning seeing to that very matter."

He meant it? "How?"

He smiled again, more disingenuous than before, with a measure of cockiness. "By whatever means I may." He straightened his gray linen coat and gave her his profile. "I'll be out most of the day."

She nodded. "Mr. Beck."

He turned with a frown.

"Berkley," she corrected. "When will you see to my house?"

Eyes dropping, he lowered his chin with a sigh. "Carina, you force my hand. I intended to keep your hope alive, but — and I do regret this tremendously —"

"You can't get it back for me?" She sounded like a child in her disappointment.

"If you want someone else to try . . ." He spread his hands in supplication.

"What can someone else do?"

"Nothing inside the law."

Surprisingly, her heart did not sink as much as it might. Maybe she had expected it. Maybe she'd grown accustomed to her small space. It was time to face reality and make of it what she could. "Thank you for trying." True regret shadowed his face, and she was reminded again of his kindness. "I'm sure you did everything you could."

"Under the circumstances. You see . . ."

"It was a forgery."

His eyes widened.

"Another man came in with a deed exactly like mine. I sent him away."

Beck took a step toward her and lifted her hand. His palm was warm and dry. "I'm terribly sorry you were victim to such a cruel hoax." Eyes gently holding hers, he brushed her knuckles with his lips. "Were it in my power . . ."

"I've no doubt of that." For a moment Carina thought he would press his advance as he lingered, lost for words, yet saying more with his eyes than she wanted to hear.

Then he smiled with apparent regret and took his leave. Carina took a long slow breath and released it. Now how would she pray?

Fifteen

What is fear but an irrational longing to retain what I do not want?

Rose

The wagons rolling in reminded Carina of the gypsy trains she'd seen in her travels, Romany wanderers with colorful ways, though why she drew the comparison, she couldn't say. The two wagons were not colorful, though the sign painted on the front wagon was quality workmanship. *Preacher Paine's Tent Revival.*

The women walking after were modestly covered, neck to wrist, skirts hanging to the dirt, not at all the short-skirted gypsy women who danced behind the garish green and gold and red of the caravan wagons. Perhaps it was the tambourines, though these were employed almost militantly and not draped with ribbons and jangled amid swirling skirts.

Still, there was an air of excitement in the passing band, the wagons moving purposefully through a street remarkably clearing before them, and the women, faces aglow, banging the tambourines with determination. Carina heard Mae's breath like a bellows beside her and turned.

276

Swiping her face with a handkerchief, Mae stopped beside her on the boardwalk. "Now you'll see for yourself."

"See?"

"Don't you remember I told you Preacher Paine was coming?"

Yes, Carina remembered, but she had no intention of experiencing it.

"They'll put the tent up in the field west of town, just up the gulch along the creek so Preacher Paine can use it to baptize those who need it."

Carina shook her head. He would douse people in the frigid rocky creek? That might be worth seeing.

Mae cracked her knuckles. "All the townswomen cook up something to donate toward the picnic. I suppose I'll bring —"

"No." Carina surprised even herself, but she couldn't bear to hear Mae say she'd bring stewed beef. Somehow it seemed . . . sacrilegious. "Let me make something."

Mae cocked her head in surprise. "You? What would you make?"

"You'll see." What on earth was she saying? How would she find anything she needed to create the sort of things she knew how to cook? Quillan. The thought was incredible, but she didn't dismiss it. "When is the picnic?"

Mae rested her hands on her hips. "Well, they'll spend today setting up the tent and passing the word. Not that they have to do that, as folks hereabouts spread it faster than brushfire. But the women go around exhorting people to think of their souls and prepare themselves for Preacher Paine."

"And Preacher Paine?"

"He keeps to himself until Saturday night — fasting and praying, is what they say."

Carina raised an eyebrow. "You don't think so?"

"Oh, I believe he does it, just not sure exactly why."

"His suffering opens his spirit to God's will." Carina thought of *i padri della Chiesa*, the Early Fathers who fasted and prayed and lived as ascetics, denying themselves material comforts to bring spiritual growth.

"Seems to me there's suffering enough without doing it to yourself." She shrugged. "It's his choice."

"The picnic is tomorrow afternoon?" Carina was warming to her impulsive plan.

"That's right."

Somehow she would get together the ingredients for something special. Why? She would not even be there to see it eaten. She drew a long breath and released it slowly. Perhaps it was just the making that mattered.

Quillan was surprised to find Miss DiGratia at the stall where he kept his

278

blacks. A quick glance about the livery did not reveal Tavish anywhere, and he was annoyed by his reaction to encountering her alone in the dimness of the stable. Did she know what the muted light did to her features?

He raised a sardonic eyebrow and cocked his head. "Waiting for me?"

"Yes."

He had meant the question in jest, so her answer took him by surprise. He recovered with a brusque business tone. "What can I do for you?"

"You said you could replace things from my wagon."

He waited.

"I need certain ingredients."

"Ingredients?"

She combed her hair back with slender fingers, held it there while she waved the other hand elegantly. He'd noticed before that she spoke as much with her hands as with her mouth.

"Plain flour and salt Mae has, but I need eggs and olive oil and spinach and butter. Most of all I need ricotta and *grana* . . . parmesan cheese. Then I will need tomatoes, garlic, and anchovies, mint, basil, and parsley —"

"Whoa." He put his own hand up. "All this was on your wagon?" He saw her flush. So she was trying to dupe him.

"Well, I didn't have eggs or spinach . . . or anchovies or ricotta . . ." The truth came reluctantly.

He tucked his tongue between his side teeth, enjoying her discomfort.

"But the rest —"

"You want at my cost."

Though she drew herself up, her eyes still leveled out at his collarbone. "You made the offer. I'm only accepting it."

Both of her hands waved this time, and he found himself liking it, as though it took all of her to express what others did stiffly with only the voice. This was the opening to win her trust, but it wasn't an easy task.

"And where, Miss DiGratia, did you think I would find these things?"

She sagged. "I . . . you would know that better. I thought you would know."

"This isn't Sonoma, California, with vine ripening tomatoes just waiting to be plucked." Her eyes widened as he'd expected. So she didn't like to be found out either. He didn't tell her Mae had offered only that small piece of information without his even asking. "Why exactly did you need the ingredients?"

She patted Jack's nose as he jutted it into her shoulder. "I'm making a dish for the picnic. Preacher Paine's picnic."

"That's tomorrow."

She nodded.

"You think I can fly, too?"

Her eyes flashed. "So you can't make good your promise?"

"Now, wait a minute." He leaned against the stall. "You said yourself half these things weren't on your wagon —"

"Some were."

"And I never said I could have them overnight."

She raised her chin with a haughty scoff. "I should have known."

What she needed more than anything was a shaking, but he was not the one to deliver it. Not if he wanted her cooperation. "Did you write up your list?"

"I can." She held her condescending pose.

He pulled a pad and pencil from his pocket and handed it over. "I'm not making any promises. But there's an Italian in Fairplay who might have some of it. God knows where he gets the stuff and how he keeps it. But if you're paying for my trouble, I'll make the trip."

She wrote the list, then handed it back to him. "How long?"

"I can be to Fairplay and back by late tonight." He'd have to trade horses and leave his four in Fairplay.

She nodded. "That will do."

Jack nuzzled her neck, and Quillan pushed him away. "Mind your manners,

281

Jack." It didn't help at all to have the horse acting out what he only imagined.

She smiled into the horse's forelock, stroking down the bony nose. "He remembers me."

As if anyone could forget. "Well, I'd better hit the road if I'm going to make it back."

She turned briefly to the gelding and caught his head between her hands. "Fly for me, Jack."

To Quillan's annoyance, the horse bobbed his head exactly as if he were accepting the mission.

Carina felt satisfied as she left Quillan Shepard to hitch his horses and start on her business. They hadn't discussed cost, but she knew now he could be bargained with. It was a shame he had guessed her ploy. In fact the only things on the wagon were the jarred tomatoes, the olive oil, and the *parmigiano* cheese.

No, she'd had some packets of dried herbs as well, and she was fairly certain basil and mint and garlic had been among them. So that left only the eggs and butter and spinach and . . . she shook her head. Whatever he named, she would talk him down. Then soon — in the morning even — Mae's kitchen would fill with the smells of rich Italian cooking.

Carina breathed the air, imagining the

aroma of pungent garlic and tomatoes, the spicy basil, the unforgettable parmigiano . . . The sight of Berkley Beck across the street jarred her back to the present. She had forgotten. He would expect her to work tomorrow, the same as today. But if she did, when would she simmer the sauce, mix and roll the pasta, stuff and cut the ravioli, bake the bread?

Why hadn't she thought of that before she commissioned Mr. Shepard's business? And now Mae was expecting her to provide for the picnic. Carina squared her shoulders. There was no help for it. She would have to request the day off.

How Mr. Garibaldi had bellowed the only time she had dared make that request of him. He wanted to know if she were on her deathbed. If not, why could she not work? Eh? Eh? His fingers had smelled of garlic as he'd extended them toward her, demanding.

Surely Mr. Beck could be no worse than that. She crossed the street and met him in front of his office window. "Good morning, Mr. Beck."

"Carina . . ." He cocked his head disapprovingly.

"Forgive me . . . Berkley."

His smile spread like the keys on a piano, and he cut a pose in his fine beige gabardine suit and starched white shirt.

She could accomplish so much with one small gesture? Now was the time to strike. "I must make a request of you."

"Oh?"

His smile took on a look of anticipation that both daunted and encouraged her. She would get her request, but what would he require in return? "I need the day off work tomorrow."

"Oh?" he repeated, and his eyes went casually across the street to the livery from which she'd come. Quillan had just emerged with his horses in tow.

"I'm cooking for the picnic."

"What picnic?"

The question surprised her, and its sharpness. "Preacher Paine's tent revival."

"Ah." He seemed suddenly relieved. "Yes, of course. The revival. It slipped my mind."

"The wagons came by this morning. They only just passed."

"Did they? I must have been buried in the newspaper." He caught her elbow and turned her toward the office door.

Quillan passed them on the street as Berkley Beck led her inside. "Now then, you need the day free, you said?"

"It is a Saturday and —"

He raised a hand. "Carina, you have only to ask." His hands folded across his chest as he studied her a moment. "Under ordinary circumstances I could deduct your daily wages, but our agreement is rather loose, isn't it? Just consider it my generosity."

Her chest tightened irrationally. "That's kind, but I'll be happy to make it up."

"Then it wouldn't be a gift." He caught her hand and brought it slowly, effectively, to his lips. He was holding her captive by this gift and meant her to know it.

Carina wished now she had never started any of this. Mr. Beck was kind, but he expected too much. Her fingers stiffened in his hold. It was on her lips to say she would prefer to make up the hours, but she knew he would take offense. It was better to say nothing.

Though the discussion had ended and was not mentioned again, Carina felt uncomfortable throughout the day. How much easier it had been to take Mr. Garibaldi's uproar. Then she had felt satisfied, vindicated even by the hours she shorted him. Now she felt . . . what? Concerned.

But why? Mr. Beck had been nothing but gracious, if a little overeager. By his goodness she had a roof and employment. And she had kept would-be suitors at bay before. Why now did she worry?

Berkley Beck stopped before her desk as she finished entering figures into the ledger. "Carina, I've noticed you have a fine hand and a good eye. Do you think you could duplicate this?" He held out a form with some detailing at the top and bottom.

She studied it a moment. Nothing too intricate. "I think so. Why?"

"You've noticed, I'm sure, that Crystal has no printing press. I could have these done easily if we had a press, but as it is, I need them reproduced manually. Unfortunately, the man I had for the job met with an accident. He broke his hand."

Carina glanced up. "That makes it difficult."

"Quite."

"What are they?"

"Claim forms. Something I need immediately and constantly on hand." He spread his hands helplessly. "You've seen the numbers of claims each day."

She nodded. "I'll try."

His teeth flashed in his full smile. "Carina, I bless the day you arrived." He reached for her hand, but she took up her pen and a clean sheet of paper. "Just set it there." She indicated the space on her desk.

With a quirk of his lips, he laid down the paper but continued to hover.

She glanced up. "Did you want to watch?"

His mouth parted to answer, then closed again. With a slight bow of his head, he left her.

Her chest eased when the door closed behind him. Why so tense? She shook her head and started to copy the form. For a moment she wondered how the man who had made the copies before had broken his hand and how soon he would heal. Then she shrugged it off. Mr. Beck would find plenty for her to do. Already he was depending on her for more each day. She was secure in her position.

Making her way back to Mae's at noon, Carina forgot some of her trepidation. She could see the tall poles of the tent rising up beyond the roofs, and she passed the boardinghouse and went on to the field where the revival would be. Was it foolish to see this Preacher Paine for herself? Could she watch it like a show, a booth at a fair?

She had heard once of a revivalist who used snakes. Did Preacher Paine do the same? Would it be like the fair in Argentina with the fire-eaters and contortionists? She cringed. No, it was better she send the ravioli with Mae. She turned back and met Èmie heading home from the baths.

"I can't stay." Èmie squeezed her hands briefly. "I have to get Uncle Henri's supper."

"Come soon," Carina called after her. "We'll read." She'd been delighted to learn Èmie appreciated good literature, though she owned no books at all. She doubted many in Crystal did. It was hardly a cultural center, in spite of Mae's opinion. She was happy to share her own rescued books with her friend.

Carina watched Èmie's back, straight and unbending as she hurried off to the small cabin she shared with her uncle. For a long moment she wondered what life was like for Èmie, working in the caves, then slaving for a grumpy old uncle.

Why didn't she marry? There must be any number of miners willing. Perhaps Henri was unwilling to let her go. Carina frowned. That was unfair and unkind. Already it was late for Èmie. In Italy she would be past the age. With a shrug, Carina turned once again for Mae's.

Quillan had pushed the horses harder than usual, though Jack seemed disarmingly willing. He made Fairplay in good time and sought out the Italian market he'd mentioned to Miss DiGratia. The proprietor, Emilio Lanza, sucked in his shriveled lips around his nearly toothless gums in his version of a grin as he looked over the list.

"For a lady?"

"Yeah."

"She'll wanta the best."

Quillan didn't doubt that for a minute. As the man puttered through heaps of cans and cloth wrapped wheels of cheese and jars of olives and tomatoes and strings of garlic,

Quillan breathed in the scents. Whatever Miss DiGratia was planning with the things on her list, it would likely be an improvement over the fare of Crystal.

He noticed the storekeeper was choosing the largest jars and wheels and strings, piling high the travel crate. Quillan hadn't asked amounts, nor had he arranged a cost or limits of any sort with Miss DiGratia. Rather than worry about it now, he made his way to the street to collect whatever else could be had for a deal to make this trip worthwhile. Somehow he suspected the profit he would make off Miss DiGratia would be less than prime.

Leaving his horses at the livery, he took the four replacements he usually used on the next leg down. This time he'd be heading back toward Crystal with Miss DiGratia's load secured near the back, where it could be unloaded first when he reached town.

When he returned to the market, Mr. Lanza finagled the sale of a few extras that "the lady would not be able to resist." Quillan succumbed without knowing why. He was not one to be outdealt. But he was shopping for Miss DiGratia this time, and unless he'd missed his mark, she would appreciate and pay for quality and service. Hadn't she tried to buy him off from the start? Oh, she haggled and quibbled, but everything about her spoke money. Why shouldn't some of it come his way? This was business. So why did the squat, smug-faced Italian look at him with that knowing grin? If he imagined some moonlight *amoré* . . .

"And for this — she willa kiss you." Lanza held up a wheel of cheese pungent enough to draw wolves.

Quillan doubted very much Miss DiGratia would do any such thing, but he figured if she didn't want that cheese, he could use it to keep the roughs at bay. He closed the deal before the man could sucker him further, then mounted the wagon box, slapped the reins, and settled in.

Shortly past dark, Carina heard the wagon creak to a halt outside of Mae's. She closed her book, then hurried down the stairs and reached the door as Quillan set the brake. He jumped down into the circle of lantern light on Mae's porch.

"Good, you're handy," was all his greeting.

Carina was too excited to care. "Did you get it all?"

"And more." He made his way around the back and lowered the gate. "Maybe you can make your way through it and see what you need."

Carina pressed in, drawn by the wonderful aromas emerging from the crates when he tugged the tarp free. *Ah, Signore, cielo!* It was heaven indeed. She fingered the papery garlic bulbs, then with a small cry lifted a wheel of Gorgonzola and pulled the wrapping back.

"I'm afraid that one's not good anymore, but Lanza insisted you'd want it that way."

Carina laughed. "It's best with the blue veins. The more blue, the better."

He raised his brows. "Well, that shows what I know."

"There's more here than I wanted, but I can't let any of it pass. How much did you spend?"

His mouth pulled sideways. "You mean how much will it cost you?"

"Of course." She waved a hand, but it irked her that he had so easily thwarted her. If she could have tricked him into naming his cost . . .

"I fetched the eggs and butter from another store. They were cheaper there." He reached for a crate wedged in a little deeper where the eggs would be shielded from the worst of the jolts. He had purchased a full dozen.

Carina could hardly believe her good fortune. If he asked for the sky she would give it. But she fought hard to keep that from showing on her face. "How much for all of it?"

"Thirty-five dollars."

The sky came falling down. "Thirty-five! That's robbery!"

His brows lowered and his eyes flickered fiercely in the lantern light. She realized with a start what she had said. Did one accuse a robber of robbery? She had spoken without thinking, but thirty-five dollars . . . that would wipe her out.

He pulled a paper from his back pocket. "Look, this is what I paid for the goods." He held out the receipt. "I had to board the horses and take on these four. Along with that, I lost a day on my regular schedule by coming back this way."

She stared at the figures on the paper. It was impossible. He had been cheated. Didn't he know the first thing about bargaining? The man must have been a Sicilian to get so much from Quillan Shepard.

"Not to mention breaking my back to get it all here tonight for you, Miss DiGratia."

His point was taken. "I'm sorry. I didn't mean . . . only . . ." She sighed. "I can't pay thirty-five dollars. That's more than I have." She hadn't meant to say that. What concern was it of his? She pulled a single bottle of olive oil from the crate and ran her palm along its shape. "I'll take only what I asked for."

He stood silently with a surly expression as she picked through the crate for the items she'd requested. She laid each on the back gate of the wagon as she chose and examined it, then gathered them into a small pile. "How much for this?"

"What am I supposed to do with the rest?"

"There are others in town. Find a black-shawled nonna. She'll buy."

He jammed his fingers into his hair. "That's more trouble than I need." He yanked the crate to the edge and loaded her things back inside. "Take it all for thirty."

Carina stared up at him. Even thirty she couldn't do, but it stuck in her throat to say as much again. With Mr. Beck's dollar a week she was scarcely putting anything by. Thirty would deplete her small reserve.

Quillan's eyes narrowed slightly. "Twenty and that's my final offer."

She shook her head. "Then you lose money."

"I'll make it up on the other things."

"No."

"Miss DiGratia, I've had a very hard day. I'd like to get some shut-eye. Now will you take this stuff before that cheese brings every dog in town?"

Carina trembled. It was one thing to be indebted to Mr. Beck, another altogether with Quillan Shepard. But the truth was she coveted everything in the crate, things she'd not tasted since leaving her family. "Will you let me feed you?"

"Beg pardon?" His arms paused in their lifting.

"What I cook with this." She waved her hand over the crate. "I'll make your suppers."

His face was inscrutable. "Well, I'm not here for most of my suppers. I'm on the road the better part of the week."

"When are you here?"

His throat worked as though he hesitated to tell her. "Most Friday nights. Sometimes through the weekend." He looked away. "Actually, it varies."

"I'm making ravioli for the picnic. If you like it —"

"I won't be here for the picnic. Tent revivals aren't for me."

Carina dropped her gaze to the wealth in the crate. If he would be stubborn, she should take it. It was his offer, after all.

He took hold of the crate. "I'll carry it in for you while you fetch your money. Has Mae an icebox?"

"In the kitchen." She stared at his back as he went inside, then realized he would be waiting for payment. Even twenty dollars was more than she should use. She'd had no idea it would come so dear. She hurried up the stairs and dug into the hidden compartment of her carpetbag for the last of her greenbacks.

Twenty dollars for a crate of food. She

clutched the bills and wondered if she could part with so much. Then she pictured again the treasures he had brought her. Why had he brought more than she requested? For profit? Or because he guessed how pleased she would be? She suspected the first. But whichever the case, she must have that crate of wonders. Gripping the money, she went back down.

Quillan Shepard was in the kitchen making enough noise to wake the house, yet she heard Mae's snoring through the wall of her bedroom. He had unloaded the crate on the board and set the small one that held the eggs in its place. The eggs were nestled in sawdust, and he fished them out, then brushed them off and laid them on a cloth. "Here's the butter. Oh, all Lanza had was canned pureed spinach." He motioned toward the cans, four of them.

She nodded, holding out the money. "I'll cook again next Friday."

He leaned on the board, looking tired. "I'll think about it." He lifted his hat and shook his hair back, then released a sharp breath and straightened. "Good night, Miss DiGratia."

"Good night, Mr. Shepard."

He turned at the door. "Quillan."

Her throat felt tight as she watched him walk out. He had given her a piece of home. Not given, sold. But not for what he wanted. Without even trying, she had cut him down to nearly half his price. What a victory! Why didn't it feel that way?

Quillan kicked the dirt of the street. How could he have so misjudged things? Just because she came from privilege didn't mean she'd brought wealth with her. Oh, she could be duping him, but if she had the money, she was a consummate liar. Watching her fondle, then part with the things she hadn't ordered was more than he could stomach. Still, he was a fool to take it in the teeth that way.

"Well, we're even, miss. Matter of fact, more than even. In fact you owe me," he muttered as he drove the wagon to the livery. He could stop feeling guilty for dumping her things. He'd more than made up for it with this trip. And he wouldn't do it again no matter how she smiled at him in the dim of the livery. He'd learned, and he had the ill humor to prove it. If the roughs jumped him tonight, he'd take them down no matter how large their pack, and if they pulled heels on him, he'd fire back. No one was getting one cent of the measly twenty bucks he'd made on that fiasco.

Twenty bucks he'd made? What twenty bucks? He was in the hole! He pulled the wagon inside the livery and parked without waking Tavish. He unhitched the horses himself and sent them to their stalls. He could leave the wagon for the night and square up in the morning. He rubbed the back of his neck and climbed down.

So she'd cook for him, would she? He scowled. As if he needed that. He'd been fending for himself a long while, and he didn't need some foreign debutante to feed him suppers. He forced his way through a rowdy bunch of revelers at the corner and cut across toward the creek.

His tent was almost lost in the dark between two dimly lit neighbors. Quillan yanked open the flap and stooped. His small stove stood ready with the pipe venting out the back. He stared at it a moment, then at the cans of victuals ready to heat. He dropped down to the cot, dog tired.

What would she make with that moldy cheese and oil squeezed from olives? And garlic? He'd smell for weeks. He rubbed his forehead and sighed. It would be well to avoid her for a time, even if she was the key to Berkley Beck. Every encounter with Miss DiGratia proved far too costly.

Sixteen

A prayer in the darkness might go no farther than the pillow. But a prayer in the
morning comes back to slap you.

Rose

In spite of the cost, Carina's heart swelled the
next day when she began her work in the
kitchen. She had needed to wait until Mae
fed all the miners their bacon and hot cakes,
scoured the dishes, then set the beef into the
giant kettle to stew until lunch and continue
on until supper. Some, at least, would not attend the picnic and would serve themselves
from the pot.

But now the kitchen was hers, and she tied
on Mae's apron, wrapping it twice around
her small form, then began, first chopping
and mashing, then heating the olive oil with
the garlic cloves, emptying the jars of tomatoes into the pot with the slivered anchovy fi-
lets and herbs to simmer and thicken.

Next, she made the filling for the ravioli
with the canned spinach, eggs, and
parmigiano and ricotta cheese. The Italian
market in Fairplay had a source for some of
the best ricotta she'd seen. But it was the
parmigiano, her own dear grana from the

north country, its pungent flavor with a slight bite, its pale, creamy yellow color and grainy texture that brought tears to her eyes.

How she had longed without knowing she longed. Her dissatisfaction with Mae's fare was no more than knowing inside how much better it could be. Eating was more than filling your belly. It was an art of blending and releasing the gift of each food to complement another until the right perfection had been reached. And it was savoring the experience of each bite.

As she worked, mixing the pasta dough and rolling it thin, marking the raviolis with Mae's biscuit cutter, since her own square fluted ravioli cutter was lost with the rest, Carina thought how it was as much an art as Flavio's painting. The mix must be just right. Too much flour and the stuffed pillowy pasta would be dry and heavy. Too much oil and they would sag. A poor seal between the layers of dough and the boiling water would ruin the filling.

She could feel with her fingers that she had made it just right. The dough had the consistency of fragile skin — elastic, yet powdery. She brushed the first layer lightly with water, then dabbed the filling into the centers of the circles she had marked. Then she laid the second sheet of dough atop, forming small mounds over the fillings.

As she cut the raviolis, she set them aside,

then covered them all with a towel to wait. Normally the ravioli would be boiled and eaten simply with melted butter, but she couldn't keep them hot that way, so she had decided to serve them in the sauce. After boiling, she would layer them into the cast-iron pan and douse them with the steaming tomato sauce, then sprinkle grated parmesan and basil on top.

She had to leave the kitchen for Mae to serve lunch to the miners, more today than usual, since many were having a holiday in anticipation of the day's events. After that, she made the bread. When it came out of the oven in long crusty loaves, she did cry. For this day only, she had made Crystal home.

And she knew already she would not send the meal with Mae. She must be there herself to see it tasted and savored as she knew it would be. They walked up together, Mae carrying the bread already sliced and spread with olive oil, basil, and salt and heaped on a wooden board, Èmie with one pan of ravioli and Carina with the other.

Carina felt like a child with butterflies in her stomach. What would she do if the men simply shoveled it in as they did anything else? She must not stake too much on this. But as she laid the offering on the table and people gathered around to sample the new aromatic fare, her heart swelled again.

She saw the looks of surprise, then delight, heard the murmurs and exclamations. Her heart swelled with both pride and pleasure. And then Quillan was before her, and all the crowd seemed to dim in importance as he scooped a helping onto his plate. Carina's breath hitched, but she forced an even tone. "I thought you weren't coming."

He shrugged slightly, suspending the fork with his first bite ready. "I figured I ought to get some return on my investment."

She waited, holding her breath. His was not the exuberant expression of the easily pleased. He finished the bite and swallowed, then swabbed his lips with the napkin he carried. Still Carina waited, though why did it matter?

"I don't taste the blue-veined cheese."

She released a short laugh. "No. That will be for desert next Friday if you bring me fresh apples."

"It's a little early yet for apples."

"Then dried will do."

He stood quietly, finishing every bite and swabbing the sauce up with an oily slab of crusty white bread. He would say something, praise some part . . . He covered his empty plate with the napkin, then nodded. "I'll see what I can find by way of apples."

Carina watched him walk away. Somewhere in his unstated praise was a tacit approval. He had accepted her offer, and she knew he would not have if it hadn't pleased. She watched him milling through the crowd, saw him stop and speak to the old man on the crutch with a white-and-brown dog at his side. It was the same man who had pulled his son from the street, the son she had nursed the next time he was beaten. She felt a small connection, not as strong as that growing between Mae and Èmie and herself, but something to lessen the awful aloneness.

She watched the old man grip Quillan's shoulder, and Quillan shake his head, then reluctantly shrug and walk with his friend toward the tent. Was he going inside? Did he mean to hear Preacher Paine after all? The tambourines had started and now voices were raised in hymns.

Praise God from whom all blessings flow . . .

People were filling the tent — men, women, and children. Carina saw Èmie start for the opening and caught her arm. "Are you going inside?"

"Of course." Èmie spoke over her shoulder as she had the first time Carina saw her.

"But what would Father Charboneau say?"

Èmie smiled. "He says if you're not against God, you're for Him."

"But . . ."

Mae pushed Carina from behind. "Come on, or we won't have a good seat."

Like a branch on the creek, Carina was carried along by the two of them. They entered the tent, and the music encircled her. The women wielding the tambourines seemed more animated than when they'd marched in, though still stiff, as though the music had a purpose but failed to move them. Thankfully Carina's companions sat near the back where the breeze through the open flaps would keep Mae as cool as possible in the stuffy tent. Carina took the aisle seat.

Two rows up, also on the aisle, sat Quillan. He didn't look back but sat straight with the dog lying at his feet. The song ended and Preacher Paine mounted the platform and raised his hands. Carina studied him curiously. He was not a large man, average in height and slightly gaunt. His eyes were green and protruding, his hair a thin mat of brown. What was there to recommend such a one?

But when he opened his mouth, it all changed. "People of Crystal!" His voice was a trumpet. "Thus says the prophet Ezekiel: 'Now is the end come upon thee, and I will send mine anger upon thee, and will judge thee according to thy ways, and will recompense upon thee all thine abominations. Violence has risen up into a rod of wickedness. The day draweth near. None shall preserve his life, neither shall any strengthen himself in his iniquity. For my wrath is upon the multitude!' "

The tendons on his neck stood out, and he raised his arms like Moses casting down the stone tablets. "The day of the Lord is upon you!" His eyes were fire, green flame passing over the crowd.

Carina trembled. They sought her alone, or so it felt. He must see her sin, her hatred toward her sister, her unforgiveness. But she felt stubbornly resistant. Why should she forgive? Had Divina asked it? She had laughed! And Flavio. He'd called her foolish and temperamental. No. The only way she would forgive was if he, Flavio, came to Crystal and went down on his knees before her.

"You have the heart of a harlot!"

She riveted her eyes once again on Preacher Paine's face, reddened now with fury.

"You have left your first love for the love of gold."

Carina released her breath. At least that was not directed at her. She had not left Flavio for gold.

Preacher Paine's tone became entreating. "Have you not heard? You cannot serve God and manna. Will your greed buy you one day more? I tell you even the hairs on your heads are numbered. Will gold give you one breath that is not allotted you already? No!"

He bellowed this last with such force Carina jumped in her seat. She was mesmerized by his voice, by his quick stride back and forth across the stage, as though he could have no peace until all the words inside had found release. He was John the Baptizer, gaunt and uncomely, but filled with a holy rage.

She saw people squirm and was only glad his words didn't apply to her.

Then, "You are all doomed. Not one is without sin. Not even one."

Bene. She wasn't perfect, but . . .

Preacher Paine suddenly stopped moving and stood, eyes closed, hands clasped at his throat. Carina waited, scarcely daring to breathe until his eyes shot open. He stretched out his arm, one finger pointing like a spear at her heart. "Behold, the judgment is upon you! Your hands are red with the blood of your brother whom you have slain!"

Or your sister. The thought seemed to come from within her. Was wishing for Divina's misery the same as killing her? No. But a trickle of sweat ran down Carina's chest, which rose and fell sharply.

"In your hearts you have slain the unfortunate, murdered those who opposed you, butchered those who stood in your way. I say unto you, as much as ye have thought vile thoughts, so have ye done it. As much as ye have disdained charity, so have ye wrought evil."

So. Carina shrank inside. She was guilty.

"I tell you, as ye have done to the least of these, so ye have done to me. And I will spit you from my mouth, sayeth the Lord!"

Carina trembled.

"You adulterers. You thieves. You who covet and bear false witness. You who worship the idols of gold and silver. You gluttons and fornicators. You who traffic in the dark arts. The flames of judgment await you in the fiery pit unless ye repent of your sin! Cast yourselves upon the mercy of the Lord, for the day of wrath is upon you!"

The very air trembled as he invoked the wrath he spoke into being. Carina's heart was pounding in her chest. Never had she heard such words pronounced with such force, never seen one so possessed of supernatural power. She could not doubt it was God speaking through him. Dread and terror seized her.

"Lazarus, come forth! All ye who are dead, come forth from your tombs, for you are surely damned! Come forward if you would live. Kneel before the King of Heaven and confess your sin. Be washed in the blood of the risen Lamb!"

The singing burst around her again and rose to a throbbing pulse. People streamed into the aisle — a trickle, then a flood. Carina saw Quillan stand, but he turned and walked out the back, his face troubled and angry. She wanted to run, too, to escape the horrible voice, but she was held mesmerized as Preacher Paine touched the heads of each person in turn, exhorting them to lay down their sinful selves and take up the cross of Christ, to die and be reborn.

What did it mean? What did any of it mean? Unconsciously she gripped the crucifix until it cut into her flesh. *Signore* . . . was God a wrathful being waiting to devour her?

"Freedom only comes through laying down your life! If you would keep your life, you will surely lose it! If a seed does not fall to the ground and die, it cannot live."

These were words she knew, but they suddenly had a force, a power unknown before. How? How did she lay down her life? Only through repentance. And she couldn't repent. Wouldn't. She was not sorry for hating Divina. Instead, feelings of vengeance swelled inside, carried her up from her seat and out the back of the tent.

She would die. She would die in sin, but Divina . . . Divina would pay in everlasting pain for stealing Flavio's love. Carina staggered, caught herself by the rope of the tent, and gulped for air. It was cold in her lungs, the evening chill already advanced.

Her head cleared, and she stared about

her. Quillan was gone. She was alone. Swallowing the bitter feelings, she stalked away even as a new hymn started, a hymn of triumph and salvation. Behind her in the red-gold rays of the setting sun, a procession started for the creek, but she hurried away. She no longer cared to see those washed clean in the blood of the Lamb.

The feeling inside him could best be called bleak. Quillan slumped on the cot. Once he had wanted to believe. Sometimes as he'd sat listening to his foster father, Reverend Shepard, he had wished so hard that it was true. If he became a new creation, would it take away the stain of his birth?

Would it win him his mother's love? No. She was not his mother. His mother was dead, and the woman who might have taken her place despised him. To spite her, he refused the call and played out that refusal in countless transgressions, though Reverend Shepard applied the rod again and again to bring wisdom and obedience.

Tonight's call was easier to resist. There was little he hadn't already heard about hell's fire, death, and damnation. There were no gaps in his understanding of the alternative to serving God. It was the gentle moments, those few times alone with Reverend Shepard when he'd explained the love of God . . . Those were the times Quillan had almost given in.

But never quite. There was in him an errant flaw, maybe the seal of his parents, Wolf and Rose. The sins of the father . . . He dropped his face to his hands. He'd known better than to go tonight. Cain would never have cornered and cajoled him if he hadn't shown himself at the picnic.

Miss DiGratia again. All day he'd meant to set out; all day he'd found one thing or another that needed doing before he left town. And then it was time for the picnic and it had been an easy thing to satisfy his curiosity. The meal she'd made with his ingredients was both flavorful and satisfying, and he'd been fool enough to make her expect him next Friday.

He hadn't said it though, hadn't actually agreed. Starting out late as he was, he wouldn't make it back by Friday, especially if he drove all the way to Denver for supplies. But he'd sold the goods from Fairplay at a decent profit. He could do that again and accept Miss DiGratia's offer.

He lay back on the cot. She was his link to Berkley Beck. If he could just win her trust . . . He scowled. Yes, it was her trust he wanted. And what information she could provide him. The things he suspected were hard to prove. No one credited Beck with the ruthlessness Quillan believed he possessed. A wily scoundrel, yes — but violence? That lanky rake?

Quillan could argue his suspicions all day, but Beck's boyish demeanor, his all-too-polished manners and fastidious dress — these were enough to put the others off. Was it his own personal run-ins with Beck or a true gut instinct that made Quillan think otherwise? He couldn't answer that. All he knew was that Miss DiGratia provided a chance to know for sure.

He closed his eyes and heard Preacher Paine. *"Lazarus, come forth!"* But what if you were already too long in the grave?

It was as Mae had said. Sleep would not come. Carina huddled in the blanket expecting the flames of judgment to overcome her at any moment. Why? What had she done that compared to the sins against her? Was she not chaste? Could Divina say so? Had she broken her betrothal vows? No. Could Flavio say so? Were they not both deserving of the hatred she bore them?

Carina had done no more than wish God's own judgment upon them. Why then did it seem the wrathful eyes of God were upon her? *Il Padre Eterno* . . . Almighty God. All mighty, all knowing, all seeing. Was He not wise enough to see the truth? She had been His messenger, damning them in the act. It was a holy mission.

Her heart lurched. No. She didn't mean to damn Flavio, not . . . not forever. Not once he came for her. Then she would forgive, when he knelt remorseful at her feet. She would forgive and free him. Didn't God's word say what she held bound was held bound and what she forgave was forgiven him?

Could she not of her own choosing free Flavio and hold Divina bound still? But what if Flavio didn't come? What then? The sick, sticky feelings of betrayal and rage cloyed her throat. Then he could not be forgiven either. What she did was right. Then why wouldn't the fear of Preacher Paine's words leave her?

Carina did not go to Mass the next morning, and that, more than her refusal to repent the night before, tormented her as she rode Dom up the gulch. If she was right, then why did she avoid worshiping God? Why dread encountering His messenger in Father Charboneau? Hadn't the priest been called and answered the call? Hadn't he turned from his ways to serve God with his whole being? If she was serving God also by pronouncing judgment on those who had wronged her, then why did she flee to the mountain?

Preacher Paine had poisoned her, his words like slow-acting hemlock eating away and dulling the edge of her righteous anger. But why should she be washed, she who was blameless? Was she not the one wronged? Had she her sister's blood on her hands? It was the other way around! Divina had stolen the life from her.

She dug her heels into Dom and started for the Rose Legacy. He plodded up as though he knew the way and where she would go. She no longer asked why. It was her refuge, a place for outcasts and those who banished themselves.

Cain made his slow, lurching way to Quillan's tent. He'd let him go last night, disappointed but not surprised. He'd hoped for, but not expected, a conversion. Still, morning brought new hope, always new hope. God's love was like the sunrise, chasing back the dark and piercing the heart with joy.

Cain felt it overflowing this morning, all the souls saved last night, all the names written in the book of the Lamb. Not the names he'd wanted, maybe, but who was he to choose? God called whom He called. And each man had the free will to say no.

Cain stumbled on a tussock, and the crutch dug into his side. No, it hadn't been D.C. washed in the creek like so much gravel from a shovel leaving only the gold behind. Nor had it been Quillan. But

Cain's hope was as fresh as the brisk air of the new day.

He reached Quillan's tent and knocked the head of his crutch against the door post. "Are ya up, Quillan? It's Cain Bradley."

The flap pulled free. "I know it's you, Cain. No one else puts a dent in the wood, knocking." Quillan reached down and gave Cain's dog an impatient pat.

Cain grinned. Preacher Paine had had some effect anyhow, or Quillan wouldn't look so fiery and disheveled. Good, good. Better he be cold than lukewarm, or God would spew him from His mouth. The Almighty Lord loved a good fight, and from the looks of it, Quillan would give him that.

Cain followed him inside. "You spent a miserable night."

"I slept fine."

"You were tormented in body and soul."

Quillan grinned. "Coffee?"

"Does a dog have fleas?"

"Not yours." Quillan reached for the pot. "They wouldn't dare desecrate the dog of such a holy and righteous man." The dog wagged as though he understood every word.

"Ah, Quillan." Cain dropped to a crate beside the cot. Sam laid his head across Cain's knee, and Cain rubbed the dog's floppy ears. "I'm an old sinner, as black-hearted as the worst desperado, don't ya know."

"No, I don't." Quillan handed him a cup. "You're a good man, and you mean well, but this is not fertile ground."

"Ain't it, though?"

"I'm afraid not, my friend." Quillan tucked a box of cartridges into the pack that stood open on the cot. "Preacher Paine did nothing but convince me I should have driven out early. His brand of salvation puts steel in my resolve."

Cain slurped loudly the strong, bitter brew. "How so?"

"All those threats and warnings. I won't come groveling because I fear some punishment I can't bear."

Cain considered that. It was a fair judgment. Preacher Paine's words were meant to awaken the unenlightened to the peril of their condition, but one such as Quillan who knew already the consequences of sin . . . "You left before the baptisms in the creek, before he shared God's love, grace, and mercy."

"Doesn't matter."

"What would bring ya, then?"

Quillan added several jars of victuals to the pack. "I don't know."

Cain thrust a knobby finger at him. "He's got his eye on you, son."

"Oh, I don't doubt that." Quillan tugged the pack shut and tied down the flap. He was running off again, as though shooting out of town could somehow keep God away.

"Then why won't you open your heart to Him?"

"I can't, Cain." Quillan raised his gray eyes, dark in their intensity.

Cain saw the honesty there and his heart stirred. "It's the surrender, ain't it?"

Quillan didn't answer.

"I remember layin' down my arms at Appomattox, puttin' my rifle on the pile. I felt only half a man, stripped and bare as a new-born babe. I'd left the gold fields to fight the good fight, run the race I thought God had called us to. But I hadn't won the laurel. Hadn't won a thing." He picked up the book of essays Quillan had on the pillow. "And I'd lost Gertie while I was off fightin'."

He turned the book over in his hand, feeling the old wound as though it were new. "Took me years to see how God had brought me through unscathed, whole in body if scarred in mind. But He sent me back off to the gold fields with my newborn son, who I hardly knew what to do with, and every day He brought a measure of peace and understanding. He was with me through it all."

Quillan reached for the book and tucked it into the side flap. "I'm glad for that, Cain."

"Just not interested yourself?"

"I don't want to disappoint you —"

Cain raised a hand. "It ain't me who's callin', Quillan."

Quillan stood and walked to the back of the tent. As he reached for the bedroll nestled there, Cain saw his silhouette on the canvas wall: a fine, strong profile, tall, muscular build, quality workmanship all around. No wonder God wanted the use of this particular vessel.

Quillan turned slowly. "I don't hear it."

Cain nodded solemnly. He knew what Quillan was saying. Cain's own faith had come without trying. But Quillan would have to wrestle God and have his hip broke. "You will, son. You will."

Èmie descended on her as soon as Carina stepped out of the livery. "Where have you been? Father Antoine was asking for you."

Carina jerked her head up, then dropped her gaze, the weight of guilt suffocating the freedom she'd found alone on the mountain. What would she say to him? How could she describe the tempest inside her? Èmie looked as fresh and cheerful as she could with her long face. Had she not heard the scathing words, the dire threats?

Carina caught Èmie's arm. "What did you think of Preacher Paine? It didn't frighten you?"

"No." Èmie shrugged. "Should it?"

"How could it not, with all that talk of wrath and judgment."

"Only for those who refuse God." Èmie covered Carina's hand with her own. "I've known all my life I belong to Him."

That was an uncomfortable thought, too close to Papa's faith. Papa believed his work on earth was only an extension of God's own mercy. He healed because God healed through him. He lived and breathed because God willed it. Carina had preferred Mamma's faith. She prayed, and if God answered it, she thanked Him. If not, she blamed and scolded. He would do better next time.

"Besides" — Èmie pulled a twig from Carina's hair — "I don't think God wants people to come to Him through fear."

Just hearing the word kindled its effects as Carina pictured again the green eyes seeking her out. "Through what, then?"

"Love. If we serve out of fear, it isn't really serving because it's ourselves we're concerned with. We serve because we love. We serve God as our heavenly Father, and we love Him as we would an earthly father."

Love God as she loved her own papa? Impossible. Papa was real and warm and good and gentle. God was — what had Preacher Paine said? — a wrathful being waiting to cast her into the fiery pit. Carina didn't want to think about Father Antoine or Preacher Paine or what either thought of God. To talk of loving God was more confusing than fearing Him. Fearing one who could bring judgment she understood. How did you love such a one?

Èmie touched her hand. "Where were you, anyway?"

Carina sighed. "I was riding."

"Where do you go?"

"Up to Placerville and beyond. There's a mine high up on the mountain. It's quiet there."

Èmie nodded. "Why don't you come for supper? Father Antoine said to ask you."

"No." Carina searched for an excuse. "Mae's expecting me."

Èmie eyed her a moment, and Carina realized she saw more than she said. "If you want to talk . . ."

"No. I have an early morning. Mr. Beck has more for me to do all the time." Now she was avoiding her friend. Had Preacher Paine bewitched her?

Èmie smiled. "Another time, then. I want you to teach me how to make whatever that was you brought to the picnic."

Carina nodded reluctantly. She wished she had never opened her mouth, never promised a meal for the picnic, never asked Quillan to find the ingredients, and never set foot in that tent.

When Èmie had gone ten steps, Carina almost called her back. But she didn't. Because if she told Èmie what troubled her about Preacher Paine, she would tell her about Divina and about Flavio, and she couldn't face the humiliation. Wasn't that why she had left the verdant hills of Sonoma and all she knew and loved? Her pride had driven her. And pride would keep her silent.

Èmie turned at the corner and waved. Carina also waved, then trudged to Mae's door. The smells of cooking greeted her. Stewed beef and potatoes. Her stomach rebelled. What was Èmie cooking for Father Antoine? Carina pressed her palm to her forehead. She had no appetite anyway. She went upstairs to her room and lost herself in *Agamemnon*. Just now someone else's tragedy was a welcome escape.

Seventeen

I am no longer what I might have been,
nor can I ever be. Yet this body is stubborn in resolve. It will not cease.

Rose

The next day the wrath came. It came with
such violence Carina jumped, feeling the jolt
of lightning through the floor. She rushed
from the desk in Mr. Beck's office to the
window to watch the sky darken unnaturally
to a frightening dim. Lightning flashed again,
a straight bolt from sky to earth, and the
crack of thunder shook the glass.

Carina felt the awful power. Was this the
judgment Preacher Paine had called down
upon them? His contingent had packed up
the tent that morning, and the wagons
rolled out of town, leaving the grass of the
field flattened and dry. But now the sky was
rent and rain fell in huge punishing drops
like bullets striking the ground.

No. It was ice. Hailstones leaping and
bouncing from the ground they struck,
mules braying, men shouting, everyone
rushing for cover. The backs of men pressed
to the window blocked her view.

She jumped back when Mr. Beck pushed

through the door, bringing the spray and wind with him. He closed it and turned, smoothing his soaked hair with a calm, practiced motion. "My word, it's a deluge."

She stared. Was he immune to God's wrath? Couldn't he see the sky was falling? How could he coif himself with such nonchalance?

He held his arms out from his sides. "I'll just change into something dry." He passed through the door that opened to his private rooms, speaking as though it were nothing more than a spring shower.

However, he had not attended the revival. He didn't know. He was like those who perished in the flood, eating and drinking and giving each other in marriage until the rains came. Carina shook herself, annoyed at her own fear. *Follia.* What foolishness. As Mr. Beck said, it was only a storm.

But she stayed at the window, uncomfortable with the thought of Mr. Beck changing clothes just beyond the wall. Yet why should she be, when only canvas separated her from the boarders at Mae's? Still, when he returned in shirtsleeves and trousers but no vest and coat, her discomfort increased.

The din, the lightning, the pouring rain; she felt trapped, closed in. It was dark in the office, and she reached for a lamp. Somewhere in the sky there was still a sun, but . . . A horrific crack of thunder shook the walls, and she cried out, dropping the lamp. Glass shattered and the oil spread over the pine boards.

Rushing forward, Mr. Beck caught her hands. "Leave it!" He hollered over the staccato hail on the roof.

"But . . ."

"It's nothing, I assure you." His hands on hers were warm and firm. "Come away from the wall." He drew her carefully around the shards of glass. "If lightning does strike, you shouldn't be touching the structure."

Though she shouldn't allow the familiarity, Carina stood with her hands in his while the sky fell on Crystal. Most of the men had now run for the saloons, and the window was clear enough to see the ground, white and drifted with ice. The street ran like a river, swamping the sidewalks, gushing up in miniature geysers at every obstruction. Splintered shingles flew from the roofs.

Carina trembled at the ferocity of nature set loose. She realized Mr. Beck was staring at her and turned her face from the window to his. Her hands suddenly felt trapped. She had given a little, and he would take more. "Mr. Beck . . ."

"Berkley."

His eyes were deep, bluer than before, the pupils enlarged by the darkness. His face was smooth, a slightly oily sheen on his cheekbones, the cleft in his chin a pale gray.

His lips parted and held that pose a full breath before he spoke. "My rooms would be better shelter."

Carina's stomach tensed. His rooms? Did he think her so cheap? A contadina with no name to protect? "Mr. Beck . . ."

"Berkley." There was an edge this time.

Lightning crackled, an explosion of light glowing through the window, imprinting on the back of her eyes. The air tingled, and Carina's hair stood out. She looked up and saw Berkley Beck's hair standing like quills around his own head. Terrified, she gripped the hands that held hers. "It has struck us!"

Her nostrils flared at the sulfurous burning smell, though she saw no fire, no smoke, and the rain kept pouring. Had such lightning caused the fire in Rose's cabin? Had it engulfed it so swiftly they couldn't move, couldn't run?

Berkley Beck pulled her close. "I'll keep you safe, Carina."

His voice was smooth as he wrapped her in his arms, yet she felt panic within. Would they find her charred body entwined with Berkley Beck's? Her breath came in gasps. She felt the fresh starch of his fine shirt, crisp against her cheek, the smooth buttons and the tiny pleats pressed flat.

His thumb traced a line down her back. "We'll be safer in my rooms."

She smelled the pomade on his hair, some eau de toilette at his throat. She felt his arms tighten, and though they didn't trap her as Quillan Shepard's had, they seemed more menacing, more purposeful. No, she was not safe, and the hungry, fierce look in his eyes confirmed it. She pulled away, staggering back and pressing into the wall.

"Carina . . ."

"I must go." Go? Out into the storm?

He waited a long moment, his eyes blinking once, heavy lidded. "No."

Her heart thumped her chest.

"I require you." His tone cut.

She had insulted him. She could see it in his stance, the tension in his jaw. "Require?"

He frowned. "Is it so much to offer shelter and protection?"

She jumped at the flash and crack of thunder that came almost at the same moment. The storm had somehow moved inside. Not the rain or the hail — only the malevolence, the power, the danger of it.

"After all, I put a roof over your head; I pay your board. Where would you be without me?" His voice was studied, forcefully reasonable. But he had lost his mind.

"I work for —"

"Do you think I need your little filing services?" He thrust himself toward her, and she shrank back. "It's a favor I do you."

She burned with sudden indignation. "I —"

"And if I didn't, what then? Do you think Mae would keep you for charity?"

Carina brought up her chin. "For friendship."

He laughed, an ugly, harsh laugh. "Mae is a businesswoman. She would gently, but firmly, boot your little backside right out the door. There's no room in Crystal for charity, or half the population would be on it."

Carina flushed with fury and humiliation, tempered by the nagging thought that he could be right. Mae did not show compassion to miners who forfeited the bills. Berkley Beck smiled, reading her thoughts. Incensed, she threw up her hands. "You think I need you?"

"I know you do."

"I don't!"

He laughed again. "And where will you go next? Madame LeGuerre, perhaps?" He gave her a moment to absorb his words. "I promise you no one else in Crystal will give you a position except the position she offers."

An indignant breath burst from her chest, and now there was no mistaking the feral fire in his eyes. She backed against the wall as he advanced. If lightning struck she would at least be spared his touch. But she could retreat no further. Her throat pulsed and hitching breaths worked her breast. She had to do something, say something to make him stop. "You would take me by force? Do you think the miners will not come running if I scream?"

He paused at that with a slow, deliberate smile. "You *are* a legend now, aren't you?"

She hadn't thought of that, hadn't considered the recognition Joe Turner's story had given her. She had thought only of the natural reaction men such as those in the mail line would have for a woman in distress.

"Yes, Carina, I've heard all about it. How you turned his luck and made him rich." He reached a hand into her hair, coiling it in his fingers. His face came close.

She could feel his breath and inhaled it with the air she gasped into her lungs. No man, not even the crudest miner, had given her fear for her virtue. Yet this man she had trusted . . . She tensed herself to scream.

With a sigh, he slid his fingers free. The hunger left his face and turned it gray. "Carina." His voice scratched and he swallowed hard. "I admit I lost my heart to you the moment you walked into my office. How could I not when I looked up from the floor into the face of an angel?"

The sincerity was back in his eyes. Her muscles went slack. She could believe him.

"Have you never been in love?" His voice begged understanding.

In love? she thought. *Most of my life, Mr. Beck.* But she wouldn't tell him so. "I'm not here to be won."

He laughed painfully, waving his hand with forced carelessness. "Yes, I know. It is your sole desire to be my clerk." He pronounced it "clark" like an Englishman.

"I —"

He raised a hand. "Spare it, my dear. I've acted abominably."

Carina's throat tightened. She was unversed in courtship, knowing only Flavio, who wore his heart like a banner. Yet hadn't he also had his dark moods? Times she couldn't penetrate his thoughts? Had he not also worn that look of hunger more than once? Could she forgive Berkley Beck when she could not forgive her one love? But she put on the best face she could.

Mr. Beck drew a shaky breath. "I believe the storm is clearing. You'd best go."

Though the rain still fell from bruised and swollen skies, Carina made her way to Mae's, thankful to be away from Mr. Beck. His intentions had been all too clear. Or had the storm made him say and do things he normally wouldn't have? Papa said a shock from lightning could affect the brain. One man who'd been struck had walked around for three days thinking he was someone else.

With the way their hair had stood out and

the tingle in the air, she could well believe the storm had done likewise to Mr. Beck. She pressed her eyes closed. Thank goodness he came to his senses when he did. Carina stopped suddenly at the sight of Èmie huddled at the side of Mae's house. What was she doing standing there in the rain? "Èmie!"

Èmie startled, then looked quickly behind her. With a swift motion, she beckoned.

Che ora? What now? She hurried to Èmie's side. "What is it? Why are you out in the rain?"

Èmie gripped her arm, the long fingers strong in their need. "Something bad is going to happen."

The words chilled Carina more than the rain soaking into her skin. Had everyone gone crazy? Had Preacher Paine loosed all of hell on Crystal with his parting? "What? What is happening?"

Èmie shook her head. "I only know Uncle Henri is part of it. And Father Antoine is gone. He left this morning." She sagged. "No one else will stop Uncle Henri."

"Stop him from what?"

"I don't know. Only that he's been paid — a lot. I saw the money."

Carina shrugged. "Maybe he found good ore."

Èmie shook her head. "He only pretends

to mine. He hasn't brought ore out of his hole in months."

"Then how do you live?"

"I make some at the baths." Èmie licked the rain from her lip and laid her soul bare. "Uncle Henri . . . steals."

Carina gasped. "He is one of the roughs?"

Èmie pressed her eyes closed. "He picks pockets. When the mine played out, Father Antoine tried to help us, but Uncle Henri won't have it. He forbade me to take one cent from the priest. And in truth, Father Antoine hardly has a cent to spare. I bring home every dime, but it's not enough. It's never enough." Èmie pressed her hands to her face.

Carina stroked her arm. "It's not your fault." How could she have imagined Èmie so serene and complacent? It never occurred to her that Èmie faced something like this. Suddenly she felt angry, angry with an uncle who would torture the soul of someone as pure and selfless as Èmie Charboneau. "Why don't you leave him?"

Èmie opened tear-filled eyes. "When I was very small my parents died. Uncle Henri found me alone and terrified. He wrapped me in his coat and carried me to his home. He didn't know how to care for me, but he did. By the time I discovered what kind of man he was, I already owed him so much. You may not believe it, but I love him. I hurt for him. And Father Antoine and I made a pact that neither of us would give up on Uncle Henri. Inside . . . inside he wants to be good."

Carina shook her head. How could Èmie be so naive?

"But now I'm afraid for him."

"Why do you think he's been paid? Maybe he stole the money."

Èmie suddenly gripped her shoulders, no longer the tall, stoic girl, but a woman shaken. "They've bought him!"

"Who?"

"I don't know. But he's getting drunk, mean drunk, ugly drunk. And he's mumbling about doing their dirty work. I'm scared."

Carina looked off in the direction of Èmie's cabin. Hadn't Èmie said she didn't fear God's wrath? But this was not God's wrath; it was man's. And she felt Èmie's need. "Stay here tonight. You'll share my cot."

Èmie's chest moved up and down. "I don't know what to do."

Carina sent her gaze down the rain-soaked street to the marshal's office near the end. She knew what had happened that night in the street, knew the marshal had been beaten. She knew also what Berkley Beck had said, to bring her concerns to him. She could hardly do that now. Not after what had transpired between them. "We'll tell the marshal what you know. He can stop it."

Èmie resisted. "I can't, Carina. He's my uncle."

"Don't you want him stopped?" But she saw Èmie's dismay. She couldn't betray Uncle Henri even for his own sake.

Carina drew herself up. "I'll go." When Èmie's grip relaxed, Carina freed herself. "Here's my key. Go inside." She wasn't certain what she could tell the marshal, but she stalked through the rain to the dreary police building.

The single lamp shed a sooty light on the front office. The cell in the back was walled of stone, but the ceiling was sod, dripping now onto the packed dirt floor. It smelled like a cave. The front office was clapboard with a lone window that let in what dismal daylight there was. A man sat hunched in the leather chair, one eye swollen shut, his arm in a sling, and a gash on the side of his head that was beginning to fester.

With one look at him, the words died in Carina's throat. She would get no help here, but at least she would try. "Marshal McCollough?"

He laughed, a hoarse, choking laugh that went on and on. "Donald McCollough here." He patted his chest at last. "But marshal? That, lassie, is a myth."

She felt angry and sorry for him at once. "I have a complaint to make. Or rather a concern."

He just sat there as though he hadn't heard. What could she say? Could she tell him Èmie's fears? Something bad might happen. You must act, must stop it. She couldn't bear to see him sit there looking more helpless than she felt.

Turning on her heel, Carina went back out into the rain. Her hair was a wet mass already, the ends dripping down her skirts. The street was rushing mud, and she held up the denim to step off the stoop to the boardwalk, then cried out when a rough hand gripped her arm and swung her around.

"What do you want with the marshal, woman?"

Her heart jumped to her throat as she looked into the face of the scarred Carruther, his lip drawn up more than ever like a cur. Blood rushed in her ears and no sound would come as he shook her hard, demanding, "What did you want!"

She tried to scream, but he had literally scared the breath from her. She fought to break free, but his strength was brutish. His horrible animal smell washed over her as they closed in combat.

"Let her go." A voice broke through her panic, but she continued to fight, her shoulders wrenching and twisting.

Abruptly, the huge paws released her, and she staggered, then turned and rushed to the outstretched hands Mr. Beck offered like a rope in a tempest. What madness, running to him for safety after just . . . But his face was firm now, detached, showing none of his earlier emotion.

Still, her heart thumped within her chest, and she realized Beck was waiting for some explanation. At last her voice came. "Emie's uncle is drunk. She's afraid for her safety."

Berkley Beck's expression eased. He cupped her hands between his, then looked past her head to the huge Carruther. "This woman is in my care. Any man who accosts her in any way will answer to me. Is that understood?"

To her amazement, the brute nodded and turned away exactly as a hound might obey his master after laying a rabbit at his feet. Did Berkley Beck wield such power? If so, he was the one to help them. He could do more than the wretched man who wore the marshal's badge. As if reading her thoughts, he met her eyes boldly.

"I told you it was useless to go to the law."

"I see that now."

"You should have come to me."

"I didn't know —"

He held up a hand. "I understand. But tell me again what the trouble is."

"Èmie's uncle . . ."

"Oh yes. He's drunk." Mr. Beck's expression was noncommittal. "Men get drunk. Èmie's uncle is no exception, nor is this the first time she's seen him so. Why run for help now?"

"She's afraid he'll do something terrible."

"Like what?"

Carina shook her head. "I don't know. She thinks he's been paid to . . . to do something."

He didn't answer at once, just led her down the boardwalk and under the streaming roofs. Then he spoke in carefully measured words. "You understand how preposterous that sounds."

It was true. "I know that, but . . ."

"Carina, the marshal can hardly go about arresting everyone who might do something terrible. Until a crime is committed, he has no power over a free citizen. He can't act on someone's fears alone."

"But Henri Charboneau has money."

"He's a thief."

She stared a moment. Was there nothing Mr. Beck didn't know?

He walked her along briskly, turning the corner at Drake. "If you're concerned, keep Èmie with you. I'll see what can be done about the rest."

"Can you do something?"

"I assure you I can. At the very least I'll

see that no harm comes to Èmie." He spoke with such confidence, such knowing. How could he be sure, when men like the Carruthers roamed the streets? But then, he had cowed the huge Carruther with words alone. Mr. Beck was more than he seemed. But could she trust him? He stopped her at the boardinghouse steps and faced her squarely, every bit the man she had first put her faith in.

"Carina, I know I behaved poorly. And I understand your hesitance in seeking me out. But I trust you understand now that I'm your best hope. Surely you have seen how capable I am of seeing to *your* safety, my dear. You would do well to consider my affection."

His narrow face was earnest, the eyes neither angry nor demanding. How could she have thought he would force her? Or was he a chameleon changing colors to suit the moment? She drew a shaky breath. "Thank you."

By his lowered brows, that was not the answer he'd hoped for. Her arm dropped to her side as he released her hand, tipped his derby with a flick to its brim, and walked away. She looked up into the storm-torn sky and felt a few scattered raindrops on her face. The storm had worn itself out and turned its face away like a woman who rages, then can't remember why.

"You got a burr in your hide?"

Quillan turned and realized he'd left Cain some distance behind. The ground around the Boundless was rough and broken, rutted from the new rain, and the slag was treacherous for a one-legged man with a crutch. "Sorry, Cain."

"What's your rush, anyhow? You think I'll stick a shovel in your hand and say dig?"

"It wouldn't do you any good." Quillan looked back at the hole bored into the hillside. His aversion to it was almost as strong as D.C.'s, though with less reason. He'd not spent one day working a mine with pick, shovel, or even pan. He didn't know the backbreaking labor or the mind-numbing effect of the darkness, the still, heavy weight of the mountain all around. Nor would he. *I see it in you. The same gold-grubbing greed of your father.* My father's a preacher. *Your real father, idiot. Your savage father. You're no more Mr. Shepard's son than you are mine. Your father was a savage, your mother a harlot. And you're the worst of them both.*

If for nothing more than to prove her wrong, Quillan would never work a gold mine. He'd come up here only to satisfy Cain, to have a look at the hole he was now half owner of, worthless as it was. The rain and ground water would have kept them out of it anyway. But Cain wanted to make sure none of the new shoring had washed away.

D.C. and his partners had done well enough with that, and it held soundly. Now Quillan was ready to go. But he hadn't meant to move so fast he caused Cain difficulty.

"Ain't she a purty sight?"

Quillan looked again at the gap in the hill. "I don't know, Cain."

"She's gonna make you rich, don't ya know."

Quillan didn't answer. It was too close to the real thing. Did investing in a mine count as gold-grubbing — even if he didn't work it? Was there gold greed in him? Didn't he hoard his savings just the same as if it were gold nuggets he guarded at the end of a rifle?

No. He worked for that money. Honest labor. Diligence. And thrift. He swallowed the sourness from his throat. "Come on. It's getting on to dark."

Cain shrugged the crutch back under his shoulder. "I know D.C.'s determined to stand his ground, and I know you're not for working her yourself, but there's silver in that hill. I feel it calling."

Again Quillan kept silent. Gold. Silver. It amounted to the same thing. He wouldn't touch either.

Cain stared at the hillside. "It's there, and I'm gonna find it."

He wouldn't call Cain a fool. For all he knew, the old man might be right. It just didn't matter. He'd bought in to help Cain save face, nothing more. They reached the wagon, and he helped Cain aboard. Then he walked around with a pat to Jock's neck. He'd made a quick run to Fairplay yesterday and returned to Crystal this afternoon with his horses.

He didn't admit to himself that it was partly to take advantage of Miss DiGratia's offer. He couldn't seem to keep it straight that he meant to avoid her. How could he, if he needed to learn what she knew? From the livery, he'd seen her leaving Beck's office in the rain and almost said something, then turned for his tent instead. That's when Cain had halooed him to go have a look at the mine.

But something nagged at him, something in the way she'd moved, almost as though fleeing. That was ridiculous. She couldn't hate her job that much, even if it entailed working for Berkley Beck. He was just jumpy. The storm probably, the charged sky that left everything feeling more intense.

Jock noticed it, too. Still, he felt an uneasiness inside that made his step quicken and his hand eager on the reins. Beside him, Cain whistled a tune. Quillan wished he

338

could be more like that, taking in the moment, savoring it even.

He turned to Cain. "Where's D.C.?"

Cain shook his head. "Went off with that threesome of hellions he calls friends."

Quillan didn't make a judgment. D.C.'s moral conduct wasn't his responsibility as long as it didn't directly hurt Cain. He hadn't taken D.C. with him this time, since he'd known when he started out it was a quick turnaround. Maybe he should have, given the frown between Cain's brows.

"Alan's hankering for some checkers. Why don't I leave you at the livery?"

Cain rubbed his palm over his crutch. "Why don't you join us?"

"Don't think I can sit."

"What's got you so worked up?"

Quillan turned Jock onto Main and flicked the reins. "I don't know. Just a feeling inside."

Cain sighed. "If you were on talking terms with the Almighty, you might better understand those urges."

Quillan didn't want to go down that road again — it was the one place Cain seemed intent on rubbing raw. He pulled Jock up to the livery and jumped down, then led the horse inside. Alan Tavish tousled the head of the boy who mucked stalls and sent him off with his pennies. Quillan walked around and helped Cain down to the packed dirt floor. He raised a hand to both men, then left them.

Outside, the gray-shrouded evening drew on. Even though the mud-thickened street was once again crawling and honky-tonk plinked from the saloon doorways, there was a heaviness in the air, almost a collectively held breath. In anticipation of what?

Eighteen

Death is a wily opponent, sneaking up
on the unwary, yet eluding the deserving.

Rose

Carina woke to Èmie's screaming in the
morning half-light. They were pressed into
each other on the cot, and Èmie's large bones
were rigid with fear. Rolling over, Carina
shook her. "Stop. Èmie, stop." She shook her
harder.

Èmie shot up with a sharp exhale. "Something's happened."

Carina had slept poorly, squeezed between Èmie and the hard edge of the cot.
She was in no mood for hysterics. She
waved a hand in annoyance. "If it's happened, it's happened. What good to scream
about it?" At Èmie's stricken look, Carina
felt remorseful. "You were dreaming. Your
uncle is probably sick in his head and won't
show his face today." She slid from the cot
and stretched out the kinks, then looked out
at the gloomy dim of an overcast sky. "You
ought to be a rooster. Only a rooster would
know it's morning already."

Èmie was silent, sitting stiff and
unmoving, very like she'd been when Carina

first saw her. The thin braid that hung down her back was only slightly mussed, and Carina examined her own. Stray wisps were everywhere, dangling beside her face, curling from last night's rain. "Come. We'll wash and eat."

Èmie sat still, unbudged.

Dio, give me patience. "Èmie . . ."

"I don't want to see it."

"See what?" Carina brushed the wisps from her face.

"What my uncle's done."

"*Oofa!* You don't know anything. Do you borrow trouble?" She tugged Èmie by the hand, the taller woman following like a doll with limbs of sawdust. "Come. I'll show you."

Firmly, Carina led her outside. Their skirts were wrinkled, their hair mussed, and their faces unwashed. But she pulled Èmie out the front door and swung her arm. "There. You see? No fire and pestilence. No —" Her eyes lighted on a gathering near the corner of Central and Drake, men shouting and rushing over, pressing into the mob.

Èmie's eyes were bleak as she, too, took in the scene. "I'm going home." She stepped off the porch and walked stiff-legged around the side of Mae's.

Carina stared after her a moment, then started for the street. Anything could draw a crowd like that. A snake, a . . . Her breath

342

caught as Quillan Shepard stepped out from the alley behind Fisher's Mercantile and raised a hand. Why did he always appear so abruptly? She stopped short, though he didn't touch her.

His face was grim, and he looked as though he'd slept worse than she. "Don't go over there, Miss DiGratia. A man's been killed."

His words stunned her. "What man?"

"William Evans, owner of the Emporium Gambling House."

Carina looked at the backs of the townspeople huddled together. Had Èmie known? Guessed what lay at the center of that crowd? Carina shuddered. What morbid fascination brought them to view a dead man's body?

Quillan's voice grew rough. "It's — his throat's cut."

Carina brought a swift hand to her own neck. *Com' é terribile!* For a moment she thought she'd be sick.

Quillan caught her elbow. "I'm sorry. I shouldn't have told you that."

Carina had seen plenty of death. Not even Papa could save them all. But except for the gunshot man, they had been natural deaths — sickness or accident or old age. Not murder. She swallowed hard and lowered her hand, then met his gray eyes. "Why?"

He shook his head, jaw cocked. His eyes

343

held the same intensity she'd seen in them the day they rode to the lake, some unexpressed bitterness.

Carina looked over her shoulder to where Èmie had disappeared, then returned her focus to the man beside her. "But who would do such a thing?"

The eyes sharpened, not unlike those on the rattler's head he'd severed. "An animal, Miss DiGratia. In human form." He turned and left her, heading not for the street, but through the field away from town.

Carina felt the breath leave her in a slow sigh. A man dead. Throat cut. Lying in the street where people gathered like vultures. She shuddered. Where was the sense of it? She turned and hurried back to Mae's. She hadn't meant to be seen in her disheveled state. She'd been drawn, unthinking, toward the crowd.

Once again Quillan Shepard had blocked her way. But what was he doing there? Why was he even in town? It was Tuesday. Should he not be miles away? She found Mae on the porch, hands on her hips and hair as wild as Carina's own.

"What is it this time?"

"A man was killed last night. William Evans, of the Emporium."

Mae's eyes widened. "Grizzly Will?" Her mouth opened and hung there, gaping. "What would someone kill him for?"

344

Carina shook her head. "I only know what Quillan told me. His . . . throat was cut."

Mae's flush vanished; her cheeks went limp and pasty. Carina feared she might faint, so swiftly did the blood leave her. But she only sagged against the post and mumbled, "Not again."

Dread crawled Carina's spine. "It's happened before?"

"What?"

Carina stepped forward. "You said 'not again.' "

Mae rubbed her face like a flabby dough. "I'm not myself. I . . . I knew Will a long time." Her voice trailed off like a bygone memory.

Carina took the stairs and helped Mae to sit on her porch chair. It began to drizzle, but Mae made no move to go inside. Carina was in no hurry to reach Berkley Beck's office, though she supposed she must go eventually. Right now, she simply sat with Mae.

"I haven't called him Grizzly Will in years. He'd grown too respectable." Mae shook her head. "After all he survived, why now?"

Mae didn't want an answer, and even if she did, Carina had none. She didn't know this man, nor did she understand such evil. She startled when Mae suddenly laughed, a low, almost strangled laugh. "His arms were so thick in those days, the men dubbed him Griz, and he could wrestle every one of them into the ground."

Carina shook her head. How could such a powerful man have his throat cut? It couldn't be Èmie's uncle. He was large, but not . . . surely not capable of this. He was a thief, not a murderer. She couldn't believe Èmie lived with a man who could cut another's throat. "What will be done?"

"Done?"

Mae wasn't thinking straight, and Carina asked it more plainly. "Will they find who did it?"

Mae's eyes closed and she rocked back in the chair. "Can't say. They didn't the last time, although that was a long time ago." She shook her head. "No, I can't say as they will." And then Mae ground her knuckles into her eyes and cried.

Carina waited, but it was clear Mae no longer wanted her, hardly even knew she was there. It frightened her to see Mae cry — Mae, who callously shrugged off the deaths of so many. People die. Isn't that what she said? But then, most people don't have their throats cut.

Carina stood up and, when Mae made no notice, went inside to wash. She had slept in her skirt in case Èmie's fears proved more widespread than her uncle's drunkenness. Now she changed into her only alternate and put on a fresh blouse. She brushed the tangles from her hair and quickly rebraided it.

Mae was gone from the porch when Carina went back out. She considered checking Mae's rooms but didn't. Some grief was better suffered alone. Hadn't Mamma shut herself away when the two babies after Carina died?

There was no longer a crowd on the street. They must have moved the body, but she made no effort to learn where. Mr. Beck was not in the office, so she took her place at her desk. She would work as though yesterday's conversation hadn't happened.

Did he need her filing services? It was a favor he did her? Though it humiliated her to consider the triviality of her job, especially as Mr. Beck had described it, she must do it still. If it were true no one else would hire her, she must make the most of this chance. She would show him he did need her assistance.

The rain came again, insistent, falling from skies dark and menacing, but not violent as it had been the day before. Still, Carina felt trapped, stifled. Though she wanted to, she couldn't ride out to seek the solitude of the snow-streaked mountains. Of the mine.

Why? Why would she seek a scene of tragedy when right here in the streets of this city was death enough? Yet the more she thought about it, the more she wanted to go. She had opened Pandora's box, and now the Rose Legacy held a strange fascination for her she couldn't ignore.

She stared out the window of Mr. Beck's office through the rain to the rushing streams in the street. If only it would stop. She'd leave this moment, Berkley Beck notwithstanding. He hadn't yet shown his face, and no one solicited his services. The office was a tomb, and she had run out of things to do. It made it harder to believe she was necessary.

Carina threw up her hands in frustration. *Innocente!* She was in his debt. She bunched her hands into the hair pulled tight on her head. She would not leave it loose again in his presence. The last thing she needed or desired was his affection. Her heart was too bruised already.

And she thought of Flavio. She thought of his times of melancholy, his silent brooding that left her separate, not knowing what to say, how to reach him. He was an artist, temperamental, moved by forces within him that she couldn't understand. Sometimes his smile was easy, sometimes his gloom so dark it overshadowed her. Yet she had loved him since they were children, seeing in him a depth, a genius other men lacked.

She pressed her fingertips to the window,

its streaming rivulets flowing over them, not touching her for the glass between. So it was with Flavio's love. It flowed, yet couldn't reach her. Divina had come between. Carina remembered her own vicious words, words spoken in anger and heartbreak, yet words only. Had they changed anything at all?

Yes, her own spirit cried. *They changed you.* She was stunned by the thought. But it was true. She had unleashed a hatred she didn't know she was capable of. Years of envy, of bearing Divina's cruelty, her sharp tongue, her insults . . . all of it had come out when she saw the depth to which her sister would stoop.

Carina shuddered. Every step she'd taken since that night had been treacherous. A vengeful journey, as Father Charboneau had guessed. *"Are you given to revenge, Carina?"* It was Quillan Shepard to whom Father Charboneau had referred, but it was Flavio her heart condemned. Was that not her sole purpose in coming? To punish him? To hurt him as he'd hurt her? To make him come for her? To leave Divina?

"You must be washed in the blood of the risen Lamb." Had Preacher Paine seen through her as easily as the priest? Seen how she hated Divina in her unforgiveness. Divina, the darling, always the shining one. The one who lied, who demanded, who received.

Divina who slapped, whose insults hurt because she knew the weak places to probe.

But something had changed, though Carina wasn't sure when. Some subtle shift, and Carina had gained power. People noticed her, petted her. She grew into Mamma's likeness, and Divina seemed . . . dulled, sharp-tongued, spoiled. She grew defensive — picking, picking, always picking.

But Carina had found a new strength. A belief in herself. And Flavio became her banner. The Romeo, the one who could not be reached: he loved her. In his fourteenth year he told her so in poetry. She was only twelve, but she knew what she had. Something Divina could never have.

Sciocca. She pressed a palm to her forehead. Why did she think he would come? What did he care that she went so far? Wasn't Divina close — and willing? Carina stalked across the room and back. Nine years she had loved him, waiting while he proved himself, became a man. Waiting for him to make good his promise and marry her.

Did Divina wait? No. She skulked in the shadows and laid a trap. And gladly he walked in.

Bene! She could have him. He deserved her sharp tongue; it would rouse him from his shadows. Wake up! See what you have chosen. You will wake to it every day.

✳ ✳ ✳

Father Antoine Charboneau stood in the rain over the grave, freshly dug and turning to mud, into which they had committed William Evans, deceased. So it had come to murder. He'd seen it before, the camps never teeming with violence, but never free of it either. Something in this, though, was different, darker, ominous.

As he prayed over the grave he felt a weight on his spirit that sapped his strength. There was something personal in the grief he felt for this heinous act, though he'd not known Evans well. It tapped a depth in him not disturbed for some years. Not since that other time so long ago.

Had an ancient evil wakened? Lord God . . . Antoine swallowed thickly, knowing the truth of it. That ancient evil never slept, never stopped pacing the earth, traveling to and fro, searching for someone to devour. And this was one more example of it.

This was not a simple case of robbery gone sour. The man had forty dollars still in his vest when they found him. No, this was deliberate, premeditated murder. Yet Marshal McCollough was at a loss, bless his wretched soul. Like his predecessor, he'd been bought through pain and fear.

Whatever questions he raised would stay far from his true suspicions, or even what he knew for certain. And what Donald Mc-

Collough confessed would be held in the protection of the sacrament. Father Antoine would carry it to the grave. The weight grew heavier.

He looked up at Èmie standing off some twenty paces as straight as the sapling beside her. She was not a comely girl, yet his heart clung to her, his brother's child. Jean had been the best of them, marrying for love a plain woman he came to know late in life. Èmie was the only fruit of their union.

As he watched her, their gaze met. What did he read there? Horror for what had happened? Or something else? Did she fear for herself? Surely Henri would see to her safety. He would not risk the one who made his meals and kept his home. And Henri loved her to the best of his ability.

Antoine sighed, the feeling of ultimate failure seeping in with thoughts of Henri. Oh, they sparred, and that sparring enlivened him. But underneath lay a desperation, a thought that maybe if Henri went unsaved, his own soul was forfeit. Why did he feel responsible for an older brother who continually resisted, who stubbornly chose the wicked path and kept to it in spite of the prayers, the sacrifices, made for him by his priest brother? What more could he do? Antoine was feeling his fifty-eight years.

He left the grave and sought Èmie. Taking her hands in his, he drew her into his embrace, kissing the crown of her head. "How are you, child?"

"I'm fine, Father."

"And where's Henri keeping himself?" Did he imagine the shudder in her spine? He held her back from him. "Èmie?"

She waved an arm. "He's somewhere. At the mine perhaps."

Antoine lifted her chin and studied her face. She was a woman grown, no more deceived by Henri's mining ruse than he. They both knew what occupation Henri practiced. Yet Antoine didn't make her speak of it. "He treats you well? No . . . harm comes to you?"

"No harm to me, Uncle Antoine."

The familial endearment touched him. "You would tell me, Èmie, wouldn't you?"

She nodded. And he believed her. Though she kept much to herself, he knew she trusted him. He glanced back at the grave, then turned away. "How is your friend Carina DiGratia?"

"Fine, Father."

Fine. Such a nondescript word, saying nothing really, containing none of Carina's fire and depth. Was Èmie even aware of it, the discrepancy? Did she know how she faded next to Carina's vibrancy? Her physical beauty alone, so remarkable. Yet to him Èmie was more dear.

Forgive him his human weakness. Should he prefer one soul to another? Did ties of blood allow a greater concern for some than others? And then he considered Carina DiGratia in her own right. She had not once received the sacrament of Holy Communion at his hand. And that meant something separated her from the Lord. Was it the vengeance of which they'd spoken?

If so, how did he bring peace? But maybe not he. He met Èmie's eyes, felt their gentleness, yet recognized their distress. He felt impotent. This woman, his niece, and Miss DiGratia, both struggling, both searching. Maybe they would find peace together.

He squeezed Èmie's shoulder. "I'm glad you have her. You need a friend."

"Yes, Father."

"Èmie, I prefer Uncle Antoine."

She smiled, the first that morning. He was a priest, but to this girl he was family. And given that her only other family was his brother Henri . . .

"Come on." He patted her shoulder. "I'll treat you to lunch at the hotel."

Èmie's eyes widened. "Should we?"

"Of course. Life is too short to forgo its few pleasures." And if he could bring joy to Èmie today, the Lord would forgive any excess.

After waiting most of the day in the silence of the office, Carina could stand it no longer. She had to get out. Snatching up the

354

canvas miner's jacket she had purchased as a protection in the rain, she reached for the door. Mr. Beck's hand was on the other side, and he stepped back in surprise.

Startled, she, too, shrank back, and he came inside, wet and dripping. *Not again.* Carina frowned. She would not wait while he changed and put himself in the mood for other things. She pulled the jacket closed.

"You're not leaving?"

She waved an arm. "What is there to do? You said yourself it's unimportant. I sat here all day with nothing to do."

He closed the door against the rain. "You were making yourself available. In case I should need you."

So he was again the indebted business-man. Which one was she to believe? "Don't you mean require, Mr. Beck?"

"Berkley." He raised a single brow as he looked at her sideways. "And I mean need — in the business sense."

She sighed, flinging her arms wide, and paced the room. "I don't know what I'm doing here. Why am I here?" She threw the question to the air, but Berkley Beck answered.

"Because I employed you."

"I don't mean here, in this office. I mean at all. What place is Crystal for me? I should go. I should leave."

"You can't."

355

She stopped pacing. Did she imagine the threatening current beneath his words? "What do you mean, I can't?"

"You're upset —"

"Upset?" She shrugged. "Why should I be upset? Men beaten outside my window, robbed and lying in their own blood. Throats cut —"

"Carina." He caught her arm. "You don't understand what's happening. There's something . . . uncivilized out there."

"I don't know that?" She tugged free and walked to the window. "I should never have come." She turned. "I'm leaving now."

"Believe me, Carina, it wouldn't be safe."

"Safe!" She threw up her hands and stalked across the room. "And I am safe here?"

"Yes. You're under my protection."

She started to scoff, but he held up a hand.

"Nothing will harm you. I give you my word."

"How can you say that? How can you know?"

He went very still, his eyes the cold blue of a mountain lake. "I believe I know who's behind all this."

She stared. How could he know? Had he gone to Èmie's uncle? Had he seen . . . "You know who killed Mr. Evans?"

"Not just that. This is bigger than one murder."

Her breath came out hard as her stomach knotted like a clenched fist.

"You don't need to fear. As you learned last night, I can protect you. And very soon I will extend that protection to others."

"What others? What are you saying?"

Beck's eyes warmed to the color of the Mediterranean sea. "Trust me, Carina."

She swallowed her protest. It would get her nowhere. "Whom do you suspect?"

Very subtly his gaze changed, drawing her in like a riptide that drowned. "It would be premature to say."

"Why? If you know . . ." She pictured Èmie's uncle being dragged off to judgment.

He caught her hands, bringing them together to his chest. "I don't know. Not for certain."

She searched his face, felt the firm grip of his hands pressing hers to his chest, but she felt no heartbeat. She didn't trust him, not down deep where she needed to, but she was afraid. And he was a powerful man like her papa.

"Right now I need your cooperation."

A different tune than yesterday. Carina was too confused to gloat. "What cooperation?" Again, the shifting in his eyes, something deep she couldn't read.

He closed his mouth, swiftly licked dry

lips. "I must know that you will be impersonal. This can't be a vendetta. Things could too easily get out of hand."

He had left her behind again. "What do you mean impersonal? How can it be personal for me?"

He half smiled. "Because, Carina, you've already expressed the desire for vengeance."

Vengeance? What was he talking about?

"Or should I say . . . reparation?"

Her mouth dropped open. Quillan Shepard. He wasn't meaning Èmie's uncle at all. He thought Quillan Shepard . . .

"My dear, I see your doubt."

Doubt? Did she doubt? Had she not already wondered this herself? Why had he been out there in the dark the night the marshal was beaten? What part did he play before he grabbed her? Maybe his snatching her was not for her sake, but to keep her from interfering with his plans. And this morning, his voice when he spoke of the murder . . . Had it been his own guilt that repulsed him? *An animal in human form.*" A Wolf? Or the son of one? She shuddered.

"Think, Carina." Again Beck gripped her hands between his. "A man wanted for robbery at fourteen might be capable of far more at twenty-eight. And a man of questionable parentage with dark things in his past . . ."

"My father was a savage, my mother a

harlot." Mr. Beck was spinning a web, but what if . . . ? Cold fear crawled her spine. "What things?"

"I could tell you. But I'd rather you heard it from others."

"Heard what?" Her head was spinning.

"About Wolf."

"My father was a savage." She knew there was something terrible in those words. She'd heard it in Quillan Shepard's voice. But how could she delve into a secret so painful to him, a secret both Mae and Father Charboneau guarded? "How will I hear it?"

He smiled slowly. "Ask the miners."

Ask about Quillan's past. Had she not done so already? But that was before she knew him. Did she know him? She pictured him tasting her ravioli, how she had waited for his approval. Was he a monster in disguise? There was only one way to know.

"Bene. I'll ask."

Nineteen

Is there a God? An author of this madness?

Rose

Quillan watched Miss DiGratia leave the office and make her way through the falling rain. She was wrapped in a miner's jacket twice her size, though her head was uncovered. He vaguely recalled a wide-brimmed hat sailing over the cliff and felt a twinge inside. Her walk was purposeful this time, yet it unsettled him more so than the last, and he turned to follow.

If he could just learn what he needed from her, something to prove his suspicions. Now that it had come to murder, they had to act or the whole thing would escalate. He'd seen it before, vigilantes hanging anyone they suspected and becoming in the end as heinous as those they had set out to stop.

He had the ear of one man on the board of trustees. Ben Masterson was level-headed and well respected. Quillan trusted him. But Beck as likely as not had others of them in his pocket, though Quillan didn't know which ones. Unlike the marshal, the trustees weren't beaten into submission. They were bought.

And Beck was wily. He'd have his trail covered. Miss DiGratia was the key. She must see who met with Beck, maybe even hear their discussions. If she had Beck's confidence and Quillan could win hers . . .

He lowered his hat brim against the rain. Like a shadow he crossed the street behind Miss DiGratia, his footsteps melting into the steady patter. He was surprised when she turned into the Boise Billiard Hall. Had Beck sent her on an errand there?

The place was packed with men, the rain driving them from their holes like rats, no one having pumping equipment adequate for this sort of ongoing deluge. The noise was substantial, though hardly jubilant, with the murder of William Evans hanging in their minds.

From the door, he watched the crowd part for Miss DiGratia. Hats were doffed like a wind passing over. Their conversation ceased, and they closed in behind with murmurs and smiles. She was gracing them with her presence. One Italian called out something in dialect, but she merely smiled and nodded her head, a legend walking among them.

Quillan had heard three versions already of Joe Turner's tale. Miss DiGratia probably had no idea the weight such superstition carried. Then again, maybe she did. A seat was brought and she took it, regally.

From the back of the crowd, Quillan watched, amused. A humble silence seemed to have fallen, the men waiting for her to speak. They had to be as puzzled as he. What brought her there among them? To what did they owe the honor?

"Might I trouble someone for a root beer?" Her voice was sweet and plaintive. She'd have forty glasses in her lap. The first came almost immediately, and she sipped the foamy brew.

Joe Turner pushed through to her side, raising his hands for attention. He'd earned the right to speak first by making her what she was. "Boys, for those of you who don't know, this is Miss Carina DiGratia, better known as Lady Luck. She found my hole for me simply by putting me out of my room. Now gather round and I'll tell you how it happened."

The men pushed in, eager to hear the tale even if they already had, now that the flesh embodiment of the heroine was in their midst. Quillan's mouth quirked. She couldn't have played it better. But what was she doing there? He cocked his head and listened as the tale grew more incredible than the last time.

When Turner finished, she laughed and shook her head. "It isn't true. I was only in need of a room."

Her smile dazzled, but she wouldn't dissuade them. There was too much superstition inherent in the prospector spirit. They would believe she floated on air if Turner told them so, his incredible earnings so far bearing him out. A bluster of voices burst in when Turner finished, each eager to catch Miss DiGratia's attention.

She tipped her head playfully. "Surely someone can top Mr. Turner's tale?"

Again the voices stampeded, but one rose above them. "Well, there's the one about Jessie Rae." It was Daniel Fletcher, looking dapper in a bottle green vest and twill trousers.

"That's too sad for a lady," someone called out, but Quillan couldn't see who.

"No, tell me." Miss DiGratia held up a hand. "I love a sad tale."

"Well." Standing, Fletcher raised his foot to the seat of the chair and rested his arms on his knee. "There was a miner in old Placer, name of Benjamin Huff, and he come up with his wife and daughter, Jessie Rae. Now the rigors of the camp proved too much for Mrs. Huff, and sadly she succumbed within the first months of their coming. They buried her under a tree as there was as yet no proper cemetery."

This tale, also, Quillan knew. But Fletcher was a good raconteur, less self-conscious than Tucker. He looked around the circle, then back to Miss DiGratia and continued. "It broke the daughter's heart to have her mama pass on so, but she knew it was even worse for Benjamin Huff, on account he blamed himself."

Nods all around. The men understood the difficulty their life-style placed on the womenfolk they brought along and the guilt that went hand in hand with it. "She was a perceptive child and knew her daddy might break under the guilt. So she did all she could to keep his spirits up, a-singin' and a-playin' for him on a little mandolin she'd brought along."

Fletcher paused for effect. "Her voice was so sweet, men would gather at their door just to listen to the angel sing. It put them in mind of all things gentle and good and made them want to do right by one another. There wasn't a heart untouched by that girl's magic."

He tipped his head to the side. "Yesirree, it was a marvelous thing. Then in the summer of '61, a bad rain came and the tunnel collapsed, taking Anthony Huff and three others. They were buried so deep it was days before the bodies were retrieved. Well, that little Jessie Rae 'bout broke down right then. But she took her mandolin under her arm and walked off up the mountain. No one could stop her — she just kept walkin'."

He hung his head and paused. "Some

months later her bones were found in a stony crevice. We buried her under the tree next to her mama and pa. But that night, there was music and singin' coming from the hills, a voice so sweet it brought men to tears. Folks say whenever the rains come, if you listen well, you can hear it still, and around the tree where those folks are buried, a light shines small and willowy, walkin' about a-pluckin' the strings."

Quillan watched to see what effect the story had on Miss DiGratia. She sat in the stillness, properly moved. He even imagined the sparkle of a tear in her eye, but then the rich brown orbs in the thick black lashes were always inordinately bright. He tried not to notice the shape of them now, the arch of the brow. Not that anyone would have blamed him. Every man in the room was trapped in her spell, every one of them awaiting her word, her whim.

Drawing a thin breath, she said, "Now tell me about Wolf."

Quillan's throat cleaved, surprise and anger surging together. Had he heard right? What was she doing? His heart beat his ribs, hands clenched at his sides. He wanted to press through and demand an answer. But his feet were leaden and stayed where they were.

Several men looked uncomfortable. Joe Turner circled the group with his eyes.

"What's she talking about? Who's Wolf?" Other voices echoed the same.

Clive Johnson shook his hoary head, his beard a forkful of frosty straw resting on his chest. "That's a bad one, miss. A gory tale and not for delicate ears."

Miss DiGratia seemed to close in a little at that, and Quillan was glad. He hoped she shuddered and writhed. Surely she'd demur, and no more would be said. But she only spread her hands. "Can it be worse than what happened last night?"

Quillan felt cold with anger. *Yes, it's worse, Miss DiGratia. But you'll have it now in every morbid detail.*

"Well, not worse maybe, and maybe there's some as will find it pertinent in light of Old Griz." Johnson cleared his throat and searched the group for approval. "It was around '51 or '52, if I recall. Again, this was in Placer. Upper Placer, the first camp in this gulch, a wild vagabond sort of place. Not an upstanding city like this here Crystal." He laughed and the beard jumped on his chest.

"It was peopled with mountain men like myself and decorated with a few fair faces painted up for color. One such face was named Rose. She'd come up herself, not in the chippy wagon like the others, and we all felt her story must be some tragic. But, mind you, she meant to do her part same as the others, else why would she be there?"

366

Quillan's throat tightened as the old man dropped his face and looked uncomfortable. "She meant to, only the night of her comin' to town another stranger blew in. This one of even more interest. He said his name was Wolf, and he wore a head of golden hair long down his back, Indian style. He was all dressed up in buckskins and moccasins, too, and he wore strings of claws and teeth around his neck. He carried a knife for skinnin' that would take the hide from a buffalo were there any roamin' these parts a'tall. He was what you'd call a handsome man and stern. Oh, Moses, he was a sight."

Again the laugh bounced the beard, but it was short and a little forced. "None of us felt too comfortable askin' him to drink, but he showed no inclination. He walked right through the cabin that was servin' as saloon, looked over the women, and reached for Rose."

Quillan watched Miss DiGratia's eyes and saw she was hanging on every word. His throat tasted sour.

"We all thought she'd put up a fight, scream and holler in sheer fear. But she just took the hand and followed like it was her fate or some such. He took her up the mountain where he'd set up a teepee of sorts. There weren't a one of us goin' to fetch her back." He scratched the side of his beard. "No, sir.

"They lived up there like that while he built a cabin and started a mine. He mined that mountain with a vengeance. We got to thinkin' he was okay, just a little rough around the edges. It come out he'd spent most all his life with the Sioux. That was bound to make a man queer. But we didn't know how queer nor . . . how deadly he'd prove."

Johnson leaned forward to the table. "You sure you want me to go on?"

Quillan's jaw tightened when Miss DiGratia nodded. He felt his pulse in his left temple.

"It was some while they lived among us, but not quite part of us. Rose, she hardly ever spoke when she come down from the mountain, which wasn't often. Wolf would talk, but not about himself except sometimes a comment here and there on how the Sioux did one thing or another. Soon it was evident he'd got Rose with child. Believe it or not, they seemed right pleased."

The old man smiled. "Rose took on a sort of glow, walking with her hand resting there on her belly."

Quillan pressed his eyes shut. He should leave, walk out before they saw him standing there. But all eyes were on the tale spinner and Miss DiGratia.

"Well, sure enough, she had the baby and all went well. Until it started in to cry. And then Wolf, see, he started a howlin', the fiercest, loneliest howlin' ever heard. Folks in town shuttered up their windows and bolted their doors. But it wasn't enough."

Here the old man's eyes slowly circled the faces around him, sensing the tension of the moment. "No, it wasn't enough. A man was found dead in the woods, all torn up, his throat ripped open . . . by teeth."

Quillan saw the shudder pass through her. His eyes burned into her until he was sure she'd look up and see him there. But she didn't. Her face had paled, but her attention was riveted on Johnson, who leaned forward again. "There were no witnesses, nothing by which we could accuse a man. No witness, no crime. That's the miner's law. But no one wanted anything to do with Wolf after that. We'd shy away like girls when he came down the mountain. The room would clear as though a wind rushed in and blew the men out. Not a tornado-type wind, just a steady blow that took one man after another silently out the door."

Johnson's eyes held Miss DiGratia's. "Rose, she kept to herself with that new baby and did all she could to make him happy. But whenever the baby cried, Wolf went off his head, howlin' and swearin' and breakin' things."

He shook his head. "We waited for another body to turn up, but before it happened, Rose gave the baby away to a missionary family. They took him away from the gulch and away from Wolf. We all knew she done it so Wolf wouldn't kill again, but it seemed the life went right out of her."

He cleared his throat. "It shames me to say it, but we were relieved that baby was gone. None of us thought what it would do to the woman. But then there was the fire. Wolf had been to town to get supplies. He was most of the way up the mountain when he saw smoke. Some of us from the nearby mines had seen it, too, and were already headin' that way. By the time he got there to his house, the walls were all aflame."

Quillan tried to stop his ears. He'd heard the story too many times not to visualize it in detail.

Johnson's voice lowered. "Wolf went inside and we heard him pleadin', but she wouldn't come out or couldn't. We thought he'd drag her or come out without her. But he didn't. He just laid down with her and they perished together."

Quillan felt the anger inside like a living thing. Who were they to lay out his past like a rag to be trampled? Who was she to ask it? He wrenched himself away, out into the rain that poured over his hat and down the hair hanging at his back. It ran over him, washing off the dust of travel, not making him clean, never making him clean. But he held his face to the rain, eyes closed, and let it run over him.

Carina sat in stunned silence. It was worse, far worse than she had imagined. *"My father was a savage, my mother a harlot."* They weren't just words. They were true.

"You don't want to be out on the mountain after dark. Folks hear him still, howlin' that lonely song." Johnson shook his head. "We never knew what made him do it."

She drew a shaky breath, forcing her voice to come. "You were right. That was not a story I should hear." She felt fouled. Why had Mr. Beck insisted? Did he know what she would hear?

Their apologies washed over her.

"I'm sorry, ma'am."

"Have another root beer."

"Here, ma'am. Let me serve you one."

She shook her head. "No, grazie." She was dazed, uncertain now what she was doing. What purpose did it serve to learn the dark secrets of a man's past? What did it mean for Quillan? Was he like his father, an animal able to tear a man's throat? Had he killed William Evans?

She stood up, and all around her the men rose like a flood, clamoring to their feet and whisking the hats again from their heads.

"Join us anytime, Miss DiGratia."

"Anything you need, just let us know."

"Sure appreciate your comin' in like this."

She passed through them, scarcely hearing, not seeing more than a flood of faces. As she reached the door, she heard the questions begin and the suppositions. What did this story mean in light of William Evans? Was there a new monster among them? An old monster returned?

She stepped out into the rain and walked. Could the story be true? Why had she not sensed evil at the mine? Sadness, yes — a haunting lostness — but not such evil as she had just heard. What of Rose? Giving her baby away to protect —

Steel gripped her arm, a fierce face, teeth bared, hair hanging wet across his shoulders. She screamed but no sound came, sheer terror holding her mute as Quillan Shepard, Wolf's son, yanked her close.

"Perhaps you'd like the rest of the story." He spoke through clenched teeth, narrow and straight. "How my own mother gave me away and the Shepards took me in, illegitimate spawn of reprobate parents. How their natural-born children died not two weeks later of the cholera, but somehow the cursed baby lived. How that poisoned the mother against me, and how she believed I was the devil incarnate, no less than the cause of her sweet children's deaths. Mr. Shepard's rod might purge me of my sins, but it never changed the fact that I lived when the others didn't."

His fingers clawed into her arms, his eyes black with wrath. "She loved to tell me the story you just heard, lest I somehow forget I wasn't really theirs. Mr. Shepard tried sometimes to show me kindness in a stern, well-meaning way. He did his Christian duty. But you see, they just couldn't change my parentage."

Quillan's rage seemed to deflate. Carina heard it seep out of his lungs in a low, sighing breath. He let her go and turned away. "So now you know."

Carina felt a stab of conscience, a dirtiness inside her like the whole of Crystal infecting her heart. Rain ran down inside her collar where the jacket had fallen loose when he released her, soaking her neck beside the braid. She had wanted this, wanted to see him hurt and shamed. But her victory was bitter.

"I'm sorry." The words came of themselves from a place inside her not tainted.

He looked at her sideways, a strand of brown hair clinging to his cheekbone, drops of rain falling from his mustache. "Would it have mattered if I'd carried your things?"

She stared at him, confused.

"Would you have been so bent on this if I hadn't sent your wagon over?"

Carina closed her eyes, shrinking inside. She had not thought what it would do to him to have the story told. His name was not mentioned, but those who knew . . . All it would take was the connection to be made, father to son. She looked again, seeing the wreckage of her deed. He was a man, not a monster.

What could she do? What could she give in return for what she'd damaged? "Mr. Beck suspects you."

His gaze merely held her.

She spread her hands. "Of the murder, of all the violence, I suppose."

His eyes were flat, lifeless. "And you, Miss DiGratia? Is that what you think?"

"I don't know what to think." She raised a splayed hand. "I don't know violence, murder, greed." She waved both arms. "I don't understand this place, these people." She wiped the rain from her eyes. "I should not have come."

"Why did you?" He had the right to ask, the right to know.

"To hurt someone."

His eyes narrowed, not comprehending the details, but not doubting the truth of it.

Looking down, she pressed her palm to her forehead, fingers curled. "I thought I mattered to him. I was mistaken." Her hand dropped.

Quillan looked away, searched the street

slowly with his eyes. They stood alone in the rain, stripped of pretense, yet strangers. After a moment, he blew out a slow breath, and she thought he would speak, but he simply stepped off the walk and strode away.

The air grew cold in his wake. Pulling the canvas jacket close, Carina hurried for the livery.

Alan Tavish snored in the chair inside the doorway with a look of pain even in his sleep. The rain must torment his swollen joints. She didn't wake him, saddling Dom herself. She heard Mr. Tavish stir, but she passed by like a shadow. Leading the mule out, she swept Crystal with her eyes.

Piles of stone next to the Exchange showed where the new opera house was being built. Across from it a haberdashery had opened its doors in the weeks she'd lived there. Crystal was growing, thriving, coming into its own. She thought of the miners gathered around her, good men, sincere. Yet at its heart, Crystal was rotten. Where did the poison come from? Mounting, she urged Dom up the street, up the gulch. It was inevitable. The mine drew her even now, even knowing.

"Carina!" Mr. Beck called from his office, but she ignored him, heeling Dom past with an urgency he sensed and responded to. She headed for Placer, the tale of Wolf and Rose spinning in her head. She had asked about Wolf, but it was Rose her thoughts clung to. Who was the woman, and what had brought her to this place?

"We all felt her story must be some tragic." Had Rose gone to Placerville to find peace? Impossible. *"She meant to do her part, same as the rest."* Carina trembled. What could make a woman choose that? And then to go with Wolf without a fight, to take his hand and go . . .

She tried to picture Wolf but could only see Quillan, teeth bared, gray eyes burning with fury and bitter rage. And then the despair that had quenched him. But it wasn't the woman he described that held her thoughts. It was the one who had given him up. Rose. What hold did she have on Carina's thoughts? A hold strong enough to bring her to the mine named for her.

The way was steep and slippery. Dom struggled. After one treacherous stumble, Carina dismounted and led him, but it was slow, difficult footing. Lightning seared the sky, the rain coming harder. The crack of thunder made her jump. She was *pazza* to be out in this.

She headed for thicker trees to shelter in as she climbed. Dom balked, hanging his head stubbornly. *Bene.* He need not come. She twisted the reins around a branch and left him, then climbed alone. He gave a plaintive bray, but she went on, determined to reach the Rose Legacy.

Perchè? What did it matter? She should go back, take Dom, and ride home. Home? This was not home, could never be home. She was without her people, without those she knew and understood. She was like Rose — alone and in the hands of some force bigger than herself.

Her foot slipped. Lightning flashed again, and it seemed the very ground rumbled beneath her. Her feet slipped again, and she realized the ground did shake. She felt it in her hands when she caught herself. What was it? She had felt tremors in Sonoma, but this was different.

Looking up the gulch where it narrowed, she saw something her mind could make no sense of. A trick of the rain perhaps, but no — it was a wall of water where no water should be. And it was rushing down the gulch. Dom!

She heard him scream as the water crashed over the place she had left him and kept coming, rising at a terrible speed, trees falling, crashing with a roar until she realized she, too, could be swept away. She staggered up as the water climbed, dragging herself up toward the mine, gaping now above her.

With bloody fingers and aching legs, she fought the weight of her soaked skirts and scrambled to the cleared land before the mine. The black mouth opened, and she rushed inside even as the water struck the mountain, flying up into the sky with a roar of white foam and tree trunks.

She staggered backward from the horror outside, groping the walls on either side. Then suddenly the ground was gone and she fell.

Quillan felt heavy, as though the very muscles under his skin had taken on a weight not of flesh but of lead. He needed distance and solitude. Why had he come to Crystal in the first place? He couldn't remember, couldn't think of one good reason he'd dragged himself back to this gulch to make a living.

Of course, he'd only been an infant when he left Placer. It was hardly a homecoming to set up freighting in Crystal. Only he knew, somewhere in the back of his mind, that up the mountain lay the mine. He'd looked on it only once when he first came. The Rose Legacy. His legacy.

He'd known there were old-timers in Crystal who remembered the tale. Even some, like Mae and Alan and Cain, who knew he was that baby, grown. But some aberrant need had brought him here, kept him here, as though by proving himself he could remove the stain of his father. Wolf.

He swallowed the bitter taste in his mouth. There were other towns, places he could go. Leadville, Fairplay, Denver. Even Colorado Springs, the little London. He had choices. Crystal meant nothing to him.

Some of the people maybe. Cain and D.C., Mae, Mrs. Barton, and Alan Tavish. And others, though not many. Not enough to keep him here. Why was he risking his neck to discover who was behind the roughs? What did it matter to him?

Berkley Beck suspected him of the murder? Well, that made it mutual. And Miss DiGratia was the pawn they each used against the other. Had Beck sent her off to pry into his past? Had he planted suspicions he knew she'd pursue? Why? So the men would start to wonder, to whisper, to find in their superstitious memories fuel with which to burn him?

Quillan reached his tent and ducked inside. Crouching near his cache under the floor, he pulled the canvas aside and considered taking it all. He could clear out of there and not look back. It wasn't his affair what happened to Crystal, and he wasn't responsible for fixing it. Cain was right. It was eating him, his need to set things right in the community his father had violated.

He hunkered back on his haunches, the muscles in his thighs taut. He was not one for hasty decisions. If he packed up in the rain, he'd have to unpack it all and let it dry out. Better to wait until the sun did the job, then pull stakes and move on. He closed up the flooring. Jabbing his fingers into his hair, he went back out into the rain. A flash, then thunder rumbled.

The rain fell harder. He would check on his horses and find something to eat. Mrs. Barton would have something cooked up at the hotel. Another flash — this time a straight bolt that hit ground — brought his head up. Thunder cracked, then rumbled and continued, seeming to grow louder and not diminish.

He frowned, feeling the ground tremble. What on earth . . . High up the gulch he saw it, churning, foaming, rushing toward them like doom. Every nerve inside jolted, and his muscles responded. "Hey! Flood! Flood!"

He ran for the livery, wrenching open the door. "Flood, Tavish!" He shook the old man, then ran on. Most of the city was holed up in the saloons and gambling houses. He hollered as he ran past, banging the doors open, then running on. Others ran with him now, hollering as they bolted for higher ground.

A sudden thought froze Quillan's feet. Cain. He changed direction and sprinted for the tents. Already the roar of the flood filled his ears. "Cain! D.C.!" He reached their tent and flung open the flap. Cain slept, one-legged on the cot.

D.C. jumped to his feet, the dog jumping with him. "What is it?"

"Flood!" Quillan rushed in, shook Cain awake, then grabbed him up beneath the arms. The water hit them as they cleared the tent, Quillan's arms tight around Cain's chest. They were tossed like rubble, dragged under and spun, but he held tight, fighting with his legs, kicking them to the surface.

White foam, thick with debris, pushed them along. A body slapped against him, stripped naked and lifeless, then spun and churned by. Shuddering, he kept Cain afloat and searched for D.C. He opened his mouth to holler, gulped the torrent and gagged, then searched only with his eyes whenever they came up again. An uprooted pine trunk swung around and thunked the side of his head. He grabbed it, pushing Cain upward, and the man took hold, gasping and choking.

Quillan let go and searched the rushing water for D.C. He was there, among those fighting their way to the edge, climbing the sides of the gulch. He saw horses and Alan Tavish clinging to one of his own blacks, Jock. Jock would carry the old ostler to safety, but where was Jack? He couldn't worry about that now.

He took a new hold of Cain and worked

them both toward the shore. The water was a living force in deadly combat with him, sapping his strength, numbing his mind. Again and again it almost tore Cain from his grip, but each time he gained a new hold and struck again for the shore, reaching it at last and slogging down in the mud.

Chest heaving, he felt his head where the tree had struck him, sticky with fresh blood now that the water no longer doused the cut. His arms shook and his legs were numb. His throat was clogged with mud. But he lived.

A thousand shall fall at thy side, and ten thousand at thy right hand; but it shall not come nigh thee . . .

Why the words came, he couldn't say. Panting, Quillan rose up to one elbow to search the water, still rushing by, taking with it the disintegration of the city. He saw men caught in the flow, boards and trees and horses. *Only with thine eyes shalt thou behold and see the reward of the wicked. . . .*

Cain groaned. Twisting around, Quillan saw D.C. scrambling toward them, the dog dragging free of the water and limping alongside.

There shall no evil befall thee, neither shall any plague come nigh thy dwelling. Frowning, Quillan stared up the valley, where his tent had stood with the others, all of them lost now beneath the running water. And not just his tent, but everything — everything he'd worked for and saved. But he was alive.

He could see buildings beyond the flood, those far enough from the creek, those built of brick or stone that had held and protected others beside them. The water must have built up by the falls where the gulch narrowed. Breaking loose, it had spread out some before reaching Crystal, though still rushing with a deadly force unimpeded by the debris it collected.

Half of Central Street had vanished in the torrent pouring by with terrible strength, the buildings crumpled like paper, wrenched apart and carried away, leaving only the brick bank and hotel and those buildings shielded by them. The livery was gone, and that would be a blow to Alan. But even that seemed small compared to their lives.

Quillan rubbed the muck from his eyelids, stretched his leg, and winced. Cain's palsied hand gripped his shoulder, and Quillan met the old man's eyes. Neither spoke. Neither had to.

Twenty

What is a lie but a shade of the truth?
Rose

Rose, Rose, don't leave me here. Carina staggered behind a woman who moved away, deaf to her cries. *Show me the way out!* If she could just reach her, Rose would lead her out of the darkness. She ran her hands over damp, stony walls that closed in on either side. A chill ran up and down her spine. *Rose!* Rose turned, and Carina strained to see her face, but it vanished in the dark. And then she was falling. . . .

Carina woke, but in the darkness she couldn't tell if her eyes were truly open or if she still dreamed. The pain in her shoulder was real; the cold, dank air more keen than she could imagine. She tried to move, kicking a stone with her foot. Pulse throbbing, she listened to it strike the walls, down, down below her before it plunked into water and the echoes died away.

Reaching tremulous fingers, she found an edge. She was on a stone shelf, with the shaft yawning beneath, but how far? Her head spun. *No, no, no.* She must not allow even a moment's dizziness or she would fall again. She willed it away, feeling about with her left hand to gauge the size and shape of her refuge. It was narrow, scarcely wider than her body lying parallel to the wall.

Shifted slightly by her searching, her right shoulder shot fire down her arm and across her collarbone. She gasped with the pain. The joint was not right. Her arm would not move. She tried to sit up and screamed with the pain in her damaged shoulder.

How far down was she? There was no way to tell, but by the movement of the air she guessed not so far. She could hear sounds from outside, water rushing . . . the flood! No. It wasn't forceful enough for that. Water certainly, but probably running down the mountain, maybe the falls. It was strange how things were magnified, a dripping somewhere, a creaking timber. She dropped her face to her hand, trying to think.

Was it night? Or was she just so far from daylight it didn't matter? She felt the timbers that formed the wall. They were laid flush into the side of the shaft, inset one above the other. Even without her damaged shoulder, she couldn't climb it. It was useless to try with one arm.

She laid her head down, aware now of other aches — her neck and back, her left shin and elbow. A dull throb started in her head. But she was not so battered she would die of it. Death would be slower, more agonizing. Hunger and thirst. Maybe shock. She closed her eyes. *Per piacere, Signore.*

Who would think to look? And even if they looked, who would come so far as to look here in the Rose Legacy? Then an awful thought stopped her breath. Was there even someone to look? What if the flood had struck Crystal? What was there to stop it rushing down the gulch, taking the town by surprise?

She trembled. She must try to get out. In spite of the pain, she pulled herself to her knees but shook so hard she couldn't stand. The throbbing grew insistent like the roar of the flood in her ears. She was too weak from the fall. She must wait. Alone. In the darkness. She pressed her palm against the timbers in terror. "Signore, per piacere."

Like a child she begged the God who either gave or punished. A capricious God who sometimes deigned to answer and sometimes not, a God she needed, yet feared. In the darkness, she was stripped of all but the fear. "Please, God. Per piacere. I'll do anything if you take me out of here."

Forgive.

She startled, staring into the blackness, certain the voice had been real. But there was no one, nothing. Forgive? Flavio? Divina? Divina. Divine. Belonging to God. Even God preferred Divina. Carina slumped

386

against the wall. The pain grew unbearable in her shoulder, and she cradled her arm and moaned. But the echoes coming up from below so frightened her, she bit her lip against the sound of her own voice and reached for the crucifix at her throat. Her fingers found empty flesh.

The dog's soft tongue slowly lapped his ear, and Cain raised a shaky hand to pat its head. He couldn't speak, and a sharp, throbbing pain immobilized his other arm. It was gashed almost to the bone and blood ran freely from the wound. But for some reason best known to God himself, he'd been spared by the flood. *Oh give thanks to the Lord for He is good: for his mercy endureth forever . . .*

He met Quillan's eyes, raw with emotion in the wake of his struggle. Cain wasn't surprised when Sam scooched along on his belly and employed his tongue on Quillan's hand. That hand had held on tenaciously, not letting an old man slip away. Caked with mud and bleeding, that hand was God's own mercy enfleshed.

"Are you all right, Daddy?" D.C. dropped to his knees beside him.

Cain could only nod. He hadn't the breath for words, and the pain was growing sharper. The blood had started to congeal, but the gash needed sewing. D.C. took the scarf from his neck and tied it tightly around the wound. That brought some small relief. Cain tried to rise but failed.

D.C. caught his shoulders and sat him up. "Thank God Quillan saw the flood."

Thank God indeed. Cain surveyed Quillan still lying in the mud. When push came to shove, that young man did the right thing every time. He could have saved himself and climbed to safety, but he'd risked warning others. Yesirree, God had His eye on Quillan.

Cain looked up the gulch. He'd seen a lot of things during his years on the mountain, even seen floods, but none like this one. None that took buildings and made matchsticks of them, roaring down the gulch like a monster devouring everything in its path, changing the landscape until he hardly knew it. The water must have been clogged somewhere high, building and holding until its force could not be contained.

Lives had been lost, he knew. It was impossible they hadn't in a cataclysm of nature such as this. But some had been spared on account of Quillan. Cain's heart swelled. He loved that man like a son, same as he loved D.C., God bless him.

He gathered his strength as Quillan and D.C. helped him to his feet, or rather his foot. The peg was somewheres down the mountain. He hooked his arm around Quillan's neck. But then, what need had he of a wooden leg when he had a friend like Quillan?

Quillan felt mauled, battered, and torn up as he helped Cain stand. The rain had stopped or mostly so, and people crawled from their holes, congregating at Central, or what used to be Central Street, now just a scattering of buildings beside a flowing mire of debris.

One side of the city had fared okay; the other side was simply gone. The sight shook him. How easily the work of their hands had been swept away. A house built on sand. What had the foundation been? Greed?

All around them small vignettes played out, people surveying the aftermath with looks of disbelief and disorientation. He supposed he and D.C. looked much the same. Cain just looked gray.

They sloshed through the mud toward Central and found Mae perched on a stool, an island amid the slag. Somehow her perch didn't look any queerer than the rest of it. He started by her, too weary to speak. His boots sucked in and out of the mud, each step an effort.

Mae gathered herself. "Have you seen Carina?"

Quillan turned. "She's not with you?" He shifted Cain's weight.

Mae shook her head. "Berkley Beck claims he saw her riding up the gulch before the flood."

Quillan looked up the gulch where the water had roiled and rushed. Only slowly did her words dawn on him. "Where can I take Cain?"

"They're setting up infirmaries at the hotel and my place." Mae's voice softened. "Take him to my bed. The old coot looks half drowned."

Quillan turned away without response, starting up the way that used to be Drake, Cain half hopping between D.C. and him. Like a seed germinating, concern for Carina DiGratia grew inside him. Soon it was a weed, twisting his stomach.

When they reached Mae's, Quillan laid Cain in the bed as gently as he could. The arm would need stitching, though how Cain had cut it, Quillan wasn't sure. But he couldn't wait now for the doctor. He glanced at D.C. "You'll stay with him? Have Dr. Felden see to his arm?"

D.C. nodded. "I'm not going anywhere."

Quillan gripped Cain's hand briefly, then went out. No telling how long it would be before Dr. Felden made his way to Cain. Many others would be brought in. Many in worse condition. Many beyond any doctor's help. He'd intended to join the search himself for injured and dead down the gulch.

But it appeared his first direction was up. Why had Miss DiGratia ridden up the gulch in the storm? Though his strength was sapped, there was no time to rest. She could be injured . . . or dead.

If she were dead, there was no hurry. So why did he force his legs to move, even with the left one shooting pain at every step? He'd pulled or torn something on the side of the knee, though the joint was whole. He sighed, passing the knot of men Berkley Beck was organizing.

He wanted no part of anything Beck had a hand in. He kept on until he found Tavish with Jock. They'd made it to the near side of the flood, and Jock's strength must have pulled them out. Tavish held tight to the gelding, as though letting go even now might mean death.

Quillan reached a gentle hand to his shoulder. "I need to take him, my friend."

Tavish nodded, letting his arms slide away. "You'll be finding the lass?"

Quillan drew his brows down. "What lass?"

"Miss DiGratia. She came for Dom just before the flood." The old man's eyes were softened with worry.

"How much before?"

Tavish rubbed his chin with the side of his hand. "Time enough to reach Placer."

"You think that's where she went?"

He shrugged. "It's where she always goes."

Quillan led Jock. He wore only a halter bridle, but it would have to do. Reaching solid ground, he mounted bareback, turned him up the gulch, and started off. If Miss DiGratia was in Placer when the flood hit . . . He frowned, not certain why it mattered. She'd been nothing but trouble for him, especially today.

But then, he'd been trouble for her, too, starting with their ill-fated meeting on the wagon road. He shook the hair back from his face. He'd lost his hat along with everything else. Not everything. He patted Jock's neck. Maybe Jack had swum free as well.

He hoped all four horses had survived. He didn't expect to find the wagon whole, but maybe. Somewhere down the gulch things would wash ashore, tangled up and waiting to be retrieved. Things . . . and bodies.

He dropped his chin, acknowledging the thought he hadn't wanted to face. He didn't want to be the one to find Miss DiGratia, didn't want to see her broken and still, she whose life seemed to pulse in her, strong and tenacious. Even if that tenacity made him crazy sometimes.

What was she doing up the gulch? Didn't

she know the danger of a storm like this, how the water could build so fast in the narrow canyons? No, of course she didn't know. How could she? He felt a shiver of dread. If he hadn't scared and upset her . . . He shook his head, too tired to think about it.

Jock climbed the gulch strewn with rubble and oozing mud. The creek ran high, twice as high as normal, bursting its banks, but nothing like the churning madness it had been just hours ago. Looking up, he blinked, unsure his mind wasn't playing tricks. His eyes searched the gulch from side to side. Placer was gone.

Jock stopped, sensing his confusion. Quillan stared. It was washed away, every building gone as though they'd never been there. No mining works, no town, no hotel, no cabins — nothing. The flood must have been a wall of water through here. His throat tightened painfully. There was no way she could have withstood that. Unless . . .

He turned and looked up the mountain. Was it to Placer she went, or somewhere else? He felt a grim hardening inside. Why? Why would she go there? What could the Rose Legacy mean to her? He turned Jock, purposeful now in his movements. The horse responded accordingly, huffing heavily with the digging of his hooves into the steep, slippery slope.

Quillan reached the clearing and stared dully at the gaping mine, empty, no huddling figure awaiting him. Fool, to think she'd gone there. Part of him was relieved, the part that was shamed by this piece of ground. He didn't want her here, seeing what he came from. He dismounted, dropped the halter rein, and walked slowly from the mine to the foundation. He'd never set foot inside the square of his birthplace, not since he could step at all.

He looked down at the blackened stones and felt the familiar quiver in his spine. Every time he thought of them dying in the fire, lying there and dying . . . Mrs. Shepard had described it too well and too often, the smell of burnt flesh, the blackened, charred bodies. Yet standing there, he felt something else. A sadness at his loss, and a deep loneliness.

His arms were heavy at his sides, his mind and body weary. But it was his soul that hurt most. He was alive, but why? *For he shall give his angels charge over thee, to keep thee in all thy ways.* When he was small he had tried so hard to believe, to trust, to do what was right. But it was never enough to satisfy her, the woman who held him and whispered poison in his ear.

He sighed. It was getting dark, the clouds overhead clumped together, leaving patches of indigo sky spattered with the first faint stars. He should have brought a lantern if he could have gotten hold of one. But what use was it now? If Miss DiGratia had ridden up, she was washed away.

Angry and hurt, he started back for Jock. He bent to pull a twig from the left rear hoof and caught the glitter of something in the muddy gravel. Taking a step toward it, he made out the shape, reached, and pulled it from the dirt. A silver crucifix. Carina DiGratia's crucifix.

Snatching it up, he raised his head and searched again the clearing of the trees, the mine. Was she inside? "Carina!"

Nothing. He stepped into the opening, nearly pitch black and void. "Carina?" He knew better than to holler into an old tunnel. The timbers might have rotted and the sound could bring it all down. A few more steps. "Carina?"

He felt the wall along one side and gingerly placed his feet. "Miss DiGratia, are you there?"

A whimper from below. His heart leaped as he dropped to his knees and felt the floor until he found the shaft. How deep? "Carina?"

"Sì. *Son qui.*"

She sounded dazed but not as far down as he'd feared. And she was alive. He took a moment to digest that. It seemed unbelievable, and he realized he'd steeled himself to find her dead. His mind had to make the shift, but it was sluggish in doing so. Then suddenly it burst on him. She was alive!

Emotions churned, the natural elation of having somehow accomplished what he believed he wouldn't, then the surge of anger. Why was she here? What morbid fascination brought her to this shaft? He pictured her face riveted on the tale of his parents' evil. His throat tightened, and he clenched his hands at his sides.

"Are you hurt?" His voice sounded odd, tumbling down the shaft.

She moaned, mumbling again, in Italian he assumed. Whatever his feelings toward her, she needed help. A lantern. A torch. Rope. How had he left with nothing? He stood and groped his way back toward the opening. Most tunnels had an alcove somewhere near the front. Maybe, though unlikely, he could find what he needed. He found the opening in the wall with his hands and felt for shelves.

They were there, his palms running over rough boards thick with dust and cobwebs. Empty. He turned and felt the next, and then the last. Long cylinders, tallow by the feel. He grabbed one up and felt for matches. None. But a metal box. Well, flint and steel were better than nothing.

He opened the box, found what he needed, and struck until his spark lit the candle wick. By its light he saw the lantern on the floor, but it was dry, whatever oil it once contained long since evaporated. Cupping the flame, he carried the candle back to the shaft, its light a pallid glow in the inky darkness.

He held it out over the shaft and saw her, caught on a shelf with the main shaft yawning black beside her. He went back, searched the alcove for rope, and found a short length, somewhat rotted but not past use. Stuffing extra candles and the tinder-box into his pocket, he brought the rope back to the shaft. "Miss DiGratia?"

No answer. She was shocked, dazed, and probably injured. "Carina, can you hear me?"

She moved, her head tipping up until her face came into the light. "I'm here."

English! Good. "I have a rope. I'll drop it down to you."

"I can't climb. My shoulder, it's *ferito*." She mumbled again, a string of Italian, then collapsed against the wall in pain.

He would have to go down after her. He looked for a place to attach the rope but found none. Frustrated, he returned to the alcove and rummaged the piles on the floor. The sacking fell away and he found what he needed: a handful of bent, rusted spikes. Outside he felt around for a rock that fit his hand well enough.

He headed back in. Propping the candle against the tunnel wall, he used the rock to drive two spikes, angling away from each other, into a timber across from the shaft. He tied one end of the rope around the spikes in a double hitch, then yanked it hard. It held, and the timber seemed sound. He'd have to take the chance.

With the lit candle between his teeth, he let himself down the shaft, hand over hand, feet finding whatever crevice they could. Some twenty feet down, he lighted on the narrow shelf beside her. She stared as though trying to piece together what she was seeing. Did she recognize him? Maybe it was better she didn't.

He took the candle from his teeth and held it upright over the shaft. The light was swallowed up, never showing bottom. It would have been a silent grave, the mystery of her death adding to her legend, how she disappeared during the flood but her body was never found.

He crouched down, all too aware of her body right beside him now on the narrow shelf. Her arm was cradled against her, and he reached a hand to her shoulder.

"Aah," she cried and slapped at him.

By the hang of her arm, he guessed the joint was out of place. He could jerk it back in, but not here on this precarious perch. He wedged the candle into a knothole, where it dripped and sputtered. Swiftly he took off his shirt and tied it around her, immobilizing the damaged shoulder. She fought him with her free hand, but her movements were weak, ineffective.

The candle's flame reeled and staggered as he looped the rope around her waist, then drew her up against him and brought the rope between his legs and around his own middle. The flame shrank and died, leaving only the thin acrid smell of smoke, but he couldn't have carried the candle anyway. By touch, he tied another double hitch and yanked the rope for give. It held for now.

Slowly he stood, drawing her up with him. It was just as well the darkness was complete. "Hold on to me with your good arm." He put her hand behind his neck, and she must have understood because she clung, awakening feelings in him it was hardly the time or place to acknowledge.

Using his feet on the wall, he climbed the rope, straining with their combined weight and his already depleted strength. His muscles burned and shook, bunching and seizing. He wouldn't make it, couldn't . . . The connection between mind and muscle felt severed. His arms knew what to do but wouldn't do it. Come on! Finding a strength beyond his own, he reached the top, pulled them to the tunnel floor, and collapsed, dragging her down with him.

She cried out in pain. "Per piacere, Signore. *Misericordia.* Misericordia, Dio."

Hearing her language come in broken tones tugged his heart with a compassion he hadn't felt before for her. Yet she seemed so small and harmless . . . and soft, tied against him. He smelled her fear, but also her, felt her breath on his neck. His own breath wouldn't come naturally. Clumsily, he fumbled with the rope, the knot easier to make than unmake. At last it came free and he untangled them.

Carina rolled only enough to take her weight from the shoulder, then lay still. He couldn't see, but he guessed she'd fainted. That was probably best. He dragged himself to his feet, then with a resolve that went beyond normal strength, he lifted her into his arms and carried her outside.

Though only the rim of sky just above the mountains glowed azure, it seemed almost bright after the inky tunnel. The rest of the sky had settled into a starry black, mostly clear and moonlit. The storm had passed.

Quillan stood with her in his arms and breathed the night air into his lungs, the clear, pine-scented air. He was keenly aware of all his senses. The night breeze in the pines, the chill of it on his skin. *They shall bear thee up in their hands, lest thou dash thy foot against a stone* . . . The words again. Why?

Why would angels watch out for him when he'd gone out of his way to prove himself anything but angelic? The weariness settled back. Carina DiGratia's insubstantial weight wore him down. He looked into her face, still in the moonlight. Maybe it was for her sake. The silvery light lined her face like a marble statue, only the dark brows and lashes breaking the pallor.

He stood for a moment, lost in the sight. *There is a garden in her face where roses and white lilies grow* . . . Thomas Campion's words at a time like this? He was past exhaustion.

Jock turned his head and nickered, and Quillan carried Carina to the horse. She stayed limp as he lifted her up and mounted behind her. The air was sharply cold on his shirtless back, but he was warm enough where she leaned against him. Too warm, too aware of her. He would get down the gulch as swiftly as possible.

But that proved an impossible task. The mud and debris were more treacherous going down, and in the dark, crazy to attempt. When they reached the Gold Creek mine, he reined in. What was the sense of breaking her neck now, if she hadn't in her fall? He jumped down and took her weight into his arms.

If she knew or cared, she made no sign, only whimpering in pain and muttering words he didn't understand. He carried her into the mine entrance and sat her against the wall. The candles were in his pocket, and with some difficulty he struck a spark that lit one. In the flickering light, he found a storeroom and pushed open the door.

A lantern and a can of kerosene. It sloshed when he shook it. Someone must have used the mine in the last several years, maybe for shelter as they were now. Dropping to his knees, he filled the lamp and lit it. Light jumped into the small enclosure, throwing the walls into rough relief. A pile in the corner might have been a blanket once, but it was rotted and ragged, and there were no others. Whoever had come took anything else useful with them when they left.

He headed back toward the entrance, the light from the lantern swinging up and down the walls as he approached Miss DiGratia. Her eyes were open, watching him approach. Seeing her conscious put an end to his poetic musings. She was clearly in pain. He set the lantern on the rough dirt floor and began to untie the shirt that held her arm.

"What are you doing?"

English, but still he wasn't sure she recognized him. "I need to fix your shoulder. It's out of joint."

She started moaning as soon as the pressure was removed. He worked swiftly, pulling down the canvas jacket so he could see the shoulder where the blouse was torn through. She cried and struggled. Without warning he jerked the arm, and she screamed, then closed her eyes, gasping as the pain subsided.

Easing her from the wall, he pulled the jacket back around her. It was adequate to keep her dry, but not so effective against the cold. At ten thousand feet in the cool of evening, his own wool flannel shirt, which he now put back on was hardly adequate. But between them . . . Well, propriety had no place in survival. He sank down against the wall and pulled her close to his side, careful not to jar her shoulder.

She didn't open her eyes. In her shocked state, the night chill could be enough to finish her off. But with his arm around her neck and his own body heat tight against her, he just might get her through. Her mouth had lost the tight, pinched look of pain, and he knew he'd brought her some ease at least. Her lips were full and slack. *There cherries grow which none may buy, till "Cherry-ripe" themselves do cry . . .*

He allowed himself the moment. After all, he was a man, and she . . . well, only a fool would hold her close and not be moved to poetry. Thankfully he was too bone-tired to act on anything. His eyes closed on their own. His knee throbbed and his leg was shaking again. He'd be stiff in the morning. Morning. He didn't want to think about it. He just wanted to sleep.

Twenty-one

I am lost and despair of being found.

Rose

Carina felt the rhythm of breath, heard its sound in her ear. First, she thought it was Divina as they nestled together in their bed when they were small, sometimes back to back, sometimes arms entwined. But there was something masculine in this breathing, and consciousness seeped in.

Her eyes flickered open to a beard-roughened jaw. Brown hair, dull with mud, lay across the shoulder where her own head rested. She felt his warmth.

In her sleep, she had been thankful for that warmth, clinging to it, absorbing it. To continue so in the first light of morning was *vergognoso*. Disgraceful. Yet she seemed unable to move away, and she realized his arm was around her shoulders, holding her close to him. It was that weight she had struggled with in waking.

His eyes opened. Quillan Shepard's slate gray eyes, blending to a charcoal ring that added definition and depth. The lids were lined with black lashes and the brows had a slight peak before cutting darkly toward his temples. She had never seen his eyes close enough to study their shape and color, and suddenly she realized what she did. He was awake! Her breath caught sharply.

He half smiled. "It can't be much worse than yourself."

What was he saying? Why did he taunt? She didn't understand the innuendoes, the irony. And then she did. She brought a hand to her face, felt the grime, her own matted hair. She looked swiftly around. Where were they?

"No, it's not home." His mouth had a rascal's tilt. He pulled his arm away and scrubbed his face with his palms, then held his head a moment, elbows resting on knees. He groaned a little as he stretched, then pulled himself to his feet. One leg wouldn't bear his weight, and he limped a few steps back and forth, wincing with the effort.

Carina watched him, unsure how she came to be in a mine tunnel with Quillan Shepard. Maybe she dreamed it. Maybe she was in the shaft still, and this was delirium. She pressed into the wall in case the darkness yawned somewhere out of her deluded sight. But if she dreamed, why was it Quillan Shepard her mind conjured?

He stopped pacing and reached a hand to her. She hesitated, not sure she dared take hold. What if it was some demon luring her over the edge? Her head spun at the thought. But the hand remained extended toward her. She reached up, and his grip was firm and real. He raised her to her feet and released her immediately.

"Can you walk?"

She quickly assessed her strength, noticing the earlier unbearable pain in her shoulder was now a dull throb. "How do you think I got here?"

Again the half grin. "How do *you* think you did?"

She looked around, disoriented. Where was she? It wasn't the Rose Legacy. But she had only disconnected thoughts. She touched her shoulder and recalled him pulling the joint into place. She recalled him wrapping her in the jacket, but she didn't recall . . . or did she? A flash of them tied together, of her arm around his neck as he climbed . . . A sense of his arms lifting and carrying her. She flushed with the realization.

"I guess you're determined I haul you no matter what."

That was unfair and she bristled. "I did not ask your help."

He laughed, actually laughed. "No, Miss DiGratia, you just set in to bargain. 'How much to haul this?' " he mimicked. "And waved your arm imperiously as though I were . . ." He shook his head. "It doesn't matter. I'd say we're even now. A square deal." He pointed a finger at her face. "I put your wagon over, but I've pulled you out. Good enough?"

What was he going on about? Either he had hit his head or she had. "You make no sense." She stepped to pass him but caught her boot in her torn skirt and stumbled. He caught her fall, but it jarred her shoulder, and she cried out, gripping the joint.

"Hold on. Let me get you untangled." He stooped and freed the skirt from her boot toe, then held her elbow as she straightened. "Besides your shoulder, are you injured?"

She shook her head. She hurt all over — every muscle stiff and sore, bruises and scrapes, her head throbbing again now that she stood. But she wouldn't say so. It was enough to be out of the shaft and alive.

He eyed her doubtfully a moment, then nodded. "Good. Stay put." He turned and walked out of the mine.

A moment later she heard him hoot. She hurried painfully to the opening and saw him standing under the spring gushing from the rock. The icy water rushed over him, slicking his hair to the back of his neck and muscular shoulders, which he had bared by tossing the shirt onto the pants and boots he had also removed. He stood in nothing but his long johns under the spring, and Carina realized she was staring.

She had never looked on a man while he washed, and she shouldn't look now. But Quillan Shepard was beautiful. His form, his strength, the way the muscles and sinews moved . . . She turned away, staring into the dimness of the tunnel until her heartbeat returned to normal and she heard him huffing through pursed lips as he pulled on his clothes.

"Cold. That's cold."

She stepped back out while he squeezed his hair, then shook it back over his shoulders, an unruly mane, tamed now by the water that dripped from its edges.

"Ready?"

She eyed him dubiously. "For what?"

He motioned to Jock grazing nearby. "To ride down."

She touched her own matted hair. "If you would wait, I might do the same." She motioned toward the spring.

"It's cold. Bone-chilling cold."

Bene. She would not ride in her grubby state with him clean. She held her head straight and walked toward the spring. At its edge, she took off her jacket and paused until he made a show of turning away. Then she bent her head into the rushing water and felt her bones chill.

Quillan watched her sidelong. He couldn't help it. Her hair came loose from the braid and shimmered like a crow's wing in the sunlight as she worked her fingers through it, then turned her face to the spring, fending the water off with her small hands and staunch fortitude.

She was an enigma, in some ways naive and gullible and helpless, yet determined and feisty at the same time. He'd scrapped enough with her to know she didn't back down, yet she'd accepted his help last night with the innocence of a child. Maybe only because she was dazed. She was anything but a child now.

When she stepped out of the spring, she gripped the injured shoulder, and he knew it was as much to cover her wet blouse as to give aid to the painful joint. He reached for the canvas jacket on the ground where she'd discarded it and wrapped it around her shoulders. She pulled it close, looking for all the world as though it was his fault he noticed her form.

What did she think? He was blind? Water ran from the bulk of her hair hanging in front of one shoulder, and she tried to squeeze it one-handed. His unease became impatience. The sooner he had her on the horse the better. "Here." With both hands he caught her hair and twisted. It was thick and springy and resisted him. Wonderful hair.

She stood frozen as he worked the water

from it, but he wasn't sure it was the cold that did it. Well, if she was the protected daughter of some high-ranking don, she'd probably never had her hair squeezed dry by a man. For that matter, it was new to him, though he wouldn't show it. He dropped the dark heavy mass, wishing now he hadn't touched it.

"Thank you." The quaver in her voice matched the feeling in his chest.

This was altogether precarious ground. "Don't you mean to say *grazie?*"

She frowned. "Why should I?"

He pulled off his boot and shook the stone from it. "You were certainly going on in Italian last night."

She raised her chin. "And what did I say?"

He tugged the boot back on. "Well, I don't know. Maybe you were thankful for my efforts in not only finding but extricating you from your predicament." He saw the fire in her eyes. She was too easy, rising to every taunt without reserve.

"Oh *sì, un gross'umo. Così importante.*"

Her defiance intrigued him, and he allowed the grin. "What did you call me?"

"A big man. So important." Her tone was anything but sincere. Again she tugged the jacket close. "I'm ready. You can fetch your horse."

Now he heated. Who did she think she

411

was? But then he saw the drawn look of pain and exhaustion on her face. Compassion stirred, compassion she didn't deserve and he didn't want to feel. If he could feel sorry for her, what else might follow?

The morning light and the icy spring had cleared the poetry from his head. But there were more corporeal instincts at work just now. And those he would not allow. She was the woman who had made more trouble for him than he'd yet seen, he was sure.

Riding down, Carina was painfully aware of the solid chest behind her back, the arms that enclosed her while guiding the halter rein, the breath on the crown of her head. This was closer to Quillan Shepard than she had ever hoped to be. *Ingrata*. Was she not thankful?

She could be lying in the dark shaft with nothing but her thoughts to make her *pazza*. She could be starving, dying of thirst, waiting for someone who would never come. Who would look there? Who but Quillan Shepard?

It was a miracle of God that he found her. But why had he? What had brought him up the gulch? Was he searching for her? Why?

"Here." He dug into his pocket. "This is yours."

She stared at the crucifix he held in his palm and took it reverently. The cross she

412

had worn and lost. It *was* a miracle. "Where did you . . ."

"Outside the Rose Legacy. I was leaving when I saw it."

Oh, Signore. Her breath fled her lungs. He was leaving? The impact of his words struck her, and she shuddered. If he had come there and gone away, who would have looked again? It would have been as she imagined. She winced at the jarring of her shoulder.

"Tuck it up here against you." He pulled her arm across her waist. "Try not to let it swing."

He had noticed her pain. Did he also see the discomfort, the unease she felt with him so near? Was this shaking fear? Did she still think him a monster, the son of an *animale?* He hadn't looked like one. And if he were, why had God let him find her? Why this man and not another? "How did you know where to look for me?"

"You hardly kept your intentions secret." His voice was gruff. "Half the town knows you ride up to Placer. And after your curiosity about Wolf, it was an easy deduction."

She cringed when he said it. Suddenly the whole scene of their last meeting came fresh to her mind, his angry face, his wounded tone. And she deserved it. Her guilt wrapped her like a cloak. "Then why?"

"Mae sent me."

Mae. Why would she go to Quillan? Why

413

not Mr. Beck or Joe Turner or any number of others? Carina could have faced anyone more easily than Quillan Shepard.

He was solid against her back. "Carina, what is it with you and the Rose Legacy?"

She felt her throat tighten at his use of her name, and she realized he had used it last night. She remembered him calling out, and hearing her name in the darkness had brought her out of her dreams. Hearing it now in the daylight, she knew something had changed between them, something she didn't want changed. But how could it not? He had given her back her life.

"At first I thought to hurt you, to learn something to use against you to retaliate for my wagon."

"The tale of Wolf worked well." His tone cut.

She sagged. "I didn't know it was —"

"Well, now you do. And most of Crystal with you. It won't be long before connections are made."

She remembered the faces of the miners, some reliving the tale, most hearing it for the first time. She had made the connection for them, saying it could be no worse than William Evans' murder. Worse or not, it was far too similar.

What would they think? How would it hurt Quillan? *Forgive me,* she wanted to ask, but couldn't. "What can I do?" It sounded self-serving and presumptuous, as though she could undo the wrong. She was learning that a deed done had consequences, no matter how much she might come to regret her action.

He was quiet a long moment. "You can tell me what you know of Berkley Beck's activities."

The answer surprised her. "His work?"

"If that's what you call it."

"I told you already. It's land claims and disputes."

"Not that work."

She half turned in the saddle. "What do you mean?"

His face was stern, unyielding, uncomfortably close and well proportioned. "I mean the other things he does, the forged deeds, the scams, the racket."

"Forged?" Could he mean . . .

He smiled grimly. "That's the irony, isn't it?"

He believed Mr. Beck had forged her deed? "How do you know?"

"I don't for sure. But I suspect, and I'm not the only one. The trouble is, he has the rough element in his pocket. Anyone who tries to speak out meets with an 'accident.' You don't think Norman Crawford fell down his shaft and broke his neck by mistake, do you?"

She shook her head. "Norman Crawford?"

"He had a room at Mae's. I thought you knew."

A quiver ran up her spine. The man who fell and broke his neck, whose bed she'd changed that day with Mae, whose bed Joe Turner now slept in . . .

"He traced a forged deed back to Beck, tried to find justice through the law. When that failed, he spoke out for vigilante action against the roughs. Had to be silenced before the idea caught on."

She didn't want to ask the next question but had to. "And William Evans?"

Quillan's arms tightened as he gripped the halter rope. "I don't think Beck dirtied his own hands."

Her breath was coming in short bursts. "But you think he ordered it?" She recalled Beck's curt words to Carruther and Carruther's immediate response.

"I don't know what's behind Evans' death. If it was meant to send a message to others, then I'd wager long odds Beck's involved."

She trembled. "Why are you telling me this?"

He reined in and turned her to face him. "I'm hoping you'll help me."

Help him? Hadn't Berkley Beck said the same? Which of them spoke truth? Whom could she trust?

"Unless, of course, you still think Beck's the golden boy he pretends to be."

416

She recalled Berkley Beck's hand coiling her hair, his dark innuendoes. "I'm not deceived."

"Then why do you stay with him?" He seemed honestly curious.

She sighed. "I'm waiting."

"For what?"

The words came with difficulty. "For Flavio."

Quillan slid the back of his fingers over the side of his jaw. "The one who doesn't care?"

She dropped her gaze, ashamed to have told so much. Why did she blurt things she didn't admit even to herself whenever Quillan held her with his eyes? "He may still."

"And until then, Beck pays your keep."

He made it sound cheap, dishonest. "He employs me in his office." She flushed.

His laugh came readily. "Don't worry. I mistook you that first time, but I've realized my mistake."

"That first . . ." Her sudden fury burned. "That was why you wouldn't help? Why you sent my wagon . . ."

"I sent your wagon down to clear the road. There was no other way."

The tears that sprang to her eyes angered her, but they seemed to soften him, the lines of his face losing their edge, the brows drawing together.

His voice thickened. "I wish I'd come on

you with an empty wagon." He released her and started Jock again.

She swallowed the tears. It was as close to an apology as she would get. Her shoulder throbbed, sending shards of pain through her arm and down her back. She felt drained and weary but held herself stiffly, so as not to rest against him. Even so, with the motion of the horse they brushed, a constant reminder of his presence. As though she could forget.

He cleared his throat. "About Berkley Beck, will you keep your eyes open?"

"I've seen nothing that —" Jock stumbled and she slipped to the side.

Quillan caught her, his arm tight around her waist, and firmly reseated her. "You best sit tight to me over this rough ground. It's a little late for appearances."

"What do you mean?"

"Never mind. Now about Mr. Beck, I'm just asking you to keep your eyes open. Whom does he see? What do they say? There might be something you missed while having your hand kissed."

"*Omaccio.*"

His laugh deepened. "I don't want to know."

"Cad."

"I guess I deserved that. Seriously, Carina . . . Miss DiGratia . . ."

"It's foolish now to stop." And somehow

she didn't want him to. As Mr. Beck said, calling her Miss DiGratia put such distance between them.

"All right, then, Carina. If you should see or hear anything besides land disputes, those beyond Beck's own devising, will you tell me?"

She considered carefully. Out of fear, she had promised to help Mr. Beck. How was she less fearful now of the man Beck had accused? If what Mr. Beck said was true, she was in the arms of a ruthless killer. But if what Quillan said was true . . . Could she truly play both sides? "*If* there is anything to notice, I'll tell you."

They broke out of the trees, and she realized he had so held her attention that they had reached the gulch floor without her once feeling the dizziness of the steep decline. At the same moment, she caught her breath and stared. Where was Placerville?

Cain sat on the stump outside Mae's, where he'd landed with D.C.'s help, his arm bandaged and his belly full of hot cakes. He raised a hand to Doc Felden as the man jumped down from the door to the ground where Mae's porch used to be.

The doctor adjusted his spectacles after his jump. "How's the arm?"

"Hurts like the dickens. Guess that means I'm still alive."

The doctor smiled and passed by, striding swiftly on to his other charges, going to and fro between the infirmaries with the vigor of a man of younger years. Just like Quillan — always on the move.

And where was Quillan anyhow? Most the town owed him a big thank-you. The minutes he'd given them with his alarm had saved plenty of lives, folks scrambling up the mountain before the flood waters could carry them away.

Cain shook his head. He'd be plucking a harp right now if it weren't for Quillan rushing in and carrying him off like a baby. D.C., too, maybe. Most of the dead had been men tangled up in their tents, unable to break free. Thirty-one mounds had been added to the graveyard, and there were still some missing.

Quillan, for one. Cain frowned. Where'd he gone off to? No one had seen him since the flood, since he'd carried this old bag of bones to the safety and comfort of Mae's bed. And plenty had looked to shake his hand and thanky-kindly if he'd been anywheres around. Of course, it was like Quillan to avoid all that.

Squinting up the gulch, Cain made out a black horse that might be Quillan's Jock or Jack. At that distance he couldn't tell them apart. But he was fairly certain it was one or the other, and it was carrying double —

Quillan and a lady, her long black hair flying out in the breeze like a sail.

"Hee-hee!" Cain cackled. Quillan had snagged himself the DiGratia woman, probably plucked her from some hidey-hole like a hero from the storybooks. And he looked the part, all straight and dour. Was it pleasure or duty that had her in his saddle? Though on second look there was no saddle, and their expressions were a little rough around the edges.

Quillan reined in. "Mornin', Cain. Where's the doctor?"

"Just moseyed down to the hotel infirmary. He'll be back, though. He's flittin' back and forth like a bee what can't choose his poison."

Quillan jumped down from Jock — it was Jock, Cain saw now — and lifted Miss DiGratia down. She stifled a cry, cradling her arm.

"She hurt?" Cain motioned with his own bandaged arm.

"Dislocated shoulder." Quillan steadied her at the elbow and eyed the front door four feet off the ground where the hill had washed away.

"Try the back." Cain grinned. "It's still connected to earth."

Quillan's leg had stiffened, riding down. He tried not to limp as he walked Carina to the back door. He felt awkward already, all too aware of the gleam in Cain's eye and exactly what it meant. And Cain wasn't the only one who had eyed them riding in. Thankfully the disarray of the city would keep most folks minding their own affairs.

And now that he had time to think of it, his affairs would keep him busy, too. Seeing Crystal in the daylight recalled to him his loss. His equipment, his tent, likely his wagon and possibly his team. It would be some time before he was back on the road.

Carina looked stunned and shaken. He guessed not having seen the flood in action, she could hardly fathom the damage in its wake. At the sight of Placer washed away she'd been full of questions and her own descriptions of the wall of water she'd escaped, but seeing Crystal half demolished had left her speechless.

"Let Mae know you need the doctor." He pushed open the door for her. "I'll see you Friday."

She was too tired or too dazed to get his meaning, and she only stared up at him, the brown of her eyes like strong coffee.

"I expect your offer's still good?"

"My offer?" She searched his face.

"Don't want that cheese too blue, do we?"

Her eyes registered cognition and a little alarm. But he couldn't back out now that he was close to getting what he needed. "I'm afraid there might not be apples, though. I doubt I have a wagon left to haul them in."

Turning before she could speak, Quillan left her. Jock needed grain, but whether or not there was grain to be had, he didn't know. And what would he use to pay for it? His savings, his very future, was buried under mud and water or already washed away. He growled a word under his breath. So much for affliction staying away.

He should have known. What sort of fool keeps his savings in a hole? He passed the bank, solid and unscathed, standing as an island amidst the destruction. All of Crystal's residents who had their money there were secure. But he? No, he didn't trust the banks, and with good reason.

Another bitter thought to chew on. His own youthful stupidity. His need to be accepted, a fourteen-year-old's understanding of loyalty, a wild streak run amok. And a pardon that didn't undo the deed. He'd stood before the judge with wide-eyed terror, caught red-handed in a robbery he hadn't known was happening, his "friend" having left him to take the blame.

By some miracle, the judge had seen it for what it was and canceled the warrant, issuing a pardon that resolved him of legal responsibility. Reverend Shepard hadn't been so forgiving. But then it did rather blight his reputation to have his ward in such a spot. So Quillan had left home for good, but not without learning a powerful lesson.

He shook his head. It had been too easy for Shane Dennison to clean out that bank. And since then Quillan had trusted his own means of securing his future. He looked over the swollen creek bed shrinking now innocuously, leaving tons of mud and gravel where the tent city had stood. A new lesson. Nothing was forever.

He blew out a disgusted breath. A rope corral had been stretched alongside the creek and horses gathered into it. As Quillan neared, he searched the herd, hopeful in spite of himself. His eyes brightened. Jack! The first stroke of luck this morning. Now if it just continued.

Carina stood in the doorway where Quillan left her. It was too much, the old buildings of Placerville washed away and half of Crystal as well. What if she had not made it to the mine? The Rose Legacy had saved her.

"Upon my life, I thought you were gone."

Carina spun at Mae's words, looked into the violet eyes unusually deep and moved. Gone. How close she had come to it! Did Mae care? Would anyone have missed her, mourned her? Tears sprang to her eyes, and when Mae spread her arms, Carina rushed to her embrace. Overwhelmed, she buried her face against Mae's neck, ignoring the shooting pain from her shoulder.

Mae rocked her, crooning, "There, there. There, now."

Carina sniffled, warmed and soothed by Mae's voice and arms.

"You're safe now." Mae smoothed her palm over Carina's hair, stroking, stroking. "Did Quillan fetch you down?"

Carina nodded, her face still pressed to Mae's neck. Then she pulled away, the pain in her shoulder finally more than she could stand.

Mae cupped Carina's face. "What is it? Are you injured?"

Carina reached to the throbbing joint. "My shoulder. *Non c'è nulla di grave.*" At Mae's questioning frown, Carina realized she had slipped once again into the language of her youth. What was wrong with her? "There's nothing much the matter. A dislocation only."

"I'll draw you a bath. And we'll have the doctor up directly."

Soaking in the large metal tub filled with warm, scented water, Carina closed her eyes and pictured the spring gushing from the rock and soaking her with its icy force. Though shockingly cold, it had also been invigorating, stripping away the grime and blood and leaving her skin tingling and fresh.

This was different, soothing the aches and dulling her thoughts. She drifted, and it was Flavio at the top of the shaft, his face twisted with fear as he called down to her. *How could you go so far? I can't reach you. Why,* tesora mia, *my darling? Why?* And she had no answer, because every time she tried to speak, his face became Quillan's and she would have to tell the truth.

She jolted awake at the doctor's voice outside the door. Climbing from the bath, she dried herself and dressed. She had only one blouse again, the one she had rescued from the mountain and sewn back together. The one she had fallen in was too badly torn to repair.

She pulled on her blue denim skirt and admitted Mae and the doctor, wincing when he examined her shoulder. She was less stoic when he treated the abrasion with carbolic acid and packed it with alum. She gasped at the terrible stinging burn. *Bruto!* He was too rough, not like Papa's gentle hands.

"Quillan tended this?"

Teeth clenched, she nodded.

"Well, he got it connected again." He snickered.

That was funny? She sent him a dark look.

He laughed a dry, cheeky laugh, as though it started in his mouth and stayed there. Then he rubbed his eyes, which looked puffy and dim, and blew out a slow breath. "We'll sling it for a week to let the tendons heal. Don't put any weight on the arm until the pain stops." As he packed up his medicine bag, she wondered how long he'd been without sleep and how many injuries he'd treated already.

Again it made her think of Papa, coming home so tired sometimes that he walked in his sleep. And Mamma guiding him in and taking his coat and his bag and his hat while he stood like a small boy without raising a hand.

"Thank you," she said, meaning it.

"On to the next one." He gave her a brief smile, then walked out.

Carina lay back on her cot, more fatigued than hurt. "Are there still people missing?"

Mae shrugged, dipping a bucket into the bath and emptying it out the window. "I don't know the latest count. If someone comes up missing, their name gets posted on the board. The trustees send searchers." She dipped the bucket again. "When they're found, they're crossed off and announced alive or dead."

Carina shuddered. "Was my name posted?"

Mae nodded. "And taken off this morning. Didn't you hear the hurrahs?"

Carina lay back smiling. No, she hadn't heard. But she could imagine.

427

Twenty-two

I am become most despised.
Rose

Joe Turner arrived not an hour later with a posy of wild flowers he must have picked above the level of flood damage. "I'm so very glad you're safe, Miss DiGratia. It gave us all a terrible scare."

The Italians brought small food offerings, cheese and pastries baked by wives and mothers, offering encouragement in dialects she had to strain to understand. And miners, slouch hats pressed to their chests, with no offering but their good wishes. Carina was moved to tears.

How could they all care? What could it matter to them that one foolish girl was safe? And then Mr. Beck came. Carina lay now on the sofa in Mae's parlor exactly as she had the other time she'd been nursed back to health. And again she heard Mae through the door. "She won't be working until she's healed, Berkley Beck."

"Of course not, Mae. What do you take me for?"

"And she's had far too many visitors trotting through already. She's resting now, and in dire need of it."

"Only just a moment."

"Come back tomorrow." Mae's tone was unyielding.

"Tomorrow I have other duties."

"So much the better. She's plumb worn out."

"Have a heart, Mae."

Carina felt as though no time had passed. Had she just imagined these last two weeks? Had the flood really happened? Did she truly fall down a shaft and spend the night in the care of Quillan Shepard? The pain in her shoulder and nearly every other part of her body told her it was so.

She sank back into the cushions, thankful Mae was not permitting Mr. Beck. Things were too confused with Mr. Beck telling her to spy on Quillan and Quillan asking her to spy on Berkley Beck. How did she get into the middle, when all she wanted was her dear Flavio to come and take her home?

The thought jarred her. It was what she had told Quillan, but was it what she wanted? If he did come, would she go? Could she be again the innocent, trusting woman in love? She pictured the vine-covered slopes of Sonoma, the sunlight like melting gold, warm on her forehead.

No, it was Mae's palm on her head, and she was in Crystal, Colorado, rescued from the mine shaft by a man as changeable as the mountain weather. Monster or man, he stirred her dangerously. If Flavio would come, it better be soon, before she forgot him altogether.

Carina walked among the men lying on makeshift beds in the hotel restaurant, the tables having been pushed aside and stacked to make room for the injured. The men lay on bedrolls on the floor, as the women and children housed at Mae's were using all the extra cots that could be amassed. Some of the women and children were injured, but many had simply lost their homes.

With her arm immobilized in a sling, Carina was no good for changing bandages or any of the other tasks that required two hands. Instead she carried messages, refilled water glasses, mopped brows, and kept spirits up. It humbled her to see the faces of the men brighten when she stopped beside their beds.

Some of them would touch her hand with gentle reverence when she felt for fever or checked a pulse. All of them thanked her, and she heard it whispered among them that they'd be sure to heal now, as though something in her touch could change their fate. Simple men, dreamers.

And the women. How had Carina misjudged them so? The Italian wives with their black dresses and shawls, their old-world ways and old-world speech. The other women making homes with their men with crude determination, making the most of their loss to keep the light in their children's eyes. It was as though her own blindness had been healed in the darkness of the Rose Legacy mine shaft, and now she saw them for what they were: fellow seekers.

Carina tousled the head of a small boy come to visit his papa, whose legs had been broken in the flood. "What is that you have?"

"A coon." He pulled his shirt open a little more to show her the baby raccoon nestled there. "It's ma died in the flood. I'm showing my pa."

"He'll like that."

"I'm feeding it canned milk."

At thirty-nine cents a can, Carina wasn't sure how much the boy's papa would like that. With one finger Carina petted the scratchy fur of the coon's head, softer to the eye than the touch. She smiled as the boy scurried off.

Crouching low, she felt the fevered brow of an Irishman whose name she didn't know. He'd been found late Thursday morning and had yet to regain his senses. *Per piacere, Signore, heal this man.* She prayed the same for each of them, knowing little or nothing of who they were. Only that it didn't matter.

Èmie came toward her with a tray of fresh bandages and ointments held perfectly level in her unwavering gait. "I'm off to Mae's with Dr. Simms."

Carina looked behind her to the young doctor who had come to Crystal to prospect but found himself needed now in his first profession. His overlarge ears and slightly bulbous nose did not enhance a stern bedside manner, but that wasn't his way regardless.

He gave her an awkward smile. "Doc Felden said not to overdo it. You'll need rest to heal that shoulder."

Carina nodded. It was true her body needed rest. She felt every movement in a dozen places. But it could have been worse, far worse. And she felt obligated to repay the debt. God had saved her, and she had promised what? Anything.

Some of that time in the darkness of the shaft was a blur. But she recalled her desperate plea. She had begged and bargained with God. He had done His part. She reached up and touched the crucifix that hung at her throat on a new chain, given to her by Joe Turner. The cross reminded her of Quillan's words. He had been leaving. God had turned him back, sent him inside to search for her. Yes, God had done His part. Now she must do hers.

"Carina."

She looked up to Father Charboneau and flushed. He must know her burden. Was it not so with him as well? God had stretched out His hand in both their lives. The priest repaid it daily.

"Are you feeling all right? Èmie's worried you're pushing too hard with your own injuries not healed." He smiled. "She sent me down to badger you into resting."

"I'm fine, Father," Carina stated, though she ached badly.

"You look as though you need some air. Will you walk with me?"

She stood slowly. The sunshine would feel good. She followed him out and blinked in the brightness. She wouldn't take the sun for granted again, not after the black skies full of hail and rain. Though clouds built now in the west, they were fluffy and white with no menace in them, only playful frivolity.

They started toward the creek, where salvaging work was well under way — small piles of undamaged goods, larger piles of slightly damaged, and then parts and pieces, the largest piles of all. They passed a group of men hauling a freight wagon upright from the water, where it had been towed upstream.

She recognized Quillan among them and dropped her gaze before he saw her. Too many feelings were conjured when their eyes met. And she was nervous already knowing he was coming for supper. Why had she ever offered such a thing?

The priest saw Quillan also but made no greeting. Instead, he drew a long breath and released it as they passed, then turned to her. "You've been asking about Wolf." The priest's face grew stern, and she quailed inside.

"I did ask, but —"

"You've awakened suppositions that were better left forgotten. Especially on the heels of this week's violence."

She knew it was true. Even with the flood, William Evans was not far from the miners' minds, and the tale of Wolf had become interwoven in their mutterings. She dropped her gaze.

"You're meddling in things you don't understand."

Carina shook her head. "I'm not asking anymore. I don't want to know."

"It's too late for that." Taking her arm, he led her to the shade of a bench beside a partially erected building. Yesterday it hadn't been there. Thanks to man's industry, today its wall kept the sun from burning down on them. Father Charboneau seated her, then motioned to the bench at her side. "May I?"

"Of course." She nodded, though she wished he would walk away and leave her.

"What you heard was not the whole story. I'm going to tell you another, and you can judge between them. Wolf's story. He gave it to me one night on the mountain in the dark. I say gave, because it took so much for him to share it. To my knowledge he told no one but me."

The priest's eyes found hers a moment, held them captive, then released her. "I recall him sitting under the stars, the firelight playing on his face as he spoke of a small boy traveling with his parents and baby sister. Two other wagons were in the train, none of them experienced, but all determined to better themselves in Oregon, the great land of plenty."

Carina pictured the two men sitting by the fire on the mountain under the night sky, Wolf with his mane of golden hair, Father Charboneau unremarkable except for his vigor.

"For a boy of five years, such a journey is a magical adventure, something new every mile. But it's also grueling and long, especially for the women and the young. One night as they camped along the river, the baby began to cry. Perhaps it was colic, perhaps something else. She wouldn't be soothed."

Carina swallowed the tightness in her throat, hearing again the old prospector's voice. *That baby started in to cry. And then*

Wolf, see, he started a-howlin', the fiercest, loneliest howlin' ever heard."

"Wolf, though that wasn't his name at the time, had crept some distance from the wagon to find a bush and take care of nature. But he heard his father scolding in a low, harsh voice. 'Quiet that baby, Judith, before she brings God's wrath upon us.' "

Carina shivered, though the sun was hot. Without knowing why, she dreaded the next words the priest would speak.

"Wolf never returned to the wagon. A Pawnee raiding party swooped in upon them in the darkness, and, though I won't give you the details, which he described with agonizing recall, the deeds done that night were something no child should behold. The horror of it would turn a strong man's mind."

Father Charboneau groaned. "Think, Carina, what such a scene would do to the innocence of a child. As Wolf watched, his family was destroyed. Not a life was spared, not even the baby, whose cries had betrayed their position."

Looking down, Father Charboneau raised his brows and sighed. "When a party of Sioux found Wolf two days later, he was sitting on the ground beside the burned out wagons, howling in fear and hunger. They named him Cries Like a Wolf."

Father Charboneau stood, linked his fingers together, and hung his hands. "Wolf showed me the scars he bore for being a white slave among the people. I'll keep the memory of them always, though I don't doubt the scars in his mind were more brutal."

Here the priest fixed her with his blue eyes. "But he was a gentle man, a deep and compassionate man. He wanted no part in violence, only to live in peace." He eyed her a long moment, then spoke very low. "I don't believe Wolf killed that miner. He was no animal. He was the most humane man I've ever met. It wasn't in him to kill."

Hearing the priest, Carina believed it. Wolf was not the monster the miner had described. He couldn't be. Nor was he the savage Quillan thought him, or Rose would not have loved him. And somehow, Carina was certain she had. Father Charboneau stood a long moment, and Carina thought he would say more. But then he turned and walked away.

Carina closed her eyes, picturing the child Cries Like a Wolf. A child who became a man but carried in him the fear and heartbreak that howled when his own son cried. And that son was Quillan. She knew now what Mae and Father Charboneau had meant. Leave it alone.

"Carina. Thank goodness you're well."

Startled, she opened her eyes to Berkley

437

Beck. She hadn't spoken with him since before the flood. He had not come back after Mae sent him away Wednesday evening. He was too busy restoring Crystal. A man of importance and duty. And what else?

He reached a hand to her. "I looked for you at Mae's, but she said you were helping with the injured. At the hotel they told me you'd gone out with the priest."

Reluctantly, she took his hand and stood, trying unsuccessfully to retrieve her fingers.

He tucked them into the crook of his arm and held her to his side. "I'm thankful to find you alone at last. And I must say I'm dismayed by your injury."

"Others are much worse."

"Yes." He sighed. "It was a grisly business finding the wounded and less fortunate. You can't imagine my concern when your name was added to the list of missing." He led her back along the creek.

From the corner of her eye, Carina saw Quillan examining the wagon. It must be his own, though the tongue was gone and the wheels demolished. The irony was not lost on her, though she took no pleasure in it. He glanced over only briefly as they passed, but Mr. Beck noticed.

"It was Quillan who found you, wasn't it?"

Her pulse jumped at the accusation in his tone. Did Mr. Beck suspect the pact she had made with Quillan Shepard?

"Mae sent him to look." She sounded defensive, insecure. She was not skilled in deception.

Yet he visibly relaxed. "Mae? Well, that explains it. She was concerned when I told her you rode out. I thought you must be somewhere near." He stopped and covered the fingers he held in his arm with his other palm. "I would have dropped everything and searched for you, had I known."

Would you? Carina met his eyes and saw through his earnest façade. If there were true concern for her, it was second to what he felt for himself. His honeyed words failed to convince.

"And if I'd known she meant to send Quillan Shepard, I would have stopped her."

That she believed. "Then I would be in the mine shaft still."

He looked startled by the thought. "I only meant it must have been terrifying for you to be alone . . . with someone capable of atrocities."

"It was terrifying to be alone."

"Yes, of course." His tone chilled.

She waved her hand. "And we have no proof of atrocities." What gave her the boldness to speak so?

Berkley Beck frowned. "No. But it's come to my attention that William Evans was a customer in the bank Quillan Shepard robbed."

439

Carina stopped short. "He robbed a bank?"

"He and a partner, Shane Dennison. I saw the warrants myself." He paused. "I believe Evans was holding it over him."

Blackmail. That was a motive. And the method of Evans' death . . . Carina looked away. It was *ridicolo*. What could she believe?

"You're tired."

"Yes." Let him think that.

"I'll see you back to Mae's."

"Thank you." She walked beside him in silence, reluctant to face the evening that would come. Was she choosing the wrong side? Was Quillan Shepard not the more likely of the two to be involved in foul play? How could she know? And why had she ever gotten involved?

Quillan watched Carina pass by with Beck. She looked especially small next to Beck's lanky height, her arm tucked close to his side. An intimate stroll, their heads turning in conversation. He'd caught only a glimpse from her, but she didn't look put out by Beck's attention.

He frowned. Why should that bother him? He had more important concerns. Yet the annoyance wouldn't pass. He rested his hands on the wagon. It had been a trying day until he'd located his freight wagon,

440

battered to be sure, but salvageable. Better than Carina's had been.

He frowned again. What had that to do with anything? Why did every thought have to come back to her? He'd spent a restless night under the stars in a canvas bedroll, and his dreams had wrapped around her again and again. It was time to get his head back to business.

Once he got the wagon repaired, he would hardly be able to make the trips for supplies fast enough to satisfy the demands. There would be more business than he and the others could handle, which would jack the prices. And that was good, as he had much to recover. He scowled at the muddy ground where his tent had stood.

If he could figure exactly where, he'd dig like a miner for his stash. But that was ridiculous, of course. Likely his savings were washed down the gulch and on their way to Mexico. And then he realized many others were in that same position. The ones who needed the most would have nothing to pay for it. He sighed. Well, it couldn't be helped. He'd have to wait for profit.

He stretched his back and thanked the men who had helped haul the wagon. The afternoon sun was overly warm and he needed a drink. Rubbing a hand over his face, he made for the nearest pump and worked the lever until water gushed. He splashed his face and neck, then cupped his hands and drank.

Looking up, he saw Alan Tavish beside him. The salvage of livery parts and pieces had kept Alan and those helping him busy. Quillan had worked with a fervor to recover everything he could for Alan, and he'd help raise the walls again when the salvage was completed. A livery was necessary to his business. And Alan was a good friend.

"Aye, and it's yer own wagon ye've trundled up this time."

"A little the worse for wear."

"But not beyond repair."

"No." Quillan took off his hat and shook back his hair. "Though where I'll find a wagon tongue . . ."

"Find you a straight, strong pine, lad."

Quillan laughed. "It may come to that." He shook his head, looking over the landscape. The mud was cracked and turning to dust. Everywhere were heaps of rubble, some left by the flood, others gathered and deposited purposely.

But Crystal would survive. There was an air of determination, and men worked together today who had been at rifle point over a claim dispute before the flood. Nothing like catastrophe to draw a town together, he thought. Then Alan ruined it.

"Don't know that ye've heard, but there's ugly talk about."

Quillan turned. "What ugly talk?"

"Concernin' yerself."

Quillan formed his features into nonchalance. "Something I should care about?"

"Hearkenin' can't hurt."

"Let's have it, then."

Alan rubbed his left shoulder joint. "Concernin' the manner of Will's death, some are drawin' the string to that other. There's some as think ye've kept overmuch to yerself."

"So?"

" 'Tis queer to some ye won't drink and wench. 'Tis queerer ye don't play the cards. But the worst of it is their knowin' ye're Wolf's own son."

Quillan frowned. "I guess it was bound to come to light."

"There's some sayin' right out ye should be strung up before the madness takes ye again."

Quillan's throat tightened more with anger than fear. "We know which ones they are."

"Aye."

"What do you think?"

"T'wouldn't hurt to bide awhile somewhere . . ."

"Hide, you mean?"

"Nay. But once yer wagon . . ."

"Once my wagon is operational, I'll be hauling supplies badly needed. Half of

443

Crystal is without necessities. By the way, how's the boy?"

Alan smiled. "Springin' back with all the grace of youth." He was clearly relieved his stableboy had suffered no worse than bruises and a few cuts. Quillan's warning had given him time to drop the shovel and help release the horses. Then Alan had lost him when the water hit, fearing for his recovery.

"Quillan . . ." Alan gripped his forearm.

Quillan laid a hand over Alan's. "Don't worry for me, my friend. Just keep your ears open."

Alan's throat worked, then he nodded. "Aye."

"Daddy, you're not goin' to believe this."

From his perch on Mae's newly erected porch, Cain gazed up to his son. "What is it, boy? Cuz I'd believe about anything after Tuesday."

D.C. straddled a stool across from him and shook the hair from his eyes. "Your mine — the Boundless? The tunnel's all closed up, filled in, and covered over." The boy sounded halfway jubilant.

"That ain't remarkable, seein's we just had a flood," Cain said flippantly. "I'll dig it out again."

"That's just it, Daddy. Remember I told you there's no ore worth beans in there?"

"That's what you say, but —"

"Listen to me, Daddy. I'm telling you, just alongside it there's a patch of ground opened up that looks to me like silver bearing lead ore with gold leaf." D.C. held out a chunk of black rock that brought Cain's heart to his throat.

The old thrumming he'd felt once before just from raising a pan of nuggets from a creek spilled through him and softened his throat. "Is it on my claim?"

D.C. nodded. "It sure is."

Cain felt the grin take over his face. *Oh, Lord Jehovah, in the midst of this devastation, you have seen fit to multiply my loaves. Let it be enough to keep my boy beside me in my failing years. And Quillan, too, if it ain't askin' too much.* "Son, you just run along and show that rock to Quillan."

From his stump, Cain watched his son skip down the hill toward the creek. He knew well enough the look he'd seen in D.C.'s eyes. Some might call it greed. Cain called it hope.

Twenty-three

My heart is a blind guide. Why did I
follow?

Rose

Carina glanced up when Èmie plopped
down at the kitchen table. The look on
Èmie's face was a curious blend of desperation and boredom, but Carina didn't ask.
She had learned that Èmie was more forth-
coming when she could do so in her own
time.

Èmie stuck out her lower lip and blew the
breath up her face to the damp hair on her
forehead. "I'm worn out. Working the baths
was tedious, but at least I didn't have to talk
from sunup to sundown. If I say another
word I'll scream."

Carina measured out the flour and salt
into Mae's yellow crockery bowl. "Talk is
good. Language is what separates us from
the animals. My papa used to tell me so
when we studied English together. He said
we must communicate to rise above the
dumb creatures."

Èmie sighed. "Right now I envy the dumb
creatures."

One-handed, Carina cracked an egg into

the well she'd made in the flour. "The injured men don't know what to do with themselves. They can't work and they can't drink or gamble." She waved the eggshells. "They must talk."

Èmie looked at her sidelong. "You seem . . . different."

Carina raised the bottle of olive oil. "How different?"

"I don't know. More . . . accepting. I saw you this morning with the Italian women. The way you held the old grandmother whose son was lost — it just didn't seem like you."

Carina frowned. It hurt to hear it. Was she so *trista,* so wicked, a simple act of kindness was a thing to notice and remember? Had she been so self-important? So wrapped up in her own woes she closed her heart to others?

That had never been her way. Always she was the one to tend the injured bird, the scraped knee of a small cousin, the wounded pride of one or another of her brothers. Papa had named her his *infermiera* and called for her help with his more difficult patients. She could soothe them when others failed and calm the despairing with a gentle touch, a soft word.

Yet here was Èmie holding the glass to her face. She had come to Crystal with her eyes darkened, full of her own heartache and the anger that went with it. It had shown as haughtiness and disdain.

Èmie touched her hand. "I'm sorry. I didn't mean to upset you."

Carina drizzled the oil into the well with the egg, a dessert spoon's worth, only she couldn't measure it properly with her arm in the sling. "You haven't. You spoke the truth. In Italy the lines are drawn more sharply. My papa is a landlord, and they are peasants. Here in America, I sometimes forget things are different. We are all pilgrims."

Èmie smiled, her teeth slightly protruding. "I like the way you talk. It's kind of poetic."

"I'm not poetic. Flavio told me too many times I lack the tortured spirit."

"Flavio? Is he one of your brothers?"

Carina blanched. She did not want to discuss him with Èmie. She had already bared too much to Quillan Shepard. She waved a hand. "He is my cousin." *Distant cousin, and only love.*

She thought of the photograph of him hidden away in the black satchel under the cot. The photograph and his letters, filled with true poetry and beautiful pictures drawn by him, freehand. Pictures and letters and one thing more. She closed her eyes. What if it had been washed away in the flood?

Carina reined in her thoughts. It was foolish to imagine she would need it, foolish to have brought it at all. And what were the letters and pictures but torment? She was spurned. What did she want with reminders? She poured hot water into the dough and worked it with her fingertips into a ball, then tipped it onto the floured board. How would she knead it with only one hand?

She looked up at Èmie. "Come. You wanted to learn. Wash your hands, and I'll teach you to make pasta that will win the heart of any man."

Èmie flushed, then stood and scoured her hands. Carina laughed when minutes later Èmie's hands were thick with dough, the weariness gone from her as they chattered and worked elbow to elbow. Carina instructed as Mamma had instructed her, as Nonna had instructed Mamma and so on for generations back.

Together they made a meal fit for the king of Sardinia himself. How Papa would have praised her efforts as her brothers fought for the choicest servings. How Mamma would have swelled with pride to see her daughter performing the duties she would need as a wife. And how Flavio would have taken it for granted that she had done it for him.

Beh! She had not done it for Flavio. She and Èmie had labored to please the palate of a man to whom she owed her life. A man she scarcely knew and more than a little feared. Yet it mattered in a way it shouldn't, and Carina's stomach fluttered with anxiety. To cook for Quillan Shepard. Whatever had possessed her?

In the gloaming, Quillan examined the rock D.C. had brought him. He'd hauled enough ore to know it was promising, the silver rich, the gold leaf visible even without crushing. "Well, Daniel Cain, how do you feel about mining now?"

D.C. grinned. "I guess it's not so bad."

"Not as great as freighting, though." Quillan patted the box of his wagon, which was now upright across two poles beside the creek.

D.C. grimaced. "Freighting's hard on the backside."

Quillan wrapped an arm over his shoulder. "You know, D.C., there's no perfect world. You have to take the bad with the good. It makes you a man." Even though there was a whole lot more bad than good.

"This . . ." D.C. held up the ore. "Is gonna make me a man."

"Maybe. But remember what happened last time. There's always someone bigger, someone tougher. Don't rest your happiness on something you can lose."

D.C. nodded slowly. "Like your tent and Daddy's."

"I wish it were only my tent." The loss of his cache had been eating him all day. Stupid thoughts like wondering how much had been in there and trying to figure it without having ever counted. And thinking maybe he ought to dig out around the area where he thought his tent had been, just to see if maybe . . .

"You got your wagon back." D.C. patted the wooden side.

Quillan smiled grimly. "In a manner of speaking."

"Aw, you can fix it up. And we can use it to haul the ore to the smelter. We won't have to pay freight, and that'll be so much profit."

Quillan yanked a splintered axle loose and laid it in the mud. "By 'we,' I presume you think I'll be working the mine with you."

"Sure. Now you see what we've got. You're half owner."

Quillan straightened. "As I told your daddy, I'm not working the mine. It's an investment only. I'll haul your ore, but you'll have to hire on some men to work the mine. From the looks of it you'll need an engineer and a manager and a crew."

"But why won't you —"

"Don't you know when to let it go?"

The boy shrugged. "I just expected you'd

jump in. Not a man in Crystal wouldn't be shouting the news if he'd found ore like this lyin' on the surface."

"Well, I suggest you keep it to yourself, or the roughs might strip that surface for you as neatly as they stripped your daddy's money from your pocket."

D.C. frowned. "Aren't you ever goin' to let me live that down?"

"Soon as you demonstrate what you've learned from it."

"Quillan?"

Quillan leaned an elbow on the wagon side.

"I'm gonna make my daddy proud."

Quillan looked at the earnest eyes, pale as Cain's, though lacking the old man's wit and wisdom. Maybe the boy wasn't hopeless after all. "You do that, D.C."

Watching him walk away, Quillan wished it had been so easy for him. Cain's sun rose and set on D.C. No matter how many times the kid messed up, Cain was there to shake him off. Not a bad thing, family.

He remembered Reverend Shepard showing him how to milk the cow, placing his hands on the udders, then covering them with his own and making the motion, squeeze and tug, squeeze and tug. Quillan remembered the thrill he felt when the milk squirted out, a sharp *fft, ftt* and the brief touch of his foster father's palm on his head. If only it could have all been like that.

★ ★ ★

With the eye of a mother for a newborn child, Carina eyed the cannelloni Mae removed from the oven. She had not meant this project to involve Mae and Èmie, but with her arm in the sling, she could not have done it alone. Now, breathing the aroma of the cannelloni stuffed with stewed beef, which Mae had provided but Carina minced and seasoned with parmigiano cheese, egg, and nutmeg, she felt the pleasure rise up again.

Mae thumped the pan unceremoniously onto the stovetop and closed the heavy oven door. "Well, there it is, and a lot of work to be put into someone's stomach."

"But worth it for the pleasure it gives the mouth." Carina smiled, feeling proud and thankful.

Mae rubbed her forehead with the back of her hand and laughed. "Can't say I'm not eager to try it. Only I have to finish shoveling out for the men first. And now all these women and children, too. I'll just be glad when they're all back where they belong." She bustled back to the dining room with a third pot of stewed beef that included carrots and potatoes this time.

Èmie had already left to prepare her uncle's meal, and Carina stood alone in the kitchen, hoping Quillan would come soon while the pasta was hot and al dente. Then she hoped he would forget altogether. But the knock on the kitchen door dashed that hope. She felt as flustered and self-conscious as a goose. What was she doing?

She threw up her free hand as he knocked again. "Yes, I'm coming." She pulled open the door.

Quillan stood there with a jar in one hand and the thumb of the other hooked into his suspender. He held out the jar. "It was the best I could do. Caramelized apples. Mrs. Barton's from last season."

He was hatless and his hair was tied back, showing the darker hair at his temples and neck. He had trimmed the length of the mustache, though it was still full. His lip had a good line, and she realized she was doing it again, staring at Quillan Shepard.

"Oh." She reached for the jar. "They'll do."

The side of his mouth quirked slightly. "May I come in?"

"Sì. Yes." She was acting a fool. "Have you washed?" What was that to ask a man?

"Yes, ma'am." Now the rascal's tilt was back in his smile.

"I only meant the food is hot and ready." She motioned to the table, wishing Èmie had stayed when she begged her. But Uncle Henri must be fed.

"If you'll sit . . ." Carina swept up his plate, then realized she couldn't hold it and

454

serve the cannelloni both. Dr. Felden had ordered her not to put any weight on the shoulder until it stopped aching.

"Why don't I hold that while you serve?" Quillan was at her side, taking the heavy crockery plate.

Bene. She was pazza to be in this position at all. He held the plate while she scooped the steaming cannelloni al gratin. Then he took another plate from the stack, and she saw he meant for her to eat with him. She hadn't thought to share the meal. Where was Mae?

Carina scooped a second fat cannelloni onto the plate and watched him set them on the table. Then she reached for the long loaf of crusty white bread and laid it on the cutting board with the knife. Now there was nothing else but to sit down across from him.

"Do you have any of that oil and . . . green stuff you put on the bread for the picnic?"

Carina had to smile. "Olive oil, salt, and basil." She set the items one at a time on the table.

Quillan sat down and eyed his plate. "I think I could get full just smelling this."

"Your stomach would not agree."

"My stomach rarely has much say over what goes into my mouth." He sliced the bread and held out a piece.

455

She drizzled oil over it. "Now take a pinch of basil from the jar and crush it between your fingers over the bread."

He did as she instructed, then salted it lightly. "Miss DiGratia, I can't say when I've anticipated the first bite of any meal the way I am this one."

She looked to see if he was teasing, but he had a way of masking his intentions unless he wanted them known. "Then try the cannelloni first."

"Cannelloni?"

"The pasta. Rolled and stuffed that way, it's cannelloni."

Quillan cut the cannelloni with his fork, took a bite, and let it tantalize his mouth as a true Italian would. The pain in her chest as she waited showed Carina just how much his opinion mattered.

He swallowed just as Mae came in with an empty stew pot. "Well, well, Quillan. If the others knew what you were getting in here, they'd revolt. They all keep saying something smells different, then looking down at their plates with the sorriest faces you ever saw."

Mae's entrance had interrupted Carina's observation of Quillan's first impression. But he spoke with closed eyes. "If they knew what I had here, they'd forget all about gold and silver."

Carina's breath caught. It was a beautiful

compliment, something Papa might have said. Or Flavio.

His eyes opened. "But they hadn't the good fortune of hauling in the supplies . . . gratis, I might add."

Taunting. She knew him better now. He might trim the jaunty mustache and put on a clean shirt, but he was still the man she met on the wagon road.

"Well, I may as well see what all the fuss is about." Mae slogged a cannelloni onto her plate and sat down at the table. "Hand me a slice of that bread, will you, Quillan?"

Carina almost laughed. Mae might have been one of the men, so coarse were her manners, but Carina blessed her now for easing the situation. She tasted her own serving and found it quite satisfactory. It brought to mind the first time she'd made cannelloni, and without thinking she told them the tale.

"It was my papa's forty-fifth birthday and I was eight. Nonna had already cooked the meat, but I diced it and crushed the bread crumbs and grated the cheese. Then I added the nutmeg. The recipe read one quarter teaspoon, but a drop of oil had marred the one and all I saw was the four. So I added four teaspoons of nutmeg." Carina sipped her tea.

"I watched for Papa's first taste, knowing he would praise me well. And he did, though his expression didn't seem to match the words. My brother Tony started choking, grabbing his throat and making a big play of it. I tasted it myself, certain it would be as wonderful as it looked."

She waved her hand. "It was not. Mama told Tony to eat it. She said it was a different recipe, a little more on the nutmeg. Lorenzo claimed he liked it better, but I saw him forcing it down with wine."

Carina dropped her gaze to her plate. "I'm ashamed to say that when my sister, Divina, laughed, I ran from the table in tears." She took up her fork and cut into the tender, perfectly seasoned cannelloni on her plate.

"Well, honey, this might bring tears, but not through any fault of yours." Mae patted Carina's slinged arm with her warm palm. "It's the best thing I ever tasted."

Carina smiled and glimpsed Quillan through her lashes.

His gray eyes were studiously on her as he held a bite aloft. Then he took it without speaking and continued until his plate was finished. "I don't suppose there's more?"

It was impossible not to feel pride as she filled his plate a second time. But after all, hospitality was a virtue, one of the highest in Mamma's esteem. Carina told them of the wondrous foods her Mamma prepared, how she herself learned at Mamma's hand.

She spoke of the long, sweaty days in the kitchen filled with laughter and stories.

It was a woman's world that a man penetrated at his own risk. And, laughing, she told of Mamma's spoon smacking Papa's knuckles when he snuck in and tried to sample the wares. None of her brothers but Tony ever followed that example, and Tony was close enough to Carina's age that she sometimes stole him a nibble or two.

Her words brought her family so close she ached for them to walk through the door and see for themselves . . . see what? What would they see? What would they think of her, sitting at the board table with Mae and Quillan Shepard? They suddenly seemed far away.

When Quillan had finished his second portion, Carina cleared that plate away and served dessert. The caramelized apples and blue cheese were a stark contrast, but pleasing to the palate after the rich cannelloni. "Take only a small piece into your mouth," she instructed Quillan when he looked dubiously at the cheese. "It's flavor is strong."

"I don't doubt that." He tasted it, moving it around between his tongue and the roof of his mouth.

Carina waited.

He met her eyes. "It's different than any cheese I've had before, but . . . I like it."

"Now a bite of the apples, then the cheese again. All we lack is the Chianti." Carina felt a glow she'd not felt since arriving at Crystal. It was almost like dining with family, the warm camaraderie and laughter, Quillan telling tales of his own food mishaps, Mae's wonderful laugh filling Carina's heart. Good food, good friends. What more could she want?

And then she caught Quillan's eyes, saw in them the smoldering warmth, and she felt her stomach liquefy. What was this feeling inside her? *Innocente!* She knew the feeling, but it had no business being there.

Quillan hadn't expected to enjoy the evening so much. He wasn't sure what he'd anticipated, but a motherly Mae and a dazzling Carina DiGratia . . . He wasn't sure what to do with that. He'd hoped to work her closer to solidifying the tentative agreement they'd made on the mountain.

He hadn't thought to find her so real. He didn't want to know her talents, her mistakes, her family, her laugh. He didn't want see her as a real person. He needed her, and intrinsic in that need was risk, even danger. If he was right about Beck . . . But there was no "if." He knew. And the man must be stopped.

Yet here was Carina, making him see, making him care. In the same way he'd held

460

her on the mountain to keep her warm, safe, protected, he now discovered something inside that wanted to continue that role. Listening to her talk, to her laugh — it gave him a warmth, a depth he hadn't tapped in years, if ever. He almost felt that he belonged.

Mae pushed up from the table. "Well, I'm not long for this night. These old bones need their sleep even if your young ones don't."

Carina started to rise also, but Quillan caught her hand. "Sit a moment." He didn't want it to end, but that wasn't why he held her back. He would convince himself of that later, that he only needed to complete what he'd started when they rode down from the mine. It wasn't just for himself. It was for all of Crystal. Carina included.

She sat, but she looked again as she had when he first came to the door, afraid to be alone with him. Did she think him such a scoundrel?

"Good night." Mae sashayed to the doorway and fixed him with a look as clear as any warning. "I'm just next door."

Did she think he'd make a play for Carina right there in her kitchen? His chest gave an unfamiliar lurch. And why not? He was alone with a beautiful, enchanting . . . He forced the thoughts away. He was as redblooded as the next man, and those thoughts would only get him into trouble. Besides, Carina DiGratia was only waiting to be claimed by the one she loved before, loved still. It had been obvious when she spoke of her Flavio.

A surge of jealous anger caught him by surprise, and he felt Carina startle in his grip. His thoughts had shown and frightened her. He let go her hand, but she didn't fly. Instead she sat looking at him with those large, expressive dark eyes. How long they sat, learning each other by sight, he didn't know. But he realized one of them had to say something.

"Thank you for supper. If I'd known it would be so good, I'd have come before Friday."

"If you'd come before Friday you'd have had stewed beef."

They laughed. It felt good and natural to laugh with her, and that surprised him. He'd imagined a number of scenarios for tonight, but none the way it had been. None half so pleasant, and none that made him feel so perilously close to her. Now it was time to return to business. Quillan pushed back his bench a little, then crossed his arms on the table. "You're going back to work soon?"

She seemed to close in. It couldn't be a pleasant thought, spending all those hours with Berkley Beck. But maybe it was something more; maybe she'd changed her mind. Maybe she wanted no part of his plans, his plotting. Then she raised her eyes to his, and they were full of emotion, even concern. "I must warn you, he's suspicious. Especially since you found me after the flood."

Did he imagine the flush that came to her cheeks? She was grateful certainly, and with reason. She would have died in the shaft of the Rose Legacy. He had saved her life, and it brought a fresh rush to his system to think of it. "Does he know about the Rose Legacy?"

Carina shrugged, then winced at the pain. She held the injured joint. "Does it matter?"

"It might."

She considered that, then shook her head. "I don't know. He knew . . . that is, he told me to ask about Wolf."

Quillan restrained the anger that memory conjured, anger at her and now fresh anger at Beck's bidding it. "Why?"

"I told you before, he suspects you're behind the violence in Crystal. He said a man who . . ."

Quillan saw the sudden caution in her eyes. "A man who what?"

Her voice came on a rush of breath. "Who robs a bank . . ."

He pushed back from the table, hanging his head back and studying the corner of the ceiling, tongue caught between side teeth.

His anger toward Beck reached new bounds, and he fought to contain it. "Who else knows?"

"Then it's true?" The pulse throbbed in the hollow of her throat.

"I was fourteen. I was taken in by a friend." *Desperate to be accepted, needing to prove myself, wanting to be a man.* "I was duped, and the charges against me were dropped, the crime pardoned, the warrant rescinded. I did not rob the bank." *But I did learn to trust no one but myself.*

He saw her eyes deepen, almost as though she looked inside him, saw his unspoken thoughts, his shame. He bristled. "If you think I'm guilty, why are you helping me? Or have you changed your mind about that?"

She shook her head. A strand of black satiny hair fell across her injured shoulder. He remembered squeezing the water from it, remembered it springing to life in his hands, remembered her lips shivering and her hands fending off the water. He remembered her nestled against him, and the need he felt to keep her warm. Why hadn't they stayed up there on the mountain, in the mine, just the two of them? The thought caught him short. It was too much like Wolf and Rose.

He turned and studied the night-blackened window. So Beck had one more piece against him, but how? "How did Beck find out about the bank?"

Carina shook her head. "He left town and came back knowing. He said he saw the warrant."

"Then he must have known it was canceled."

"If he knows, he's not saying. He said William Evans recognized you. That he knew about the robbery and made you pay to keep him quiet."

Quillan smiled wryly. "He wouldn't get much these days." But that didn't matter. The story was plausible enough to provide motive to a death that shook the town. Add to that the nature of the killing and the relationship of Quillan Shepard to the infamous Wolf, villainous killer and madman. It made sense. Perfect sense.

Who wouldn't connect the two in the superstitious way of miners? Like father, like son. He should clear out as Alan said. It was obvious Beck could garner more support for his arguments than any Quillan could raise.

"What are you going to do?"

Her question was his own. "I need to know more. Beck's obviously done his work on me." He saw her flinch, remembered her throwing Wolf and his own disreputable birth in his face. Had she given Beck the information? Was she even now working to trip him up, to learn more to use against him?

The thought sent cold steel through him. He could well believe her duplicity. She was a woman. But the look on her face was concerned and earnest. And she was still his best hope. "In his papers, his ledger, was there anything . . ."

"I told you. Nothing but land disputes."

"There must be more."

"I've filed everything in the office. All the papers. I regularly balance his ledger. There's nothing —"

"It might not be obvious."

Carina waved her hand, frustrated. "Unless it's in his rooms — and I'm not searching there."

"I'm not asking you to. Only there must be something somewhere." He jammed his fingers into his hair. How could he refute the case Beck was building against him without any proof to substantiate his own claims against Beck?

She suddenly paused as though a thought had caught her. "There is something. When I brought Nonna's silver back from the hillside, I gave it to him for safe-keeping."

Leaning forward, Quillan anticipated her words. "Where did he put it?"

She shook her head. "He didn't want to say."

"Then you have two reasons for searching."

She waved her hand. "I need only ask for my silver."

"I wouldn't be so sure."

Carina turned away, shaking her head. "I don't know what to think. He has protected me. He is powerful. When that awful Carruther . . ." She shuddered. "He sent him off with a word."

Quillan spread his own hands. "What do you expect? He's his lapdog. He and others."

Her brows pulled together. "What others?"

"Henri Charboneau for one." When she startled visibly, he drew even closer. "What is it?"

But she only shook her head. "No, I shouldn't say it."

"Carina, if you know something . . ."

"I don't know."

"But you suspect."

"No. Èmie . . ." She stood suddenly and walked across the kitchen and back.

Quillan waited, watching, thinking again of the sprightly Morgan filly he'd seen in Golden. Carina had the same fire, the same spirit. What would it be like to love her? The thought was so incongruous, he forced it away. "Whether you know for sure or not, why don't you just tell me." He used his most winning tone, though by what she'd already said he guessed the rest.

She frowned. "You and Mr. Beck. Always talking, telling me what to do." She stalked as she spoke, holding the sling with her other hand, stopping directly before him. "You think this, he thinks that. I don't know what to think."

Quillan stood up also, stepping around the side of the table. "Don't think I'm like Berkley Beck." Besides the obvious insult of the comparison, he felt compelled to make her understand their differences. "If you want me to back off . . ."

She closed her eyes and expelled her breath. "Émie thinks her uncle . . ." Her free hand came up again, so expressive. "She thinks he killed William Evans."

Quillan digested that. He'd guessed right, but, as Carina said, it was only conjecture. "Does she know it?"

"No. She was with me that night. Right in my cot. She neither saw nor heard, only dreamed a bad dream."

"But?" Quillan leaned his hip onto the cupboard.

"But . . . she said her uncle was paid to do something, and the next morning there is Mr. Evans with his throat —" She broke off abruptly, her mind making the jump, just as others had and more would.

Quillan scowled, his anger taking the lead. "His throat what? Torn by teeth?"

Her eyes came to him, large and deep. "Is that what Mr. Beck wants? For people to think —"

Quillan's laugh was low. "What do you think, Carina?"

Again her gaze was penetrating, but this time his armor was in place. She'd see no more than he showed. And he'd show no more than a shell.

Her voice was scarcely more than a whisper. "I don't know."

What could he say? If she didn't trust him, didn't believe him, what words could make it so? "Then I'm wasting my time." He turned for the door, paused a moment as the night air came over him, then went out into the dark.

Twenty-four

If there is a hell I have found it. Yet here I find a welcome, and the price is no more than I paid to lose everything before.

Rose

It was a wonderful thing the way Crystal healed. Just one week past the flood, new buildings were being erected. Stone from nearby pits was quarried and used for more substantial business establishments, and many of those who had lived in tents now built small cabins. All the families who had been huddled into Mae's dining room were back in some sort of shelter.

All around her, Carina heard the blows of hammers, the rasp of saws, the strokes of axes. Though she grieved that the slopes were further logged, she saw that the small trees would grow up again as had those at Placer. And much of the wood used had been stripped by nature herself, pines uprooted by the flood and carried down the gulch. So much lumber was salvaged from the old buildings of Placer and Crystal that Carina felt the two had somehow merged. And since Placerville was truly no more,

Crystal seemed the stronger for it.

Carina didn't mourn Placer, didn't miss the gray buildings that had housed the shades. Perhaps the flood had been a warning, a judgment, as Preacher Paine had said. But the men of Crystal gamely rebuilt. In the same way, Quillan had repaired his wagon and acquired new wheels. From the looks of it across the street, it was better than new. She suspected the wheelwright was only too glad to oblige him, as the freighters were the most popular fraternity at present, so needy was Crystal of supplies.

Carina looked for Quillan by his wagon, but it stood empty, the horses waiting quietly for their driver. She made her way down Central, once again bordered on both sides by new construction, men working together to erect the buildings so swiftly it made her head spin. She didn't see him anywhere along the street and chided herself for her foolishness.

They hadn't spoken in the last week, not since the dinner they'd shared. But something had happened that night. Since then, she had been overly aware of him, catching a glance across the field, hearing his voice in a group of men, watching him help Cain to his stump where the old man could see the happenings. She had become attuned to Quillan Shepard in a way that concerned and frustrated her.

471

And there he was now, tossing a small rubber ball with three ragged boys. He launched the ball high into the air, and all three vied for position. The tallest of them caught the ball with a whoop. Quillan laughed, then waved them off when they clamored for more. He turned and caught her watching.

Carina felt the blood burn up her neck and into her cheeks. She was too far away for him to see her flush, but not too far to notice her watching. He made a slight bow with his head, but she was already turning away. What must he think to find her watching him so? And what was it that held her every time she did see him?

Hurrying on, she passed Cain's son on the street. His full name, she had learned, was Daniel Cain, and though they never spoke of the night she'd tended him, he did occasionally seek her out and talk. She knew they were close in age because he told her the day he turned twenty. She would be twenty-two in September. Twenty-two years old and not married.

At home Mamma's worry would be extreme. *"What do you wait for? Choose!"* And the truth was that she could choose, she being favored with Mamma's beauty and Papa's position. She didn't have to wait, hoping someone would choose her. Someone had. Should she have stayed and married Flavio in spite of it all? Impossible!

Here in Crystal, she had only to show she was willing and hundreds of men would propose. This last week as she tended the injured and gave solace to the homeless, she had been embraced in a way she hadn't thought possible when she first walked the streets of Crystal, seeing only the squalor and degradation.

In Sonoma she'd been surrounded by her people, Papa's contingent, most of them carrying on as they had in Sardinia. Life had changed little more than location. They worked the vineyards, they made the wine, they made the music and the art and carried the renaissance inside them to the new world.

Here in Crystal, the Italians were less her people than simply Crystal's people. She watched them playing bocce behind the barns, but she didn't long to jump in. She didn't need to. The spirit that joined the citizens of Crystal after the flood reached out and included her . . . if she wanted it.

Carina felt Mae and Èmie opening up, the three of them forming a cord, a friendship so different from those she had known before. Mae with her brusque, coarse ways that hid a heart both soft and vulnerable; Èmie with her stiff, dutiful manner. Both learning to laugh, to cry, to feel as alive as Carina did.

And she did! Somehow this time away from those who had sheltered her, coddled her, told her how to feel, to think . . . somehow it was forming her in a new way, independent of her family, of Flavio. For the first time she knew there was a world beyond her own, and she could be part of it.

Stopping outside Mr. Beck's office, she drew a long breath and went inside. He wasn't there, and she felt instantly relieved. That whole week he'd been out more than he was in, and she was glad for his absence. With him there she was constantly on edge, feeling his eyes, sensing his thoughts, his suspicions.

She watched for anything amiss, but there was nothing. Mr. Beck was only what he seemed, a busy attorney who was now a city trustee, replacing a man who had drowned in the flood. Mr. Beck was more respected and powerful than before. She walked to his desk, heaped again with papers. *Bene*. There was some comfort in things that stayed the same.

She took his seat and began sorting. Some of the papers were land claims, but many had to do with city business. Mr. Beck's quick action following the flood had earned him much respect. And with that came expectations.

Crystal was far from peaceful. There was a new undercurrent of suspicion, and

though on the surface people worked together, Carina noted them also watching
their backs. The roughs took full advantage
of the disarray, and the trustees were under
fire. Mr. Beck had assured her he intended
to bring order to the situation, but how?
And how did it involve Quillan and Berkley
Beck's suspicions toward him?

Carina sighed. She wouldn't think of that
now. Any thought of Quillan brought a
tremor to her belly. It was the risk of playing
both sides. It was the position he'd placed
her in — they'd both placed her in. So why
did she feel it only in considering Quillan
Shepard?

Enough. She must focus on the task before her. The city business she filed in a
separate pile. Complaints. Almost as many
as land disputes. She would get a new
crate to hold them. Why didn't Mr. Beck
buy the cabinets so many kept their files
in? Surely he had money enough for that.
Yet his office was Spartan. Were his rooms
the same?

Since her discussion with Quillan, she had
wondered more and more. Was that where
he kept her silver? Was there some hiding
place in Mr. Beck's rooms that held the
proof Quillan wanted, proof of misdeeds?
She got up and again her skirt caught on the
loose board. She tugged it free. She should
nail it down. Maybe he had a hammer and

nail. Slowly she walked to the door and reached for the knob.

A jolt ran up her spine. Suppose he were inside! She withdrew her hand as though scorched. *Pazza!* What was she thinking? She turned back, her heart thumping in her ribs.

She looked around the room where she stood. It was obvious nothing was hidden there. The crates were her own devising. The desks had no locked drawers, no secret panels. They were simple — two drawers and a top. She sat down in the chair and pulled open the right-hand drawer of Mr. Beck's desk; pens and nibs and ink, his seal and other such things.

The left drawer held paper and envelopes and his ledger. His legal books were on the shelf along the far wall. That was all. Frustrated, she stood, and the skirt snagged again, irking her. Was the man too cheap to fix his floor?

She reached down and felt the board. She would leave it on his desk for him to repair. She pulled it free and froze. Beneath it was a sizable space, and inside she saw a ledger and other things, including the box that held Nonna's silver. So this was his safe place?

Frowning, she lifted the ledger and beneath it saw deeds, exactly like her own. Illustrations of her property and others and advertisements such as the one she had answered. Quillan had been right. Mr. Beck *was* responsible. He had known from the first moment she would not have her house.

He was the one who had cheated her! Lied! And kissed her hand! Heart pounding, she replaced the ledger and reached for the box of silver, then stopped. She couldn't take it without revealing that she'd found his hiding place. She would request it. And once it was returned . . . She replaced the board, then climbed out from under the desk and stood, shaking with fury. She spun when the door opened and Berkley Beck stepped in.

"Carina!" His smile stretched, his teeth white, straight, his eyes wide with delight and blue as a baby's.

Bestia! Animale! Demonio!

In three strides he had captured her hands and brought them together to his lips. "I have great news. The trustees have decided to organize into a council, and it seems Crystal will have need of a mayor." He paused, sensing at last her fury. "Are you all right?"

No. I am not all right. But she knew better than to show it. She tugged a hand free and waved it. "A touch of fever maybe. I'm well enough." But she shook with anger, and he could feel it when he took her elbow, she was sure.

"Here, sit." He walked her to her chair.

"I'm fine." *Animale*. "Please don't concern yourself."

His blue eyes softened. "You know I can't help it."

No? *You think I don't know you? I would not learn the truth? You think me stupida?* She said nothing.

His eyes deepened. "Carina." He dropped to his knee beside her where she sat, captured her hands in his. "If things fall out the way I think they will —"

"Please don't." She wanted to kick him as hard as Giusseppe's mule.

"I must."

"Then I must refuse." Or slap him. Her hand itched for it.

"Marry me, Carina."

"No."

She saw the anger flicker in his eyes, felt his grip on her hands tighten. His eyes burned as though he would change her mind by staring alone. "They're considering me for mayor. The trustees want a leader. The city wants —"

"That changes nothing."

His jaw tightened. "You should think well before refusing me."

"I have refused you already."

His eyes turned cold. She had overstepped herself, and he seethed as he stood up stiffly. She stood up as well, her chest

478

heaving with all the invectives she would like to shout. *How dare you woo me when you have lied and cheated and deceived me. Omaccio!* Mr. Beck was not the man to anger, yet how could she help herself? He was everything Quillan thought him and worse. She couldn't bear to be in his presence a moment longer.

She stalked out of the office and searched the street, but Quillan's wagon was gone. Lifting her skirts, she ran back to Mae's, her back stiff with rage, as much at herself as Berkley Beck. How had she been such a fool? How had she thought Berkley Beck kind when he did nothing but serve himself?

She saw Cain sitting on the stump and made her path straight to him. "Have you seen Quillan?"

"And good day to you, too, little miss."

She released an exasperated breath. "I'm sorry. I don't have time."

"That's the trouble with you young folks. Always rushing to and fro." He raised a pointed finger. "Quillan's the same. He's got a fire under him and not a minute to spare, don't ya know. Off about his business with hardly a fare-thee-well."

"Then he's gone?"

"Hee-hee. You don't miss a step." He waved the finger in her face.

"Please." Carina was losing her patience. "Has he left town?"

"I don't know that he's left. He's a-haulin' some ore from the New Boundless. I reckon he's filled up by now and headin' down for the smelting works. After that he's on to Colorado Springs. He'll be gone a good piece."

She turned and hurried back toward Central.

"And good day to you!" Cain hollered after her.

Carina made no reply. She hadn't time for courtesy. She must catch Quillan before he left town, must tell him what she'd found. Tension formed a pain between her eyebrows, but she needn't have worried. As she reached the street, she saw him standing outside the new livery, which was mostly rebuilt and again housing horses.

He stood with Alan Tavish. His blacks and two new Clydesdales were hitched to the wagon loaded with ore. If he was in such a hurry, why did he delay to chat with an old ostler? Carina shook her head. She should question good fortune?

Raising her skirts, she fought her way across the crowded street. Some things hadn't changed since the flood. The dust and traffic remained. Disgusted, she stepped around a mound of mule droppings. After one week, the smell, too, was much the same.

Both men stopped talking when she

480

rushed upon them. Alan Tavish smiled his stump-toothed smile. Quillan simply appraised her.

She ignored Mr. Tavish and confronted Quillan Shepard. "I must speak with you."

"Business or pleasure?" he asked with a half smile and taunting eyes.

"In regard to business we discussed before. Concerning a mutual . . . friend." She put a hand to her chest and stilled her breath. She had sounded foolish, but his eyes flashed understanding.

Quillan glanced sidelong across the street to Mr. Beck's office. "I'm on my way out of town. Why don't you check on your mule . . ."

"Dom was lost in the flood." Though she'd had little enough chance to mourn him.

"I'm sorry to hear that. Perhaps Alan would loan you a horse."

"I don't want a horse. You wanted to know —"

Alan touched her arm. "Come inside and see what I have."

Carina stared as Quillan tipped the broad brim of his new hat and started off without hearing what she had to tell him.

"Come on, lass." Alan Tavish tugged her gently.

Carina followed, frustrated.

As soon as they were inside Mr. Tavish's

demeanor changed. His face grew serious, though still the same kindly features. "Give him a moment to be on his way, then meet him by the creek. Less eyes and ears that way."

Sciocca. Again she had proved her foolishness, rushing to him as she had in plain view. What if she had blurted what she knew right there across from Mr. Beck's office? She dropped her forehead to her palm.

Tavish slipped the bridle over the head of a sorrel mare. "This mare's a soft ride. Why don't ye take her for a wee trip about the gulch. Up a little, then down." Tavish saddled her and tightened the girth.

Now Carina understood. Alan Tavish must know what Quillan Shepard suspected. He must be in the man's confidence. How many others were included in Quillan's circle of conspirators?

"If you're ever in trouble, lass, Alan Tavish is here."

"Thank you." She took the reins he handed her.

He grinned. "Aye. Daisy's her name."

Carina led the horse out and mounted. The mare had a gentle stride indeed after Dom's leggy plod. Instead of fighting her way up the street, Carina walked the mare around the back of the livery, threading through the tents and shacks. Why didn't

Quillan build himself a house? He could afford it with the prices he charged. Why live like a gypsy when he must be growing rich freighting? Mae had told her the freighters who owned their own outfits amassed as much as the successful miners, if not the millionaires.

She rode along the creek, then turned and started down. She left the town behind without seeing Quillan's wagon. She kept the road on her left and followed the creek. How far would she have to go?

She rounded the bend where the creek deepened into small falls and rapids and came on the wagon suddenly. It was just off the road so as not to impede traffic. She reined in and looked about for Quillan. He stepped around the huge wagon, looking taller and sterner than before. With no greeting, he reached up and swung her from the saddle. She had only a moment to grasp his shoulders, then she was down.

"Ever heard the word surreptitious?" He led her by the elbow around the side of the wagon.

"Yes."

"Know what it means?" He was not smiling.

"Yes."

He backed her to the wagon and planted his palms against the wood on both sides of her, arms straight, but still far too close.

"Does everything you feel always show to all the world?"

She couldn't answer with him so close.

"Or did you intend the show for Mr. Beck?"

"I —"

"Never mind." He shook his head. "You had something to tell me?"

"If you would move your arms . . ."

He hesitated a long moment, holding her with his eyes until her breath wouldn't come. Then he pushed back from the wagon and stood before her, waiting.

"I found things. Under a loose board in the floor. A ledger and deeds. The same deeds as mine, forgeries." Her hands clenched. "He lied to me. Cheated me. He —"

"What else was in there?"

She frowned, spreading her hands. "I didn't see it all. There was no time."

"Do you have the ledger?"

"Do you think me pazza?"

He grinned sideways. "Maybe. A little."

He was teasing. At such a time. "I must be, to help such as you." She waved her hand at his face and started to push past.

He swiftly snatched her back, pulling her into his arms, tight to his chest. "Act like you like it," he hissed in her ear, and she heard the rumble of wagon wheels. His arms were strong and unyielding as trail dust enveloped them, swirling up and around in a cloying cloud. The ore wagon passed so slowly she could count each beat of her heart.

At last the rumble faded, and she staggered back. "You have spoiled my name!"

"Better that than anyone suspect our real purpose. Besides, I hid your face." There was more than a hint of amusement.

Carina clawed her hair and leaned her head back to the wagon, more shaken than angry. "I should thank you?"

He glanced back along the road. "I need to know what's in the ledger."

She shook her head.

"Why do you think he has it hidden?"

"I don't care why. I'm not going back there."

"What about your silver?"

She was silent. She hadn't considered that.

"Carina, you can't quit now. It would be dangerous."

"Dangerous? He wants to marry me!" She splayed her fingers at him, palm upraised.

Quillan cocked his head with the start of another grin. "Did he ask you?"

"It was more of a demand," she scoffed, "though he was on his knee."

Quillan's laugh surprised her. It so changed his face when he laughed, lightening and softening it at once. "So you told him about Flavio."

Blood rushed to her face. "No." How did

he remember even the name? She had said it only once. She turned away, frustrated. "You asked me to tell you what I found. I've done so. I can do no more."

"Then I won't ask you to." He took off his hat and shook his hair back, the light catching in it like wild honey. He replaced the hat and smiled. "Take the scenic way home."

He was satisfied? She felt a slight disappointment. "Are you leaving?"

For answer he waved at his full wagon.

"How long will you be gone? And what am I to do about Mr. Beck?"

"You've done all you can."

He walked her to the horse and helped her mount. Looking down into his face, she wanted to explain, to make him understand. All that came out was, "Good-bye, Quillan Shepard."

"Just Quillan." He stepped back from the horse, touched his hat, and headed for his wagon. He pulled himself into the box and took up the reins, then paused. "If you did change your mind, you could find me through Cain or Alan. Otherwise I won't bother you again."

Bene. She should be so lucky. Only . . . it didn't feel that way. And as he drove away, she knew her heart had rushed with more than surprise when he pulled her into his arms.

486

★ ★ ★

Quillan left the ore at the Malta smelting works and started down the Colorado Springs road over Trout Creek Pass. He was torn now about leaving. The need was still great for supplies, and, though most of what he brought up he donated to those worst off, some was earning him huge profits.

The Denver merchants had jacked their prices when they learned about the flood. That was why he headed now for Colorado Springs. And time away from Crystal would give him time to think about Carina's information. It both amused and annoyed him that Beck's hidey-hole was under the floor as his own had been, but then, maybe it wasn't as original as he'd thought.

Anyway, now that the spot was found, what would he do about it? Seize Beck's books himself? He'd already ascertained that Beck's place was watched — or rather, guarded — by one or another of the roughs always lingering near. He frowned. If only he could have convinced Carina . . .

But maybe she was right. If Beck had declared himself, he wouldn't take her rejection kindly. He paused for a moment, realizing she hadn't said she'd refused Beck. She must have, though. She was hotter than a pistol when she came flying across the street. Of course, Beck hadn't helped his suit by swindling her out of her house, and Quillan grinned at the thought of him on his knee to the furious Italian belle.

He shook his head. The man must truly believe himself invincible. And frankly, with the way he'd handled things since the flood, wiggling onto the board of trustees and now posturing himself for mayor, not to mention the physical control he wielded with the roughs in his pocket . . .

Quillan slapped his thigh. If he could just get that ledger! Would it show payoffs and bribes? Crooked deals? Would it reveal which of the trustees were in his pocket, the judges, the merchants? Would it name the thugs? He realized he was making the horses tense and forced himself to relax on the reins.

Well, time on the road would help him sort things out and maybe cool the rumors about him, rumors Beck was fanning into flame. Quillan had rarely cared what people thought of him, but he noticed now when conversation ceased and heads turned away. For the first time he imagined how Wolf must have felt. He pushed the thought away.

He wasn't running. He was doing business as usual. He'd had to replace his tent and furnishings and supplies, much of it on credit, something he'd never done before. But it didn't matter. He could load up just about anything he wanted in Colorado Springs and find a buyer for it in Crystal. At least some were loyal to him still.

Cain grimaced as the new crutches dug into his armpits. It was easier to fashion them than a new peg, but hopping along on one leg with two ill-fitting poles . . . *Ah, Lord, it's hard, don't ya know. But if my right hand offends thee, take it. If my right eye offends thee, gouge it out. If my peg is better off down the way, keep me from a-grumblin'.*

He reached Alan Tavish outside the livery and stopped. "Has he gone?"

"Aye."

"Will he stay gone?"

The old ostler's features were careworn and tight. "I dinna think so."

That brought a mixed emotion. Cain valued Quillan's company, and not just for himself. D.C. fairly fawned on him, admiring the strength and purpose Quillan demonstrated. The boy might love his pappy, but it was Quillan he emulated. But if anyone could make a man of D.C., it was Quillan. And that in spite of his resistance to God. It was only a matter of time before Quillan stopped fighting, and then D.C. would know that a strong man could surrender to God without shame. That religion wasn't just for old cripples and women.

Alan gave the saddle across his knees another rub. "Do ye remember how we celebrate St. Patrick's Day?"

"You mean the brawl?"

"The Irish all lined up along the street one side, the Orangemen along t'other."

Cain grinned. "Craziest thing I ever saw. Fists flyin', feet kickin', hair pullin' until everyone's so bloody and bruised up you can't tell who's who."

"Ye can tell, man. But what I meant is the linin' up. Now plain folks are choosin' camps, linin' up for or against Quillan."

It chilled Cain that rumors of Quillan being a monster like his pappy Wolf were taking shape in folks' imaginations. Once people got it into their heads one way, it was sorely difficult to get it out. Even if there weren't one piece of truth to it.

"The marshal ain't made an accusation. Far as I know he ain't inquired of Quillan at all."

"Father Charboneau forbade him."

Cain raised his eyes to Alan. "Forbade?"

Alan nodded. "Donald McCollough may fear Berkley Beck, but he fears God more. Sure he looks aside at Beck's villainy, but the priest put the fear of hell into him if he so much as questions Quillan on William Evans' death."

Cain leaned against the wall. "Father Charboneau. He was with us in Placer, wasn't he?"

"Aye. Came through in his wanderings."

"Knew Wolf, as I recall."

"Well as any."

Cain cast his memory back to the days of gravel shoveling and sluicing. The priest had come and gone between the mining camps as had others. The Reverend Shepard for one, who'd taken Quillan into his home and raised him. But as far as he knew, Quillan had no dealings with the priest. "Why do you suppose the padre's protecting him?" He was asking himself as much as Alan.

Alan Tavish turned slowly. Their eyes met, but neither had the answer.

Father Antoine Charboneau stood over the grave. This stone was older, part of the mountain itself, hewed from its bed and crudely carved by his own hand. He bent and touched the names there. More and more, that grave weighed on him.

In the years between, he'd put it from his mind. Best forgotten except in his prayers on the lonely nights when memory returned. But now . . . why couldn't the past remain buried? Why had Miss DiGratia asked questions that brought the horror alive once more?

Father God, what am I to do? Must the son pay for the sins of the father? Your own son you didn't spare. But this one, this one who weighs so heavily on my conscience . . . surely this time I can save him?

A chill passed through him. What if he were wrong? Antoine dropped to his knees in the clumpy mountain grasses. He clasped his hands at his chest and dropped his chin. Was he wrong about Wolf? Had the tortured spirit of Cries Like a Wolf struck out with cruel and deadly force in some madness Antoine could not comprehend? And had that curse passed to the son?

His hands came up and covered his face. Antoine groaned. *What more can I do? God, what more can I do?*

Twenty-five

His name is Fate.
Rose

Carina tossed in her bed, her dreams feverish and confused, feelings of falling, falling through the darkness, then arms catching her. Yet when she tried to see the face of the one who saved her, he was gone and she was falling again, no rock shelf to catch her. She jolted awake in the darkness.

Beside her, Èmie slept, softly solid. How could she sleep after once again fleeing her uncle's drunken fury? When Carina had returned from meeting with Quillan, she'd slipped quietly into the livery. Neither Alan Tavish nor Cain Bradley asked her what she had told Quillan, but Alan again assured her he was there if she needed him.

It disconcerted her to hear it. Why did he think she was in trouble? And if she were, why had Quillan left town? *Innocente*. She was not Quillan's responsibility. So he had saved her — not once, but three times. From the snake, from the roughs, from the mine shaft. Did that mean she could depend on him? She felt his arms around her. It was a ruse only to keep the freighter who passed from guessing their purpose. Yet . . .

Èmie sighed in her sleep, and Carina eased herself up on one elbow to see her friend. The evening had scarcely deepened when Èmie had once again sought her. This time her uncle had ordered her out, and Carina had seen the fear, that same fear as the other time.

Carina trembled. Did she still doubt Èmie's intuition? Was it possible Èmie's uncle had murdered William Evans? Was the priest's brother capable of slicing another's throat? With a sigh, Carina lay back on the pillow and studied the ceiling by the brightness of the full moon. The wood planks were tightly grooved and narrow, a defense against the elements, but what defense was there against evil? *"You must be washed in the blood of the risen Lamb."*

Signore, what does it all mean? Why am I here? I thought you had answered my prayers, but it was all a lie. A forged deed, a fraud. Are you a fraud, Signore? Pinching the bridge of her nose, Carina rolled to her side and stood.

She made her way on silent feet to the window. The streets were brightly moonlit, the shadows sharp. As she watched, the shadows moved and formed themselves into the shapes of men, stealthy and full of violence. She must be dreaming. Her head

494

swam and the dizziness came on her, though she stood only one story from the street.

She was on the roof with Divina. *"Don't sway so, Carina . . ."* And this time she heard the fear and concern in the voice, felt the hands reaching to clasp her, to stop her fall. No, it couldn't be. Divina had wanted her to fall. Then why the grasping arms, the worried plea?

Carina gripped the windowsill. Had she misunderstood? Had her memory played her wrong? They were on the roof, but why? To see the nestlings under the rafter. A vague image of the nest, ragged and cone-shaped, the sharp beaks bobbing up and parting with noisy squawks . . . Divina's arms lifting her to see.

Carina pressed her forehead to the glass, eyes closed. They were on the roof to see the baby birds. And she had fallen. Was it Divina's fault, as she had told herself all these years? Except for the falling, the memory was too vague. She couldn't make it out, yet she had believed Divina caused the fear of heights that she never had until that day.

Carina shivered. The window glass was cold against her skin, no remnant of the day's heat present in the thin night air. It was cold, and she shivered again, her gown too thin for the mountain nights. She should climb back into the blankets, warm beside Èmie.

But she looked out to the street instead. The shadow men were still there, and now she realized they were real. One sprang upon another, cutting him down with blows. Farther down, yet still in her view, two more attacked a second man. It was happening! There before her!

Pressing her palms to the glass, she felt helpless, watching, unable to change what played out before her eyes. From somewhere in the night a howl came, long and lonely and savage. She shuddered, staggered back from the window as though the wolf might see her there and bound through to catch her throat with its teeth.

She backed into something warm and shrieked, then Èmie's hands were on hers and they pulled each other close, an embrace of fear and helplessness. Then Carina pushed away. "We must do something!"

Èmie clung to her. "We can't."

"You know we must."

"They'll kill us. Uncle Henri and all the others working for —" Her eyes widened and she turned away, her breath ragged.

"For whom? For whom does he do his wickedness?"

Èmie shook her head.

Carina grabbed her shoulders, though Èmie stood a full head taller. "Tell me!"

"I can't. God forgive me." Èmie dropped to her knees.

Carina stood over her, hands resting on Èmie's shoulders. She willed her friend to listen. "Tell me, Èmie."

The answer was scarcely more than a whisper. "Berkley Beck."

So Quillan was right. Carina was amazed by the cold stillness that stole over her. Berkley Beck was the monster. Berkley Beck, whom she had trusted, even touted to Mae and others. Did anyone know? Did Mae, who thought him conceited but harmless? Did Alan Tavish? Cain Bradley? Father Charboneau?

Quillan knew. But he needed proof. What proof could there be for this? She stared out into the night. Surely Mr. Beck would not keep a record of such acts. Yet what did the ledger under the floor contain?

The very thought made her quail. She was not foolish nor brave enough — it was out of the question. She crossed herself. *No, Signore, I cannot.* And she absolved herself with Quillan's words, *"Then I won't ask you to."* He was not asking.

She turned to Èmie. "You must tell Father Antoine what you know."

Èmie's eyes widened, and she slowly shook her head. "I can't, Carina."

"Who else can stop your uncle?"

Èmie pulled herself up and stood stiffly. "He can't stop Uncle Henri. Not after what's been done."

Carina looked past her to the window. Was Henri out there wielding a club? A knife? Slicing men's throats? "You don't know he did murder."

"I know it."

Carina threw out her hands. "You didn't see him do it!"

Èmie's face went still as marble. "I saw the knife."

Carina's breath stilled, and the chill spread through her. "You must tell the priest."

"I won't."

Carina waved her arms in sudden frustration. "Why are you protecting him after what he's done?"

Èmie's reserve broke. "It's not Uncle Henri I protect. It's Uncle Antoine, Father Antoine. It would kill him."

Carina pictured the vigorous priest and doubted that.

"Every day he blames himself for not reaching Henri. If he knew . . . Swear you won't tell him, Carina."

Carina paced across the rectangle of moonlight on the floor back to the window. She could see bodies lying unconscious, but the shadow men had passed from her view. "Something has to be done."

498

"There's nothing we can do. He's too powerful."

Carina knew Èmie didn't mean her uncle. She was suddenly aware of evil, palpable and present. The evil Mr. Beck wielded. At his command men robbed and plundered, maimed and killed. Because of him, men huddled in their tents, afraid to set foot outside after dark. He was a bully of the worst sort. And he had cheated her.

She straightened and turned. "He must be stopped."

Èmie spread her hands, pleading. "He's the devil."

The words should have terrified her. But Carina's breath came evenly now, slow and steady, as though all the fear and horror had been drained from her. She knew what she must do. She didn't have the courage, but somehow she must find it. She had told Quillan she wasn't going back and had intended to tell Berkley Beck the same. But she had to. At least once.

Lying awake in the moonlit tent, Cain waited for D.C. to come home, staring at the canvas walls dim in the moonlight. More than ever he felt his age. His arm was healing badly, the muscles growing weak and pulling away from the scar that caved into his flesh. He felt phantom pains from a shin and ankle and foot that were no longer there, and he was unable to get to the privy groping for crutches that pressed into the ragged skin of his sides.

He sighed. Sometimes living was hard. He rolled over on the bedding. D.C. had been all for building a fine house right beside the mine, but Quillan had said wait. Wait until the first assay confirmed the expectations, wait until the extent of the ore was ascertained, wait and see.

And it was sound advice. For once the boy had listened. But he didn't listen tonight. With everything coming out just as he'd hoped, the money weighting his pocket from the early ore shipments, and Quillan not there to gainsay him, D.C. had left his daddy in the tent and gone to town.

And now Cain waited. The moon waned and still he waited. In the waiting, he realized how little the silver meant to him. The fever that had burned in him for two decades had burned itself out. For the first time, he had prospects worth tens, hundreds of thousands, maybe more. And it didn't matter. He just wanted his boy to come home.

The morning sun fought for its piece of sky through the clouds crowding in from the north, carried on the wind. With her mind set, though bleary from lack of sleep, Carina made her way toward the office. Knots of men clustered on the walks and streets in angry discussion while the mule teams and ore wagons, the calls of the hawkers and tinny pianos, all seemed a part of a discordant opera with no libretto.

There were no bodies in the street. No murdered men with crowds gathered around. She almost believed she had dreamed what she saw the night before. Then her skirt swished over blood-spattered dirt, and the reality of the night's events returned. Now she heard the conversations, the fear in the men's voices, the anger.

"By gum, we won't stand for it. We've got to put an end to it."

"And end with our throats cut like Evans?"

"Or just wait till it happens anyway?"

"I say lynch them all."

"And you'll be the next with a slit throat."

She crossed herself and walked by, wishing her feet might travel on for miles, rather than stop where they did. Per piacere, Signore, one minute only, a quick look, nothing more . . . Carina touched the office door, gripped the knob and turned, then went inside. Her heart sank at the sight of Mr. Beck, sitting at the desk with his feet on the board. So it would not be easy. She shot her silent disgruntlement to heaven.

She wanted only one chance to give Quillan what he asked for. But God would not make it easy. Bene. She walked in, trying not to tremble, knowing what she knew. Did the knowing show in her face?

Berkley Beck stood but did not extend his usual greeting, nor did he smile. She had hoped to be in and out while he lingered over coffee and his newspaper. Why this morning must he be prompt?

"Good morning." Her voice sounded small.

Still he didn't speak. His eyes were cold blue ice.

As he made no effort at cordiality, she chose to be direct. "I would like my grandmother's silver."

He quirked an eyebrow but didn't reply. Did he think to intimidate her with his silence?

"My silver, Mr. Beck."

"I heard you the first time. Unfortunately . . ." He stood and walked around the desk. "Since you made clear yesterday that you refuse my offer, I must hold the silver as collateral against your debts."

"My debts?" Carina glanced at the floor where both her silver and the ledger lay. So close.

"Your keep has come dear."

Her mouth fell open, her poise deserting her. Blood rushed to her face. "I demand my silver."

He half smiled. "You're hardly in a position to be making demands."

He was right. She could not browbeat him. She forced a reasonable tone. "How much is my debt?"

"Two hundred dollars."

"Two hundred! For room and board at Mae's? You're pazzo."

"Room and board was trivial. Your protection was not."

"My protection . . . from what?" She spread her hands.

"Surely you don't think you roamed these streets unscathed because of some universal chivalry, do you?"

She stared. That was exactly what she thought. She didn't fear the men of Crystal, the miners, the simple men who had welcomed her to their hearts. But she did fear Berkley Beck and those he controlled. If she was safe it was because he had not ordered it otherwise.

He picked a piece of lint from his sleeve. "No, Carina, it was my goodwill that safeguarded you. And after last night, others will put their trust in me."

"Trust?" She spit the word.

"Yes, Carina, trust. And they'll pay to be protected as you have been."

"They will pay to be cheated, swindled —"

"Temper, my dear. In what way have I cheated you?"

She almost blurted what she knew. But then he would guess she'd found the deeds, the ledger. "You . . . you never said I must pay for protection."

He dropped his gaze. "I never thought it would come to that. As it is, you asked for my aid and you've received it." He raised his head. "And you'll continue in my service until the debt is paid. Unless, of course, you reconsider your refusal?"

She clamped her mouth shut. What she wanted to say would be dangerous.

"I thought not. In that case I have a task for you. Some collections to be made."

He held out a large leather pack. It had a shoulder strap and a hand grip, two buckle closings, and a keyhole. In his other hand he proffered the key. "You may use this purse to carry them."

Trembling with fury, she took the bag, then secreted the key in her pocket. As she did, she felt the Sharps Pepperbox Quillan had procured for her. *What you won't know until it comes to it is if you can point at a man and pull the trigger.* Quillan's words stung her. Had he guessed she might have to find out?

She drew her fingers away from the metal. She hadn't used it since he had showed her how. Except for the one time Quillan had grabbed her in the night, she'd had no thought to use the gun in her defense. Now it seemed Berkley Beck must guess its presence. Could she point at him and shoot?

He held out a list. "These are the addresses you'll visit. The owners are expecting you." His arrogance was appalling.

A surge of anger filled her. "No." She thrust the bag at him. Let him withdraw his protection.

His eyes pierced her suddenly, terrifyingly real. "You'll make the collections and bring them here. Otherwise, I can't be responsible for Èmie's safety. Henri Charboneau is . . . unbalanced."

Carina's spine went cold. He would threaten Èmie? *Sì*. It was in his face. She felt the gun against her thigh through the skirts. *"Try it from your pocket. Don't take time to close your eye. Just point and shoot."* The thought horrified her. To send a bullet into Berkley Beck. *Oh, Dio*. She couldn't do it.

Then he softened, nearly becoming the man she had first seen, first implored to help her. "It doesn't have to be this way. I had other plans for you, for us. . . ."

Oh yes, Mr. Beck. You had plans. But I have plans, too. She raised her chin. With her blood running high, she gripped the bag and stalked toward the door. For now she must do as he said, but at the first opportunity she would get the ledger and give it to Quillan. As soon as he returned. She sent up a silent prayer that it would be soon.

She started down the street, glancing up

at the rumbling thunder from the dark mass of clouds rolling in, battling the sun for the sky. The wind buffeted her. There was no rain yet, but it would come. Maybe this time it would wash away the rest of Crystal, Berkley Beck included!

She turned into the Emporium, walked straight through the nearly empty room to the counter and stopped. What would she say? How did one speak for Berkley Beck? But she didn't need to.

The man behind the bar eyed her sourly. "It's you he's sent, eh?" He muttered an oath under his breath. ". . . pay his doxy . . ."

The blood rushed to her face at the insult, but what could she say? Would he believe she was as constrained as he?

The man shoved a stack of bills at her. "There. Now get out."

Furious and humiliated, she snatched the money and shoved it into the bag. *Porca miserio.* She reached the street, shaking, then moved on to the next. Her welcome was no better at the Boise Billiard Hall, though Bennet Danes didn't insult her to her face. He waited until she turned her back, then let loose a string of names that made her shake with rage.

She cringed when the owner of the Gilded Slipper glared her way, then snarled, "You'd earn it more honestly working for me."

His words hurt the worst yet. A saloon girl more honest than she? If they were so eager to trust Mr. Beck, so thankful for his protection, why did they treat her like the plague? Because they didn't trust or respect him. And in their eyes, she and Berkley Beck were one. With this task, he had destroyed her name, her reputation. It didn't matter that none of the things they said were true, only that they believed it.

And suddenly she thought of Quillan and the things being said about him, about Wolf and about Rose. Had Rose been maligned this way? Surely she was ruined. Why else flee to Placerville as . . . as the sort of woman the merchants now thought Carina? How long before everyone said such things of her? Holding herself defiantly, she started down the walk.

"Miss DiGratia." Joe Turner doffed his hat before her. "I'm boring a new shaft, and I wondered, would you be so kind as to take a look before we dig?" His face was humbly earnest.

The knot in her stomach eased. His faith in her, no matter how silly, returned to her a measure of decency. She smiled. "Where is it?"

"Just a little way. I brought my carryall." He motioned to the small carriage pulled by a single gray.

She had five more places from which to

collect, and Mr. Beck would be angry at the delay. Well, let him be. She would show him he couldn't bully her. Joe Turner helped her into the off side, then climbed in himself and drove her to his mine. The works were substantial already, with many men laboring. They all doffed their hats when she climbed down, and her heart sang over the noise of steel on steel and blasting powder.

Here were the men who believed in her, the men she trusted. To them she was still Lady Luck. Grazie, Signore, for these people. Mr. Turner walked her through the shaft house and out again, skirting the tailings. "Here it is, the spot I've chosen for the new shaft. And I'd like to name it after you."

Carina looked up, amazed.

"The *Carina DiGratia*. I know it'll bring me luck . . . again."

Luck? Her throat tightened. The Rose Legacy had been named for Rose. Had it brought Wolf luck? Or Rose? Why did thoughts of Quillan's mother keep intruding? Because Rose, too, had been shunned. All the buoyancy left her. "Mr. Turner, you've brought your own luck."

He shook his head. "No. I intended to dig the next hill over, only I couldn't find it in the dark. You're my luck, Miss DiGratia. Please say I may."

The money bag was heavy on her shoulder, as she hadn't dared leave it in the wagon. What if Joe Turner learned of it? What if they all learned? She sighed. "You may name it anything you like." *But my luck may have run out.* It certainly felt that way.

He whooped and tossed up his hat. "The Carina DiGratia it is!"

Carina forced a smile, though her heart grew heavy inside her. *Why, Signore? Why do you strike me? What have I done?* But she knew the answer, and it weighed on her mind as heavily as her heart. *Forgive and be forgiven.*

As Joe drove her back, she sat silently, perilously close to tears. When he left her she felt bereaved, standing alone in the crowd on the walk. The next two stops were as bad as the first ones; the last three were less painful. By that time she was numb. As she carried the bag back to Berkley Beck, she thought again of the gun in her skirt pocket.

What if she shot him? Would they hang her? The owners of the saloons knew what he was doing, but would they speak for her? She pressed her eyes closed, hearing the names they called her, the innuendoes. No. They would not defend her. She was now as guilty as he.

Drawing a long, bitter breath she went into the office and dropped the bag at Mr.

Beck's feet. Without a word, she turned and walked out. She had never felt so low, so wretched. Even Flavio's betrayal had not taken away her self-respect. She was aware in a way she'd never been before of what flimsy fabric reputation was made. Born into respectability, one's virtue was assumed until such slight breeze should snatch it away.

How would she hold up her head? How would she look people in the eye? She lifted her skirts and ran to Mae's. Surely Mae wouldn't judge her.

Cain sat beside his son, every year heavy in his limbs. The premonition had kept his eyes from closing in sleep last night, and he'd been wakeful and ready when they came for him. He knew by their faces it was bad, but he hadn't guessed how bad. *God, if it's a life you want, take mine. What good am I anyhow? An old, legless broken-down fool.* He sagged, feeling the sob building in his chest.

The doctor and the young doc together had helped him up the hill to Mae's, and he'd sat there through the rest of the night and most of the day, alone with D.C. and unmindful of all around him. No pain, not even when he'd blown off his leg, compared to what he suffered now. He'd felt so secure in his faith. But now . . . "Lord, don't take my boy. Don't . . ." He dropped his face to his hands and wept.

Sam's brown mottled head was on Cain's boot, his eyes large and sorrowful. Sensing Cain's distress, the dog whined softly. But D.C. lay still, no sign of life in his battered body but a faint pulse and breath too slight to notice. The gash on his head was stitched closed, but the swelling behind it was the demon, though it hardly showed. Under the skull, the doctor'd said.

Cain grasped D.C.'s hand as though he could hold him there as he'd held him back from so much as a youngster. "Don't you leave me, boy. You hear? Don't you leave me." And he cried again, frustrated, frightened, and far too angry.

Who did this to my son? Who put his life on the scale? I'll kill them! Then he realized what he'd thought. *Oh, God . . . I'm a weak and wretched man. But my boy . . . he could be something wonderful if you'd just give him the chance. Just give him the chance.*

Twenty-six

What strange quirk of fate, to be saved from disgrace by a savage.

Rose

Carina hurried to Mae's rooms, but upon hearing voices, she paused. Dr. Felden stood at the door with a grim countenance. What was he doing there? Was Mae ill? Carina thought of her labored breath, her easy fatigue. Had her heart . . . ? She rushed forward, but it wasn't Mae in the bed. It was D.C.

"What is it? What's wrong with him?" She stared at the boy who thought his dreams had come true. The boy who had twice already suffered at the hands of the roughs.

"He was attacked. Robbed and beaten, hit with something hard and sharp, but blunt enough to cause a contusion to the brain. I fear the swelling is internal, beneath the skull."

Mae stood in the corner shaking her head. Cain sat crumpled at the bedside, looking almost as bad as D.C. except that he looked totally miserable, while D.C. looked dead already, pale and discolored. He was a victim of last night's violence, violence Mr. Beck had used to scare the merchants into paying. And she had collected the payments.

Cain looked up, turning slowly, his pale eyes meeting hers, his hand clasping his son's. "Can you help him?" His voice was a ghost, but she saw in his plea the same hope she'd seen in the infirmary, men thinking she could do something she could not. What did she know? But suddenly a thought came to her of a case her papa and Vittorio, her brother, had discussed. Not the same perhaps, but similar. If the swelling was beneath the skull . . .

Her voice came weakly, unsure. "There was one man Papa treated with a swelling on the brain. A hole was drilled through the skull and a shunt inserted to drain the fluid." She saw the doctor's avid attention and spread her hands. "To take the pressure off the brain."

"Did the man live?" It was Cain who spoke, his voice impressing on her his need.

"He lived, yes, and recovered. Vittorio said he would drill the heads of all the numskulls and make them right as he had this man." She looked at Dr. Felden. "He meant it as a joke."

The doctor stroked his chin, his brows drawn together in thought. "It could work. Seems barbaric, but if the pressure were relieved gently, gradually . . . How does one do it, though?"

Looking at D.C., Carina shuddered. Had she just spoken his death sentence? Or was it his only chance? Life was fragile. Papa learned too often just how fragile. But the times he beat death, the times he won . . . *Per piacere, Signore* . . . There she was again, asking and begging like a child, waiting for Him to do what she wanted. Yet she was unable and unwilling to do what He required.

She went out of Mae's rooms and started for the stairs. But a knock sounded on the front door. Who would knock? Didn't people know it was open? Carina changed course for the door and opened it to find Èmie. She felt a sudden, irrational anger toward her friend. "What is it?" If Èmie told her one more time something bad was going to happen, she would scream.

"I thought you'd like to take the air with me. It's such a lovely evening." Èmie's face was eager.

Take the air? Promenade like two winsome girls without a care in the world? Did Èmie have any idea? Carina looked at Èmie's long, plain face and wanted to cry. Instead, she snatched a shawl from Mae's hook and went out.

What she wanted was the peaceful quiet of the mine. She rarely noticed Crystal's din anymore. It was a constant barrage that no longer drew her attention except at times like this when she longed for the mountain's silence. Why had Èmie come? Had she any idea what Carina had suffered for her sake? Sacrificed for her friend's safety?

Would Mr. Beck truly harm Èmie? Would he stoop so low as to endanger a woman? How could she believe otherwise if he ordered the murder of William Evans? She thought of Quillan's suspicions that other accidental deaths were also ordered by Berkley Beck. If only Quillan would come back. . . .

"What is it, Carina? What's troubling you?"

Carina startled. Had her distress been obvious? *"Does everything you feel always show to all the world?"* Quillan again, his words filling her thoughts, unsettling her mind.

"Carina?" Èmie stopped walking.

Carina waved a hand. "It's been a difficult day."

"I'm sorry. Maybe you'd rather be alone."

As you are all the time? Carina thought, looking at her friend who had so little pleasure. She hooked an arm through Èmie's. Whatever it took to keep Èmie safe, she would do it. "Shall we parade Central and show the young men what they're missing?"

Èmie laughed. "I'd rather walk the creek."

"The creek it is. The men can eat their hearts out."

Èmie pulled the braid over one shoulder. "I doubt anyone's losing rest over me."

"Do you? Well, you're wrong. You just haven't given them the chance."

"I have Uncle Henri to think of."

Carina snorted. "Uncle Henri can think of himself. You have your own life."

"I owe him so much."

Carina didn't argue. Èmie's face had that beatific peace she'd seen the day Èmie told her she belonged to God. *Bene.* Let her belong to her uncle as well. "Do you ever complain? Ever want to . . . throw something or kick someone?"

Èmie laughed. "I see it was a very difficult day. Do you want to tell me about it?"

Carina pressed her hands to her face. Tell Èmie? Let her know she had lost her reputation and self-respect because Berkley Beck would order Uncle Henri . . . The thought was too horrifying with Èmie beside her. And it would crush her friend to know. "I just wish . . . I wish I'd never come."

Èmie sagged. "It must be hard to leave all those you love behind. But, Carina, why did you come?"

Carina stopped walking and dropped her hands to her sides. She sighed, then looked into Èmie's sympathetic face. How could she give her anything but the truth? "I was

516

hurt. By someone I trusted." *And loved, and believed in. Someone in whom I'd put my faith . . . and who proved faithless.*

Carina spread her hands. "I prayed, 'Lord, what do I do?' And then I saw the advertisement for a house in Crystal, Colorado, the diamond of the Rockies. Oh, I thought, that will show him! First he will beg me to stay, saying how sorry he was, can I ever forgive? But he didn't."

Shaking her head, she continued. "He got angry. Called me a foolish girl for making so much of it. Told me I knew nothing of life. That I was innocente. It was true." She kicked a stone and walked swiftly toward the water sparkling in the streambed, the same water that had almost cost her her life.

"I thought God had sent me here. Now . . ." She shrugged her shoulders.

"God works in mysterious ways." Èmie joined her at the edge of the creek. Her voice was soft. "Before you came, every day was the same. Sometimes I thought I would die of the boredom. Then I felt so ungrateful. I had a home. I was needed, even loved by my uncles."

She glanced over. "But when I saw you that day in the bath, you were like some wonderful bird from a land far away. I felt a longing to know you, to have . . . a friend."

Tears stung Carina's eyes.

Èmie smiled impishly. "Perhaps it's for

my sake you've come. Should I apologize for wanting it? God knows my desires."

Swiping a tear, Carina laughed. "And so He whisked me out of California and carried me here?"

Èmie shrugged. "I'd believe anything of my God."

My God. Carina felt a pang, a hunger inside. Èmie believed what she said. Could she know God so well? Trust Him so fully? Love Him so intimately? It was in her voice as though God were her dearest friend.

Oh, Signore . . . But no. What if He proved as faithless as Flavio? Besides, Èmie was good enough for God to love that way. *"You must be washed in the blood of the risen Lamb."* She looked at the creek water mumbling over the rocks in the fading light. *Forgive,* it seemed to say, *forgive.*

Father Antoine Charboneau laid a hand on Alan Tavish's head and pronounced the blessing. The confessions of such a one always humbled the priest and left him feeling wanting in his own walk. He with his robust vigor and hardly a sick day in his life — what could he say to one who spent every hour in pain, then asked God's forgiveness for ingratitude and discontent?

He was only God's ear, Antoine reminded himself, and the compassion he felt for the ostler's suffering must dimly mirror the

Lord's own. "Go in peace, my friend. Kneeling this long is penance enough."

"Aye." Alan's breath came thickly as he stood. "Thank you, Father."

"God bless you." Father Antoine walked Alan to the door of the cabin, noting the stoop of the shoulders, the disfigured knuckles and wrists. *Forgive me, Lord, for ever grudging a single ache or weary muscle.*

"Father . . ." Alan stopped at the door and turned. One sandy gray eyebrow bristled up like a comb above the rheumy green eye. "There's one more thing. I'm worried about my friend."

"Your friend?"

"Quillan."

Antoine's own concern flickered. "Why?"

"The talk, Father. 'Tis growing ugly."

Antoine looked out into the street. "Yes, I've heard."

"I know ye've done what ye can to stem it, but each day that passes without findin' Will's killer . . ."

"I know, Alan." Antoine tugged at his long black cassock, which he wore to hear confessions. "Is he in town? I haven't seen him for a couple of days."

"He's buyin' supplies."

"Maybe he'll stay away."

Alan shook his head. "He knows he's needed."

Antoine nodded once. From what he'd

heard, Quillan Shepard was serving those hardest hit by the flood. Yet still the rumors persisted. He frowned. What more could be done? He patted Alan's shoulder. "What does it avail us to worry? The Lord knows our needs."

Alan looked unconvinced. "Maybe that's so. But there's a devil among us."

Again Antoine felt the chill, the personal responsibility he'd felt over William Evans' death. "I'll see what I can do with your prayers behind me."

"Aye, Father." Alan tugged the flat, nearly brimless hat onto his head and started for the street.

Antoine watched him go, then followed reluctantly. It wouldn't hurt to try once more with Donald McCollough. The marshal was not in his office, but Antoine found him with two of his constables in the Boise Billiard Hall.

McCollough raised his glass in toast. "Come to join us, Father? A glass for the priest."

Antoine waved Bennet Danes away. He was not averse to a French Chardonnay, especially the fine vintage they'd produced at the monastery. But he wouldn't poison himself with the shoe polish that passed for whiskey in Crystal's bars. "No, thank you. I came for a word with you."

McCollough's face darkened. He was already into his cups and took affront at Antoine's refusal. He probably also guessed what word Antoine meant to have. "If it's concernin' me work, I'm off duty." He downed his shot and called for ale. "Not that I'll find a decent drop. Oh, for a mug of black ale —"

"Donald." Antoine spoke sternly. "I want to know what you've learned concerning William Evans."

"Do ye now?" McCollough lurched forward, and the wave of his breath caught Antoine full in the face. "And maybe ye'd not be so eager if ye did know, eh, boys?"

The others with him shared an awkward glance. What did McCollough know? Suddenly Antoine felt the chill deep in his entrails. It turned to anger. "Where is your pride, man? Do your job. If you know —" The blast of sour breath that flew on the laughter made him step back.

"Do me job, is it?" McCollough held up his plaster casted arm. "Do me job? Me job is to look t'other way. And ye might be thankin' me for it."

The man beside McCollough dropped his gaze and flushed.

Antoine pinned him with a glare. "Out with it, Kelly. What is it you know?"

"Nothing, Father. It was some devil off the mountain that killed William Evans." The man's eyes never once met Antoine's.

"Is that what you've been told to say? By whom?"

Kelly squirmed. "No one, Father. I swear it."

"You'll burn in hell for lying, Gerald Kelly." Antoine rarely used such words, certainly not with such anger as compelled him now.

The man paled and wet his lips, but he didn't reply. Antoine turned back to McCollough. "Because you delay, an innocent man is being maligned. If it turns violent, his blood will be on your hands for eternity."

McCollough's jaw grew rigid. "Look to yer own hands, Father. And leave mine in peace."

There was a meaning behind his words, but Antoine couldn't catch it. He turned with a frown and left them to their drink. He'd done what he could for Quillan. So why was his spirit dark with fear?

Quillan woke with a jolt, soaked with sweat and chest heaving. He held himself up on his elbows and willed his breath to slow. It had been many years since that dream had tormented his sleep. But it was as fresh and virulent now as ever before. He could almost smell the smoke and feel the scorching flames.

He rubbed the sweat from his forehead

with the back of his hand and settled back to stare at the underside of his wagon. If he closed his eyes he'd feel their arms around him, the arms of his parents holding him between them as the cabin burned down upon them. He'd see their blistering flesh peeling off the bones, and the bones turning to black and charred skeletons.

At least he hadn't wet himself. The first time the dream had come he awoke soaked in his own urine. He'd continued wetting for three years, even on the nights he didn't dream of the fire. It was a deep humiliation. Lying there, waiting for the shaking to stop, he supposed it was natural the dream should return. He'd thought so much of Wolf these last days.

He hooked his arms behind his head, closed his eyes, and drew a long breath to compose himself. Then he once again studied the undergirding of his wagon. He'd be in Crystal soon. Why? Why go back to the rumors, the hushed suppositions? People knew him now. He couldn't hide who he was.

But there were Cain and D.C. and Alan, and all the others in a bind since the flood. And he'd had a stroke of luck this trip. He'd met a mule train on the road and relieved them for a fair price of all edibles save their own. They'd also been hauling a supply of steels and sledges that he took as well. That saved him driving all the way to Colorado Springs, the prospect of which had grown heavier and heavier with each mile.

He couldn't focus, couldn't put his mind to it. He was worried about his friends. Crystal was a powder keg ready to blow. And there was Carina. He shook his head, not wanting to ponder that again. Carina Maria DiGratia. Prima donna. Yet at times so achingly real.

The dreams she'd invaded were hardly less disturbing than the one he tried now to forget. And even his waking hours weren't free of her. What was his obligation? Had he endangered her by telling what he suspected, by asking her to help him? The thought left him more agitated than before.

He sat up and hit his head. "Ow!" He rubbed the spot, gritting his teeth, then threw himself down on his side. Even if he didn't sleep, the horses needed to rest. He reached into his pack for matches, lit the lantern he'd hung from the rear axle near his head, and pulled out the poetry anthology he'd purchased.

He let it fall open and stared, surprised and a little annoyed, at Thomas Campion's "There Is a Garden in Her Face." Why should it open there, on the very poem that brought Carina DiGratia's visage to his eyes as she'd been that night in the moonlight in his arms? He could hardly think of that poem, of which he had every word in his head, without seeing her.

He flipped the page, then flipped it back. *There is a garden in her face where roses and white lilies grow; A heav'nly paradise is that place wherein all pleasant fruits do flow* . . .

Well, she wasn't all pleasant fruits. There was certainly a persimmon or two. Even a prickly pear. Cherry ripe her lips might cry, but were they chokecherries? He closed the book and took out *The Prisoner of Chillon* instead. That was more like it. Quillan settled onto his back, holding the book above his face. No more love poems or he'd have no chance of sleep at all tonight.

The next day, Mr. Beck added the houses on Hall Street to Carina's collection list. She stood before him, stone-faced. "You can't mean it."

"Of course I mean it." His tone was clear. It was punishment, she knew, for refusing him. He was breaking her, making her pay for his humiliation with her own.

With the blood of sheer incredulity rushing to her face, Carina gripped her hands together at her chest. "I will not go into a house of that nature." She stood obstinate, but he was equally unmoved.

"I offered you an alternative."

Did he truly believe he could humiliate her into marrying him? "I won't do it. I'm leaving Crystal with or without my silver."

His face turned to flint. "You won't get as far as the lake."

She flung a hand toward him. "Who will stop me?"

He was silent, but his eyes held such malice, she quailed.

"Why are you doing this?"

His face softened. "Carina, you force my hand."

So he would force hers. It would only get worse. Berkley Beck would use all his power to subdue her. It infuriated her to feel so helpless against him. Everything in her wanted to fight. Her hands longed to slap, to scratch, to shake him.

But she was a lady, constrained not only by size and strength, but also training. She could not fight him like a street urchin; she must use her brain. Berkley Beck was no fool, but neither was she, and it was time to stop behaving like one.

Very subtly she let the fight drain from her. What if she said yes? What if she accepted his proposal of marriage? The thought sickened her, but it would buy her time and save her further degradation. Did she dare? A breach of promise would not be taken lightly.

But then, she had already broken one —

to Flavio, though for reasons of his own making. Anger flickered inside at what his betrayal had brought her to, but the pain of it was lessened somehow. If she could break off with her darling Flavio, what was it to breach a promise to Berkley Beck, who was dishonesty itself?

She looked at him holding out the purse. Yes, she dared. She forced herself to look him in the eye. She must convince him of her sincerity, if not her desire. She let her hands drop to her sides. "You leave me no choice, Berkley. I accept your offer of marriage." At least he would know she bore him no sentiment.

His brows came up, then his smile spread broadly. "You won't regret it, my dear. When I've accomplished what I intend —"

"Please." She raised a hand. "I know what you're capable of." *Oh yes, I know.* "Now if you'll excuse me." She snatched up her shawl.

"Carina."

He caught her arm, and for a moment she thought he would press his advance. Inwardly she cringed, but she showed only a cool control. "Yes?"

"We'll have dinner tonight and discuss arrangements."

She nodded. There was no use protesting. For now, he had the advantage. But soon . . . *Oh, it would be sweet . . .* She caught herself. She was in no position to anticipate victory when she had no idea how to accomplish it.

Twenty-seven

To find beauty is to know mercy.

Rose

Berkley Beck wore a daisy in the lapel of his gray linen suit, and Carina was reminded of the first time Mae had sent him away. If only he'd stayed away. Now her fingers trembled with revulsion when he brought them to his lips, then tucked them into his arm and began walking. She said nothing all the way to the hotel.

Again Mrs. Barton seated them with tight lips, and now Carina knew why. Mrs. Barton recognized Berkley Beck for what he was. Had Quillan told her? What would he think of her engagement? She shuddered. It was only a sham.

Mr. Beck held her chair and she sat. He smiled suavely as he took his own seat. She didn't return it but tried not to glare. Mrs. Barton returned with a pad. Berkley Beck turned his smile on her.

"We'll have the trout in almond butter. Make sure it's not dry."

Carina's eyebrow twitched. Who was he to speak for her? But she held her peace. Let him enjoy his victory. It would be short-lived.

"My dear." He reached across and clasped her hand in his. "I spoke with the judge, and he agreed to perform the ceremony next Saturday."

Her breath fled in a rush. "No! That's too soon. I can't possibly be ready so soon."

"What's to be ready? We'll honeymoon in Denver, and you can buy whatever you need there." He leaned slightly forward. "I'm not without means."

Carina shook her head in disbelief. "That's too soon."

"A week in Denver, or perhaps you have somewhere else in mind?"

"You can't expect —"

"But I do." Now his veneer grew thin.

"Propriety —"

"Propriety be hanged. This is Crystal, Carina. We make our own rules."

She looked down at the plate Mrs. Barton slid before her. The steamy aroma of the fish turned her stomach, and she pressed her fingers to her mouth.

When Mrs. Barton had gone, Berkley Beck cut into his trout and inspected its flesh. "Hmm. Not perfect, but it will do. How is yours, Carina?"

She stared at him speechless, then slid her fingers to her throat. "I'm not feeling well." She groped her way to her feet, and he was instantly assisting her.

She extricated herself from his grip.

"Please don't trouble yourself. No sense missing your meal. I can see myself home."

He examined her a long moment. "If you're certain . . ."

"Of course. I'm a little indisposed, that's all." And tomorrow she would be deathly ill, and Mae would keep Berkley Beck away. Or would she, when he told of their impending marriage? Carina hurried out.

She should tell Mae everything. But then, out on the street, she saw Quillan, returning from his trip, his wagon half full, his hair uncovered and blowing in the brisk evening breeze. It was sooner than she'd expected, but none too soon. When his eyes met hers, she felt an irrational elation.

She didn't have the ledger. But she would tell him what she knew, how Mr. Beck was extorting the merchants, how the latest night of violence had made them pay. He could act on that. He must. Quillan passed with a short nod, a half smile. Would he go first to his tent? Or would he make his deliveries?

She struck across the street, fighting the evening melee. Though it was not the weekend, the city crawled with men, more and more each day with reports of Joe Turner's success and others. Cain Bradley had hired enough men to hollow a bowl of surface ore from the hillside he claimed. Now the street teemed with them. Some tried to make a way for her, but there were many who didn't know her, didn't care that Joe Turner's second glory hole was named for her.

She thought wryly how the Carina DiGratia was rising in fame and glory while the woman he'd named it for faced possible ruin. She cut across the field, then navigated through the tent city until she stopped outside the one she needed. She knew it was his; she'd seen him emerge from it once before he'd left. Now like a shadow, she went inside.

Quillan's place was sparse, plain, and orderly, containing the bare essentials and nothing more. But then, whatever he had before had been lost in the flood. One thing caught her eye: a crate of books, water damaged. Had he rescued them from the flood as she'd rescued hers from the mountain?

She lifted the top book. *Tales from the Brothers Grimm*. She had read those herself. She looked through the others: *Moby Dick* by Herman Melville, *The House of the Seven Gables*, Nathaniel Hawthorne, and also Hawthorne's *The Snow Image*. There were several anthologies of poetry. Some of the books were ruined, yet he'd kept them as well. She smiled at that.

His tent seemed less forbidding. She took up one book that seemed hardly dampened, the first of the *Leatherstocking Tales* by James Fenimore Cooper. She paged through it slowly, circling the tight space with her steps. How long before Quillan came? It could be hours. It could be dark before he found her there. She shrank inside.

What was she doing? It was not only foolish, it was dangerous. If Berkley Beck learned of it . . . Suddenly the tent flap opened, and she spun. Quillan's reaction was so swift and immediate it staggered her, the gun free from the holster and aimed for her heart. *Madonna mia* . . .

Releasing a sharp breath, he holstered the gun and looked swiftly about. Then he stooped to enter and closed the flap behind him. The tent was not large enough for them both. His presence shrank it unbearably. She was pazza, out of her mind.

"Well." He smiled. "This is a surprise." He motioned toward the cot, the only thing in the tent on which to sit besides the ground covered with tarps.

She shook her head.

He pulled the pack from his shoulder and set it on the cot, then opened the flap and took out two books that he dropped onto the cot beside the pack. She couldn't help looking. The top one was Lord Byron's *The Prisoner of Chillon*.

"Have you read it?" He'd noticed her glance.

She shook her head.

"I'll lend it when I'm done." He rubbed

the back of his neck. "Unless you'd prefer that one." He motioned to the copy of *The Pioneers* that she still held.

Carina looked down at the book as though it had come into her hands on its own, then set it on the cot beside the other.

He pulled a cloth-wrapped ham and several jars from his pack, then tossed it aside. "I could flatter myself that you're here to see me, but I suspect you had a purpose?"

Must she always act the fool in his presence? "It's Mr. Beck."

He turned from the low shelf where he'd set the jars. "I figured that much."

"He's selling protection." She could think of no better way to explain it.

Quillan's eyes narrowed. "Protection?"

"The ones who pay are not harassed; the ones who don't . . ." She spread her hands. "They all pay."

Quillan studied her. "What proof do you have?"

She felt the blood flush her cheeks and stared at the corner of the tent. "I collected the fees."

"What?" His face intensified.

"He threatened Èmie." She turned away, hating to seem weak.

Quillan turned her toward him, his hand on her shoulder gentle but insistent. "You know that makes you an accomplice?"

She trembled. She was more than an accomplice now. "It's worse than that. He thinks we're to be married."

Quillan dropped his hand. "Why does he think that?"

"I accepted his proposal. It was either that or collect fees from the businesses on Hall Street." She saw him flinch. "Please, you have to get me out of here." She hadn't even formed that thought until she spoke it. But now she earnestly prayed he would.

He looked away, his expression pensive and stern. "I might get you out, but that wouldn't solve it."

"Solve what? He thinks we'll marry on Saturday. If I —"

"Give me a minute, Carina." He strode to the end of the tent and back, holding his jaw, which sported substantial whiskers. He stopped again before her. "He must be recording these collections in the ledger."

The ledger? How could he think of the ledger now? "Didn't you hear me? He wants —"

"I heard you. If he thinks you've accepted him, you'll have no trouble getting to the ledger. It would be perfectly natural for you to come and go as you've been."

She spread her hands desperately wide. "I don't work there any longer."

"That's irrelevant. What eager bride-to-be wouldn't drop in to see her betrothed?"

"He knows I'm not eager."

535

Quillan caught her arms and pulled her close. "Pretend."

Her heart raced in her chest.

"Get me the ledger, Carina." His eyes commanded her attention.

She couldn't look away. "And then?"

"Then we'll see how the cards fall out."

Carina pushed against his chest. "What kind of promise is that?"

He let her go. "I'll see that Berkley Beck doesn't marry you. If I get the ledger into the right hands —"

"You mean the marshal?"

Quillan shook his head.

"Who then?"

"Someone level-headed enough to deal with it quickly and not let it escalate."

"I don't understand." A strand of hair caught in her lips and she pulled it free. "Escalate how?"

"Vigilantes. Some who are calling for my neck right now. They want justice. They've had all they can take of the roughs and they're scared. Beck has them believing I'm behind it. William Evans knew different, and he was silenced. The merchants won't stand much more."

Carina was silent. It was madness.

"Just get me the ledger, Carina. It's got to contain what we need to stop Beck before it all gets out of hand." His voice softened. "Trust me in this."

Trust Quillan Shepard? As she had trusted Berkley Beck? Trusted Flavio? *Signore, it's too much.* She dropped her gaze to the small space between them. She felt his hand on her shoulder, in the hair at the nape of her neck. He tipped her head up, and their eyes met.

"You have to trust me. Plans might already have been made, plans that include you."

She gasped with sudden fear. Was it possible? She heard in her mind the invectives against her and knew it was. A high moan started in her throat, and Quillan pulled her into his arms. Pressed close to his chest, she smelled the dust of the road on his shirt and didn't care. He would protect her. She had to trust him. She had nowhere else to turn. But could she do what he wanted?

The rap on his tent post brought Quillan to his senses, and he released Carina abruptly. "Who is it?"

"Alan."

Quillan glanced at Carina, but there was no place for her to go. He opened the flap to Alan Tavish, who hurried in and saw Carina at once.

Quillan closed the flap. "Miss DiGratia brought me news of Beck."

Tavish's face was grave. "Dark news no

doubt, but not so dire, I'm afraid, as what I bring ye."

Quillan frowned.

"It's Daniel Cain, Quillan. He's dyin'."

Quillan's breath left his chest. D.C. dying?

"And it's maybe part of what the lass was tellin' you. T'was the roughs last Tuesday night."

The night he left. He'd ridden out and left Cain and D.C. . . . No wonder he'd felt so anxious to return!

"There's a surgery been done, but the lad won't waken."

Quillan searched Alan's face, hoping to see there something that lightened his words. He didn't. A hollowness stole over him. Nothing Carina had said mattered now. He was too late. Whatever he'd meant to do would not save D.C. He suddenly felt tired to the bone. "Where is he?"

"At Mae's. And Cain with him, closer to the grave maybe than his boy."

Carina stood alone in the tent after the two of them left. Quillan had not even realized she remained. How deeply he must care for that boy and his papa. She felt selfish for running to him with her news, her hopes that he would take care of everything. She had not even thought to tell him of D.C.'s condition, not considered his distress. She had thought only of herself.

Carina pressed her palm to her forehead, then let it drop. Now what would she do? She had told Quillan her news, and his answer was the same. Get the ledger. It was all he cared about. And it was impossible.

Bene. She must make it possible. Pretend? She'd never been a pretender. As he said, everything she felt showed to all the world. Well, she must learn to hide it now. She stepped out of the tent, staring at the ground as she hurried away.

The step beside her startled her, and she looked up into a rough face, not one she knew, but she recognized evil. The man didn't touch her, but his words did. "Mr. Beck wants to see you."

Her breath left in a rush. Her heart raced in her chest. "Why?"

He only waved her toward the street. Annoyed, she started that way. *Had he seen her go to Quillan?* Her legs shook as she walked in silence to the office door, then with only a slight hesitation, she pulled it open. Berkley Beck stood inside and turned when she entered. He nodded the man out, and the door closed behind her.

"A miraculous recovery, my dear."

She recalled her half-feigned illness. "The air helped."

"So they claim. Remarkable climate." He

was toying with her. He walked to the window and surveyed the street. "Why were you in Quillan Shepard's tent?"

Her heart lurched, but she didn't show it. She must not seem defensive. Pretend. She contained her fear and took control of her voice. "I had things to purchase."

"From his tent?"

"From him."

"What things?"

"It's not your business." Daring, but convincing.

He turned. "Why Quillan instead of another freighter?"

She fought the panic in her mind. Be clear. Tell as much truth as possible. "I don't know another freighter."

"But you know Quillan Shepard."

"It would be hard not to. He saved my life."

Berkley Beck was silent so long she squirmed under his gaze. Then his chin came up slightly. "I forbid you to see him again."

Carina stared, her natural defiance rising. "Would you suggest blinders?"

His left cheek twitched. "I would suggest you guard your tongue."

"You don't own me. Even in light of our . . . agreement."

"Don't I?" His eyes turned cold, hard as glass.

She felt her breath stop, her throat tighten. Her hands quivered at her sides. Then she walked out of his office. She wanted to run, imagined all kinds of ruffians gathering behind her. But she kept her back straight. Pretend!

Cain sat beside his boy, exhausted and used up. He'd stopped praying in words. He'd said all the good Lord needed to hear. Now the prayer just ached and swelled in his soul as he looked at his son. The shunt had been removed when the drainage ceased, and D.C.'s color was better, his breath coming stronger. But that was all. He just lay there, never moving except for a sporadic fluttering of the eyes.

Cain glanced up as Quillan came into the room. He must have just returned, just heard the news. Cain saw him react, knew what he thought. The boy was closer to death than life. And it showed. Each day that passed diminished their hope.

Quillan came and squatted down beside him. "How bad is it?" His voice was hoarse with concern.

"Ain't good. Doc Felden fears he's done the boy a disservice, savin' his life when this may be all he has left to it."

Quillan's jaw tensed.

Cain fought a wave of despair. "It didn't

use to be this way. You don't remember, but up in Placer we had a miner's law. Hardly needed enforcing. Folks could leave their gold dust dryin' and no one would touch it. Life was precious. We depended on each other. Now . . ." He squeezed his hands together. "It's gotta stop."

"It will."

Cain looked up. Something in Quillan's eyes, the set of his jaw . . . he was Wolf all over. The Wolf who had stanched the whispers with a look, withstood the insults, and left men dumb who thought to provoke him. With the same quiet intensity, Quillan was the image of his father. He was a force to be reckoned with. But it was a force without brutality.

Quillan took Cain's hand between his. "It will, Cain."

Father Antoine felt as though his heart had been ripped out. He prayed to Almighty God that his eyes lied, but he knew they didn't. He knelt beside the bed in the pale morning light and reached a shaky hand to touch Èmie's. Her swollen eyelids quivered. Her upper lip was the size of his thumb and split in two places.

Tears came to his eyes, brimmed, and ran over. "Èmie . . ." His voice was choked and rough.

She was curled into a ball on her bed, but now she tried to roll, and one bruised eye opened a slit.

Antoine gripped the bed frame. "Who did this to you? Was it Henri!"

Her eye blinked slowly, and her tongue dampened the damaged lips. "Please. Find Carina. You must —" She winced with the effort.

The priest brushed her hair with his hand, forcing a calmness he couldn't feel. His rage would not help her. "Lie still. I'll bring your friend." He rose. How could he leave her alone even for the time it would take to find Miss DiGratia? Where was Henri? Would he return?

Antoine shook with anguish as he hurried out of the cabin and made his way toward Mae's, praying that Carina would be there. *Holy God.* He climbed Mae's porch. *Mighty God.* He rapped on the door, then remembered this one was kept open. *Merciful God.* He yanked it open and went in. *Precious Savior.* Carina was there before him, speaking with Mae at the desk. They both turned, and by their expressions he must look like death. He felt like death.

"Father?" Carina's eyes were wide.

"It's Èmie."

Carina gave a little cry and rushed for the door.

"Carina!" Mae called after, but Miss

DiGratia was already running toward the slope where Èmie's cabin stood.

"What is it, Father?" Mae demanded, hands on hips.

"Èmie's been beaten. I need the doctor."

"Well, they're here, both of them." She ushered him into her rooms.

Antoine stopped in the doorway of the bedroom where Doctors Felden and Simms were discussing Daniel Cain. The boy lay in the bed, a victim like Èmie. Haggard beside the bed sat Cain Bradley.

"What's the matter?" Dr. Felden asked.

Antoine told them.

"Èmie . . ." Young Dr. Simms paled. "Are not even the women safe now?" He snatched up the medical bag.

Antoine took the slope as though he could conquer the mountain itself, but it wasn't enough. *Why Èmie, Lord? Why?*

Carina felt sick as she dropped to her knees beside her friend. A wail started in her throat, and she didn't stop it as she looked at this woman she had endangered. Better that she had never come, never befriended her, never brought her to this. . . .

One swollen eye opened, and Èmie reached for her. "Carina."

Carina dropped her head to Èmie's hand, clutched between her own.

544

Èmie's tongue parted her lips. "You must do what Mr. Beck wants."

Carina shook with rage. "I will tear his heart out! I will —"

"Listen to me."

"I won't listen! I will put a bullet in him and your uncle and —"

"Carina." The voice from the doorway was intense.

She spun and faced the priest defiantly. "I don't care. He will pay for this!"

Dr. Simms pushed through behind the priest. "Èmie needs healing, not vengeance."

Carina resisted, then allowed Father Antoine to pull her aside. She covered her face with her hands. Sciocca! She had defied him at Èmie's risk. "It's my fault," she moaned.

"It's not your fault." The priest's eyes were intent.

"I angered and defied him."

"I left her here and went traipsing after lost souls." The priest's hand on her shoulder shook with emotion.

"Will you two stop blaming yourselves and get me boiled water?" Dr. Simms spoke with more authority than Carina had heard from him before.

He was right. The first thing must be tending Èmie. She hurried for the stove. "I need wood, Father. There are coals." Her hands shook as she shoveled the ashes that buried the coals still glowing in the oven.

The priest chopped wood from the pile out back, and she lit the stove and heated water while Dr. Simms performed his examination. With nervous energy she scoured Èmie's place, recalling as she did Papa's admonitions on the part of cleanliness in healing. Carina swept the pressed dirt floor as though she could take it down to bedrock. As soon as the steam blew from the edge of the lid, she poured a bowl of water and took it to Èmie's bedside with the cleanest cloth she could find.

The work had helped her to think straight. She couldn't shoot Berkley Beck. Not for revenge, even though her heart burned for it. But she could get Quillan the ledger. Her rage gave her courage. Now. She must do it now before she lost the nerve.

When Dr. Simms sent them out, Carina left the priest standing with his back to the rough log wall. She stalked to the livery, turned outside the door, and searched the street. From this vantage, she would see Mr. Beck leave. Would he look for her or send one of his dogs? Would he expect her to come to him remorseful and pliant?

She clenched her fists at her sides. He would never break her. He had lost whatever hold the threat of hurting Èmie had given him. The act had made her a tiger.

She waited and watched. She would get the ledger and then —

His door opened, and Mr. Beck stepped out. Her heart clamored as two men came forward immediately to speak to him. Beck nodded twice, then went with one down the walk toward the Emporium. The other moseyed back across to the corner and stood there. She would have to enter under that one's very nose.

But what had Quillan said? She would be expected. Drawing a jagged breath, she crossed the street and made her way along the sidewalk, looking suitably subdued. A group of miners tipped their hats, and she recognized one from Joe Turner's operation. He gave her a bright smile, but she was too tense to return it.

A man in a striped coat and yellow cravat stepped into her path. "A small act of prestidigitation, miss?"

"No." She shook her head, but he reached out and drew a coin from her hair. She pushed by. If only she could secure the ledger so easily. But God would determine that. And so far nothing had been easy. She went inside, almost too tense to breathe. The room was warm and smelled of Beck's pomade. It made his presence almost palpable, though she had seen him leave.

What if he discovered her there beneath his desk? Or simply found the ledger missing? Of course he would think of her. Who else? Regardless of that, she hurried to Mr. Beck's desk and lifted the board underneath. Let him guess. Let him know. After what he did to Èmie . . . She tugged the board free. The ledger lay there among the papers and engraved plates. She snatched it up, then removed the box of Nonna's silver.

She had no idea how long Berkley Beck would be out. He could return at any moment, but she couldn't just walk out with the ledger in plain view. Quickly she pulled open the box and removed the spoons and forks and knives. These she tied into her underskirt, then pulled out the velvet forms that had held them in place. She tucked those back under the floor, and into the empty box, she fit the ledger.

With a sigh, Carina replaced the board and stood. The silver clinked when she walked, but only softly. She peeked out through the window. No sign of Mr. Beck. Was it possible the Lord had finally seen fit to aid her? *Grazie, Signore.* But it was a scornful gratitude.

She went out the door and started along the walk. The man was still on the corner, and she noticed it was the one who had escorted her to Mr. Beck the day before. She was certain he would hear her heart pounding as she passed. She waited for his challenge.

Would she run? What if he asked to see what was inside the box? She averted her gaze and came within three steps of him, then two. Then she was past. He didn't stop her, and she carried the box around the corner at Drake and, with an effort, kept herself from running to Mae's.

She went inside and started for the stairs, then changed her mind. If Mr. Beck came looking for the ledger, he'd search her room first. She went instead to the room where D.C. slept. For once Cain was not beside the bed, and she breathed her relief. Though he was Quillan's friend, she felt safer alone.

Kneeling down, she took the ledger from the box and slipped it between the mattress and springs. Then she replaced the silver into the wooden box and shoved it against the wall under the bed. She sat back on her heels and pressed her hands to her temples. Then she stood and headed for the kitchen.

The breeze billowed the curtain at the open window, but the room was still stuffy. Mae looked up from the stove, her face a steamed mixture of fatigue and concern. "How's Èmie?"

It was an innocent question, but at the thought of Èmie, Carina crumpled. The fury that had carried her through the theft drained away, leaving only pain and guilt. She shook her head with a throat too tight to answer, then covered her face in her hands.

Mae crossed to her and stroked her head, then pulled her into a soft embrace. "What's this world coming to?"

What indeed? Carina pressed her face to Mae's neck as tears stung her eyes.

Mae patted her shoulder. "There must be some rhyme or reason to it, but only God knows what."

Did He? Did God know that she had just placed herself in peril? Maybe even of her life? Did He care that Èmie lay in pain? Èmie who belonged to Him, who loved Him like a papa? She felt her heart pounding and remembered Father Antoine. *"God is all and in all."*

Not in Crystal. There was no God in Crystal. She swept out of the room, ran up the stairs, and flung herself onto her cot, releasing the tears held too long.

Twenty-eight

What miracle joins one heart to another?
Rose

Quillan rubbed the weariness from his face. He'd spent the better portion of the night sitting with Cain, the rest of it trying vainly to sleep. His thoughts wouldn't give him any peace — thoughts of D.C.'s beating, and now his struggle for life. Thoughts of Cain's agony. Quillan almost worried more for him, and it put a hollow in his belly to think what Cain must be feeling.

Quillan sat up. There was a steely taste in his mouth, and his eyes felt like sand. The thoughts still roiled. Carina's news about Beck's activities wasn't altogether unexpected, for Cain had suggested as much before William Evans was killed. What was new was her part in it.

Why had she involved herself to that degree? It was not only stupid; it was dangerous. If he brought Beck down, would it endanger Carina? He shook the thickness from his head. She was already endangered. He'd just have to protect her from the storm.

He rubbed the kink from his left

shoulder, tipped his neck to one side till the spine popped softly, then to the other. Then he forked both hands through his hair and pulled it back. With his fingers clasped through it at the back of his skull, he tried to think. Things would happen today. He could feel it. Maybe his return would precipitate them. He released the hair and blew out his breath. Better to face it head on.

He tensed at the stealthy knock on his tent frame. "Who is it?"

"Ben Masterson."

Quillan sprang to his feet and admitted the city trustee.

Masterson's countenance was troubled, the ridge above his brows dipping into a *V*. He wasted no time. "It's not wise for you to be here, Quillan. Beck's raised a hue against you, and this morning he's put the brand to the fire."

Quillan flinched inwardly. "How?"

"Emie Charboneau."

Quillan scrunched his own brow. "Emie . . . I don't know her except in passing."

"She was beaten last night. Savagely. Beck has witnesses that swear they saw you running from the cabin." Masterson's eyes veered away. "On all fours."

Quillan felt a chill and a knot in his belly.

"One of your neighbors claims you didn't come to your tent before nearly dawn."

Quillan bristled. "I was sitting with Cain. Do you know about D.C.?"

Masterson nodded. "It's not enough. Even if Cain vouches for you, there's too much sentiment against."

Quillan straightened, thinking of Carina. "I just need a little time. There's proof of Beck's infamy."

"You're beating a cracked drum."

"A ledger, hidden under his floor. If I can get my hands on it . . ."

Masterson shook his head. "You'll be lucky to get out of town alive. I'm warning you, Quillan."

"I won't run. Certainly not on all fours." He felt his lip pull into a sneer and didn't try to hide it.

Masterson sighed. "How will you get this ledger?"

"Carina DiGratia."

"Beck's mistress?"

Quillan stiffened. "She's not his mistress."

Masterson looked unconvinced. "They're to be married."

Quillan dismissed that with a snort. "Only Beck thinks so."

"Tempers are high. With this last attack on a woman . . ." He shook his head. "I can't hold them back forever."

"Give me today."

Masterson stepped back, eyed the walls of the tent, then nodded. "I'll do what I can."

When Masterson left, Quillan washed and headed for Mae's. The morning was well advanced, and he had to convince Carina to get the ledger without delay. He held himself straight, confident, ignoring the whispers and stares and more than one hard look as he passed. But underneath he felt every one.

Cain stumped into the room and leaned over the face of his son bathed in morning light. "How you doin' there, D.C.? The mine's bringin' out good ore, don't ya know. Good as any you thought would be there."

He settled into the chair and rubbed his stump, which was shooting pain up his thigh and down where no flesh existed anymore. "Cain't say it ain't time for you to be doin' your share, though. You always was one to shirk the work. Not that I'm blamin' you. It's not always been easy." He touched his son's hand.

No, Lord, it ain't been easy. I'm not askin' it to be, either. I don't need much. Nothing for myself. Just this boy here. Now, I know I'm goin' on like that widow woman haranguing the judge till he cain't stand it no more. But it's in the Good Book to keep on that way, so here I am again, askin' you to spare him.

It seemed the Lord had done that much already. Both docs guessed D.C. might live.

I'm right thankful for that much, don't ya know. But, Lord, I'm askin' just a little bit more. You said ask and ye shall receive. I'd like him back walkin' and talkin', if it's all the same to you. I'll even take his gripin' like music to my ears.

What he wouldn't give to hear D.C. argue. *You work all things together for the good of those as love you. Well, I've loved you most all my life and I'm not stoppin' now. If this is the best I get, then I'm grateful for it. But I know it ain't the best you can do, what with the loaves and fishes and all. I'm lookin' for a bit more, if you get my meanin'. And thankful for it, Lord.*

Cain sat back and closed his eyes. There were no Chinese firecrackers. Never had been. He didn't need it. He wasn't one of those that demanded a sign every time. He knew God heard him. And things would work out according to God's sovereign will. *They always do, don't ya know.*

Tears spent, Carina hid in her room. She could not go to Quillan and tell him she'd taken the ledger. She knew now Mr. Beck would have her watched. Had the guard reported her coming and going from the office? Why didn't Berkley Beck send for her?

Was it a small thing that a woman had been beaten to teach another to guard her tongue? Did he only wait until she was so tight with nerves she would break when he called for her? Carina swallowed the knot in her throat.

She would not break. But Quillan must come. Surely he would come. She got up and stalked to the window as she had a hundred times already. And this time, she saw him. The hat hid his face, but she knew his walk, so determined, so sure.

She threw open the door and rushed down. Hearing his voice with Mae's, she hurried into the room where D.C. lay atop the ledger. Mae and Quillan and Cain all looked at her, but it was Quillan's gaze she felt. Standing in the small bedroom, he seemed every bit as tall and foreboding as he had in his tent.

His hair was loose to his shoulders, his jaw still unshaved. If he'd been dressed in buckskins and carried a powder rifle, she'd have thought him a mountain man. Even so, there was something wild in him this morning, something she hadn't seen last evening in his tent. Defiance maybe, like that of a cornered animal who meant to fight. She wondered what appearance she presented. Her tears must show, and she felt flushed and agitated.

Before she could speak, Mae pushed past. "Well, I've work to do."

Now it was only Cain and Quillan, and

D.C., who lay unseeing. Cain rubbed the knuckles of one hand with the palm of the other. Quillan watched her steadily.

She met his gaze. "May I speak with you alone?"

He shifted his weight with a fluid motion from the ball of one foot to the other. "I have no secrets from Cain."

The old man looked up. "Eh?"

Carina motioned with her hand. "It's there. Under the mattress."

Quillan's understanding was instant. "You got it?"

"This morning. After . . ." Her chest squeezed painfully. She couldn't speak of Èmie. She knelt beside the bed and reached in for the ledger. She jostled the mattress, and D.C.'s arm came down, landing on her shoulder. With a cry, she jumped back.

At the same moment Cain lunged forward. "D.C.?" His voice broke.

"I'm hungry. Can't we ever have a decent meal around here?"

Carina gasped, looking straight into D.C.'s eyes. She couldn't move for amazement.

Quillan crouched beside her, taking the boy's hand. "D.C., can you hear me?"

" 'Course I can. What's going on?" D.C. looked around him and flushed. "What am I doing here?"

"Hee-hee-hee." Cain slapped his thigh.

"Son, you are a living miracle. Praise God!" He threw his feeble hands up.

Carina could only stare. Each day she had expected to hear the doctor say D.C. was dead. She had grown used to him lying there, rolled one way or another like a pillow you fluffed and tossed in place. But now here he was awake and whole, and she felt a surging joy. *Grazie, Signore!*

How could she not thank a God who could do such a thing? She tugged her arm from under the mattress and rushed out. "Mae! Mae, he's awake." She landed in the kitchen where Mae was chopping potatoes. "He's awake, Mae, and hungry!"

Mae spun. "Daniel Cain?"

"Yes!"

"Well, I . . . I never heard the like." She rubbed her hands down her apron, then pushed past toward the bedroom.

Carina went to the stove and scooped a small amount of beef with plenty of gravy into a bowl. She carried it to the bedroom but couldn't get through to D.C. "Someone should go for the doctor," she said, thinking no one heard her over the questions and exclamations.

But then Quillan stood. "I'll go." For a moment their eyes locked, and he was gone.

Dr. Felden straightened and took the stethoscope from his ears. He looked across the bed to Carina and raised his brows. "Well, Miss DiGratia, it seems your hocus-pocus worked."

She shrugged and looked at D.C. "I only told him you needed a hole in the head." Laughter followed.

D.C. grinned. "I knew enough to run from you the first time. Guess I wasn't quick enough the next."

"Well, let's see what your legs can do now." Dr. Felden pulled aside the covers and put an arm around D.C.'s waist.

D.C. blushed furiously at his bare legs under the nightshirt. Carina wondered what he would say to the sponge baths and rubs she and Mae had given. She glanced aside and found Quillan's eyes on her. He didn't look away until D.C. got to his feet and stood on his own.

"Better than I can do." Cain cackled. Again laughter.

Mae moved aside. "Can he walk?"

D.C. took a few steps, then sat down at the end of the bed. "I feel a little rickety."

"And no wonder." Dr. Felden snapped his bag closed. "Aside from the small amounts of water and broth trickled down your throat, you've had neither food nor exercise for days."

D.C. shook his head. "I don't remember anything. Not even what happened to put me here."

Quillan scowled. "Probably just as well."

Cain raised a hand. "If it's all right with you all, I feel a mighty need to bow our heads and say a little thanks, don't ya know."

"That would be right nice." Mae folded her hands, and they were swallowed up in her bosom.

Carina closed her eyes, surprised by the sting of tears. She tucked her folded hands beneath her chin and felt the crucifix against her thumb. How long since she'd prayed? Truly prayed?

"Dear Lord, I wanted to thank you with these friends here for restoring my boy. You gave up your own Son for our salvation, but I'm tickled you saw fit to pluck mine off the altar, just as you did Abraham's Isaac. I'm much obliged." Cain's voice broke and tears came to his eyes.

Carina blinked her own away and saw Mae's eyes grow moist as well. Cain spoke to God as to his closest friend. His *compagno*. One he loved and knew. Like Èmie. But how could he know God?

"Daddy." D.C. took Cain's hand. "I think this would be a good time for me to take Preacher Paine's advice. I want to give my life to Jesus, seeing how He's given it back to me."

Cain's cheeks reddened and the flesh seemed to soften with joy. "God works all things together for the good of those as love him." With his palsied hands supporting him, he lowered himself down onto his one knee, the stump resting beside it, and took D.C.'s hands in his. "Just pray the way Preacher Paine told it, son."

Carina's chest felt tight. She had ignored Preacher Paine's words, not wanting to face her own darkness. Now she was too confused to know how to feel, what to think. She looked at Quillan, but he stood quietly, his gaze on D.C. both gentle and keen.

"Well, Lord . . ." D.C.'s voice cracked. "I've messed things up a lot. I'm a first-rate sinner, and I need your pardon. Guess I need washing in the blood of the Lamb. You died for me, and now you've let me live. I'll try from here on to do what's right and hope to serve you well."

"Amen!" Cain clasped his son's hands. D.C. gripped his father in a tight hug, then Quillan helped Cain stand and got him back to the chair. Dr. Felden took up his bag.

"See you don't overdo it. No baptisms in the creek."

D.C. only grinned.

"Stay another night here, and I'll check back in the morning. Miss DiGratia, a word?"

Surprised, Carina followed him out.

He stopped at the outer door. "Dr. Simms wanted you to know Èmie's not as bad as might be. There doesn't seem to be internal damage."

"Thank God." She breathed her relief.

Dr. Felden rubbed his face with his palm. "I'm not much of a faithful man, but after a thing like this, it's hard to ignore the part a Deity plays. Look after yourself, Miss DiGratia. The trouble in Crystal is far from over." For a moment he looked as though he would say more, then he put on his hat and went out the door.

She sighed, wishing he hadn't reminded her.

Quillan reached under the mattress and pulled out the ledger. He stared at it, unopened, for a long minute. Carina had done it. He'd come prepared to beg and threaten, but she'd already gotten what he needed. Why?

He glanced at Cain, but Cain was speaking low and earnestly to his son, neither of them aware he was there. Stuffing the book into his shirt, Quillan went out and headed for his tent. He would read it there and determine what use it might be. It had to be. He'd risked enough to get it. No, not him. Carina.

He raked his hair with his fingers and realized he'd left his hat at Mae's. He drew a long breath and released it, then rested his hand on his gun to pass through town. All his senses were tuned. If someone meant to start something, he'd be ready. But no one threatened him. Not in the daylight, not in plain view. If the vigilantes struck, it would be at night with the darkness hiding their identities.

He passed Central and crossed behind the last of the buildings to the rows of tents assembled again along the creek, half as many as before the flood. The others had either wised up or drowned. He reached his tent and went inside, then sat down on the cot with the ledger across his knees.

He didn't open it. Instead he pictured the turn of D.C.'s head, the eyes opening. Only now did he realize how little hope he'd had to see the boy again. He rubbed his hand over the cover of the ledger, reluctant now to open it. *God works all things together for the good of those who love him*. Watching Cain and D.C. had put an ache in his heart and a lump in his throat. Maybe he wasn't quite the renegade he thought himself.

Carina pushed the damp tendrils of hair from her face and squinted against the glare. The day was hot, but now that the ledger was in Quillan's hands, she refused to skulk in her room. She scoured the dishes in the tub behind Mae's. At least there was a breeze. It caught in her hair tumbling loosely down her back.

Leaning back on her haunches, Carina tossed the hair back and swiped her forehead with her sleeve. A shadow passed over, but it was not Quillan Shepard this time. It was Berkley Beck. She startled back with dismay. How had she not heard him approach?

He posed himself before her. "Good day, Carina."

"Is it?" All her venom rose to her tongue. "How dare you show yourself!"

"Show myself? Why shouldn't I?"

Carina jumped to her feet. "Do you pretend you didn't order Èmie Charboneau beaten?"

"Order it? My dear."

Carina shook with fury. "I know what you are, Mr. Beck."

"Do you?" He caught her arm in a piercing grip. "I've changed our plans. You'll marry me tonight."

"What! You can't seriously think I would stoop to marry you now."

"But you will." He leaned his face close. "Èmie's still alive."

Shocked into silence, Carina stared at him. His meaning was clear, and he was vile beyond anything she'd ever imagined. "Get your hand off me."

He let go of her arm. "Tonight." Tugging his coat flaps, he stalked away.

Carina's chest heaved. She dropped her

face into her hands. God had deserted her! Why had he saved her from the shaft only to give her to Berkley Beck? God was cruel! He was unforgiving. *Unforgiving.*

"No," she moaned. Was He punishing her? She clenched her fists and shook them at the sky. "What have I done? *I* was wronged. *I* was betrayed. What right have you to destroy me?"

She sniffed angrily and swiped the tears with her sleeve. Snatching up her skirts, she ran. Banging through the bodies of men and mules alike, she crossed Central and passed into the rows of tents. She flung open Quillan's canvas flap and found him once again with a gun to her heart.

"Tonight! He thinks he will marry me tonight!"

Quillan reached out and tugged her into the tent, then peered out behind her a long while, gun held ready. Carina waited, her heart thumping from both her running and her rage.

Quillan turned back inside, holstered the gun. "He won't marry you tonight."

"You'll take me out of here?"

"We'd be cut down as soon as we left town."

She clutched her hands together at her throat. "What, then?" She'd done her part with the ledger, and he had promised to stop this farce of a marriage. She felt caught in the center of a dust devil, tossing and whirling at the whim of some force she couldn't deny. She couldn't leave; she couldn't refuse. Quillan must think of something.

And it seemed he did. The lines of his face smoothed. He went very still, yet she felt him like a force she couldn't ignore. "He can't marry you if you're married already."

She stared into his face. "But I'm not."

"But you could be." His mouth stayed slightly parted as he waited.

Her head was thick. He couldn't be saying what it seemed he was. Quillan Shepard, loner, who refused even a partner on his wagon?

"We can find the priest and have it done before Beck's rounded up a judge."

He would marry her to stop Beck? Marry her with no feelings for her, no . . . love between them? "But . . . you would . . ."

His swift motion cut her off. He gripped her arms and pulled her close. Looking into her startled eyes, he brought his mouth to hers. The chin whiskers scratched, yet the mustache was soft. His mouth, however, was not. He pulled her to her toes and kissed her so long she couldn't breathe.

He then set her back down, but their eyes remained locked. She couldn't look away if she wanted to. One hand rested on her heaving breast, the other hung at her waist, immobile.

His mouth pulled sideways into his pirate's grin. "Yes, I would. But I'd like to clean up first."

Carina took a step back, still watching him, still unable to speak.

"I'd rather do it alone." And now there was laughter in his eyes. At her.

She spun and swept out of his tent. Shaking inside, she walked to Mae's. What was she doing? Marry Quillan Shepard? Marry him? Had she agreed? He certainly thought so. Maybe her lips had told him, the hammering of her heart. Was she leaping from the skillet into the fire?

Quillan stared at the tent flap through which Carina had fled. He must have taken her by surprise if his own condition were any indication. He had certainly not premeditated proposing marriage. But when the thought came to him, it seemed the perfect thing.

Beck would be furious. It was certain to cause some action on his part. But this time Crystal would be ready. Quillan glanced at the ledger. Ready, because he would equip them with the proof. Two of the trustees were named as receiving bribes. One judge, a scattering of constables, and those less virtuous than the ones controlled by fear alone. And of course, the names of the roughs.

Some of them showed as monies owed. They obeyed orders to work off their debt. Others were paid thugs. And that's where he found the Carruthers. No wonder Carina hadn't gotten her property. Beck wanted them right there within reach.

And then there was Carina. Quillan had guessed she might be listed with the others. It was a mean trick on Beck's part, probably to dissuade this very thing. But Quillan wasn't overly concerned. His wedding would safeguard her as well as anything. People would see she was not Beck's mistress and had been coerced to collect for him. Probably the same could be said for others in the book, but Quillan couldn't worry about that.

He picked up the ledger and tucked it into his shirt. With a firm stride he made his way to Masterson's fine house. He applied the brass knocker that he had hauled for the door. Masterson's manservant opened. "Mr. Masterson is expecting you, sir."

Sir. Quillan almost grinned. A far cry from running on all fours. He swallowed the bitterness and followed the man to Masterson's study.

"Ah, Quillan. Come in. You have it?"

Quillan extricated the ledger from his shirt and laid it on Masterson's desk. "Con-

568

victing, but not overly enlightening. I'm certain you won't be surprised at many of the names."

"Still, this is the first concrete evidence. Can't act on speculation, you know. Does it mention William Evans?"

"Not by name. That would be far too careless. But it lists the players and their roles. The roughs are euphemistically guards and enforcers."

"Yes, yes, I see that." Masterson scanned the pages. "You were right, Quillan. This ledger is invaluable. Every name can be held to account."

Quillan leaned forward and rested his hands on the desk. "There's one name that needs exempting."

"Oh?" Masterson looked up over his pince-nez.

"Carina DiGratia."

Masterson frowned.

"She was compelled beyond her control."

"The same could be true for any number of these. You know how it works. A dirty little secret. Who wouldn't pay to keep certain things quiet? Threats made. As far as I'm concerned, Miss DiGratia —"

"Miss DiGratia is becoming Mrs. Shepard."

Masterson removed his pince-nez and stared. "When?"

"Today."

A long moment their eyes held. "You're forcing his hand."

"Exactly."

"And what of the woman?"

Quillan straightened. "She'll be my wife."

"This is preposterous, Quillan. You can't take a wife simply to contrive revenge."

Quillan didn't answer. He needn't point out Carina's qualities or their effect on him. All Masterson needed to know was that she was inviolable. "She is the one who procured the ledger. Without Miss DiGratia we'd have nothing."

"Very well." Ben Masterson tugged the fob and removed his watch from his vest pocket. "Except for those herein named, I'll speak with the trustees. Beck won't surrender his power easily, and it could come to war. We can only hope to strike quickly and avoid that." He replaced his pince-nez on the bridge of his nose but glanced over them. "Happy nuptials."

Quillan gave him a half smile, turned on his heel, and left. There were details to accomplish. He couldn't go to a judge, as even those not listed in the ledger might be friendly to Beck and bring word of Quillan's intention. Beck's own matrimonial plans were widely known, and it was bound to raise eyebrows.

There were several ministers, but for his own reasons Quillan preferred to avoid them. That left Father Charboneau, whom Quillan had never met personally and who was probably not in the best form today after what happened to his niece. Nonetheless, Quillan would be convincing.

If they performed the ceremony at Mae's, Cain could witness it without leaving D.C., as the two were suddenly inseparable. Mae could be the second witness, so there would be no question of legality. Beck must not presume for a moment this wedding a sham. Quillan wanted him to know that Carina was in every way his wife, and in that knowing, regret dragging out Quillan's parentage and blackening his name.

Twenty-nine

Cruelty sustained loses its barb.
Rose

Carina's legs were numb as she climbed the stairs to her room. She closed the door behind her and stood staring at the cot. Then she knelt and pulled out the black satchel. She removed the paper-wrapped garment and set it gently on the bed. Then she pulled out the packet that held her precious mementos.

Sitting down on the cot, she slid the contents onto the blanket. Her heart tugged as she eyed each photograph of her loved ones, alighting at last on the melting features of her dear Flavio. He had not come. Nor would it matter now if he did.

She looked at the bundle of letters tied in a red ribbon, letters filled with his poetry, his words, beautiful and vague. She slipped one out and read it, the words conjuring images and memories poignant and deep. One by one she read the letters, Flavio's words to her, his promises. Yet he had proved so false. Did she even know him? Had she ever?

He seemed a lifetime away. A dream. An imaginary love whom she had needed to form her self. She'd been Flavio's darling, Flavio's intended. But who was she without him?

She was no longer the pampered child who believed he would come a thousand miles to have her back. She was a woman, a woman in love with a dangerous man. Carina trembled. When had she come to love Quillan? When he found her in the mine shaft? When he shared her meal, her stories? When he bared his soul and showed her his pain?

Carina ran a hand over the paper-wrapped gown, then tugged the paper from it. It was beautiful, the fitted sea green bodice embroidered with lacy traceries of shells and spirals accented with seed pearls, the lace underskirt that extended beneath the silk skirting like foam on the waves. The silk sleeves ended beneath the elbow in layers of Italian lace. With each stitch she'd sewn, she had dreamed of wearing this dress for Flavio on their wedding day.

Now it was her wedding day, but Flavio would never see it. With a tight throat, she shook the dress out and laid it across the cot. Would Quillan think her beautiful? The thought sent her rushing to the small oval mirror she had purchased for her wall. Her hair was a riotous mass.

She had washed it furiously the night before after leaving Mr. Beck. She'd wanted no scent of him to remain on her after his threats. Now she trembled. What would he do when he learned? Her hand came to the crucifix at her throat and she stared at the silver emblem. What did it mean to her, this cross she wore?

Nonna had given it to her when she was a child. She said it would always remind her of God's love, love poured out in the blood of his only Son. Did God love her? Did He have a plan in this madness? Carina stared into the mirror. Was it His will she marry Quillan? Had He brought her to Crystal for that reason?

Carina's fingers tightened on it. What did she believe? God had used the crucifix to save her life. Used Quillan to save her. He'd gone to the Rose Legacy to find her. The mine his parents had made. They were tied together. Somehow they were interwoven in a pattern she couldn't see.

A knock came on the door and she jumped. "Who is it?"

"It's Mae, Carina."

Carina pulled open the door, and Mae swept in with her broad, rolling gait. With a glance, she took in the dress lying across the cot and turned to Carina. "So he's not telling tales."

"Who?"

"Quillan's downstairs. Says you're getting hitched."

Carina's stomach clenched in apprehension. "He's here now?"

"In the entry waiting."

So soon. She gripped her hands together. "And the priest?"

"With him."

Carina fumbled with the buttons on her blouse, then slipped it off. The skirt was next.

Mae went to the cot and bundled the gown up onto her arms. When Carina bent, she worked it over her head and down. "A nice bit of fancy."

Carina couldn't answer. Her voice would betray her trepidation. Mae turned her and started on the tiny pearl buttons up her back. Carina snatched up her brush and worked it swiftly through her hair.

"Hold still, now." Mae finished the buttons at her neck and turned her. "Land sakes, Carina. You're the prettiest thing I ever saw."

Would Quillan think so? Why was he marrying her? To foil Berkley Beck? She brushed the skirts downward from the fitted bodice, then looked at Mae. She must have looked like a frightened deer, because Mae spread her arms, and once again Carina found refuge against her bosom. What would she have done without Mae?

Mae patted her back. "Things must be different now. In my time a man did a bit of courting first." Her tone was baldly inquisitive.

Carina waved a hand. "Quillan does nothing in the normal way." That was certainly true of his proposal. But she didn't want to think too deeply on that. Carina drew herself up. There was nothing more to do but go downstairs and marry the man who had cast her wagon down the mountain.

Quillan saw her coming. Her hair was her veil, and the dress . . . he'd never seen anything so fine. It set her off like a jewel washed upon a stony shore. His blood surged, and he swallowed the sudden tightness in his throat. Until this moment he hadn't realized just how incredible she was.

Her outer beauty accented all the things about her that had kept her in his thoughts. Her laugh, her hands waving, her biting wit, her daring, even her naiveté. No wonder Beck risked so much to have her. Carina got under your skin until you wanted to shake her or . . . or just hold her close.

As she crossed the floor to him, he marveled at the delicacy of her features, the shape of her tiny waist, her deep, liquid eyes. Was he simply thwarting Beck, or had he succumbed like all of Crystal to this woman, this creature from another world? She stopped before him, and he looked down as though he'd never seen her, never carried her, dirty and bruised from a mine shaft, never snatched her out of the street where thugs waited, never tossed her wagon and all she owned over the mountain.

He was surely bewitched. She'd befuddled his mind, his senses. With an effort, he took control. "Are you ready?"

She nodded but looked so apprehensive he wondered for the first time how old she was. He turned to the priest. "Cain will witness. He's in with his son."

Father Charboneau appeared not to have heard. He looked gray and distracted. Of course he would, after the horrible thing done to his niece. But he had come. Quillan had impressed on him the importance, if not the reasons, for this hasty ceremony.

"Father?" Carina spoke now.

He came out of his reverie. "Yes?"

"We're ready now."

He frowned slightly, then followed them into Mae's parlor. Quillan waved for Cain to join them, and D.C. followed, wrapped in a quilt. Quillan eyed him dubiously, but the boy seemed hale enough. Mae took her place behind Carina, and Father Charboneau instructed bride and groom to kneel.

With a glance at Cain, Quillan went down on his knees for the first time in years.

577

$\star\ \star\ \star$

Carina knelt down beside Quillan, sensing in him a tension that hadn't been there a moment ago. She glanced up at Father Antoine. His face was stark. Did he know why she did this? Did he think it insensitive to marry on the same day Èmie suffered so extremely? What had Quillan told him?

As they knelt, Father Antoine spoke the wedding rite, the words washing over her with a solemnity that precluded all other thoughts. She knelt with her eyes closed until Quillan spoke his vows, then she dared a glance at him and couldn't look away. It didn't seem real that she was marrying this man, this son of Wolf.

She thought of Rose and Wolf entwined in the flames, their last embrace eternal. But when Father Antoine spoke the vows to her, she repeated the words with all her heart. The priest instructed them to stand, then Quillan took her in his arms and kissed her. It had not the daring or the power of his first kiss. This one was so gentle it brought an ache to her throat.

Then they separated, and she saw in Quillan's eyes a certain fire. He turned and thanked the priest, Cain, and Mae, winked at D.C., then took Carina's hand and led her out. Carina blinked in the sunshine's glare when he stopped her at the porch stairs. The blacks stood there, hides shining, manes and tails brushed. Somewhere he had found a side saddle, and he lifted her onto it now.

She settled her skirt and the billows of lace around her feet. He stood a long minute looking at her there, then mounted Jock. He turned with a roguish grin. "Want to race?"

It was just what she needed to break her stupor. She laughed and dropped her chin. "I know better."

He turned his horse, and they rode out of Crystal and up the gulch. The afternoon sun was hot and bright, the breeze wild flower scented, the Indian paintbrush's brilliant orange flecks among the fuchsia lupine and bluebells. Quillan's hair blew behind his head like silken cloth of honey brown, and Carina wanted to touch it. Were such thoughts permissible now?

She had thought sometimes of touching Flavio, had even allowed him to kiss her. Not as Quillan had, she realized, thinking back. She had kissed him as her cousin, as her darling boy, her dark poet. Quillan was her husband. A thrill passed through her.

They rode to a place where the creek tumbled over a cascade of rocks. A bluebottle fly darted over the crystalline water, and somewhere close a meadowlark sang. Quillan turned. "Far enough?"

Carina looked around at the sparkling

beauty, then shook her head. "I want to go higher." She pulled Jack up beside Jock. "Do you hear that?" She tipped her head toward the whistling birdsong. "You never hear that in Crystal. Any birds that try to sing are drowned out by the cacophony. And the higher you go, the more there are."

Quillan didn't answer, just nudged Jock on. They came to the Placerville valley, and Carina studied it again without any buildings. She was relieved they were gone. Then she looked up the narrow gulch where the wall of water had come and carried Dom away. She turned automatically toward the track that led to the Rose Legacy.

"Not that way." Quillan's voice was low.

She looked back over her shoulder. "Why not?"

"I don't want to go up there."

She could see there was no question in either of their minds where she meant to go. The mine called her as it always did. But this time she wanted to be there with Quillan. It was his mine. His legacy. "Come up, Quillan."

He crossed his wrists atop the saddle horn. "Just because I married you doesn't mean you can start telling me what to do."

"I'm not telling."

He half smirked. "What would you call it?"

She cocked her head. "Urging." She started Jack up the track.

"Carina."

She patted Jack's neck, sensing his hesitation. He didn't want to leave Jock and Quillan behind. But she nudged him on with her heels. In a moment she heard Jock following. She flashed a glance at Quillan and saw him staring up the mountain with a fixed expression. Was it a mistake to push it?

What did she know of his inner feelings? She had only a sense of his turmoil and the bitterness she'd seen. She hadn't been to the mine since he'd found her there. She'd been afraid for a time, then things had happened so quickly in Crystal. This seemed a stolen pleasure. They'd stepped outside of all the tumult, and time stood still for them.

Jack followed the track energetically now that Jock was on his heels. She suspected he enjoyed the lead spot for a change. She bit her lip on a smile of satisfaction herself. When they reached the Gold Creek Mine, Quillan reined in and dismounted. He led Jock to the spring to drink, then came and lifted Carina down. His hands remained on her waist, and he looked down into her face.

Carina felt warm under his gaze. "We've been here before."

"I seem to recall." Amusement touched

the corners of his eyes. "I should have known then."

"Known what?"

He turned and watched Jock at the spring, then released her and led Jack to drink. She held her skirts up, keeping the lace from the dirt, and followed. Quillan stood with his hands in the pockets of his gray linen pants. She hadn't noticed the fine trousers, the boiled shirt.

He tipped his chin up and worked a kink from his neck. His face was clean shaven except for the mustache, which once again reached below the line of his mouth at the sides. Had Wolf worn a mustache? Had his hair caught in the breeze and tempted the fingers as Quillan's did? What had Rose felt when he reached out his hand to her?

Quillan's eyes swiveled to the side and found hers on him. It was natural for them to linger. Just as she'd stared at him the morning they woke there together, she stared now. There was beauty in his features, the dark rim of his eyes, the angle of his eyebrows, the nearly straight line of his nose. He had a fine brow and his hair sprang from it in little arches streaked with sun.

"What are you thinking?" His voice was soft.

"You're very like Wolf." She saw him tense, almost flinch.

His eyes narrowed. "How would you know?"

She shrugged. "As I imagine him."

His throat worked and the muscle on one side of his jaw clenched and released. "How do you imagine him, Carina?"

"Strong. And mysterious. When I think of him, I see you."

Quillan turned away. "Unfortunately, so do others."

"Not unfortunately, Quillan. Father Charboneau said he was the most humane man he ever knew. He doesn't believe Wolf —"

"I don't want to talk about it."

Carina laid a hand on his arm. "Maybe if you did . . ."

He shook her off and took a step away.

"Come with me to the mine," she urged.

"No."

Determined, Carina walked to Jack, slipped her foot into the stirrup, swung up, and hooked her knee into place. Quillan didn't move. She turned Jack and started him up the remainder of the track to the Rose Legacy. She felt Quillan's eyes but heard nothing behind her.

Why did she force it? What did she hope to gain by making him dwell on something so obviously painful? She reached the clearing and dismounted. The blackened foundation was cast in shade by the westering sun. She went and sat on the edge, watching the track.

Not a quarter hour had passed before Jock's hooves clomped upward toward her and Quillan came into view. His face was set and hard. He dismounted beside Jack and returned her gaze. Then he crossed the gravel circle to where she sat. "If I'd known marriage would make you so impossible —"

"You'd have left me to Berkley Beck?" She waved her upended palm at him.

He looked down at it. "Why do you do that?"

"What?"

"Talk with your hands."

She looked also at the palm. "I don't know." She stood up. "I just do. I suppose it's in my family." She reached down and picked a tiny daisy from inside the foundation. She breathed its fragrance, then twirled it between her finger and thumb. "Maybe there are things you do that were in your family, only you don't know."

He laughed dryly. "Oh yes. The men in town believe I run on all fours."

A chill shimmied down her spine. He must have seen it because he stepped close. "Is that also how you imagine Wolf, Carina? At night, maybe?"

"No." She said it with more fervor than necessary. Looking back at the foundation, she tried to find the words. "Sometimes I imagine him lonely. Haunted by memories, experiences that marked him, changed him."

"What memories?"

She took Quillan's hand, tugged him down to the foundation with her. He seemed repelled by it, but then he relaxed as one resigned to his circumstances. Gently and carefully she told him what Father Antoine had shared with her. He listened without comment, almost without expression. How did he hide so completely?

As she finished, she laid a hand on Quillan's knee. "Wolf probably never belonged. He couldn't have known who he was before the Sioux took him, and they never gave him the personhood he longed for."

Imperceptibly, Quillan softened, then turned. "Why does it matter? To you?"

"Because it matters to you."

It seemed he would deny it, but he didn't. Instead, he pulled her to her feet, cupped the back of her head with one hand, and kissed her. Carina reached her hands up into his hair and found it as soft as she imagined, softer than her own, which was springy with curl.

He likewise forked his fingerfuls and kissed her hungrily. "Carina . . ." His voice was thick, and he pressed her face to his chest. "We have to go down."

She didn't want to. She didn't want him to stop holding her, kissing her. She looked up, and he kissed her again. Smiling, she begged, "Stay."

"No." He looked at the foundation beside them. "I know what you're trying to do. But I won't stay here. There's . . . too much . . . pain."

"For you?"

He shook his head. "For them."

Carina felt satisfied. As least he now thought of his parents as people instead of the horrible names he'd called them before. He held her face between his palms, then kissed her brow right where her hair began. "Just so you know, from now on, I'm in charge."

She smiled. "Ah. Un gross'umo."

He laughed softly, then lifted and carried her to Jack, hoisting her into the saddle.

They rode down through the lengthening shadows, and for the first time in hours, Carina thought of what they returned to. "What do we do now?"

He crooked an eyebrow, causing blood to rush to her face.

"I mean about Berkley Beck."

He drew a slow breath and released it. "There's a chance he'll accept defeat gracefully."

"You don't really believe that."

"No. But I gave the ledger to Ben Masterson, and the trustees will have determined a plan."

Carina swiped a lock of hair from her eyes. "What was in the ledger?"

"Names of those in his less reputable employ, dates, monies received, monies paid out."

Carina had a sudden thought. "Was . . ."

"Yes. But I told Masterson you were coerced."

She brought a hand to her throat. "Did he believe you?"

"It was fairly convincing when I told him I was marrying you."

She sagged in the saddle. "I don't want to go back to it. I wish I'd never set eyes on Crystal."

"Do you?" He gave her a crooked grin. "We met before Crystal, remember."

"And an auspicious start it was."

She raised her chin. "I'll expect everything replaced."

"I'm sure you will." He laughed, but she could see that he, too, was concerned as they approached town. People stared openly, and not all the stares were kind. There were whispers and dark looks. Why hadn't they stayed on the mountain?

Quillan didn't take her to Mae's. Instead, he tied the horses outside the hotel in plain view, as though daring anyone to question his right. If the muttering and glares fazed him, he showed very little. A tension in his arms when he lifted her down, a grim set to his jaw, but not enough to betray what he must be feeling. He led her into the lobby.

Mrs. Barton was at the desk. Her face lightened as always at the sight of Quillan. At least there was one person who still thought highly of him, though she scarcely looked at Carina. She held out a key to Quillan and asked, "Dinner?"

"Thank you." Quillan put the key into his pocket.

She took them to a table, and Quillan held Carina's chair. Carina sank into it a little shakily. She hadn't eaten since breakfast and was unaccustomed to the side saddle. Mostly, it was that she hadn't shared a meal with Quillan since the one she cooked for him, and she was suddenly very aware of his presence.

He smiled at her discomfort. "How are you such a tyrant on the mountain and such a cinch in town?"

Carina took umbrage. "I am not a cinch."

"You sure let Beck gull you."

"I admit I'm not versed in unscrupulous men."

"Good thing you ran to my tent." His pirate's smile.

Carina pressed her palms to the table. "I almost liked you earlier."

"You like me. Or you wouldn't have asked me to marry you."

"I asked!" Blood rushed to her face, but Mrs. Barton came and stood at their table.

Quillan demurred to Carina. "What would you like?"

"I . . . haven't looked."

"The chicken dumplings are nice tonight." Mrs. Barton gave her a thin smile.

Carina nodded and Mrs. Barton turned to Quillan.

"Beef steak. Rare." As Mrs. Barton left, he tucked his tongue into his side teeth with a mocking grin that showed he at least was not guided by someone else's opinion.

He was insufferable. She leaned forward, almost hissing, "I never asked. And as I recall, you didn't, either."

"I didn't get down on my knee. But it wasn't really necessary, was it? You'd already played that one."

Carina's heart sank. Why was he being so cruel? If he thought she was different on the mountain, *he* was two distinct men. She brushed a wrinkle from the tablecloth and refused to continue the banter. Mocking her situation with Mr. Beck was not only brazen, it was uncalled for.

She looked over and saw the empty table along the wall, Berkley Beck's table. Would he come and dine? Or did he even now search for her, thinking to make her his wife? What would he do when he learned of her marriage? She shuddered inside.

Looking up, she surprised a raw mien on Quillan. Did he know he'd been cruel? Did he care? Mrs. Barton brought their plates, and they ate quietly. Mr. Beck's table stood empty. Where was he? What was he doing? Carina felt a stabbing fear for Èmie, then recalled that Doctor Simms was sitting the night with her — armed.

Carina tried to put Berkley Beck from her mind. He was small and mean, but now he would see there was no point in continuing. As Quillan said, he couldn't marry her if she was married already. She looked up at Quillan. He offered her a conciliating smile, and she returned it.

She finished her meal just after Quillan finished his. He paid the cheque in cash and stood to hold her chair, then led her out to the lobby. She was unsure now of his intentions. Why had he spoiled the closeness they'd gained on the ride? Was he punishing her for taking him to the mine?

He led her up the stairs with a hand to her elbow. At the door he stopped and used the key. The room was a suite in blue-and-white watered silk with a lamp of blue crystal ringed with clear pendants on a corner table. It was all complementary and lovely, and the part of her that appreciated such beauty was soothed by it. There was a settee and a low marble table in the sitting room. Someone had put hothouse flowers, red and yellow, in a vase. Mrs. Barton?

Quillan closed the door, and once again Carina felt his presence shrink the room. He crossed the rug and opened the window to let in the cool evening air. The blue chintz curtain filled like a sail. Then he came and took her waist between his hands. She rested her palms on his chest. Would he apologize?

Searching her face, he dampened his lips, then, "You are the most beautiful woman I've ever known."

Her misgivings fell away. She must have mistaken his intentions, taken affront where none was meant.

He kissed her lips and then her neck. "I had Mae send over what you'd need for tonight."

Carina could scarcely breathe. But then, she'd had little time to prepare herself, and even though she'd loved Flavio for years, she was innocent of many of the details. She went into the room that held the four-poster bed and saw her gown lying across it. The gown had survived any damage, since it had been in her carpetbag and not her trunk, and it was a lovely bit of fancy, as Mae would put it. But Carina felt awkward and self-conscious as she removed the sea green gown and put on the flimsy white batiste garment.

591

Her hair was already down, so she merely brushed it with the brush Mae had set on the washstand. Then she washed her face and hands and neck, touching gently the place where Quillan's lips had been. She scrubbed her teeth and scrutinized them in the mirror. Each one shown like a slender pearl. She stepped back and waited.

It wasn't long. Quillan tapped the door, then opened it. He, too, had washed, and stood there, bare to the waist as he'd been under the icy spring. She had a flashing thought of Wolf, but it was Quillan who took her into his arms. Carina was amazed how safe he could make her feel.

Nothing could have prepared him for the wanting. Quillan silently groaned as he moved his hand beneath her hair lying like a lake surrounding and drowning him. But the visceral wanting, potent, returning even now as Carina slept, wasn't all.

Worse by far was the wanting of *her*, the essence, the depth of her, her mind, her heart, her devotion. All the things that made her who she was. And he knew this wanting would destroy him, day by day eroding the self he'd formed from denying the wants — to be known, to be acknowledged, to be loved. He pressed his eyes closed against the ache.

He'd spent the first half his life wanting

the love of a woman, and the other half purging her from his thoughts and emotions. One kind word, one motherly touch . . . he'd have lived on it for years. But the first woman who had mattered had given him away. And the second never failed to remind him.

Now there was Carina. Carina Maria DiGratia. He'd taken her body with his own in a closeness more near to love than anything before, and in that he had jeopardized all that he'd achieved. He groaned again without making a sound. How could he have known that with one rash act he would tear himself open, pour himself out, lose himself in her? And want, want so much for her to feel the same.

Thirty

Is hope a dream?
Rose

Carina woke to the unfamiliar feel of soft sheets, soft bed. She brushed her fingers over the fine linen pillow slip, not recognizing the scalloped work along the edge. And then she did. She looked furtively across the bed, but it was empty.

Was it possible she had dreamed him there? Turning swiftly, she searched the room. It, too, was empty. She sank back into the pillow, as soft and different from what she'd slept on these last nights as the rest of it. Everything was different. She was different. She was no longer Carina DiGratia. She was Mrs. Quillan Shepard in name and reality.

Closing her eyes, she slipped from the bed to her knees on the floor and crossed herself. *Oh, Signore* . . . She hadn't thought to love him. The man who sent her wagon over, the man with the pirate smile who could be dangerous, yet made her feel so safe . . .

She loved him. And it was both frightening and wonderful. It was not as she'd loved Flavio, the yearning to understand but never understanding. Flavio was a mirage. Quillan was real. She loved the realness of him, the rightness of him. She felt renewed, awakened, alive, eager for the things that would make up their life together.

He was pleased with her cannelloni, but would he like sausage and peppers? She would learn his likes and dislikes. She would tell him her stories, and he would tell his. They would laugh and maybe cry. And in the silence their hearts would join. She folded her hands and rested her forehead on the peaked fingers. *Signore, thank you for this day and for this husband. . . .*

There was a noise, and she turned to see Quillan in the doorway. He was dressed in jeans and a cotton flannel shirt. His gun hung at his hip, and his hat was in his hands. He took in her position with a slow gaze, then leaned his hip to the doorjamb. "Praying for deliverance?"

The taunt was back in his tone, the cruelty in his eyes. What was he doing? He wanted to hurt her. She couldn't mistake it this time. She stood up. Self-conscious in her batiste gown, she clasped her hands beneath her chin.

His mouth softened, and for a moment she saw the tenderness in his eyes, then it was gone. "I've paid Mae to keep you."

"Mae?"

He raised an eyebrow. "Unless you'd prefer my tent?"

"But . . ."

"I'm not around much, Carina. You'll be better off at Mae's."

She felt a stone in her stomach. He would not make a home with her?

He pushed off from the doorjamb and straightened. "I don't know how long I'll be gone."

He was leaving? "Where are you going?"

"I have a job to do."

She rushed toward him without thinking. "But what about Mr. Beck?"

Quillan put the hat on his head. "It's all about town that we married. It won't escape his notice."

"That's not what I meant." She closed her hands into fists. "What if he retaliates?"

"I expect he will. What do you think this was all about?"

He might have slapped her, so unjust and painful were his words. Her jaw dropped with the shock of it, but he didn't see. He had turned and walked away. Cinch. He had called her a cinch, and here was the proof of it. He had married her only to spite Berkley Beck, to force his hand.

Carina felt numb, stupid, unable to move or think. And then the fury hit with the force of the flood. It took an interminable time to wash and change into the beige skirt and blouse Mae had sent from Carina's room. She was thankful she didn't have to wear the wedding dress. She wished never to see it again and forced it into the carpetbag with disgust.

Omaccio. Cialtrone. What did she care? He was a rogue. She snatched up her bag and left the room. Downstairs, she smacked the key on the counter and left without a word to Mrs. Barton, who stood all smiles behind the polished wood. She pressed through the milling crowd, ignoring the greetings. She turned the corner at Drake and fairly ran. Mae was in the kitchen frying hot cakes, and Carina threw herself into her arms.

Mae dropped the spatula and held her close. "There, there. The first time's always the worst."

If only it were that. Carina's heart ached with more than maidenly discomfort. She sobbed, furious, humiliated, and once again betrayed.

"Now, lamb. It's not so bad as all that."

"He's gone." Let Mae think her heartsick.

"But he'll be back."

That thought was hardly comforting. But with a sniff, Carina pulled away and wiped her eyes. She was acting foolish, as foolish as she felt. How had she thought his tenderness real? He was Quillan Shepard, rogue, pirate, omaccio.

Mae smiled. "That's better." She bent

and scooped up the spatula. "Now I've burnt these." She turned back to the stove. Her life was undisturbed, unchanged from yesterday, the same as tomorrow.

Only Carina's existence was turned about, inside out. With a shaky breath she gathered herself and left the kitchen. Stepping outside, she saw Dr. Simms, and suddenly the weight of everything returned. Èmie. Mr. Beck. What was Quillan thinking, leaving her to face it all? But face it she must.

She hurried to the doctor. "How is Èmie?"

He turned, his thoughts obviously occupied, then he half smiled. "Èmie? Remarkable."

Carina's concern eased. "Then she's healing."

He nodded, still bemused, then seemed to catch himself with a slight shake of his head. "Yes, she's healing."

"Thank God. May I see her?"

"Yes. Yes, actually she was asking for you."

Carina picked up her skirts and ran, slowing only as she neared Èmie's cabin. She didn't see Father Antoine, but he could be inside with his niece. She didn't want to be reminded of the rite he had performed the day before, the marriage she had entered into with good faith. Good faith.

Signore . . . But the word was empty. What good was faith when no one could be trusted? What good was God, who twisted and spun her until she was reeling and bleeding inside? Carina stopped outside the door. She must go in, must succor Èmie, though her own heart was ragged.

She went inside. Father Antoine was not there. Only Èmie lay on her cot, sleeping and seemingly peaceful. Carina knelt beside her. She lifted Èmie's hand, noting the length and shape of the fingers. The ends were blunt, but they were good hands, strong hands. Her heart ached.

Èmie stirred. Carina leaned over her. Èmie opened her eyes, both eyes now, though neither as wide as they should. The swelling was less, but the bruising darker. Èmie smiled faintly. "I knew you were here."

Carina cupped her hand. "Yes, I'm here." But she couldn't be there always. Who else did Èmie have? Her uncle? Carina shuddered. "Èmie, who did this?"

Èmie's face shadowed. "It doesn't matter."

"How can you say that?"

Èmie touched the swelling along one cheekbone. "Jesus said to turn the other cheek."

"I can't believe that's what He meant."

"He meant we must forgive the wrongs against us."

Carina felt her chest clutch suddenly. Was that it? Did her own unforgiveness cause all this misfortune in her life? She recalled Father Charboneau's words. *"Justice is more noble than vengeance. But better than both is mercy."* Did the priest feel merciful now? Did he pardon his brother for this crime against Èmie? If so, he was no man.

"He didn't want to do it." Èmie's voice was low, gentle, and sad.

She pitied her assailant? Her uncle? Impossible!

Èmie closed her eyes. "I forgive him."

Carina pushed away from the bed and crossed the room. It wasn't possible. How could Èmie forgive the one who did this? She rebelled at the idea. Then she recalled her own part in it. Did Èmie know it was because of her that Mr. Beck had ordered her beaten?

"Carina." Èmie reached up a hand.

Slowly she returned to Èmie's side and dropped to the floor beside the bed.

Èmie clutched her hand. "You mustn't blame yourself."

Tears stung Carina's eyes. "Then you know. It's my fault."

"It's not your fault. But I forgive you, too."

With a sob, Carina brought Èmie's hand to her lips. "Why? How can you forgive me for causing you this pain?"

Èmie smiled crookedly. "God doesn't allow anything that isn't for my good."

Carina couldn't speak. How could a loving God allow Èmie to suffer? How could it be for her good? It made no sense. She stood when Dr. Simms returned, but her hand and Èmie's lingered together. Carina drew a long, shaking breath and broke the contact.

Èmie's eyes turned to Dr. Simms. Carina watched in amazement as the bruised and swollen face of her friend transformed. Èmie was in love.

Quillan pulled himself into the box and took up the reins. Masterson had insisted he make himself scarce until things were sorted out. There was still the matter of Beck's innuendoes, and Masterson didn't want anything clouding the picture. But Quillan didn't intend to go far, one day to Fairplay and back the next. In his absence Masterson and the other trustees would amass enough men to subdue the roughs, then remove McCollough from office and vote in another marshal, one with the guts to arrest Berkley Beck.

If the crooked trustees caught wind of it, they'd undoubtedly inform Beck, and he wouldn't relinquish power without a fight. It could get ugly, but Masterson and company were willing to take that chance. With the merchants and those who'd suffered the treatment of the roughs behind them, Crystal's notables were ready to make an end of it. It was a sound plan, and Quillan felt some relative confidence.

"Quillan!"

Quillan turned in surprise as D.C. strode up. His head still bore the bandage, but his color was high and there was a spring in his step. "What are you doing out of bed?"

"I have a clean bill. Dr. Felden thought I should take the air. I thought maybe I could ride along with you."

"I'm not taking responsibility for a kid with a hole in his head."

D.C. grinned. "That hole's as good as closed up. And if I sit around one more day with nothing to do, I'll go crazy!"

"That's strange. I thought you'd reached new heights in avoiding work."

D.C. laughed. "That's about what Daddy said."

"Get up, then." Quillan waved him over. "Does Cain know you're coming?"

D.C. looked a little sheepish. "He knows."

"D.C." Quillan was not going to be party to D.C.'s shenanigans.

"It was his idea, all right?" D.C. pulled himself into the box.

Quillan considered that. Maybe Cain felt the boy needed a change of venue. Maybe he wanted him under a watchful eye as he tried his wings again, recovered his strength. Quillan could do that. This was a short trip.

"Get comfortable. Your backside will come to know that spot before the day's over."

"I remember." D.C. looked none too pleased at the prospect.

It could have been any of the days he and the boy had started out before Cain's mine had struck ore. Then D.C. had dropped freighting like a scalding iron. But he'd helped haul the ore on occasion, and Quillan liked his company. There weren't too many he'd invite aboard, and of those he would, most were too arthritic and crippled to stand it.

But for all his youth and inexperience, D.C. was a fine companion. He knew when to talk and when to keep still. Quillan felt a degree of normalcy having D.C. on the box with him. And that was good. He didn't want to think how his life was suddenly altered, though any recollection of last night made that impossible.

He'd taken a wife, and moreover, that wife was Carina. How had she bedeviled him? Worked her way in where he'd sworn no woman would? Even now he felt the softness of her skin, smelled and tasted and felt her there. It was like a poison in his mind, the wanting. At least D.C. could distract him.

"Quillan?"

He turned to the boy. "Yeah?"

"What was it like?"

"What?"

"You know." D.C. rubbed his palms on his knees. "Last night."

So much for distraction. Quillan frowned. "That's a question no gentleman should answer — or ask." Had his thoughts somehow filled the silence and brought on D.C.'s curiosity?

D.C. hung his head. "I know that, but . . . I just wondered if it was different from, well . . . you know, the Hall Street gals."

Quillan swallowed the alum in his throat. "I couldn't say, as I've never been with the Hall Street gals."

"Never?" D.C. squinted up at him. "Not even in another city?"

Quillan shook his head.

"Why not?"

Quillan stared at the white line of road ahead, tasting the dust from their wheels. The horses' backs rolled and shifted with the step of each hoof. The leather reins were supple and smooth in his hands. "I guess it's because of my mother."

"She told you to stay away from that sort of woman?"

"No." He met D.C.'s eyes. "She was that sort of woman." He saw the impact that had on D.C.'s brain.

The boy's throat worked. "Oh. I guess I shouldn't have asked."

Quillan's mouth quirked. "It's all right. I just couldn't see my way clear to giving someone else the kind of start I had."

"Then last night was . . ."

"D.C."

"Sorry. It's just . . . I wish I'd done it that way. I mean, if I ever do take a wife, I'd like it to be, well, special."

That sent a pang more painful yet through Quillan. Special. The word recalled all the gentleness, the taking and giving, the touching and learning. The wonder of the woman he'd known last night, the joy she'd awakened . . . and the terror.

D.C. hung his head. "Now that I've come to Jesus, it just seems all the things I've done wrong are awful clear to me."

Quillan tugged D.C.'s hat brim down. "That'll teach you."

D.C. laughed. "Maybe. But the funny thing is, even though I'm more clear on what I did wrong, it don't bother me so much. I mean, I might wish it different, but it don't weigh on me like it did before."

Quillan drew a long breath and released it slowly. "Well, that's good, D.C."

"Daddy says you won't come to Jesus cuz you don't want to give up control of your life."

So now D.C. was going to rub the raw

spot. Quillan should have never let him climb up. "Well, it took too long to get control." He flicked a grasshopper from his thigh. "I'd like to keep it awhile."

"I don't think we ever really have control. I mean all kinds of stuff happens, and we can't do a thing about it."

Quillan just digested that.

"Like the flood. It seemed as though that was a terrible thing. And it might have been worse if you hadn't warned us. Even so, it looked like we lost everything. Then come to find out it opened up the New Boundless. You know what Daddy said?"

"I can imagine."

"He said God works all things for the good of those who love Him. And that's just how it was. God took a bad thing and made it good."

Quillan pictured Carina in the mine shaft, broken and delirious. The feel of her tied up against him, and again in his arms under the moonlight . . . Was that when it happened? When he'd kept her alive with the heat of his own body? He thought of the meal they'd shared, and her stories, the motion of her hands, her laugh. Inwardly he groaned.

D.C. swatted a fly. "So it seems if you have no control over the big things, why try to control the little ones? Why not just hand it all over?"

Hand it all over. Not a chance. "You ever thought of becoming a preacher?"

D.C. wagged his head. "Haven't really thought of becoming anything. Got stuck being a miner, and freighting's worse."

Quillan hunched over the reins. "Well, you ought to consider it. Your mouth's the best exercised muscle you have."

Father Antoine strode purposely in pursuit of his brother. He had held some hope that Henri could not have done to Èmie such a brutal and senseless thing. But when he failed to return all night, whatever doubts Antoine had were squelched.

Now he made his way up the steep slope, his mind filled with other times he'd followed that path, hardly more than a deer track now to the old shack he'd find at the end. Henri had never brought much out of this hole, less even than his current mine in Crystal. But he'd never been one for honest labor.

Antoine looked up. Something told him the old Placerville mine was where he'd find his brother. A surge of passion too dangerous to indulge filled him. *Please God, give me wisdom and compassion*. He wanted to kill. In his heart he knew the feelings of a murderer. He wanted to beat Henri as the man had beaten Èmie, blow for blow, pain for pain.

Waves of remorse and self-loathing filled him. He had failed to reach Henri, and now his heart was as dark as his brother's. *Forgive my wickedness. Let me not fail you now. Your will, oh, Lord* . . . The sharp report of a gun echoed from the mountain above. Antoine staggered, staring up at the shack. It had sounded like a shotgun, but he saw no one afield.

Trembling, he ran the rest of the path and burst through the door. There was a smell of cheap whiskey and a more potent smell of blood. Henri lay there, blood pumping from his side. His hand sprawled, grasping at the air above the shotgun; his mouth worked soundlessly.

Antoine rushed over and dropped to his side. "Henri! Oh, Henri . . ." Futilely he pressed his hand to the pumping flesh, knowing it wouldn't be stanched. Henri's side was a sieve his life was slipping through.

Henri drew a rattling breath. "It was me. I did it. Èmie . . ." He moaned. "And Evans. And . . ." Foaming blood covered his lips from shattered lungs. His eyes rolled. "And all those years ago . . . it wasn't Wolf."

Pain seared Antoine's own chest. He pulled Henri's head into his lap. He'd known, somewhere deep inside he'd known.

"The first time . . . an accident. I . . . lost

control. Angry. So angry." He coughed the blood from his throat. "I'll burn. Just like Wolf. I'll burn."

Antoine recalled himself. "Do you ask God's pardon of your sins?" He gripped his brother's face. "Henri?"

Slowly Henri nodded, his eyes blinking closed, then opening again with a thick, dull expression.

"Then know they are forgiven you." The priest pulled the small vial of blessed water from his coat. Dabbing his thumb, he signed the cross on Henri's forehead. *In nomine Patris, et Fili, et Spiritu Sancti.*" But Henri was gone.

Sorrow filled him as Antoine sat stroking his brother's brow as the blood congealed and the flesh grew cold.

Thirty-one

There is a God, and he is merciful. He has looked upon an unworthy soul with pity and filled my heart with joy.

Rose

Carina crept away from Èmie's cabin and headed for the creek. Except for visiting Èmie, she meant to avoid any place Mr. Beck's roughs might look for her. She half expected Berkley Beck himself to spring up without warning as he had the day before. Before she married Quillan.

She jumped at a sound and looked over her shoulder, but it was a crow cracking a beetle on a rock. She stayed to the shadows and edges, but then she supposed those were the more likely places Beck's men might be lurking. Raising her chin defiantly, she hurried through the last of the buildings and entered the tent city. If Mr. Beck had her followed, she'd stay where the miners could hear her.

Then Carina realized how ludicrous it was to think anyone would hear her over the mining din. Work was not suspended simply because her life was turned upside down. No one cared that Quillan had married, then deserted her, that Berkley Beck would be furious, if for no other reason than that it was Quillan who'd spited him.

She was nothing but a pawn between them, as she'd been from the start. Was there anything left of her pride? First Flavio, now Quillan. Was she not worth loving? She walked along the edge of the creek, alone with only the voice of the running water. The air smelled of goldenrod and pine, a fresh relief from the stench of Crystal, yet it failed to cheer her.

"Praying for deliverance?" Did Quillan know how those words would hurt? Was he speaking his own wish to be free of her? His regret at taking her for his wife? She pressed her hands to the tight knot in her belly. Had she so disappointed him?

She dropped to her knees on a flat boulder at the water's edge and thought of Èmie. Even in her pain, Èmie had no condemnation, only forgiveness. She felt compassion for her friend, for her uncle. Carina was sure now it was Henri Charboneau who beat Èmie. Why else had he not shown his face since?

Yet Èmie didn't condemn him, didn't want him punished, didn't long for revenge. Carina dropped her face into her hand. Had she ever loved that way? So selflessly? She let her hand fall, then reached down and felt the chill as the water met and leaped over her fingers. She rubbed the water over her face, cooling the shame in her cheeks. Yes, she was ashamed.

She was a spoiled, headstrong woman, unwilling to forgive the injuries, real and imagined, against her. She closed her eyes. She'd become small and selfish. She'd come to Crystal, not at God's beckoning, but to satisfy her own spite. Now . . .

"Justice is more noble than vengeance, and far above both is mercy." Father Antoine. *"You must be washed in the blood of the risen Lamb."* Preacher Paine. *"God doesn't allow anything that isn't for my good."* Èmie. Carina clenched her hands. Had all this heartache been for her good? She looked up to the sky, saw the eagle circling. *God's signature.*

"He is all and in all." In her? In Divina? In Flavio? Were they all bound somehow together? Each person, Quillan and Èmie and Father Antoine? Even Wolf and Rose? Was it a cloth that included them all, that each thread could weaken?

She drew a weary breath. "Signore, show me what to do. Show me how to know you." Tears stung her eyes.

Forgive. Again she heard it. The same as in the darkness of the shaft. Could it be so simple? Her heart jerked inside her. Did she want to? Forgive Flavio? And Divina? Divina.

Her heart ached. Divina had been deceived, had given in to Flavio's desires. She could only hope he would do the right thing for her. Carina closed her eyes and pressed her knotted hands to her breast. "Signore . . . I surrender. Please forgive the words I said, the anger I harbored for Flavio and my sister. I forgive them."

She felt the weight leave her heart and breathed freely. The pain that had lodged in her chest was replaced by a peace more sustaining than any she'd known. How could she feel that way with so much trouble yet to face? But there was a presence so near, so empowering, it swept away the fear.

She no longer desired vengeance. Father Charboneau spoke truly. Vengeance was wrong. Justice was right, but more noble was mercy. She could see that now and even want it. *Grazie, Signore.* It was His presence she felt. God was more than she'd thought Him, closer than she'd believed possible. *All, and in all.* If only she would let Him be.

She thought of D.C.'s prayer, his humbling himself and admitting his need. Tears came to her eyes. Still on her knees, she bowed her head. "Signore, *Gesù Cristo,* I'm not worthy." She thought of Preacher Paine. "Wash me clean in the blood of the Lamb, the blood you shed for my sins. I give you my life."

She dipped trembling fingers into the

water. She had been baptized at birth, and she was thankful for that. She had known God, and in her own way honored Him, each day presenting herself in prayer, even if they were pettish and childish prayers. Now she felt a connection, like family, only deeper, more reverent, to Him, to God.

She drew her fingers out and signed herself with the cross, the cross that Christ had borne for her. With her fingers on her forehead, *"In nomine Patri." In the name of the Father, Almighty God.* And on her heart, *"Et Fili." The Son, the Savior, the Christ.* From shoulder to shoulder. *"Et Spiritu Sancti." The Holy Spirit. The power that restored.*

She felt it now, the restoring power, inside her where the ache had twisted around her heart. She felt the healing presence breaking down the anger, the hurt, the need to hurt back. On her knees beside the creek, she felt the sun's warmth on her face, though the air beside the water was cool. She heard the *too-whit* of a mountain bird somewhere in the trees, saw the flash of a blue-bodied dragonfly.

All around her was beauty, God's handiwork. And it was good, so good. She clasped her hands tightly beneath her chin. "Grazie Signore. Grazie." She got to her feet on the soft pale grasses. The pungent scent of the yellow goldenrod stung her nostrils.

Then she thought again of Quillan. That hurt was fresh and raw. Even now she burned with the humiliation of his words. But something in it made no sense. He couldn't have been who he was with her last night and also who he seemed to be this morning. It was like their time on the mountain, then their time at dinner. It was the closeness that made him cruel. If only she could understand why.

She looked up the gulch. She couldn't see it, but it was there, the Rose Legacy. Did she dare venture up alone? What more could she possibly learn from the vacant tunnel, the burnt foundation? How would it help her know Quillan? She sighed. It was as good a place to hide from Berkley Beck as any — if she could get out of Crystal undetected.

Well, Alan Tavish had promised his help. Maybe now she would ask it. She slipped into the back doors of the livery and found him instructing the boy on how to stroke the curry brush. She waited until he caught sight of her. "I'd like to take the mare up the gulch."

Alan Tavish frowned, not with displeasure but concern. "I dinna think it wise, lass." He tucked the curry into the boy's hand and patted his shoulder. "Gently, now." Then he came out of the stall to meet her. "What is it that takes you away up there?"

His question surprised her. Had Quillan not told him of the mine? "The Rose Legacy."

He stared at her a long minute, his eyes like soft green stones with a milky edge. "Why, lass? What good can that piece of cursed ground do ye?"

"It isn't cursed. It's . . . I don't know how to say it. I just need to go." She pressed a fist to her breastbone.

Tavish shrugged. "As you wish."

That was the first bridge crossed. Now, "Maybe would you have some trousers I could borrow?"

His old head shot up, his expression exactly what she'd expected.

"No one will notice me if I ride out as a boy."

Tavish shook his head. "No one could mistake you for a boy, lassie."

"Maybe not if they looked closely, but who will bother with one more body on horseback plodding through the melee?"

He wanted to argue, but the boy spoke from the stall. "She could take my hat." He motioned to the flat-brimmed felt hat similar to Quillan's that hung on the stall post. "Shove her hair all up inside."

Carina had to smile at a fellow conspirator. "What's your name?"

"Johnny."

"Would you lend me your hat, Johnny?"

He nodded. "Sure. Are you hiding from the roughs?"

"Something like that."

Tavish mumbled something, then hung his head resignedly. "Let's see what I have." He tossed things about in his sleeping room, then emerged with a pair of trousers, well worn in the seat, and a bulky shirt. "Change in there, and we'll see how these work."

Carina closed the door behind her, stripped down to her lacy whites, and pulled on the men's clothing. It was not unheard of for a woman to wear pants, especially in the West, but Carina had never donned them before. The trousers were hopelessly large at the waist, though close enough in length.

She searched the room for a length of soft rope and found a piece that wound about her three times. That both held the pants and added bulk where she was lacking. The shirt was oversized enough to hide her curves, old and ugly enough to escape notice. Satisfied, she went out.

Tavish shook his head at once, but when she braided her hair and pulled it up inside the hat, he admitted, "I wouldn'a thought it, but dressed like that your own mother wouldn't know ye."

Carina smiled and winked at the boy. "I'll return your hat here."

He just nodded and went back to currying the gelding. Alan Tavish had prepared the

617

mare while she changed, and Carina took her now, not out the back as she'd come in, but through the front doors and into the street. The best way to hide was in the open. She felt a surging confidence as she blended into the flow of mule trains, wagons, and men.

Some people glanced, but no one looked twice. The brim of the hat shadowed her face and muted her features. Without her skirts to show her a woman, no one gave her a thought. Carina wasn't sure how she felt about that, but under the circumstances . . .

She made it out of Crystal without incident, amazed at the relief she felt. The town had weighted her down more than she'd known. There seemed a brooding, a massing tension, though on the surface all was normal. Maybe it was her imagination.

The little mare carried Carina past the emptiness of Placerville to the slope that led upward, climbing with spry hooves. Now that she was alone, thoughts of Quillan crowded in. She might be right with God, but she was anything but right with her husband.

She passed the Gold Creek Mine and the spring where Quillan had watered the horses. Maybe she should not have pressed him to go farther. Maybe he would not have despised her this morning. But it was on farther, at the Rose Legacy, that he had listened and then kissed her for it.

She shook her head. How could she make sense of his complexity? She bit her lip, trying hard not to feel betrayed. He had wounded her, yes, but why? If she could only understand. She came to the landing of the Rose Legacy, but she wasn't alone. "Father?"

The priest sat on the stone foundation overlooking the plunging slope. His hands hung empty from arms rested on his knees. He looked up, his face gray and rutted as though he had outlived the vigor he'd once possessed. He showed no surprise at her attire, no interest in her at all.

Carina brought the mare to a halt. What was he doing there, so grim and bleak? She slid from the horse and crossed the distance between them. "What is it, Father? Are you hurt?"

He let his head hang, too heavy for his neck. "Not in body."

"What's happened? Did you find Henri?"

He groaned, caught his head between his hands, and nodded.

Carina spun and searched the woods about them. Was Henri Charboneau near? "Where is he?"

"Dead. By his own hand."

Carina dropped down to the foundation

beside the priest, understanding now his condition. "You were too late."

"To save his life." He looked up now.

She stared into Father Antoine's face. "His soul?"

"He made his confession. Threw himself on God's mercy, God rest him."

Carina clasped her hands in her lap. Surely that was enough. God's promise extended to the last breath. Yet the priest's desolation was complete. Did he mourn him so deeply? Or had that confession, as Èmie feared, destroyed Father Antoine's peace? Had Henri admitted killing William Evans?

Father Antoine sighed. "I knew. I never had proof, but inside I knew. Yet I let Wolf take the blame, coward that I was. I couldn't bear to have people know that my own brother . . ."

Was he wandering? Why did he speak of Wolf?

"And when all the town would have lynched Wolf, I spoke the voice of reason. There was no witness. He couldn't be convicted. Leave the man in peace."

The priest dropped his face to his hands a long moment, then suddenly looked at her directly. "But what peace was there for him, doubted on all sides, suspected of butchery and worse, some violent insanity? Feared and hated. I did that to him."

"No."

"Yes. If I had acted on my suspicions, confronted Henri . . ."

And now she guessed why he spoke so. Henri had killed the man Wolf was accused of killing, torn out the throat of a human being. Carina trembled. She looked at the square of burnt foundation. Is that why Wolf, like Rose, had burned? Was it too much to be hated and feared, despised and rejected? Had he not suffered that already at the hands of the Sioux who took him as a slave?

She understood Father Antoine's pain. Quillan's papa. Even his own son had been taught to despise him. And Rose? Was she not caught in the terrible web? Carina sat in silence beside the priest as the sun apexed above the mountain. Her stomach was hollow, but she wanted no food.

Forking his fingers into his hair, the priest groaned. "All these years."

Carina just listened.

"Rose came to me with the baby. She wanted me to take him, to raise him as my own. But I was new into my calling. I burned to search out the lost souls and minister God's mercy."

Tears caught in his throat. "What would I do with a baby? What would people think? How could I tramp the mountain with an infant, a child? God had big things for me. I

621

couldn't see that she'd brought me 'one of the least of these.' "

He dropped his face into his hands, held it there. "So I suggested my colleague, the Reverend Edward Shepard. He was a good man, a faithful man." He shook his head. "But Mrs. Shepard . . . she pulled aside her skirts when Rose passed, told the children not to look. And here I suggested she give her precious son to the woman to raise?"

The priest stood up and paced furiously. "What did I know? A man. A priest. How could I understand a woman's mind? And one already fragile with tragedy . . ."

He drew a long breath and spread his hands. "I was the death of both of them."

Tears stung Carina's eyes. Her heart ached, for the priest, for Rose and Wolf . . . for Quillan. Oh, Signore . . .

Father Antoine motioned to her. "Come with me."

Carina rose and followed him up the mountain. Some two hundred yards above the mine he stopped, and Carina saw there a single stone, crudely chiseled with two words, *Wolf* and *Rose*. They stood in silence before the stone, pale in the waning light.

Then the priest walked to a mound of stones and pulled them apart. From their hollow he retrieved a metal box. Carina watched as he opened the box and took out a bundle wrapped in oilcloth. He unwrapped the cloth from a book. Bound in red leather, it had a clasp and lock and tiny key tied on with a silken ribbon. He held the book out to her, and gently Carina took it.

"It belonged to Rose. She put it into my keeping should Quillan ever want to know his mother." He stared out across the mountainside, his face a mask of pain. "This much I accepted."

Carina stared at the finely tooled cover with gold inlay, the name plaque in the center of the scrollwork. *Rose Annelise De-Mornay*. She brought the book to her breast and cradled it there, her heart beating against it. Quillan's mother. Rose Annelise DeMornay. Now she had a name.

"You want me to give it to him?"

He stayed silent. That was for her to decide. He was merely passing on the trust. And now she knew why she'd had to come up there. This little book was the key. By knowing Rose, she might somehow know Quillan.

Her heart ached. How different Quillan's life might have been. She knew so little, but she would never forget the bitterness with which he'd spoken of his foster mother. His pain was raw and haunting. Father Charboneau had reason to blame himself. But then, didn't they all?

She turned to him, touched his arm gently. "Go down to Èmie, Father."

He just stood, looking lost on the mountain.

"You've done all you can here. You must forgive, even yourself."

His mouth softened, almost smiled. "Have you learned that, then?"

She nodded.

He kindled slowly, then he did smile. "Thank you for reminding me."

They walked together to the Rose Legacy, stopping a moment at the square foundation. Carina looked at the priest. "Will you tell them now? About Henri? Clear Quillan's name of suspicion?"

Father Antoine nodded. Then Carina watched him take the track down. The scent of pine was potent in the afternoon heat as Carina settled on the edge of the foundation. She looked down to where Placer used to be. She saw the gulch floor, Cooper Creek running through, new grass and wild flowers making a soft carpet where the flood had passed over.

She caught her breath sharply. She was looking down, yet there was no dizziness. No sense of falling. No twisting in her stomach. Her breath came out in a slow sigh as she realized God had healed her. *Grazie, Signore!* She pressed the diary to her breast with an overwhelming sense of peace. God would make it right. Somehow God would make it right.

With that hope, she unlocked the diary and opened to the first gilt-edged page. *This is the journal of Rose Annelise DeMornay written by my own hand this year of 1851.* The page was inscribed in a beautiful Spenserian hand. Rose had been well educated, probably gently reared, but her very next words shocked Carina.

It is the way of dreams to become nightmares. What seems beautiful is seldom as it seems. Can any who have lived not believe in death? Can any who have loved not know what it is to hate?

Carina looked up at the cloud-clotted sky. They could be her own words. Had she not come to Crystal with just such a thought, betrayed by Flavio and wanting to hurt back? Had not her dream become a nightmare? Even now her new faith struggled against the fresh hurt from Quillan. Could God bring good out of it? Gesù Cristo. She wanted to believe it, but could she?

It is a fact that the human heart differs from all other species. While its function to the body is that same of all animals, its participation with the human soul is both rhapsodic and fatal. I find myself at odds with my own heart, longing and at the same time despising myself for that longing. For I know what sort of man I love, and if I once surrender to that love, will it not destroy me? Yet he pleads his case with such skill I fear I shall succumb with the same helpless devotion of so many others. For I love him and hate him at once. I love what I want him to be, and hate what he is.

Carina pressed her hand to the page, surprised by the affinity. Could she not have written exactly that for Flavio? Wasn't it so? She had loved the dream, the might-have-been. And blinded herself to the truth of him. At least Rose had seen her love for what he was.

She turned the page.

January 7, 1851 Is there any pain an enemy can inflict that compares to the damage done by a friend? Even more so, love's injury? I am diseased in every part, no part free of the ailment. For it is as I feared. His love is a poison I cannot live without. If I surrender, will he become the man I dream of?

January 9, 1851 What joy in the sunshine. What glory fills a bird's throat that infects the air with song. I am awakened to the wonder, and I will open my ears and close my eyes, the better to listen and feel the sun's glow. For my love sings my praises and on his lips are the words I long to hear. In me he learns faithfulness and eternal devotion.

Carina closed her eyes. Was there even such a thing? Her faith in God was fledgling; her faith in men . . . Shaking her head, she read on.

To rise to higher joy is to risk a deeper sorrow. Do I dare reach for the sun? Or have I touched it already? I don't know. My experience is too small. What I know is little to what I hope to know. What I feel is already too much. Yet how can I go back to thinking and reasoning when there is such bliss?

Was love bliss? The feelings that swept in like the tide, then left the dry sand in its wake? How could feelings be trusted? Feelings had made her surrender more of herself to Quillan than she ever thought possible. Feelings had left her angry and wounded when he deserted her that morning.

Feelings were not enough. There must be more. There must be trust, respect, honor.

All that she longed to give Quillan. A warmth of appreciation filled her. She loved him with something that went beyond feelings.

She wished she could warn the woman whose words filled the page before her. Don't listen to his words. Don't act on the flight they give your heart. Think of what you first said, of dreams becoming nightmares. But the ink was set, and with the next passage, Carina sagged.

February 4, 1851 The thing is done; it can't be undone. How can one go back and change a moment passed? Even a moment that should never have come. I fear with the deed I have lost not only my virtue but my life as well. For of all life's betrayers, the heart is the worst. It flutters with joyful anticipation, leading down paths better untrod. Now that I know my heart, I must never follow it again.

Carina held the book, trembling. She hadn't expected a happy story, but neither had she anticipated such a connection to the woman whose most private thoughts she now read. It was as though Rose's struggle became her own. She stared at the journal, its pages showing her a woman she never knew, but might have known if life had been kinder, a woman who would now be her mamma through marriage to Quillan.

A large gray jay lighted on the corner of the wall and hopped toward her. Carina recalled Mae's trick but had nothing for him. He cocked his head to look at her sideways, then flew.

She dropped her gaze to the page.

February 23, 1851 It has been weeks now since he's come. I no longer fool myself. Eternity for my darling was very short indeed. But to me time is an undying enemy. No matter how much you put behind you, there is always more. I think eternity the cruelest joke of all.

How will I hide my despair? If the eye is the window to the soul, and from the abundance of the heart the mouth speaks, why can't we all be blind and dumb? Then all might stumble about speaking foolishness and no one be the wiser to my plight. As it is, all who see me must know, all who hear feel the pain entrapped within me. For the abundance of my heart is gall and my soul languishes.

Carina rested her fingers on the page, aching for one who could express such despair so poignantly. Rose was herself a poet, not writing in rhyme and meter, but in beauty and sorrow so profound it found an echo in Carina's breast. And suddenly Carina felt blessed that it was not she Flavio had enticed! Could she have withstood him?

I no longer know myself. Is it possible to live someone else's life? If so, I have left mine and entered the mind and body of a stranger . . . whom I don't much like and trust not at all. I weep incessantly, which is a great disgrace to me. Did I not know what I risked? Did I not choose it?

Carina brushed a tiny gold-bodied fly from the page. Now that she saw herself with new eyes, with God's eyes, she knew her own weakness. Even her marriage to Quillan left her vulnerable. The heart was indeed a false guide. She read on.

February 24, 1851 To think is pain; to remember, torment; but to consider the future — more than I can bear. If my suspicions prove correct, then I am lost indeed. For what woman of fallen character has ever survived the blow?

Carina's breath caught. What did Rose surmise? She was with child? Quillan?

And where is the one who led me there, who held the draught to my lips saying "drink, drink." He has found another with whom to dally, and I would warn her but I am mute beside him. My words would fall on deaf ears.

February 25, 1851 A single moment of joy can slake the throat of a dying spirit. An act of kindness, no matter how small, becomes a mercy drop from heaven. Where are these drops? Where is my joy? Each moment is consumed by fear and trembling. My angst weakens me, body and soul. Where will I turn for peace?

February 26 Of all my sins, one stands out above the others. That I ever took my first breath. My foolishness will soon be seen. What is whispered in darkness will be shouted in the light. Cry shame! You are defiled. Away from me, daughter of sin. Their voices haunt my dreams. Soon they will fill my waking, as well.

Carina read on, transfixed by Rose's plight. Her lover had gone to prey on a new victim, and Rose . . . Rose was left to bear the shame. And the child.

March 3, 1851 Is a violent deed

more heinous than a violent thought? The thought and deed spring from the same spirit. What fear have I of death? What is fear but a longing to retain what I do not want? Since I have died inside, it cannot matter what becomes of my shell.

I pray then for death to come upon me. I fill both waking and sleeping hours with that prayer. Yet I linger. A prayer in the darkness might go no farther than the pillow. But a prayer in the morning comes back to slap you. God has turned His face from me. He knows me no more. Daughter of shame. Daughter of sorrow.

I am no longer what I might have been, nor can I ever be. Yet this body is stubborn in resolve. It will not cease. For death is a wily opponent, sneaking up on the unwary, yet eluding the deserving.

Is there a God? An author of this madness? Take me if you are real. I would rather face your judgment than the condemnation of your people.

Carina closed the book and pressed it again to her breast, the pain in its pages too great. Why had Father Antoine given it to her? Did he hope she might come to know

Rose from its pages? What then? The woman was dead. But not forgotten.

She recalled Quillan's words for her. *"My father was a savage, my mother a harlot."* Did the priest think she could change his mind? If Quillan read these pages, would he feel differently? Or would he think like any other man, that Rose was to blame for her condition?

Carina stood up and stretched. Carrying the book with her, she walked to the entrance of the mine and looked into its darkness. She had no desire to go farther or see the shaft down which she'd fallen. She turned from the hole in the mountain and started back up the slope. Beside the gravestone, she sat down and returned to the journal.

March 15, 1851 What is a lie but a shade of the truth? Yet I am the basest of liars to think I would end my life because of the life inside me. It grows stronger each day, defying the shame with which it was conceived. Because it lives — I live. I am bound to the child inside by a force beyond my control, and it shames me to say I'm glad for it. What monster could kill the child of her womb even if she hates her own self for conceiving it?

Tonight I leave. For I will not bring

the shame upon my house, my loving father and mother. It would break their hearts.

Carina thought of her own parents. Mamma and Papa. What would they think of her? What would they say to her marriage? In marrying Quillan, she had gone outside her people, not sought her papa's permission, Mamma's blessing. Could they understand? Did she?

March 19, 1851 I am lost and despair of being found. Believing a lie, I severed myself from all that mattered, leaving only the one within me to share my fate. Where will I go? What will I do? Who will take me in, wretched child of sin? I am wholly unclean.

No, Carina thought. You were deceived. You participated in your ruin, but God is bigger than that. Only see the grace He offers. That grace even now brought Carina peace when the fear might overwhelm her. God had extended to her a mercy so deep and encompassing she longed to share it with Rose, to infuse it onto the page and have it change what happened.

March 25, 1851 I am become most

despised. Even the result of my for-
bidden love could not remain within
me to be born alive. Had it done so, it
would have looked upon its mother's
face in shame.

Carina started. The baby died? Then it
wasn't Quillan at all. She expelled her
breath and looked at the gravestone nestled
into the grass and tangled vines of the
mountain. What are you telling me, Rose?

March 26, 1851 My mind is a blind
guide. Why did I follow? I lie awake
and wonder why did I listen, why
couldn't I see? Why did I risk everything for a lie? And more than that,
why did I give my heart to the child
of my folly? I am weary. I fear my
feet will never light, for I bear the
stigma of my deed. Though my condition will never show now, my own
heart convicts me.

"Go home," Carina whispered to the
faded and water-stained page. "They will
forgive you. God will forgive you. Live,
Rose. I want you to live." She took up the
book and pressed it to her chest. "I want
you to live!"

Thirty-two

How does one accept a miracle?
Humbly.

Rose

They'd made excellent time, but D.C. looked
fatigued when they reached Fairplay an hour
past noon. Quillan guessed the trip had been
too much for him so soon after a serious injury. He jumped down from the box and circled around. D.C. didn't want his help, but
he'd be there if the boy lost his balance. He
looked pale enough when he lighted.

"You all right?"

D.C. nodded.

Quillan gripped his shoulder. "Get us a
room. Tell them it's Quillan Shepard and
they'll have something."

"I can help. . . ."

"No sense pushing it. Get the room and
lie down."

"This morning I thought I never wanted
to see a bed again."

Quillan smiled. "Well, one's calling you
now."

D.C. didn't argue. He headed off for the
Fairplay House, and Quillan got to work.
The purpose of this trip might be to remove

636

him from Crystal while Masterson handled Beck, but he'd make it a profitable one anyway. Buying from the merchants at Fairplay left little margin for profit. But if he was shrewd, he'd garner something.

It felt good to occupy himself. He thrived on work, hauling the heavy bags of grain, the barrels of flour and sugar and salt, straining with the box of steels and feeling the muscles in his back and arms and legs. Only when the wagon was fully loaded and the tarp tied down did he relax. And now he was hungry. He'd collect D.C. and get them a decent meal.

D.C. was asleep, but when Quillan touched his shoulder and suggested food, the boy came wide awake. He seemed to have profited greatly from the nap and sat up eagerly. "As Daddy always says, 'My belly button's sayin' howdy to my backbone.' "

"Then let's put some distance between them."

D.C. did the meal justice. Quillan remembered being that voracious. It hadn't been that long for him. But as he ate the mediocre fare, he thought of the meal Carina had cooked him. Beyond the delight of her company, the food had made a memorable impression. She had a gift and a heart for it.

He considered for a moment that he

could have that sort of meal every night if he chose. She was his wife. All he had to do was pick up the sorts of things he'd gotten for her before and . . . He stopped the thought and stared at the mealy cornbread and chuck roast before him.

"Aren't you hungry?" D.C. looked covetous.

Quillan slid him the plate. "Have at it."

"You sure?"

"No, D.C., I'm going to knock you on the head if you touch it." As soon as the words were out, he realized how inappropriate they were. He flushed with remorse. "I'm sorry. I didn't mean that." He forked the hair back from his face.

"It's okay." D.C. slid the plate close and started shoveling. "I guess you're missing Carina."

Quillan scowled. He couldn't exactly argue, because with D.C.'s words he'd felt an acute ache inside. Yes, he missed her. He wished she were there that minute so he could grab her into his arms and show her . . . show her what? That he hadn't meant to hurt her? That he loved her. Yes, he loved her. He pushed back from the table, suddenly tight all over.

D.C. waved his fork. "In some ways, you and I are alike."

Quillan glared. He wasn't in the mood for D.C. to philosophize.

"I mean I never knew my mother, and you —"

"D.C."

The boy looked up.

"Shut your mouth and eat your food."

D.C. grinned. "That's one of those things Daddy would say. How can you eat if you shut your mouth?"

Quillan gave him a look that said more than words.

"You're ornerier than I thought. Must be missing her awful bad."

Quillan was making a fool of himself to a kid too wet behind the ears to . . . and then he recalled that D.C.'s experience exceeded his own, if you considered his visits to Hall Street. Quillan shuddered inside. It was an ugly thought.

He slid his chair out and stood. "Put the bill on the room." Then he walked out.

The tension wouldn't leave him, however. As he stalked through the streets of Fairplay, Quillan felt tighter and tighter. Something wasn't right. Yes, he was exasperated with D.C. and angry with himself for doing something so utterly stupid in marrying Carina. But it was more. It was as he'd felt the night William Evans was killed. A feeling of impending doom.

It sounded overly dramatic even to himself. What could happen? Masterson would be quietly amassing his men even now.

They'd be arming themselves and passing the word to their friends and partners. Crystal had reached the breaking point, and the moment Beck tried anything, there'd be a force arrayed against him he couldn't imagine.

So why did Quillan chafe? What was he missing? And then it struck him. Berkley Beck was not the kind to take his insult lying down. Yet there'd been no response whatever to the wedding. Was Beck brooding over some particularly nasty revenge?

A chill found him even in the afternoon heat. Quillan stopped walking and stood with dread immobilizing his legs. Would Beck commit one last heinous act before going down in defeat? A surge of fear rushed him. Carina? His throat grew tight, hands clenched at his sides.

He turned on his heel and rushed back to the Fairplay House. D.C. stood outside on the porch surveying the town. Quillan strode up and gripped his shoulder. He turned him and shoved some bills into his hand. "Cancel the room, D.C. We're not staying the night."

"We're not?"

But Quillan was already crossing to the livery. He found the ostler wrangling with a customer and shouldered his way in. "I need to leave my wagon. And I need two horses, your freshest and best." Because he had a relationship with Ferguson, the man turned from the difficult customer and nodded.

"Park the wagon inside. I'll have two animals saddled and ready."

The customer began blustering, but Quillan was half running out the door. He maneuvered the wagon, already full and ready for the drive up, into the back of the livery. But Quillan didn't care what he lost from it. He paid Ferguson and led the two geldings outside to the street where D.C. waited.

He gave the boy a serious look-over. "Can you make the ride up? Maybe I should have let you keep the room."

"I can make it. What's happened?"

"Nothing that I know of. Just a feeling."

D.C. didn't laugh. He took the reins of the bay and mounted. "Daddy said to listen when you had a feeling. He said God talks to you."

Frowning, Quillan mounted. He couldn't explain the urgency he felt, but he wouldn't believe it was God. They weren't on speaking terms.

Cain hobbled into the livery where Alan Tavish stood at the open doors, rubbing his chin with slow strokes.

"Now, what would the lass be about . . . ?"

While Sam circled, then settled at his feet,

Cain followed Alan's gaze up the gulch. He saw no sign of a lass. Did he mean Quillan's bride? "What are you gawkin' at?"

Alan sighed and turned. "Sure and it's nothin'. But Miss DiGratia's away up the gulch there."

"Mrs. Quillan Shepard, you mean. Did Quillan give you any indication a'tall he meant to marry her?"

Alan grinned. "None that he intended, mind ye."

Cain raised his brows.

"Cain, are ye blind, man? He's smitten sure."

"No." Cain slipped the crutches from under his arms and settled onto a barrel. "I'd have seen if he were smitten."

"Not if ye weren't lookin'. But then ye've had other concerns."

"True enough. Still, I'm not easy in my mind about this. Seems awful sudden-like."

" 'Tis." Alan nodded. He pulled his pipe from his pocket, tapped it, and lit the tobacco that half filled the bowl.

"It's a sorry thing when a man, who you consider a son, falls in love right under your nose, and you take no notice a'tall," Cain stated.

"Aye. But then Quillan's not like other men. T'wouldn't surprise me if he's fightin' himself over it all."

Cain considered that. "That would explain his sour face this morning."

"And the way he barked at me, then apologized as though t'were St. Michael himself he'd offended." Alan laughed. "The man's in love, but he's not sure he wants to be."

"What about her?" Cain waved toward the woman somewhere up the gulch. "Does she love him?"

"Aye."

Cain slapped his knee. "You know what I think? I think there's a heap of romance wanderin' around in your head that just wants a place to fix."

Alan drew on his pipe. " 'Tis possible. But I dinna think so."

Cain leaned as far out the door as he could. "What else have these old eyes missed? You seen Beck?"

Alan swiveled his head. "Bit queer, that. Saw him last evenin' with a face like thunder. Sure and t'was for Quillan stealin' his bride."

A sight Cain would have relished himself. *Not that I take pleasure in misfortune, but even King David appreciated how the wicked had fallen.*

Alan puffed smoke from the side of his mouth. "I have'na seen him since."

"Think he cleared out?"

Alan shook his head.

Frowning, Cain said, "Quillan expected he'd respond, don't ya know."

"Aye. With the town ready when he did."

"Well, Beck's just weasel enough to save his own tail and let the others roast."

"I dinna think he's gone. I'd wager he's away inside there, thinkin' thoughts as no one wants to know."

Cain reached for his crutches, and Sam's head came up. "Let him stay there till they come and haul 'im off to justice." He pulled himself up on the crutches, and his dog leaped up, willing and ready. Cain worried Sam's ears. "Nothing like a dawg for pure devotion."

Alan smiled. "Sure, the dumb creatures know best." He tapped his temple. "Dinna think they don't."

Cain hobbled outside, squinting in the brightness. God sure knew what he was about when he made dogs. But just now Sam circled him, making every swing of the crutches difficult. "What're you doin', you fool dawg? Heel now."

Sam moved obediently behind but whined about it. Cain grinned. "You've gotten spoiled, don't ya know." He swung himself out past the livery to the backside of the new smithy. He nodded to the giant Swede inside, arms bare and slick with sweat. Then he passed on. Halfway behind the bootier, his dog began to growl. Cain stopped and half turned when he heard the swish, then the blow tumbled him down.

April 31, 1851 If there is a hell I have found it. Yet here I find a welcome, and the price is no more than I paid to lose everything before. Placerville. I rode up today in a wagon filled with wretched men. My heart quakes at what lies ahead. But I forsook all for my lover's embrace and his fleeting devotion. I have chosen my part, and now it remains to see how well I can play the fool.

The shadows grew long and Carina knew she should think about returning to town, but she felt so reluctant to leave the site of this lonely marker, this mountain grave. How could she mourn someone she never knew? Yet she did. She had felt the affinity before she loved Quillan, felt it the first time she rode up to the Rose Legacy mine. Did Rose reach out to her from the grave? Was that possible?

She thought of the tale Fisher had told of the child, Jessie Rae, playing her mandolin on dark rainy nights. Did these mountains hold the souls that passed here? Did they roam after dark? Did Rose and Wolf remain in an embrace that forever bound them to this earthly realm?

Carina shook her head. She had read nothing yet of Wolf and how they came to be together. She should go, but the thought of riding down to Crystal and facing the ugliness, the fear, even the noise . . . She could stay a while yet. There was so much still to know. She read on.

May 1, 1851 What strange quirk of fate, to be saved from disgrace by a savage. Yet is he more a savage than those who would have bought me? Who is this man? A stranger, yet when he found me with his eyes, I knew him. His name is Fate. He knew me by my pain, and I him, by his. We are bound together, he and I.

As I am bound to your son. Whether he wants me or not.

June 1, 1851 To find beauty is to know mercy. Wolf is the most beautiful man I have ever seen, his hair next to honey, his skin bronzed by the sun, but his eyes the color of a stormy sky. What miracle joins one heart to another? Standing under the night stars, Wolf wrapped a blanket around us both, the Indian way of choosing me for his wife. Then we spoke our vows with only God and the mountain to hear. Would anyone recognize what we have done? Or would they say our pact is false and consider me still what I was? It matters less than it did. Cruelty sustained loses its barb.

Carina smiled. How true. The human capacity for suffering was like that for joy. It could only have the greatest impact in small doses. After that, mind and body could no longer take it in. Hadn't Papa told her that?

June 13, 1851 Wolf is solicitous in every way. I've told him more than I ever thought to share. When I spoke of losing the baby, he grew quiet. Maybe he, too, has lost a child. He tells me little about himself but speaks readily about the things he knows. He is wonderfully versed in nature and all her aspects. In every way we live at one with the mountain and forest, every way but one. He mines the ground from dawn till dusk, delving deeper and deeper with a ferocity and energy both wondrous and frightening. He will not relent. He tells me he must. I think he fights to find his identity.

Carina thought of Quillan, always moving, always working, tirelessly seeking something. His identity? Perhaps there was more of Wolf in him than their storm-colored eyes.

June 15, 1851 Is hope a dream? I've named the baby Angel. Wolf says his spirit must have a name to find its way to heaven. Imagining him there with God eases my pain. Yet I long still for the life that was lost, though I despised it, wishing even to do it harm. How perverse is the human spirit. I would give my life to have it back again.

July 1, 1851 There is a God, and He is merciful. He has looked upon an unworthy soul with pity and filled my heart with joy. I have yet to tell Wolf, but I entrust my secret to this page. I am once again with child.

Quillan. Carina knew it without reading on. He was the fruit of Rose and Wolf's union, not that of her unconscionable beau. Would he be as glad to know that as Carina was?

I cannot find it in me to regret. Is there a marriage on earth more blessed by God than the joining of two hearts in simple fidelity? Yet when Father Charboneau came to us a fortnight ago, Wolf insisted our marriage be sanctified by the Christian rite. For my part I accepted his wisdom, and this child is proof of God's blessing.

Father Charboneau. He had married Wolf and Rose? Then Quillan's wasn't an illegitimate birth as he thought. Carina turned the page and read on. Rose's writings at this point were devoted to many things. She began detailing the flora she found in her walks on the mountain. Did she only now begin to see what was around her? Did the life inside awaken her to the beauty?

Carina imagined it so. With Quillan growing inside her, Rose seemed to have recaptured the joy she had lost. She described the falls and the sunrise over the peaks. The pages were filled with prose and attempts at verse. There were even some drawings of wild flowers. These were labeled with names Carina guessed to be Sioux.

Did Rose bring them home for Wolf to name when he came out of the mine? Rose wrote of her concern for him. What did it matter to her if he found gold? They had everything she could want already.

I told Wolf that, but he only looked at me with his stormy eyes. He needs something he thinks he can find only by bringing gold from the ground.

September 12, 1852 I know why Wolf plumbs the earth. He is searching for his soul. The Sioux never accepted him. Though others were adopted into the people and became Sioux, Wolf was always separate. He is caught between two worlds, not Sioux, not white. It is the *needing* of gold he seeks. If he needs it as they do, he will be one of them. For my part, I would as soon he were not.

The sun continued its westering. Still Carina read. She read Rose's account of the aspens turning golden, the leaves falling. Snows came, one perilously close to burying them alive in their cabin. Father Charboneau spent Christmas eve with them. Rose cooked rabbit.

January 8, 1852 How does one accept a miracle? Humbly. The child grows large within me. I no longer fear his fate will be that of my Angel's. This one is strong and eager for the world. He will make his own name.

Carina touched the page with quivering fingers. Quillan. Strong and eager for the world. She felt a measure of Rose's pride. That child was her husband. She closed the journal and breathed deeply, thankful Father Antoine had given it to her. Had he known she would love Quillan better for reading it?

She knew him now, understood the force of his personality. Even in the womb he'd made his presence known. She closed her eyes and pictured him. *Oh, Signore, how I love him.* She recalled Rose's words. *Is there a marriage on earth more blessed by God than the joining of two hearts in simple fidelity?*

If only she could have the chance. She drew the mountain air into her lungs and longed for his return. Surely he would love her. Once he knew her heart.

Quillan rode beside D.C., careful not to push the horses harder than they could stand, but the need to push was inside him. He shouldn't have gone. The premonition of something bad gripped him. For once D.C. was quiet, and Quillan wondered if he felt it, too. He didn't ask, though.

He noticed the horses' strain and expelled his breath in frustration. "We've got to let them blow." The way was steep and the air thin. Pushed too hard, a horse would get spraddle-legged with ribs heaving and the breath rattling in its throat. It would be dead by nightfall. They dismounted and lightly watered the geldings, then simply let them rest.

Quillan paced. D.C. stretched out alongside the road and watched him. Then he closed his eyes, and Quillan saw the fatigue and maybe pain as well. He should have left him in Fairplay. Were all his decisions going to be wrong? He kicked a stone and changed direction.

At last he rallied D.C. and they started up again. The horses were strong. Ferguson had given him the best he had, not the crow bait the other fellow would end up with. But still Quillan chafed the time. They were ten minutes shy of another blow for the horses when D.C. lurched up in his saddle.

"Look there, Quillan!"

"I see it." Quillan veered the horse to the right and looked over the edge. A canvas-covered wagon lay on its side some twenty yards down. A woman struggled out the end with a child in her arms. It appeared the man was thrown, and he lay a short distance on the far side.

"We can't just leave them there." D.C. leaned forward over the saddle horn for a better look. "They might be hurt."

Quillan's jaw tensed. "I know that." He dismounted, left the gelding on the road, and made his way down to the family.

"Oh, thank the Lord. I thought no one

would see us. What a terrible thing. First the one horse collapsed, then . . ." The woman fluttered her hands as she spoke. She was dough-faced and ordinary in features, with a voice particularly high and breathy.

Quillan ignored her and stooped down beside her husband. The man was stunned but came to when Quillan rolled him. His face was pockmarked, and that, with his receding hairline, made him look older than he probably was. He hissed his breath in and grabbed hold of his arm.

"Anything broken besides your arm?"

The man put a hand to his head. "I don't think so. Madeline?"

"Your wife and child are fine, which is more than I can say for your horse." Quillan looked at the battered carcass. "Did it ever occur to you that one animal couldn't haul this load on a grade at this elevation?"

The man tugged his mouth down sideways. "The other one gave out. Just up and collapsed."

"Where are you from, Mr. . . ."

"Nielson." He started to reach, but his introduction hand was connected to the broken arm. "We're from Wichita. Kansas."

Quillan had expected as much. "Mr. Nielson, I'll get you and your family up to the road. You can flag someone else from there."

"What about the wagon?"

"You'll have to work that out with them." He helped the man to his feet. "It'll be nightfall soon enough. Take the first opportunity you get."

Nielson frowned. Quillan ignored it. He went and looked inside the wagon. It seemed sound, considering its rough descent. The animal must have failed the grade and slipped back, sending the wagon backward over the side and dragging the poor beast behind. They were lucky the slope was more gradual at this point.

"D.C." Quillan nodded the boy over from where he stood listening to Mrs. Nielson carry on. "Fetch one of the horses." Together, with D.C. directing the horse and Quillan's back to it, they heaved the wagon upright. It would serve the Nielsons if they ended up staying the night, though he expected there'd be traffic as long as the light held.

"We'll get you up to the road now, ma'am." Quillan reached for the child and swung him up. The little boy hooked his arms around Quillan's neck but looked back at his mother the whole way.

"Come on, Mrs. Nielson." D.C. gave her an arm to hold.

Quillan climbed with resolute strides. There'd been no help for it. They couldn't leave the family unattended. They were fortunate to have so few injuries, though he'd gotten a look at Nielson's arm and the bone was protruding. He set the boy down on the opposite side of the road.

"How can we thank you?" Mrs. Nielson's face was earnest.

Quillan was glad D.C. stepped in to handle the gratitude. He went down to help Mr. Nielson up the last bit of slope. "Use the wagon for shelter if it comes to it. But I think you'll have some wagons pass through still."

Nielson was clearly in pain.

"Let me see the arm." Quillan had been right. Though the bone didn't break through the flesh, he could see the lump of it where it didn't belong. "You want me to tug it back in?"

Nielson looked sick. "I guess you'd better. But don't let Maddie see. She's none too keen on all this." Nielson ought to have done some clearer thinking beforehand. But Quillan figured he was doing it now.

"Resist me." Quillan pressed his palm to Nielson's upper arm and pulled through Nielson's hollering until he felt the bone slide back. His wife didn't need to see; she'd heard plenty. Quillan released him. He was not a doctor and couldn't tell how well he'd lined it up. But it no longer threatened to break through the skin.

He wasn't sure whether husband or wife

was the paler, but when Quillan let go of Mr. Nielson, Mrs. Nielson looked at him with wary eyes. Quillan half smiled at the irony. Even here on the road with complete strangers, he was watched askance. He dug into his pocket, brought out a nickel, and handed it to the little boy connected to his mother's skirts. The child snatched it with a grin. His mother's face eased immediately, but before she could begin thanking again, Quillan touched his hat and started for the horse.

Riding beside D.C., Quillan observed, "Some folks should not leave Kansas."

D.C. grinned. "Mrs. Nielson didn't know what to make of you. She asked if you were always so surly."

Quillan glanced sidelong. "What did you tell her?"

"That you were pressed to get back to your bride."

Quillan flinched.

"She offered her congratulations."

Thirty-three

If I die this minute I will not have lived
in vain.

Rose

The clouds overhead blushed, then flamed,
but Carina knew she would not leave until
she'd read every word of Rose's diary. She
was compelled. She couldn't put it down,
couldn't walk away without knowing it all.

April 4, 1852 If I die this minute I
will not have lived in vain. For I have
seen the face of my child, and his
name is joy. He is perfect in every feature, fearfully and beautifully made.
Wolf said we will call him Quillan. He
has a lusty cry.

Carina's breath stilled. A lusty cry. *"And
then that baby started in to cry and Wolf, see,
he started a-howlin', the fiercest, loneliest
howlin' ever heard."* The memory of the old
miner's words chilled her, and Carina
dreaded what would come. Was the story as
she'd heard it? Could she bear to know?

April 5, 1852 I am sick with concern.

What has come over Wolf? When first he took his son into his hands, he rejoiced, his face alight with joy. But when the baby cried, a terrible change came over him. The sound of Quillan's cries has drawn from Wolf a wailing I hope never to hear again. Even now the memory of it chills me, and I fear for us.

Carina's throat tightened painfully. She didn't want to read it in Rose's own words. Yet neither could she leave Rose to suffer it alone. She would not abandon her. She had to continue.

April 8, 1852 I don't know the truth of it. Only that on the night of my baby's birth, a man was killed. Wolf is blamed, and I cannot say it's not so, for he spent that night away out on the mountain. I can only hear in my mind his howling . . . and wonder. Doubt erodes my soul. How can I hold in my heart one who might have done what they say? Did I ever know him?

Yet who am I to judge? Has he ever once looked at me as the "good" woman does, pulling her skirts aside lest they touch me and contaminate her? Has he withheld his love from me, who came to him so tarnished I would have sold myself for food? The truth of it is, even if he has done this vile deed, we are joined, heart and spirit. We are one.

Carina shuddered. Would Rose take on Wolf's guilt? Could she love him so much to share even the lowest part of him? Or would she believe his innocence, proven now, twenty-eight years later, with Henri's confession?

April 24, 1852 Whatever happens to Wolf and to me, Quillan is innocent of it. I have given him life, and I must safeguard it. I fear for him. I see the hatred in the faces of the miners. They would do violence to us if they could.

April 25, 1852 Does Wolf know what they say, hear the things I've heard? Does he know how they fear him? And when my baby cries and Wolf goes out on the mountain, I fear, too. My heart is weak within me. I begged him to take us away, but he won't leave the mine. He works like one possessed.

April 26, 1852 I know what I must do. Yet my heart aches. How can I live without my child?

Carina pictured Rose with the infant Quillan clutched to her breast, agonizing over her choice. The sorrow she must have felt!

April 27, 1852 I tried to give my baby to the priest. He alone has shown us unflagging kindness. But he won't take my son. I am in anguish, for the one he names is not one I would choose. What choice have I? I am unable to quell Quillan's helpless wailings, for what baby was ever born who didn't make his needs known? Wolf cannot bear his cries, though I will carry them forever in my heart.

A slow tear started down Carina's cheek. Her chest ached to think of Rose's courage and desperation. To sever ties with her own child after losing the first . . . Where did she get the strength?

April 28, 1852 Quillan is lost to me. I must have nothing to do with him, make no effort to see him or watch him grow. I must not taint him in any way with my presence. Those were her words. Only in this way might she deliver him from his sinful start. My arms nearly snatched him back, but I watched her take him into their home and close the door between us.

I must think of him no more or I will surely go mad. Wolf wept when I told him what I'd done, but he did not set out to recapture his son. He knows the truth of it. I can't find it in me to hate him, though my soul wants so badly to blame someone, something. There is only myself.

No. You did what you had to. Rose's love, like Èmie's, was selfless and deep. But like Èmie, would she find joy in that? Carina turned the page. The next entry was nearly a month later, and she could only suppose Rose's grief during that time was too deep to record.

May 24, 1852 I dreamed last night that I held Angel. I put him to my breast and suckled him as I had suckled Quillan. I long for him as I cannot allow myself to long for Quillan. When I heard of the deaths of the Shepards' children, I was petrified that I had killed my own son. But he lived! God is merciful! He spared my child, though they have taken him away; I don't know where. Is it wicked once again to want to die?

June 22, 1852 Angel came to me

again. Is it a dream? He is so warm and milk-scented. I stroke his head and feel its downy softness. He is older now and cutting teeth. But he never cries. He never cries.

Carina stared at the words. Had Rose's mind lost its hold of reality? Did she imagine the perfect child, one even Wolf could have borne? *He never cries.* The lump in Carina's throat ached.

October 7, 1852 Sometimes I see them playing on the floor, Quillan and Angel together. How beautiful they are. But they don't stay. I feel so cold. I feel cold all the time. The sun can't penetrate the chill. It comes from inside me.

October 8, 1852 My body is unfailing in cruelty. It is strong, stronger than my mind. Wolf holds me, but I don't feel him there. I'm so weary of it all.

Carina's hand trembled as she turned the leaf and saw there the last entry.

October 9, 1852 I'm taking this book to Father Charboneau. Perhaps one day he will give it to my son. I can only hope that Quillan will have compassion on the one who bore him. For there is another inside me whom I cannot bear to see. God have mercy on my soul.

Carina drew a raspy breath and closed the book, then gave way to the tears. Such despair. How could Quillan hate the woman who had suffered so much to give him life and keep him safe? He didn't know. He couldn't know the truth and not cherish her.

Had she taken her own life? Or had the fire simply provided the opportunity she longed for? Did it matter? Perhaps it should. But Carina couldn't find it in her to judge. God knew. God alone could judge Rose's soul. And Wolf had loved her too much to let her die alone.

Regretfully, Carina stood. She sniffed away her tears, reluctant even now to go down. Here, in Rose's place, she could forget for a time the ugliness of Crystal and her own woes. But not forever. She must face it.

Daisy was fresh and well grazed and carried her with ease. She reached Crystal just as the last evening color faded to gray. Dressed as she was, Carina had little concern she would be noticed returning the mare, so she went directly to the livery. Alan Tavish wasn't in, so she saw to the horse herself. Something seemed odd, and then she realized what it was.

Quiet. No tinny pianos, no raucous voices. The street wasn't deserted, but mostly so. She checked the back room for the old ostler. Maybe he could tell her what was happening. But the room was empty, and she looked out the back doors to the tent city and beyond. There was a gathering at the creek side. Experience brought a chill to her breast.

As she stood, more and more people gathered. What was it? What drew them? She had to know as well. It could be nothing more than . . . than . . . But thoughts of the crowd around William Evans' body would not allow her to even imagine an alternative. Her heart pumped. She reached the crowd breathless and shaking.

A blond giant turned to those nearest. "Ya, I heard the dog yelp. But that was some hours ago."

Was it only a dog? She strained to see through all those in front of her.

"Joseph, Mary, and all the saints!" It was Alan Tavish. "Why? In heaven's name, why?"

Carina's chest suspended. Alan's agony was real. She insinuated herself between the gawkers, pushing toward the front. This was some devilry, she was sure, and the knot in her stomach tightened. *Dio, not Èmie*. No, it couldn't be Èmie. Dr. Simms would keep her safe. Who, then?

"Musta lost his balance and fallen."

A man.

"Head's got quite a bash."

He was attacked.

"How could he get that from a fall face-down?"

"Water must have rolled him."

"Poor old Cain. Bad way to go."

Carina froze. *Cain?* She must have spoken it, because the men in front of her turned, and she saw Cain lying in the gravel beside the creek, his mottled dog whining softly beside him.

"I say he was murdered." It was Bennet Danes, owner of the Boise Billiard Hall. Their eyes met, and he recognized her in spite of her garb. His expression was ugly.

Carina felt sick inside, sick in a way that wouldn't heal. Why would someone murder a defenseless, crippled old man? And then she guessed. Berkley Beck. This was his retaliation, his revenge on Quillan. And it would be bitter indeed. She'd seen the love Quillan had for Cain, the gentleness and the respect he bore him.

She must have swayed, for hands caught her arms and turned her away. She let them carry her through the crowd, then shook them off and walked alone. Her legs moved of their own volition. Her mind was too stunned to direct her path. She staggered, caught herself, and kept on. A shadow moved to her right. She spun, but her arm was gripped before she could run.

"My dear. I must say marriage doesn't suit you." Mr. Beck's eyes were wide and unusually bright. His shirt was wrinkled as though he'd slept in it, and there was dust on one sleeve. "Has Quillan made you a freighter?"

"He's made me nothing but his wife."

Beck slapped her. Carina gasped and held her cheek. He would strike her? Bestia! She swallowed her cry, though she couldn't keep her eyes from tearing.

"Where is the ledger, Carina?"

Her throat constricted with fear, but she raised her chin defiantly. "I gave it to Quillan. You have no more secrets, Mr. Beck."

He pulled her very close to his chest. "Berkley."

A drop of spittle hit her lip. She was repulsed, but she refused to struggle.

He smiled broadly, then laughed. "In that case, the most I can hope is to take you with me." He set her back without releasing his grip. "Will you dine with me, Miss Di-Gratia?"

Was he pazzo? "I will not."

"You'll have to change clothes. I can't abide a woman in pants."

"Let go of my arm, and you won't have to."

He yanked the hat from her head, and her hair tumbled loose. "That's better. A woman's hair is her crown."

He'd lost his mind. She was in the clutch of a madman.

"Now, then." He walked her forcibly toward Mae's. "I think the lovely green gown you wore last night."

Carina trembled. Had he seen her with Quillan? Had he lurked somewhere out of sight, yet watched her? They reached Mae's, and she prayed there would be people there. There were always people there. But the house was quiet. Cain's murder must have drawn them away. He half dragged her up the stairs, then kicked her door open with a strength she wouldn't have credited him.

"I'll wait in the hall."

She went inside and started to close the door behind her.

"I wouldn't try the window. If the fall didn't kill you, my man would."

Carina slammed the damaged door and rushed to the window. Walter Carruther paced below. She looked at the carpetbag lying where she'd thrown it. One consolation was the dreadful condition the dress must be in.

She pulled it from the bag. It was wrinkled, but not so much as she had hoped.

Closing her eyes, she pressed her face to the silk. Had Quillan thought her beautiful? As he eyed her in the dress, had he thought of her at all? Could he have left her if he had?

A wave of self-pity washed over her as she shook the dress and laid it across the bed. Why was this happening? Hadn't she surrendered her life to God's care? Had she mistaken His presence, His promise, His peace? How could this possibly be for her good? She pulled off Mr. Tavish's clothes and put on the gown, painfully aware of the way it enhanced her.

She fastened the buttons with clumsy fingers and smoothed the skirts, but refused to check herself in the mirror. It would show only her face anyway, and she did not want to see what emotions her eyes must hold. She opened the door, futilely hoping Mr. Beck would be gone.

He was not. He looked at her with fierce admiration and hatred, then held out his arm. She refused it, and he gripped hers instead. His fingers were brutal. Down the stairs and out the door and still no one stopped them. He then walked her along Drake to Central in plain view of the few people around.

He brought her into the hotel dining room and seated her himself. Carina hoped Mrs. Barton was away with the rest, but she was disappointed in that. Berkley Beck ordered a bottle of wine and walnut-stuffed pork chops for them both. His charade was ridiculous, but who would know that?

Mrs. Barton's lips were tight when she brought the wine. If she would only look at her she must see Carina's distress, but she refused to. She left the wine and stalked away. Mr. Beck opened it himself and poured them two glasses. He raised his. "A toast."

Carina's hands stayed in her lap.

"To my able and most beautiful assistant." He raised the glass, then drank. "And if you'd married me, I would not have abandoned you to save my own neck." The muscle twitched in his temple. "I would have been man enough for more than one night. You chose poorly, Carina."

She said nothing, but his words stung. She'd known Mr. Beck would retaliate, but as Quillan said, that was the point of it all. She dampened her lips, but her tongue was like powder. Quillan had left her to this. *Signore, why?*

Mrs. Barton brought their plates. The pork chops were lightly browned, and the stuffing smelled rich and savory. Fluffy potatoes were slathered with gravy. Carina looked up, daring the woman to see her. Mrs. Barton looked, but her eyes were so full of contempt, she missed Carina's plea.

Berkley Beck cut into his pork chop, took a bite, and chewed slowly, deliberately. He cut another, held it out for inspection, then masticated it as well. Carina turned away.

"Aren't you hungry, my dear?"

She didn't answer.

"The wine is very good." He nudged her glass closer.

She had a strong urge to throw it at him. But what was the use?

"Do you recall our first meal together?" He smiled boyishly. "You looked so lost and . . . indignant." He cocked his head. "A little like now. But then you'd just been wronged by Quillan Shepard. Funny you didn't learn from it."

"I had also been wronged by you. You forged my deed. You sold fraudulent property and lied to me. You pretended to help, but you had no intention of doing so."

He was quiet for a time. "That was perhaps my mistake. I should have given you the house, but then what need would you have had for me?"

Carina dropped her forehead to her fingertips.

"What is it, my dear? Are you not feeling well?"

"You know what I'm feeling," she hissed.

"Temper, Carina. You've always had too much temper." He laid his fork and knife down. "Perhaps we weren't suited. As I think of it now, the son of a savage is more your like. And the son of a strumpet."

"She's not a strumpet!" Carina gripped the table edge. "And Wolf never killed anyone. It's all lies. And Quillan deserves better."

Berkley Beck narrowed his eyes. She saw in them unadulterated hatred. "He'll get what he deserves."

Carina was trembling, both with fury and fear. "I'm through with my dinner. I'd like to leave."

"Of course, my dear." He dabbed his mouth and folded the napkin neatly beside his plate, then stood.

Carina was too surprised to refuse his help with her chair.

He tucked her hand into the crook of his arm. "If you're ready . . ."

She nodded. Would he take her back to Mae's? Would Mae be there? No one else had come in to dine, and Carina looked at Mrs. Barton in her position by the wall. Did she imagine the look of satisfaction on her face?

"Worried?" D.C. had read his thoughts.

Quillan shrugged. No sense making more of it and having D.C. consider him some prophet of doom. They might return to Crystal and find Beck and the roughs detained and awaiting trial, the streets quiet, and the citizenry safe in their beds. Including Carina. His heart jumped.

"Daddy says, 'Behold the fowls of the air: for they sow not, neither do they reap, nor gather into barns; yet your heavenly Father feedeth them. Are ye not much better than they?' "

Quillan looked back at the gunmetal lake almost lost in the shadows behind them. Early stars shared the sky with mares' tails clouds, and soon it would be dark. The delay with the Nielsons had hurt.

"It's freeing to let God handle your business."

"It's called shirking."

D.C. rubbed his face. "Maybe. But if He really is in control . . ."

"God's had no part of my business. I take care of it and let Him run the rest of the world."

"Don't you ever get tired, Quillan?"

Quillan looked over. The boy's face was drawn. Quillan suspected he was talking again to try to shake the clouds from his head. He had definitely pushed too hard for his condition. But that wasn't the kind of tired the boy meant.

"I don't give myself time." Quillan was honest. Even at rest, he kept his mind occupied with reading and memorizing what he read. An idle mind left room for thoughts he preferred to ignore. He frowned. "Can you

say you've heard from the Lord since hand-
ing yourself over?"

D.C. was quiet a moment, then slapped
his neck where a mosquito bit. "I think
maybe so."

Quillan cocked an eyebrow.

"Not so much a voice in my ears as in my
mind, sort of telling me yes and no as I go
about my business."

"Yes and no."

"I'll pass the door of a saloon and hear
the no, then come on a begging man and
hear the yes. I avoid the one and help the
other."

"That's conscience, D.C. Every man
could say as much."

"But not every man could do it." D.C.
turned earnest eyes his way. "Before, I
knew what was wrong, but I did it anyway.
Now it's like a new strength inside. Daddy
says the Holy Ghost has got me by the tail.
I only know I want to do what's right, and I
can."

Quillan shook his head. "Anyone can conquer bad habits. I don't see anything supernatural in that."

"You weren't dead."

Quillan pondered that. Is that what it
took? To be rendered completely incapable
of helping oneself? A shiver found his spine.
He never wanted to be helpless again.

Thirty-four

I fear for us.
Rose

Carina stepped out with Mr. Beck. Suddenly the night was shattered by shouts and curses and grasping arms. Berkley Beck went down under a dozen fists. He fought and bellowed but was no match for the number that came against him. His face was a mask of rage as ropes were tied around and he was hauled to his feet.

Carina staggered back, then a voice hollered, "Get Beck's woman!" She recognized the heavy jowls of Bennet Danes and realized he meant her. Arms grappled for her, but she fought free, snatched up her gown and ran.

A faint voice hollered, "Not the lass. Not the lass, men!"

The air was filled with shouts and guttural cries, grunts and screams. Her chest burned as she ran for Mae's, confused in the torchlight, following instinct alone. She tripped on her skirt in the mud and fell hard, scrambled up, and ran again. She reached the door, but it was locked. Mae, who never locked the door!

674

She banged with her fist. "Mae!" Then she ran around to the back and tried the kitchen door. Sobbing, she banged this one, too. And it opened. Mae snatched her inside and closed the door behind her, sliding the bolt just as other fists and angry shouts met the wood. They were banging now with more than fists.

"Get your gun!" Mae hollered.

Carina ran up the stairs to the satchel where she had stowed the gun. She tugged it out and checked its load. The four chambers were filled, but her hand shook so badly she doubted she could shoot.

She went back down to Mae, who stood guard at the front door that was also being assailed. Carina shrank against the wall as she heard the wood split. Surely they weren't using an ax! But another blow showed her the shiny wedge as the wood splintered and squeaked.

Mae pressed her between the wall and her own bulk, pointing her handgun at the door. Another blow and the door shivered, then burst open. Mae stood firm. "Stop right there."

But the men surged forward. Mae fired, and return gunfire blasted around them. Carina flung an arm over her face, shrinking behind Mae. Mae jerked, then buckled. She gasped, "Run!" then fell, blocking the entry.

But Carina stood frozen, staring at Mae

on the floor. As the men pushed inside, she fired four times into those surging toward her. They would have to leap over Mae to reach her, but Carina had no doubt now that they would. Throwing down the gun, she turned and ran for Mae's rooms, burst into the kitchen, and felt the night air.

That door, too, was open wide. She spun to flee, but arms grabbed her, and a hand covered her mouth even as the shouts behind her neared. Carina fought, kicking and biting.

"Stop!" Quillan pulled her into the shadow beside the door.

She half screamed with relief, but his hand kept her mute as he searched the darkness outside, each second interminable. Carina's heart thumped with fear and hope. Quillan had come. He would keep her safe. He would . . .

The men tumbled through Mae's parlor. Something smashed. With an arm tight around her, Quillan lunged out into the night. The darkness flickered with torchlight as they ran toward the deeper shadow of the adjacent wall. Carina thought they would keep on, but Quillan wedged them into a gap between the wall and a shabby lean-to.

Pressed against him, Carina clutched Quillan's shirt and stared wildly behind them. "They're coming." She whimpered.

"Keep still." He jerked her face up and kissed her. With running feet, shouts, and spasmodic torchlight passing, he kissed her. In the darkness that followed, he kissed her. Then he let her go.

She didn't want him to stop, even if he'd only done it to silence her. She wanted him to hold her until everything was over. "Quillan . . ."

"Not now." He glanced quickly out, then pulled her with him. Her skirt snagged and she stumbled. Quillan half lifted, half tugged her to the alley and down to Central. Crouching there, she saw more men dragged along, tied and kicking. She felt Quillan tense as he watched, but he stayed still.

It was terrifying. Ugly. "What's happening? What are they doing?"

Quillan answered in a low voice, "Ridding Hamelin of the rats."

Her chest went cold. They were using the ledger, the names in the ledger. She'd provided it . . . and her name was among them. Quillan yanked her up, and they ran across the street, crouching again at the corner of the Gilded Slipper. They ran and shrank from shadow to shadow, freezing when a torch went by, then moving again in its wake.

He pressed her close to the back wall of the livery. "Stay here." Then he left her.

Carina's heart beat her ribs. Beyond the immediate fear for her life was the pain. Mae! Her heart ached with a pain so acute she couldn't breathe. Mae, crumpled and dying, shot down for her, protecting her. *Signore, why?* And now she feared for Quillan. Would the madmen take him, too? She pressed her fists to her breast and groaned.

Through the wood slats she heard voices, heated and rough. She heard Quillan, even but firm. She pushed up to her feet and found the door into the tack room. She pried it open and slipped inside, blind in the total darkness, then felt her way to the inner doorway and saw torchlight through the crack.

A man hollered angrily, and Quillan answered low. What was he doing? Did he speak for her, argue for her life? Did he, too, risk himself for her? She would not allow it. If they made one move toward him . . . She pressed the door open, but it bumped something heavy at the top.

In the torchlight, Carina looked up into the ghastly face of Berkley Beck, hanging by the neck. Sick and stunned, she fell back against a grain sack, then stared out into the room. Rows of men hung like hams from the rafters, their features grotesque and distorted. She pressed a hand to her mouth, fighting to hold her gorge as her head spun.

Adrenaline pumped in Quillan's limbs. He and D.C. had returned to a nightmare. The trustees had not collected the accused and detained them for trial. It was a lynching, a vigilante action fueled by fury and outrage. Had Masterson known? Intended it? Is that why he wanted Quillan out?

Quillan shook his head. No, it had spiraled out of Masterson's control. Something had driven it beyond reason. Quillan had felt it even before they saw the streets thick with torchlight and heard the yells. He'd rushed immediately to Mae's, seen Mae fall, then run around to find Carina. One minute sooner and he might have gotten them both safe. One minute later . . . He shook off the thought.

He had to focus. Carina wasn't safe yet. He'd argued for her, and maybe Masterson could hold them back. But violence was thick as the smoke from the torches. Not even the trustees had control anymore. Tempers ran too high. How had it escalated to this, and why?

Quillan glanced over his shoulder as another bound man was dragged into the livery. Then he darted to the place he'd left Carina. It was empty. His chest lurched as he spun and searched the darkness, his eyes strained. Had they found her? While he was in speaking for her life, had someone caught her? Groping along the back, he found the tack door open. He crept inside and stumbled across the soft heap.

"Carina?" he whispered hoarsely and gathered her up.

She stirred, gasped, and he muffled her moan against his chest as he surveyed the view that had shocked her into a faint. In the torchlight, the corpses were grisly indeed. It was a sight to turn a man's stomach. How much worse for Carina. "Hush," he whispered into her hair, turning her face from the light.

Beyond the door, the vigilantes dragged Walter Carruther to the noose, bawling and fighting like a bear. Quillan lifted and carried Carina out. She was shaking and he feared the shock might be too great. But terrible as her need might be, there was another need greater.

He headed toward the creek and found Alan standing with a pair of horses saddled and ready. He wasn't surprised Alan anticipated him, but he was grateful. Maybe the violence would not engulf Carina, but he couldn't be sure. He swept her up onto the nearest mount. "Get to the mine."

She started to protest, but he squeezed her hands around the reins. "Get to the mine, Carina." With a whack of his palm, he sent the horse off and watched her go. The moon flitted in and out through the breaking clouds. She had only to follow the creek. She would make it.

He stanched Alan's argument with a look, then hurried back to Mae's, running openly now. He didn't care who saw him. There was madness in the air, but he would not be caught in it. He found Mae hunched against the wall, breathing thickly, but breathing. He dropped down beside her.

She gripped his hand. "Carina?"

"I sent her up the gulch."

"Alone?"

He ignored her. "Where are you hit?"

"My hip and higher up." She screwed up her face. "Hurts bad."

Quillan knew he couldn't move her. She was three hundred pounds dead weight, and he couldn't risk it anyway. He went into her parlor and fetched a lamp and a blanket. He lit the lamp and set it on the floor beside her. The blood on her skirt was substantial. Sweat beaded her upper lip. He knelt and wrapped her in the blanket.

"I'll get the doctor."

"Quillan, Carina needs you."

His throat was tight and hard. "Right now you need me more." He went out into the night.

Dr. Felden was at home, his face grim. "I wondered who'd be first. How bad is she?"

"Two shots near the hip. I don't know where exactly."

The doctor snorted. "Didn't examine her, eh? Well, you can put such squeamishness aside. I'll need you to attend."

"Where's Simms?"

"With Èmie Charboneau. Not even the women are safe tonight."

Quillan knew that better than the doc. Together, they hurried up to Mae's. She wasn't conscious, but her labored breath continued. Between them, they got her onto the ruined door panel and carried her to the kitchen table, then scrubbed their arms and hands.

"Get some water boiling." Dr. Felden took out his shears and cut away her skirt and bloomers to the pale and blood-smeared flesh beneath. He frowned, taking in the angle and placement of the shots. "Her girth may be the saving of her."

It was blunt, but Quillan was glad to hear it.

Mae grunted and opened her eyes. "Any more compliments, Doc?"

"You'll be the first to know if there are." The doctor tipped her head up and gave her morphine for the pain. "Have a nice sleep. We'll be digging around awhile."

"Find any gold, let me know."

Dr. Felden smiled. "You're pure gold, Mae."

Her head lolled to the side, and she turned her violet eyes on Quillan. "Go to Carina."

He didn't answer, and soon enough she

wouldn't have heard him anyway. He worked with the doctor, fighting his gorge as the bloody probe dug around inside Mae's flesh until both slugs landed in the pan. Relieved, Quillan expelled his breath. "What do you think?"

Dr. Felden rubbed his brow. "Small caliber. No vitals damaged as the fatty tissue and the hip bone stopped both slugs. If we can avoid infection . . ." He tossed the sweaty cloth down and reached for the bottle of carbolic acid. "Her chance is as good as another. And better than those having their necks stretched."

Quillan didn't need the reminder.

"Hold the wounds open now."

Quillan pressed the flesh as the doctor applied carbolic acid. Mae made no motion as the burning liquid entered the bullet holes. The doctor packed and bandaged them, and Quillan stared at Mae's doughy face. He'd never known her to risk herself for anyone. But she'd done it for Carina.

Quillan rubbed the back of his own neck. "Where's Cain?"

The doctor looked up and removed his spectacles. "Cain? Quillan . . . he's dead. I thought you knew."

Quillan felt his legs leave him. He leaned against the wall, weak and numb.

"Whoa, there." Dr. Felden caught him by the shoulders and made him sit.

Cain, dead? Cain? His voice wouldn't come.

"I'm sorry, Quillan. They knocked him in the head and drowned him in the creek. It's what started all this hullabaloo."

Quillan sagged. So that was it. His chest filled with a throbbing sorrow. His eyes burned, and he dropped his face to his hands. *No* . . .

"It's a shock. Let me give you a powder."

Quillan shook his head, dragged himself up. *Not Cain!* It exploded inside him like a poisoned organ bursting. Who had struck the blow? Which one dragged a helpless old man to the creek and left him to drown? Hang them all! Let them kick their life away, gasping and gagging.

He staggered to the doorway, still open to the night, and gripped the frame. *Cain, Cain, Cain* . . . It pounded in his head. If he let himself, he would break down and cry. Cry for the man he loved like a father. *Cain* . . .

He passed through the doorway. He had to think. He turned and headed for Central. Before he reached the livery doors, Alan met him with the extra horse, again anticipating his need. He saw Alan's discomfort. But that didn't ease the anger.

"Why didn't you tell me?"

Alan gripped his arm. "It canna be changed."

Quillan snatched Alan's shirt and yanked him close. "Why did they kill Cain?" He shook him. "Why?"

"Ye know why, Quillan."

Quillan dropped Alan, scalded by his words. Cain was dead because of him? Because he'd married Carina? His stomach clenched up. Beck had struck back. And the pain was lethal. As Beck had known it would be.

Alan hung his head, the crags of his face deep with regret. "Dinna blame yerself, Quillan."

Quillan dropped his face to his hands and groaned. Don't blame himself? Who, then? In his hubris he'd provoked this ghastly act. To have the victory over Beck, he'd sacrificed Cain. He felt gray. "Where's D.C.?"

"With the Reverend Baylor."

"He knows?"

"Aye."

So. He'd be saved the boy's grief at least. Quillan took hold of the saddled gelding. He dragged himself up and started for the gulch. However ill-fated their pact, he must see Carina safe.

Carina sat huddled in the blanket she'd found tied to the back of the saddle. She had tethered the horse directly outside the entrance to the mine and sat so close she could smell the mare's grassy breath. She had left her saddled and bridled in case . . . in case they came after her.

The clouds had dissolved and left a palette of stars smeared at one edge while mist lingered in the east. The gibbous moon silvered the mountainside, which she searched repeatedly, shivering with more than the cold. Would they hang her from the rafters, too?

Every time she looked up, she saw Berkley Beck's ghastly countenance, his arms hanging slack, his head askew. She pressed her hands to her eyes, heard the shouts and screams. *"Get Beck's woman!"*

She shuddered. If not for Mae . . . Mae had died protecting her. She recalled the thump of bullets striking Mae, the buckling, the fall. Carina heard a low wailing and realized it was her own. She clamped a hand to her mouth. She must make no sound.

Codarda. Coward. She had let Mae die. She should have stood away, let them take her, should never have run to Mae's, led them there. It was her fault. *Oh, Signore, why?* Her mind tormented her with images. Men hanging from the rafters.

She could have hung there, too. If not for Quillan. He had rescued her from the clutches of wicked men, as wicked as Mr. Beck and all the others. The hatred was the same. Carina shuddered. Why had Quillan sent her alone?

A sound made her stiffen, fear coursing through her. Should she run? Jump on the mare and ride? Her legs were weak; her body trembled. She clutched the blanket to her chin, eyes wide and searching. A horse climbed, and in the silvery light she saw him, his hair loose, his body inclined weakly in the saddle. She felt a surge of love. Quillan was good. He was strong and brave and good.

He slid down and stood on the ledge before the mine, a silhouette against the stars. Then he uncinched and tugged the saddle from his horse and dropped it to the ground. He did the same for her mare. He must believe them safe. He untied a blanket and shook it free, then walked toward the tunnel.

Carina sprang toward him, but he stopped her rush. With a firm hand he put her back from him. "Don't."

She wanted to speak. A thousand questions burned. But he was separate in his silence. He sank down against the wall and wrapped himself in the blanket. His chin dropped, and he wept, a silent weeping worse than anything she'd seen.

What could she say, what could she do? She knew instinctively he would reject her touch, her words. *Pray.* All she could do was pray for God's peace. Did Quillan believe in God? Did he know Him? It didn't matter. She did.

★ ★ ★

Morning. A thrush opened its throat. Cold, wind-washed air. Chartreuse aspen leaves ignited by the molten orb entering the eastern sky. Carina was dazed by light and color, everything heightened, dazzling her waking eyes.

Quillan slept beside her, sitting against the wall, self-contained in his blanket. His face was haggard. His dreams were not peaceful. Neither were hers. She slipped her blanket off and stood. Quillan didn't move.

She pushed past the mare and the grulla gelding Quillan had ridden up, stopping at the edge of the circle and dropping to her knees. *Signore, thank you for this day.* She might not have had it. This morning would have come, but she might not have lived to see it. *You have spared my life, saved me from those who would have done me harm. Grazie, Signore. Grazie.* She glanced back at the mine tunnel. *And please help my husband.*

She had guessed last night that it was Cain he grieved. She knew nothing that could lessen that grief, nothing but time and tenderness and God. *Per piacere, Signore, bring him peace.*

She stood and started down the path on foot. One side of her slipper had torn out, and the lace of her gown hung in ragged strips. But she was sound, and she marveled

688

at it. She was unharmed, though the malice had nearly overwhelmed and destroyed her.

She thought of Berkley Beck. Had he known they would take her when they found them together? Is that what he'd meant, that he could only hope to take her with him? Could he have hated her so much? If not for Mae . . .

Her chest clutched, and again her throat filled with tears. Why hadn't God spared Mae? He could have. And Cain. He could have spared Quillan his pain and Carina her own. Tears filled her eyes as she struggled to accept that somehow it was right, it was for her good. But how? Her mind would not accept that. So her spirit must.

She heard the spring ahead and walked to it. There she pulled off her dress and slippers and all her undergarments. The morning air raised her skin to gooseflesh, but she stepped into the gushing water and gasped. In its biting flow, she scrubbed her hair and skin, washing away the fear-sweat and filth. She bared her teeth and opened her mouth until the spring had thoroughly cleansed it. With violent shivers and teeth chattering, she stepped out and wrung the water from her hair.

Her wet skin stung in the morning chill, and she shivered as she pulled on her chemise and bloomers, corset and crinoline. She reached for her dress and startled as a motion caught the corner of her eye. Quillan stood at the curve of the path. She clutched the ruined dress to her breast, trying to read his mood.

How long had he stood there? Had he watched her bathe? Did he think her beautiful? Could he think of her at all with the horror of last night hanging over them? He was so grim, so silent. He came around the bend, cupped his hands in the water and scrubbed his face, then doused his hair and flung it back.

He dried his face with his sleeve. "When you're dressed we'll go."

There was no cruelty in his tone, but it was colder than the spring. He started up the path, and Carina sighed. Before putting on the dress, she tore away the ragged lace she had sewn with such care. It was good for nothing now.

Quillan's chest was tight. When he'd seen her with the spring rushing over, his breath had literally stopped. He'd appreciated such poetic descriptions, but now he knew it was physical reality. Beauty in its purest form could suspend the breath.

He made his way back up the path away from her, away from what she made him feel, from the wanting. How could he want her now? If not for their union, Cain would be alive. It was a hot poker inside him. His need to win had cost him the person he loved most in the world. Maybe the only person he loved.

Cain. What good had his faith done him in the end? Cain would have an answer to that, Quillan thought grimly, but he wasn't alive to voice it. He reached the Rose Legacy, rounded up the grazing horses, and saddled them. Carina came up the path, and he knew he was wrong. Cain wasn't the only one he loved. He watched her approach. The dress that he'd thought so fine was superfluous. It detracted. He turned away, yanked the cinch, then felt her beside him.

"We're going back to Crystal?"

"That's right."

"But . . ." Her voice quavered, and her hand went to her throat, saying more than words.

He turned. "Do you think they'll string you up in the light of day?" He saw her shudder and reached a hand to her shoulder. "It's over and done."

She searched his face, but he gave her nothing. One crack, and she would seep back in. Even the feel of her shoulder in his hand was too much. He let go. She fit her foot into the stirrup, and he assisted her onto the mare, then mounted the gelding.

He led and she followed. He was glad for the separate horses. The last time they'd

691

done this was too clear in his mind. With her in the saddle against his chest, he'd first imagined how it would be to love her. Now he knew.

Thirty-five

Doubt erodes my soul.
Rose

Carina watched Quillan's back, straight and unyielding as he rode before her. All around them, the gulch was full of life, tiny birds flitting, the hum of bees, the murmuring creek, and the breeze itself carrying the scent of flowering fields. But he seemed oblivious, cut off from it, from her.

Couldn't they comfort each other, find strength and solace? At least share their grief? She thought of his silent weeping. It had not emasculated him. It had shown him capable of great love. She stared at his back. His hair hung free, flying loose with the breeze. Beyond him she saw the first buildings of Crystal, but she was too insensate to feel afraid.

As they entered, he reined slightly and allowed her to come alongside. They passed Drury, then Spruce, then Drake. Along Central before the livery lay bodies, covered in blankets, and she began to shake. They'd been cut down and awaited burial. She stared at them, lying like furrows along the street. One, she knew, was Berkley Beck.

693

She jumped when someone grabbed her waist and realized Quillan had dismounted and was lifting her down. She was vaguely aware of Alan Tavish leading the horses away. Quillan had hold of her arm and walked her toward Mae's. A sob caught in her chest. At the house, he opened the door, but still he wouldn't speak.

Carina's voice was a ghost. "Where have they put Mae?"

"Inside."

Grazie, Dio. They'd not yet put her in the grave. Carina turned without a word, made her way to Mae's bedroom, and waited at the closed door. Then drawing a deep breath, she went in. Dr. Felden held vigil, his hands clasped and head bowed. Carina would not have thought him so devout.

She looked at the bed. They had covered her in blankets to her neck. Her hands lay atop, but not crossed. Only one bent over the mound of her belly. Posed as she was, she appeared sleeping, not dead. Carina pressed her eyes closed against the grief. They flew open at the touch of a hand on her shoulder.

Dr. Felden's eyes were red-rimmed. "Would you like to sit with her?"

Carina looked again at the bed. She had attended the body of her *bisnonna* and the cook whose heart had stopped while serving antipasti to Mamma's guests. But this was different. Mae was dead because of her.

"It's not likely she'll wake with the dose of morphine I've given her."

The doctor was speaking, but she wasn't hearing him right.

"Mrs. Shepard?"

She turned to him slowly.

"On second thought, maybe I'd better mix you a powder. Mae's going to sleep awhile, and it looks as though you should, too."

"But . . . she's not dead?"

He raised his brows. "Not last I looked. She berated me this morning for spoiling her skirt. Said she could have patched the bullet holes, but I had to go and make ribbons of it." He chuckled. "No, she's too ornery to be dead."

Carina collapsed and he barely caught her before lowering her to the chair. "Young woman, I'm putting you to bed."

"No!" Her fear must have shown.

"If it's last night you're thinking of, don't. That ugly business is over and done."

Over and done. So Quillan had said also. But how could it be? Could the men who did the killing simply go back to work? She thought of the bodies lying in the street. Would they be buried and forgotten? Who were they to forget such a thing?

Carina dropped her head to her hands. "I want to sit with Mae."

He frowned but left her alone.

Slowly the realization penetrated her stupor. Mae was alive!

Quillan stood with D.C. at Cain's grave. A stone had been put in place, previously quarried from the mountain and hastily carved. *Cain Jeremiah Bradley 1810–1880.* It said nothing about the old man who lay beneath it. But then, Quillan had no words either, and D.C. wanted none. Did the boy blame him? He blamed himself. *Oh, Cain.*

He had never felt such a loss. Not when he left the Shepards, not when his friend duped him. Cain was more than a friend. He was father, mentor, companion. He was wisdom, reason, and compassion. Everything good, everything real, everything that mattered.

Quillan heard Cain's laugh in his memory. That old man had found so much to amuse him, even frequently Quillan himself. And Quillan didn't mind because he knew Cain cared. *Oh, Cain.* He felt so lost. Cain had been his anchor.

He'd given Quillan purpose. Caring for Cain had given him joy. But what had he ever given Cain? Stubborn arguments and stiff-necked pride. Surely not the one thing Cain wanted above any other. How could he?

Surrender his heart to a God who sacrificed His best and His finest? What for? A surge of anger filled him. Then he saw D.C. watching. The boy's eyes were swollen, his mouth drawn. But Quillan could see no anger there. How? How could D.C. not rage against a God who would allow this?

Quillan heard the shovels pounding against the stony earth as graves were dug, graves for those who'd paid last night for Cain's death. Cain wouldn't have wanted it. He hated violence.

Quillan pictured the corpses hanging, a grotesque and grisly sight. And it could have been worse. What if Carina had been among them? He thought of the faces they'd passed riding in, some ashamed, some still bearing their animosity, but he'd made his point, bringing her in through the center of town. None would lay a hand on her, now that the bloodlust was passed.

He dropped his chin to his chest. If only it mattered. If only anything mattered. He would leave. What was there to keep him? At whose tent would he linger for a chat?

"Quillan?" D.C.'s voice was unnaturally thick, but he struggled to keep it steady.

"Yeah?" His own sounded false and forced.

The dog at D.C.'s side whined, a more

honest reaction than either he or D.C. allowed themselves.

"I've been thinking about what you said, about being a preacher. I think I could do Daddy proud."

Quillan swallowed the tightness in his throat. "You'd do him right proud, D.C." He could almost see the old man grin.

"I talked to Reverend Baylor last night. He's going to see me into seminary."

Quillan studied the young face before him. Cain would be downright tickled. He could almost hear the unrestrained *"hee-hee"* and the slap on the knee. *"Don't ya know."* He fought the sudden sting of tears.

"I have the funds since, well, the mine's earning a lot. Daddy talked to a group from back east who wants to finance it, a real operation. He meant to tell you, only things got so crazy."

Quillan's chest squeezed. Why now? Why should it all work out for Cain now that he was gone? What a perverse God.

"I know how you feel about the mine and all. But Daddy sure was proud to call you partner. I guess his half comes to me, and I was hoping you'd look out for it."

Quillan was unprepared for that.

"I don't want to let it go. Daddy's heart was in that hole, and I can't see clear to selling it. Not yet, anyhow."

Cain's heart wasn't in the hole. It was in

the boy who stood before him. But Quillan couldn't say that now. D.C. wouldn't understand. He was grieving his daddy by doing what he thought Cain would want. Quillan felt the trap, heard Mrs. Shepard in his mind. *"At the first scratch in the dirt you'll be one of them, the greedy soul-sellers. Just like your savage father."*

He closed his eyes. Was there even one time she'd thought something good about him? One good thing she'd said? Even when she prayed, it was to lay out all his faults. *"What will I do with this burden? He's the devil's own."*

Quillan shook himself. His personal feelings had nothing to do with D.C.'s request. It was all about Cain, what Cain would want. Quillan knew what Cain would want. "You have the names of these . . . investors?"

D.C. pulled a paper from his jacket. "Here's the one talked to Daddy. He's the mining engineer. Someone named Alexander Makepeace. Daddy was awful excited." And now the boy's voice broke. "He thought he'd finally made it."

Quillan clenched his teeth to keep from giving in to angry tears himself. Last night had been enough. Yeah, Cain had made it. For what? To be bashed by thugs and thrown into the creek like so much rubbish. God's mercy.

D.C. sniffed, blew his nose in his handkerchief, then pulled himself up straight. "There's one more thing. I wondered . . . would you take Sam?"

"Sam?"

"The dog." D.C. fondled the shaggy brown ear.

Quillan looked at the animal. Cain's words echoed in his mind. *"You gotta get you a dawg."* Again tears stung. *Not this way, Cain!* He squatted down and took the dog's head between his hands. He'd never asked Cain the animal's name. *Sam.*

"It's actually Second Samuel. The first Samuel died and Daddy named this one Second Samuel, after the book, don't ya know." He said it just like Cain, unintentionally, but the familiar phrase sucked away Quillan's resistance.

"I'll take him. If you think he'll sit in the box."

The dog laid his muzzle on Quillan's knee.

"I imagine he'll sit better than I did."

Quillan shrugged. "He doesn't have to go far for that. Preaching will suit you better."

D.C. managed a grin. "You know me and hard work."

"You might find it harder than you know. Especially with boneheads like me."

D.C. squatted down and circled the dog's

neck with his arms. Sam licked his face, then returned his nose to Quillan's knee. D.C. looked at the grave. "Daddy believed you'd come."

Quillan didn't answer. He looked at the gravestone. *For your sake, Cain, I wish I could.*

D.C. stood. "Well, the reverend and I got some things to figure out."

He was trying too hard to be strong, but Quillan didn't say so. He'd been there himself. He nodded, stroking the dog's head. He stayed after D.C. left. He'd never felt so alone.

The rasp of the shovels, the gruff murmurs, even the dragging of the bodies didn't rouse him from his graveside stupor. The dog settled at his feet, and Quillan sank from the squat to sit with his knees loosely wrapped by his arms. He remembered sitting that way at the grave of his dog. What had he been, eight, nine years old? It was an old stray. Mrs. Shepard had ordered it shot when it killed a chicken. *"Once a chicken killer, always a chicken killer. You can't change what he is."*

Quillan forked his fingers through his hair and rested his forehead on his palms. What was the point of trying if he could never change what he was? Whatever he did would go wrong. Just look at Cain. Quillan stared at the mounded earth. His wedding had put Cain there. He dropped his forehead to the crook of his arm across his knees. What could he do about it now?

Carina longed for the violet eyes to open. Dr. Felden had dosed Mae heavily, but Carina wanted to thank her, to beg her forgiveness, to show her relief that the bullets had not killed. She had kept bedside vigil before, but it chafed her.

She wanted the healing now. She wanted forgiveness and reconciliation. She wanted Mae to know she loved her. Carina watched the coverlet rise and fall with the motion of Mae's ample chest.

Oh, Signore . . . A sense of His mercy filled her. *Dio, you are faithful. Working all things together for good.* She thought of the journal, Quillan's mother's final despair. If only Rose could have known. But perhaps she did. Perhaps in her last moments, in Wolf's arms, she found the peace she so desperately wanted. Surely God would have mercy on two such wounded souls?

And good had come of it. Quillan had come of it. He hadn't perished in the fire because Rose's selfless act had saved him. His mother had loved him more than her own life. And Carina loved him, too.

Sliding to her knees beside Mae's bed, she folded her hands. *Grazie, Signore, for your grace which has saved me, for Quillan and*

Mae and Èmie. Make me worthy of their love and help me to love well in return. She caught Mae's hand up to her mouth and kissed her fingers.

The door opened, and Quillan entered. With the day's growth of beard and his shirt soiled and open at the neck, he looked weary and grieved. He must ache for Cain. Could he see beyond the pain? Did he know that even in this God was working, pouring out His grace, His mercy?

"May I speak with you?" His voice was flat.

She stood up and followed him out the back door. The sun was high overhead and it shadowed his face beneath the hat, just as it had the first time she saw him.

He waited until she closed the door behind her, then spoke. "In a couple days D.C.'s leaving Crystal. You can go with him."

She searched his face. "Go where?"

He removed his hat and shook back his hair. "Anywhere. Home. To Flavio."

Her breath escaped in a rush. "Flavio?"

"We'll make an end to this travesty. Then you'll be free to —"

It hit her like a punch to the stomach. "But I don't want . . ."

His face was so cold it froze her. "I should never have married you. What happened between us was a mistake."

A mistake? Her love for him a mistake? His tenderness, his awakening her, a mistake? "Is our marriage not legal?"

He looked away. "It can be undone."

He would divorce her? Carina burned with shame and horror. It hurt. More than Flavio's betrayal it hurt, and she wanted to hurt back. But this time she knew. There was no peace in that. She swallowed her injured pride and the pain of rejection and humbled herself. "I don't want it undone."

There. She had groveled. But she loved him. Even now she loved him. Their eyes met and held, his hard and bleak, hers holding her heart. He must know, must see. "I am Mrs. Quillan Shepard. You gave me your name."

His jaw tensed. "It wasn't mine to give."

"Then call me whatever you like. We made a covenant."

He puzzled her sternly. He must see she meant it. He would not be rid of her so easily. So he was not happy with his bargain. She would make him happy. So he disdained the daughter of Angelo Pasquale DiGratia. She would be simply Carina. Like Rose accepting Wolf, she would accept his son.

"Carina . . ."

"Are you saying you don't want me?"

"It doesn't matter what I want."

"You have no feelings for me?" She saw

the crack in his façade. He did care, and her heart quickened.

He released a hard breath. "Have it your way." He put the hat back on his head. "I'll pay Mae to keep you."

Could he be so stubborn? Well, so could she. Carina raised her chin. "Where will you be?"

He didn't answer.

"It doesn't matter. I'll wait."

His face softened again. "Carina . . ."

"As long as it takes."

He dropped his chin, fighting with himself, it seemed. Which part would win? The one who had held her, whose strength she trusted, or the one who hurt, who lashed out when someone came too close? Her stomach knotted into a hard ball inside her.

He lifted only his eyes. "You're wasting your time."

"I don't think so."

He looked up and frowned. "Do you always get what you want, Carina?"

She raised herself to the fullness of her stature. "When I know what I want."

His eyes narrowed. She could see the fight in him. He would not give in easily. *Buono*. Neither would she.

He tucked his tongue between his side teeth and held her eyes, then shook his head and walked away. She knew his stride. He was determined, set on this course. As he called to Cain's dog, her heart wavered. But he didn't turn back, and there was nothing more she could do. Quillan must find his own way back to her.

It was out of her hands, but God was bigger than she, bigger than Quillan. He would have His way, in spite of them. For her part, she would wait. *Signore?* She looked up into the blue bowl of sky. The hurt of rejection stung, then eased with fresh hope. Even this would work together for good. She would wait. And she would have God's grace to do it.

Acknowledgments

I have the strength for everything
through him who empowers me.
Philippians 4:13, New Am.

I gratefully acknowledge my dependence on
the Lord my Savior and the Holy Spirit,
through whom all things are possible.

Thanks to Sarah Long and Barb Lilland,
my fine and committed editors
Thanks to Gerry Deakin for assistance
Doug Hirt and Mary Davis
for feedback and Jim and Jessie
for endurance and extraordinary love